Praise for Amit Chaudhuri's

The Immortals

"Enchanting. . . . Impressive and rare. . . . Seldom has any contemporary author invested such detail in descriptions of place, behavior, and physicality. Chaudhuri is astonishingly precise."
—*San Francisco Chronicle*

"With exquisite wit and grace, [Chaudhuri] can depict a rapidly changing India in a single life and an entire life in a single detail."
—*The Boston Globe*

"A command performance. Even in the context of contemporary Indian writing in English, much of which is outstanding, Chaudhuri is the best."
—*The Irish Times*

"The lyrical quality of [Chaudhuri's] writing is striking. The terrain of the novel is the battleground of art and materialism. In this it invites honourable comparison with Thomas Mann's *Buddenbrooks*."
—*The Times* (London)

"Chaudhuri is one of India's most distinctive literary figures. While lesser writers obsess over the heat and dust, he charts the by-ways of the Indian soul. . . . *The Immortals* is a memorable work—capacious, multifaceted but intimate, it is Indian to the core but universal in its implications. . . . Superb."
—*The Independent* (London)

"Beguiling and silently moving. . . . [Filled with] deeply etched but subtly drawn characters."
—*India Abroad*

"There are two Indian writers who are quite unlike each other, but whose sentences are immediately identifiable. If just a few words of their prose are read out to you, you will confidently call out their names—one is Rushdie, the other is Chaudhuri."

—*The National* (Abu Dhabi)

"Chaudhuri's particular art lies [in] rendering beauty from normality. His characters linger in the mind; and his prose, with its exactness and elegance, its exquisite delineation of memory and emotion, has a strange, mesmerising grace." —*Financial Times*

"An important novel. . . . There is a filigreed, Jamesian quality to [Chaudhuri's] work, an urbanity and aesthetic style not often associated with Indian fiction."

—*The Times Literary Supplement* (London)

"Amit Chaudhuri captures, as no one else can, the delicate, subtle emotions of people who inhabit an India of the past and the privileged. . . . His powerful evocations of people and places, his startling use of words and images and metaphors, leaves an impression that lingers in the reader's mind for many days, more like poetry than prose. *The Immortals* is his most beautiful and complex novel." —Wendy Doniger

"Nothing happens in the story in a rush or bustle to precipitate action, yet it generates a low-profile chain of events that, for all its apparent lack of theatricality, affects the writing as a stillness full of movement and vibrancy." —Ranajit Guha

"An enchanting novel about the place of traditional music in a modernizing India and what it means to be an artist."

—*The Star-Ledger* (Newark)

ALSO BY AMIT CHAUDHURI

The Vintage Book of Modern Indian Literature
(editor)

Real Time

A New World

Freedom Song

Afternoon Raag

A Strange and Sublime Address

AMIT CHAUDHURI

The Immortals

Amit Chaudhuri is the author of several award-winning novels and is an internationally acclaimed musician and essayist. *Freedom Song: Three Novels* received the Los Angeles Times Book Prize for Fiction. He is a contributor to the *London Review of Books*, *Granta*, and *The Times Literary Supplement*. He is currently Professor of Contemporary Literature at the University of East Anglia.

www.amitchaudhuri.com

The Immortals

The Immortals

AMIT CHAUDHURI

Vintage Books
A Division of Random House, Inc.
New York

FIRST VINTAGE BOOKS EDITION, SEPTEMBER 2010

The Library of Congress has cataloged the Knopf edition as follows:
Chaudhuri, Amit.
The immortals / by Amit Chaudhuri.—1st American ed.
p. cm.
1. Bombay (India)—Fiction. 2. Domestic fiction. I. Title.
PR9499.3.C4678166 2009
823'.914—dc22 2009024461

Vintage ISBN: 978-0-307-45465-2

Book design by Virginia Tan

www.vintagebooks.com

Printed in the United States of America
10 9 8 7 6 5 4 3 2

For Rinka

The mortals become immortals; the immortals become mortals.

—Heraclitus

Transformation

My days are pallid with the hard pummelling of work,
my nights are incandescent with waking dreams.
Arise from the clash of metals, O beautiful one, white fire-flame,
may the mass of matter become wind, the moon become woman,
may the flowers of the earth become the stars of the sky.
Arise, O sacred lotus, rise from the spirit's stalk,
free the eternal in the unfading forgiveness of the moment,
make the momentary eternal.
May the body become mind, the mind become spirit, the spirit
unite with death,
may death become body, spirit, mind.

—Buddhadeva Bose
(trans. from Bengali by Ketaki Kushari Dyson)

The Immortals

The notes of Bhimpalasi emerged from a corner of the room. Panditji was singing again, impatient, as if he were taking his mind off something else. But he grew quite immersed: the piece was exquisite and difficult. He'd composed it himself seven years ago.

From not far away came the sound of traffic; the roundabout, bewildering in its congestion. Bullocks and cars ground around it. The bulls looked mired in their element; the buses and dusty long-distance taxis were waiting to move. The car horns created an anxious music, discordant but not indifferent.

The Panditji wasn't there: he'd died two years ago, after his third cardiac seizure. They had rushed him to Jaslok Hospital; on the way, in the car, he'd had his second heart attack. He had died in Jaslok, to the utter disbelief of his relatives: they hadn't thought that he'd been admitted to a hospital to die. Now, his presence, or his absence, persisted in the small seven-hundred-square-feet house. The singing had come from the tape recorder, from the tape the grandson had played accidentally, thinking it was a cassette of film songs.

"Yeh to dadaji ke gaane hai," remarked the boy, recognising his grandfather's singing; was he surprised or disappointed? Next to him hung a portrait of his dadaji, enlarged from a photograph taken when he was fifty-seven. The face was an austere one, bespectacled, the oiled hair combed back. It was the face of—by common consensus in the family—a great man. The large forehead had been smeared with a tilak, as if someone had confused the portrait with a real person.

Already, the Panditji was becoming a sort of myth. It wasn't as if a large number of people knew him; but those who did divulged their knowledge with satisfaction. How well he sang Malkauns, for instance; how even Bade Ghulam Ali hesitated to sing Malkauns at a conference in Calcutta after Panditji had the previous day. How Panditji was a man of stark simplicity, despite his weakness for the occasional peg of whisky in the evening.

But it was certain that Panditji was proud, a man of prickly sensitivity. He had been a man silently aware of the protocol between student and teacher, organiser and performer, musician and musician. If slighted or rebuffed, he sealed off that part of the world that rebuffed him.

This severity had probably cost him. There was a story of how Lata Mangeshkar wanted a guru to train her in the finer points of classical music, and of how she had thought of him, Ram Lal, having heard his abilities as a teacher praised highly. "You must call her, Panditji," said a well-wisher. "She is waiting for your call." Panditji did not call. "She should call me," he said. "If she wants to learn from me, she will call me." The call did not come. In the meantime, Amir Khan telephoned her and said that he was at her disposal. Word spread quickly; Lata turned to the distinguished ustad; and Amir Khan became known as the man who had taught Lata Mangeshkar the subtler intricacies of classical music.

And yet, for all that, his reputation as a teacher had remained intact when he died; like something small and perfect, it had neither been subtracted from nor added to. People outside the family remembered him less and less; if asked "Where did you learn that beautiful bandish?" they might say in a tone of remembrance, "Oh I had learnt that from Pandit Ram Lal," for people used to drift in and out of Panditji's life, and some became students for brief spells of time.

Shyamji's life was to be different. This was a simple determination, but it was not a conscious plan. *Consciously*, Panditji's life was the ideal life; when Shyamji mentioned it, it was as if he were speaking of a saint, and not of his father. That was all very well; but it was a life that could not be repeated.

Tonight was a night of upaas and jagran, an absurdity enforced ritually by the women. Shyamji succumbed meekly to being a witness. The abstention from food by the women, the singing of bhajans till dawn: these were necessary observances. Done repeatedly, they were meant to lead to betterment. Instead, they led to acidity, and a grogginess and lack of focus that lasted two days. But they were undertaken in light-hearted camaraderie.

The children and the men were fed. Then night came; and they began to sing the bhajans. The children had fallen asleep without any prompting, as usual, in the midst of the chatter, their eyes closed in the bright light of the tube-light. The low, droning singing began; not tuneless, because this was a family of musicians, but strangely soothing. Half-asleep, Shyamji watched his wife and his sister and, with them, an older daughter, Neha: they were about to lull him to sleep. Nisha, his youngest daughter, had desperately wanted to stay awake, and join the chorus; but she had fallen asleep at a quarter to eleven. His mother sat in a corner, in a plain white sari, with an absent look, yet entirely alert. Shyamji had a dream into which was woven the sound of the chorus; in which his father was also present, both as a living person and as a portrait, hanging in a reddish light. This dream, about the vicissitudes of Shyamji's life, continued for a long time, taking one shape, then another. When he woke briefly, it was dawn; the women had vanished: they must have gone to bed, probably after having taken a glass of milk to break the fast. The room was silent, except for the noises coming in from outside.

Late one evening the door must have been left ajar—early evenings the doors were anyway wide open, to let in a continual trickle of visitors; people coming in and going out—but late one evening when the door was ajar, the rat must have got in. No one had noticed. But it was Neha who saw it later that night, as she was stepping out of the bathroom. It had jumped out, and scooted behind the pots in the kitchen once again. Expectedly, Neha almost fainted. It was really a bandicoot; cats were scared of them. They ran down the gutters and, at night, scurried down the narrow passage that connected the houses of the colony. They had the aggressiveness and urgency of touts.

The children danced, half in fear and in excitement at an undefined peril. Shyamji's wife, never known to be particularly violent, had managed to chase it out with a jhadu; it darted through the kitchen window. Shyamji, not moving from the divan, was a picture of patience, and kept saying, as he did during most crises, "Arrey bhai, pareshan mat hona, don't get agitated."

On the way to the city in the mornings, he'd stop at Peddar Road sometimes, at his wife's brother's place; going up a steep incline and entering a compound that was not visible from the main road. Here, they lived in a single-storey house not far from a posh girls' school.

"Hari om," he said as he entered. It was an old joke, this invocation to God, a part of Shyamji's "fun" mode: it meant he was hot, and that he was here, needing attention. "Water, jijaji?" asked the woman sitting near the doorstep; she had covered part of her face with her sari the moment he had stepped in. Shyamji nodded; then added affectionately: "Cold." He lowered himself onto the mat and sighed.

It was in this house, oddly, that he'd first seen Lata Mangeshkar. She, sitting on the little divan in her white sari, talking to the members of the household in her baby-like voice. She had seemed tiny to Shyamji. He glanced at her; although her songs often floated about in his head, he was, at that moment, curious about what she looked like, sounded like. They brought her puris and potatoes on a plate—it seemed she'd asked for them specifically—and she ate them carefully and said: "I love eating anything Arati makes."

Arati was married to Motilal, Shyamji's wife's brother: everyone knew she was a good cook. A small cordon of family members, of children and cousins intermittently talking to each other, had formed itself around Lata. He was introduced to her as Ram Lal's son, and at this she showed a passing flicker of interest. When you are introduced to the great, you have a fleeting impression that they have taken in your features and your name, and that they'll remember you the next time you meet. Shyamji was happy to pay his respects with a namaskar, then retreat into the background.

Later, when she was practising a song with Motilalji—without accompaniment, without harmonium—he was surprised that he could not hear her. He then went a little closer; the familiar voice became audible, small and sharp. So this is what a microphone could do!

Motilalji himself was a marvellous singer, astonishingly accomplished; but this was the pinnacle of his achievement—to have his talent mutedly applauded by Lata, to give her a few tunes for the bhajans she sang, to accompany her on the harmonium at the occasional public concert she gave, and to act as a filler during those concerts: that is, to sing a song or two when she wasn't singing, and the audience was distracted, going out for coffee or to the toilet. At first, they'd all thought it was a miracle—a result of "bhagya," fate—this conjunction with Lata Mangeshkar, and it was expected that, when the time came, she'd surely "do" something for him. But she hadn't "done" anything for him; he had continued to be her filler, he hadn't become a music director. What *could* she do? explained the family. But the relationship with Lata, to all outward purposes, was cordial; it could even be described as "particularly close."

Part of Motilalji's problem was drink; no use blaming others for a self-inflicted problem. Drink made him more solitary; late in the evening, he would sit alone, talking to himself. The rest of the day, if he was sober, he was abrasive; as if the world somehow displeased him. And his talent became a problematic responsibility he did not know what to do with; it was as if, having given so much to his gift—hard work, practice—he wanted something in return; and not having got that "something," whatever it might be, he had decided to punish both himself and everyone around him.

Motilalji came into the room, looked around him, and appeared barely to notice his brother-in-law. But he had noticed him of course; "Bhaiyya, at this time of the morning?" he said.

"No, I had a moment," said Shyamji, "and I thought I'd stop for a glass of water."

"Well, did you get it?"

"I did, and it gave much ananda," said Shyamji.

Motilalji seemed to mull over this remark and dismiss it. He came to Shyamji and for the first time looked him in the eye.

"Where are you going now?" he asked; Shyamji smelled drink on his breath. Although the smell revolted Shyamji, he kept his expression amenable. He noticed that Motilalji's teeth, bared briefly, had flecks of paan on them.

"I was going to see a chela of mine at twelve o'clock, but I'm in no hurry—he'll wait."

Shyamji thought of this student of his, an enthusiastic young man whose voice kept going off-key, and put him out of his mind.

Motilalji patted his hair and smoothed his creased kurta. "Come with me then," he said, glancing at a mirror, and then at his watch.

It turned out that they were going to Cumballa Hill. This was not far away, and they might have walked it in half an hour. But Motilalji had lavish tastes; as they descended from the small hill on which the house stood, he hailed a taxi. They sat at the back, Shyamji wondering if they could have taken a bus. "Arrey, who will take a bus for such a short distance! And these buses tire me—I am not well." He looked distractedly before him.

Besides, no bus would have taken them straight to the building.

Motilalji began to hum with a sour expression on his face, as if he was never on holiday from his talent and vocation, and resented the fact, as the taxi made the round from Peddar Road to Kemp's Corner, and then turned right at the Allah Beli Café and continued down the straight lane. Shyamji, by contrast, was wide-eyed and curious, as if he was still not bored by this area. He was also silent. The small intermission of the journey seemed to have mixed up daydream and reality for him. He watched the sunlight fall on the different buildings; the old, deceptively homely but expensive shops on Kemp's Corner; the multi-storeyed buildings in the lane in which mainly Gujaratis lived, with their sense of crowdedness; then the sense of spaciousness again as they turned into the hill, with its older buildings.

They came now to an old, large, three-storeyed house. "Arrey, dekho," said Motilalji, "I have only two rupees' change in my pocket. These fellows will never have change for a hundred-rupee note. Give him five rupees, will you, Shyam?" and with that he got out of the taxi. Shyamji noticed, as he fished resignedly in his kurta pocket, that Motilalji's dhoti was quite shabby. But he was not drunk; he was walking straight. They went up a single floor in an old lift, one that apparently never caught the sunlight. In a way that was both unworldly and dramatic, Motilalji rang the bell next to a large door with a brass nameplate.

The door was opened by an ageing bearer, a grey-haired Malyali, who'd grown inured to the incursion of people like Motilalji into the flat. Certain skills brought you into contact with the well-to-do, he'd decided; and in his thirty years as cleaner, boy, and bearer, he'd seen a range of skills. Besides, the lady of the house liked singing; the people he'd worked for had always had interesting hobbies, and he preferred the employers that had hobbies to the ones that didn't have any. He was accomplished enough to feign a look of tolerance and respect toward Motilalji; he didn't know the other man. Then, with an approximation of childlike enthusiasm, he padded off barefoot towards the bedroom to say, "Memsaab, music teacher has come!"

Motilalji sat on the sofa with a sort of half-smile on his face, while Shyamji turned his head momentarily to look at the flat; glancing back quickly over his shoulder, he saw the potted plants in the veranda. Motilalji leaned towards him to say something; but the lady was approaching them; he cleared his throat.

"Mallika," he said, "I hope you don't mind that I brought my dewar with me!"

The dewar, the brother-in-law, looked a bit startled; he felt, more than ever, that he was in someone else's house, and that he'd been manipulated by Motilalji for a reason only he knew. He was also surprised, and mildly offended, that Motilalji referred to the lady by her name, rather than "Mallikaji" or "didi."

The lady smiled and nodded at Shyamji. John came out of the room with a harmonium, and placed it on the carpet.

"She's been learning from me for seven–eight months now," said Motilalji. "You should listen to her—she has a good voice. She's very proud though."

Shyamji quailed. He pretended he hadn't heard.

"My dewar's name is Shyam—Shyam Lal," said Motilalji. "The late," and he glanced at the heavens, "Pandit Ram Lal's son. He's quite a good singer, and a teacher too. He's still young, though."

The lady and Motilalji sat down to sing. First the parping sound of the harmonium, not very musical; then the lady began singing, while Motilalji sat there, feigning boredom. Her voice was full-throated, surprisingly melodious.

"Wah, didi!" said Shyamji after she'd finished; then Motilalji went through the motions—they could be called nothing else—of a lesson without bothering to raise his voice, but almost humming her a tune, which she followed assiduously, nodding appreciatively.

There was a break, and John brought them tea. Shyamji stirred his cup thoughtfully, and Motilalji declaimed,

"You must practise this song, Mallika! And you have to get the pronunciation right!"

Mallika Sengupta had been trying to get the pronunciation right. In every way she liked being in Bombay; but as a singer she'd been temporarily unmoored, and had to find her bearings, and explore avenues she'd once never thought of exploring. These avenues mainly comprised bhajans and ghazals, so popular in Bombay. She'd had to take a deep breath to get round to them, of course. She'd never taken Hindi songs seriously when growing up; even though she'd heard the Hindi songs of Saigal and Kananbala, they were film songs, there was a prejudice against them in her family. Now, more than thirty years later, she found herself faced with these languages; the onus was on her, in the daytime loneliness of her flat, to get her tongue round Hindi and Urdu vowels and consonants.

Her metier was the Bengali song, the Tagore song—naturally. Everything she said in Hindi, thus, sounded a bit like Bengali. But the Bengaliness of her voice—its rounded full-throatedness—is also what made her sound charming to her music teachers; they would prick up their ears and search for analogies: "You sing like Kanandevi," they'd say; or, "You sing like Geeta Dutt!" Kanandevi had long turned to religion; Geeta Dutt had gone out of circulation prematurely; in the age of Lata, Mrs. Sengupta's voice was certainly different.

Mrs. Sengupta's voice evoked a "golden age." When people heard it in this drawing room, when they closed their eyes they couldn't believe it, they felt they'd been transported, somehow, to an earlier, to a better time. Secretly, one or two of them might think the voice "old fashioned"; but it wasn't at all; it was simply out of place in the zeitgeist. The zeitgeist was Lata's voice, thin, small, and, to Mrs. Sengupta's ears, shrill. This was the reigning definition of a female singing voice. Mallika Sengupta's voice's moment had passed, at least for now, though neither she nor anyone else could be conscious of this fact; passed, unless it was rediscovered in the distant, as-yet unimaginable future, unless a change of taste were brought about by a future generation and it cared to remember Mallika Sengupta.

Her beginnings were in a small town in North Bengal where her father had been an advocate. Her family had had social pretensions in the small town, but had swiftly fallen from grace after her father's death when she was twelve. The family struggled; but the cultural pretensions survived, as did the talent and intelligence. Her own talent was least nurtured, because she was a girl. It was almost a lucky break that she met and married Apurva Sengupta.

At first she'd refused him; she laughed now when she thought of it. She laughed; but at the time it had been no laughing matter. She was not in love, she thought; and, even as the daughter in a large family run only partly successfully by a widowed mother, she had this impractical desire—not only to be loved, but also to love the person she would marry. Then there was the matter that he was her brother's friend at college, and that was how she thought of him; and the fact that although her family looked up to him, both for being a "nice boy" and for belonging to a wealthy zamindari family, their odd cultural snobbery made them look down on his family, as not being cultured enough. But the tumult of Partition and Independence had made these histories and their nuances, her brothers' prejudices, absurd and dreamlike; the landscape changed permanently; she wisely accepted his offer, largely because she respected him, but also because she decided, shrewdly, that life with him would allow her to pursue her singing. Here she was in Bombay now, with her husband, as if they'd come from nowhere, freshly created from morning dew, the future a clean slate.

"John!" she said.

"Memsaab!" he responded urgently, emerging into the drawing room, a duster in one hand. Everything for him was a form of theatre.

"Please remove the harmonium. Is baba's food ready—the mutton stew?" The smell of the stew had drifted into the hall. She was now waiting for her son to arrive.

"Yes memsaab baba stew ready!" exclaimed John in English; then stooped toward the harmonium.

Motilalji and his brother-in-law had left twenty minutes ago; her attention was focussed on the boy returning from school. She'd feel an inward restlessness, as if at a job left undone, until he'd come back and eaten.

The music was a constant trickle in her life, not allowed to disturb her routine; in fact, the routine went on, and now and then paused decorously to make time for the music, at which point it was consigned to someone else's hands—John, or the cook; but it wasn't allowed to stop. She never consented to losing her grip on it, to handing the reins to someone else, except temporarily.

Nirmalya came in busily at twenty to one. He was seven years old. Immediately, food was served on a trolley in the air-conditioned bedroom. It was what he liked best; daal and rice and fried fish.

Ten minutes after Motilalji had left, she'd had John shut the windows of the bedroom, in anticipation of her son's arrival, and switch on the air conditioner. The temperature would be just right by the time he was here. Her mind kept going back to Motilalji's little performance—you could call it nothing else—and the way his personality always exacerbated her. "She's very proud," he'd said, or "she thinks very highly of herself," or words to that effect; and boasted the next moment, "Do you see how she holds that steady note? None of the others can do it!" She was pleased by his praise, coming as it was from someone whose gift she respected; but she wasn't certain how long she could cope with his personality.

15

Now, with Nirmalya before her, dangling his legs from the divan, eating from the trolley, a different set of pleasures and anxieties replaced the previous one.

"Do you like the fish? How was your day?"

She always asked these or similar questions; but she also viewed him, always, with a mixture of excitement and foreboding. She felt he was special; more special than other children. If asked to explain herself, she probably couldn't have done so; but, from the moment he was born, she'd held the belief with conviction. Nothing he'd done—at school or at home—had necessarily proved her right. In fact, the time he'd spent at school, until recently, had been miserable. This only strengthened her conviction—the teachers didn't have the insight to understand him.

He scraped the white fish and its black skin off the bone. He was bright and sunny—thoughts racing in his head—as he always was when he came back home; as if the reluctant boy of the morning had gone to never return.

"I want to go and fetch Baba today!" he said.

"Yes, yes."

Mrs. Sengupta saw this homecoming as an apogee of something; she didn't quite know what. Next morning it would go bad again; there would be the usual waning of enthusiasm. She would have to cope with the transformation. It repeated itself on every weekday morning.

Once or twice a week, a maulvi saheb came to the flat, a man who looked exactly like a "maulvi saheb" should. He was an extremely polite man with hidden reserves of personality, a thin man with a small skull cap on his head and a beard.

From the start, this had been a bad idea; but the maulvi saheb was such a patient man that he almost turned it into a good one. He taught her Urdu; slowly, patiently. She had no patience, but she was determined in the interests of her new life in Bombay; she must get her tongue around the words in the ghazals. "Not jim," he said. "Jeem."

In her notebook, she wrote aliph, be, and te. She forgot them the next time he came. "Oh maulvi saheb," she said, embarrassed but not unduly concerned, "I've forgotten them." He was not so much stoic as calm; he was used to rich students paying him for the ritual of learning Urdu; though he wished he had more well-to-do students. Sometimes he wished he had more; sometimes, when he grew tired, he longed for serious students.

Their business was conducted at this centre table, in this small area in the drawing room, where, you could say, many of her daytime pursuits—call them work, or hobbies—were confined. Here, too, tea came and interrupted them. He always accepted tea tentatively, with the fastidiousness a Victorian Englishwoman might have had. He was clearly thrown off-balance by the prospect of having tea with Mrs. Sengupta; he didn't know what relationship he should have to this interregnum, this moment, and to her during it: was he her equal, her co-tea-drinker, or still the "maulvi saheb"? She made it slightly easier for him by ignoring him completely as she finished her tea.

Half her mind, of course, was on whether the furniture had been dusted, whether the decorations had been moved inadvertently from their shelves. Then she would find that her eyes were staring at "jeem" and "che."

"Bas, maulvi saheb," she'd say, "enough today. I'll see you again next week."

A large sofa with floral upholstery; a patterned carpet with a rectangular centre table whose pug marks showed if it moved slightly out of place; the two dignified armchairs on either side; the shelves on the wall-unit which had been bare and became quickly populated with miniatures and objects—urns, brass lamps—released from their expected uses; the momentarily listless curtains; the dining table glimmering in the distance—this, at least for now, was *her* house.

Sometimes the boy, when he came home from school early, or on a holiday, would see the maulvi saheb and his mother, and approach them. He found the maulvi saheb uncommunicative. Yet he felt he might tell him something. He always felt that visitors from a clearly different background were his natural allies; that when they were pretending not to notice him, they were waiting for the right moment.

"But why should I sing the ghazal?" she asked herself one day. Would giving it up mean she had failed? But wasn't her forte the bhajan, the devotional; isn't that what they said? Then why was she struggling to sing these love songs? She'd never get them right, and, anyway, they were, in a sense, absolutely foreign to her; she'd never be able to enter their mood, their spirit. Once she realised this, it was as if a burden she'd carried without knowing it had gone. Overnight, the letters "aliph" and "jeem" began to disappear from her memory. She discontinued her lessons with "maulvi saheb."

That evening, they went out for dinner—the company secretary was visiting from Calcutta. Mr. Deb was in a room at the old Taj; although it was still not the old Taj—the idea for the new Taj had been floated, but it had still not been built. The old Taj was alone, and had an inviolability about it.

They went to the Crystal Room for dinner. It was good to see Mr. Deb again; they ordered naan, palak chicken, daal. The boy was there too; he sometimes accompanied his parents on these occasions. They sat, talking about Calcutta, about the company, about Bombay. When food was served, the dim light almost concealed the colours on the plate; the yellow of the daal, the green of the palak. Yet, though they tore the naan with enthusiasm, they didn't seem interested in the food. Only Mrs. Sengupta said she liked the taste of the daal. Where Mr. Deb was concerned, there was always, for them, a sense of waiting and watching. They were not conscious of this, though; but it was almost certain that once Mr. Deb retired, Mr. Sengupta would take his place. This, perhaps, gave these meetings an air of deferral, where a lot was said, but something couldn't be.

"Sir, the bill." The bill was settled by Mr. Deb; easier for him, as he was staying at the hotel. But, outside this little ritual, it came to the same thing: the meal would be paid for by the company. They—Mr. and Mrs. Sengupta—had just begun to get used to, to take for granted, the freedom of gesture this represented.

Two months later, taking them by surprise, Mr. Deb died. Death had nipped retirement in the bud by two years. He would now be fifty-six years old for eternity; he was quietly cremated in Calcutta. The company settled the dues. A chest pain, wrongly diagnosed by a family doctor as flatulence, had been followed by a heart attack. They could now talk about it—the mistaken diagnosis—forever. Mr. Sengupta flew into Calcutta, on work, but also made his visit coincide with Mr. Deb's shraddh. Mr. Deb was, in a small way, part of his private mythology; he'd been one of the people who interviewed Mr. Sengupta. He felt, within the constraints of the circumstances, the context of flux in the company the departure of one person created, a sense of bereavement. Mrs. Deb, in a white sari, gave a general impression of whiteness, as her hair was almost all white. She spoke to him as someone who was not quite a relative, someone she had got to know, but risked losing. "You must stay for dinner, Apurva," she said.

The company office was on Tulsi Pipe Road. This was a curious address—not a very distinguished address—for a company of standing. They were framed by the old, declining industrial landscape, by a sense of grease and iron, and of funnels of smoke from chimneys in deathless mills. But now, for two years, the office had become the head office; the head office had moved from Calcutta. It was strange to see, in these surroundings, Mr. Dyer emerge from the entrance, debonair, balding, not too long after his pretty secretary, Pamela, had left, and advance towards his car. Apurva Sengupta, too, could be seen coming out not too much later, his jacket on one arm.

Sometimes the boy would come to pick up his father (this was a momentous event in the week) and sit in the car watching the procession of company employees coming out of the incongruous art deco building, the secretaries in their long skirts, the junior executives in chattering groups, invisible as individuals, the directors getting into cars. One day, as they were going back home, a man in rags fell across the bonnet of the car as it paused at the turning; with one arm he banged the windshield, and turned to stare, for one protracted second, inside the car. The driver swore. Ignoring him, the man rose, and, as if he had more important things to do, swayed to the other side of the road. "He's drunk too much," said the driver, starting the engine. "Bewda!" Nirmalya didn't know what it meant to have drunk too much; he didn't know what had happened for the man to become like this, or what the strangely unseeing stare meant. He sat motionless; inwardly, he shrank with terror. Only when his father, who'd been smiling with astonishment, began to talk about the party in the evening did his sense of being at home—in the car, in the world—flow back to him; the moment receded, like a dream that no longer had the power to touch him.

Some people said that Mr. Dyer had affairs with his secretaries; but most of them would have admitted there was more exaggeration in this than truth. But they chose to suspend belief and disbelief, and continued to inhabit a mental realm in which these affairs—plunged into at some hour of the day that lay outside the flow of time as they knew it; probably when he was dictating, behind the shut door, a long letter to either Pamela or Doris—were possible.

He was a charming man. A great part of his charm lay in his physique and his manner: his height, the way he stooped forward slightly, his sideburns—that narrow, perfect-shaped fleece of gold; all things that made the fact that he was balding almost irrelevant.

He gave the impression of listening to you very carefully, his blue eyes fixed over your shoulders, his eyebrows slightly raised in interest and concern, the deep alluring lines creasing his tanned forehead. Behind this manner, he was a dictator who left final and important decisions to no one else, and carried the company, like a personal possession he didn't want to misplace, in his pocket. But he had been specially charming with Mr. Sengupta: he gave him exactly what he wanted—a chauffeur-driven car, a flat, servants, a decent salary—so as to preclude permanently the possibility of Apurva Sengupta one day moving elsewhere. Mr. Sengupta didn't think of his being here as necessarily permanent; but he was beginning to become happy in the company. He suppressed his instinct that his boss was a type of extraordinary and somewhat disrespectable English adventurer: everyone knew it was largely Dyer who'd made the company the success it now was.

"Well, A. B.," he said one afternoon, leaning over his desk (he'd begun the practice of referring to his colleagues by their initials, perhaps to conceal the fact that he had trouble getting their names right; he himself was known to them by his first name—Philip), "you know that, with poor Deb gone, there's a vacancy." He smiled; lines appeared round his eyes. An expression almost like kindness; a moment's deference to the death, but also a sensitivity to the window it had opened up. "I've thought about it, and I don't want to advertise. I've been looking at your work, and I think you're the right man for the job, don't you?"

At these moments, in the air-conditioned isolation of his office, Mr. Dyer's style was pressing: he was a seducer. He was Mephistophelean; but he made it clear that he wasn't interested in being Mephistopheles to everybody; and the alternative (which induced nervousness in those who'd seen it) was a blankness in the blue eyes.

"If you say so, Philip," said Apurva Sengupta, outwardly still but quietly elated. He saw the window as well, open, the light shining. "I'll do my best."

"Good man! I'm very pleased."

Dyer, people knew, cared for presentability and appearance as much as—or perhaps more than—he did for ability. He was an aesthete of executive appearance; he wanted decent-looking people in the upper echelons of the company. And this was part of the reason he had his eye on Apurva Sengupta from the beginning: he had the right kind of looks—a sort of measured elegance and modest style, an appearance, at once, of slightness and control, which convinced Dyer.

Parties too—this was part of the Senguptas' gradual education—were important in the scheme of things; and Dyer's tolerance for hot Indian food—another feature of his uniqueness, his charm, his slightly scandalous air—was high. When the Senguptas threw a party, he'd stand in a corner alone, perspiring, eating Mrs. Sengupta's fish preparations.

"What are you making today?" Mr. Sengupta asked this tensely sometimes before a party. "Are you making that fish?" It was Dyer, who seemed to have been weaned on curries, that Apurva Sengupta was thinking of. He cautiously sniffed the air in the flat. Pumpkin and coriander: the smell had filled the drawing room and barely arrived at the bedroom, as he stood there, still in his jacket. It soon occupied the entire flat.

Around this time, when Mr. Sengupta was promoted, they decided to move office—all the way to that new reclamation on Marine Drive, that puny strip called Nariman Point. One evening, when this strip was still coming into existence, the boy and his parents had walked down it, past coconut and peanut vendors, towards where it petered out into hunched boulders and, further, the fury of the waves. Nirmalya discovered he was scared of the ocean. The sea here had an ancient energy, as it swirled round the finger extending into the water. On both sides, as mother, father, and son stood there for a moment, Nirmalya threatened by blasts of wind, couples moved dimly and mysteriously, unperturbed, as if inside a foyer in a large building. This—the phantasmagoria of roaring, maddened waves and darkness—was what stood behind, at least momentarily, the city they were becoming intimate with.

This area, which had been water not very long ago, became very quickly populated with towers and offices. The building the company moved to was called Udayan. The offices were on the sixteenth floor. One day, in the afternoon, when he'd gone again to pick up his father, Nirmalya stood before the building, separate among the other buildings, and measured it with his eyes. He felt thrilled by it, as if it were a sword that had, strangely, pierced him painlessly. "How tall it is!" It was a significant moment in his own brief life—a grand, inward episode in the unfolding epic of his father's employment. This time, the stream of employees emerging was somehow different, larger and more diffuse. It was full of people he didn't recognise, small men in white shirts, women in saris, both going in and coming out, and then, in the midst of them, he'd spot, from the car, the suited, elegant figure of his father, shorter than Dyer but in his own way striking, then Dyer, and other known faces; his father and Mr. Dyer seemed strangely untouched by the crowd around them; they were at ease but inviolable.

Here, the ethos was that of the busy daylight world of the city; at once indifferent and absorbed, focussed and reckless. Nirmalya quickly forgot Nariman Point as he'd first stood on it nervously at night, threatened by waves. And he had no reason to visit Tulsi Pipe Road, where the old office building had been, again.

"She sings good, but pronunciation must improve." The person who said this was Laxmi Ratan Shukla, a stocky man whose thick bifocals made his eyes seem twice their size, and also indistinct. It seemed the whites of the eyes were melting behind the glasses. He spoke very softly, and hardly ever smiled. He was nondescript and boring, and this was a dimension of his dangerousness. "The words still sound like Bengali. See—'barsat' is sounding like 'borsat.' " He performed this parody of Mrs. Sengupta's Hindi pronunciation without malice or self-consciousness.

He was, of course, not dangerous at all; or he was as dangerous as he, or any human being, could be made dangerous by others. It depended on you. He was, really, a sort of bureaucrat, the head of HMV's Light Music wing. But the problem was he was a bureaucrat who thought he was an artist—he composed tunes; he taught young women; he would have liked to create acolytes who said, "I was taught this song by Laxmi Ratan Shukla." Somehow, it hadn't happened; but, secretly, he wanted to be more than just an office man.

He sat now with two luchis before him, and a cup of tea. Of course, he was unused to luchis; he pierced one with his finger; then he tore a piece and ate it. "She has stopped the maulvi saheb, that is okay," he said. "She can sing bhajan." He referred to her in the third person in her presence, as if she was a child of ten. But he spoke so softly that no one could accuse him of being impolite.

He somewhat despised Bengalis for their inability to speak Hindi, their timid forays into culture as they clung to middle-class propriety, their inability to let themselves go. Even Mrs. Sengupta's voice—it was a mistake on creation's part to have given it to *her*; when he'd heard it, he'd thought it was beautiful and lost interest in it. He was bored by beauty and by artistic gifts; he wanted something else—but if asked, would have spoken in terms of beauty and art.

He liked Bengali food, though. The luchis were interesting. He put the last piece in his mouth.

"Laxmiji, some more?" asked Mrs. Sengupta, sitting up. "John," she admonished the bearer, "what are you doing, see, the saab's plate is empty."

Laxmi Ratan Shukla raised the palm of one hand. "Bas," he said.

Two years later, as they were going down the curve of Haji Ali—a grey day, with very few cars on the road, when it seemed it was going to rain—Mrs. Sengupta said a little resignedly, "Do you know, I don't think he's ever going to let me cut a record." She didn't expect a reply from her husband; his policy, she knew, was long term: Wait and see. She was the opposite; she was impatient; there was no point in waiting and watching.

Dark clouds hung over the twin towers of Samudra Mahal. She stirred restlessly in her seat, and he gave no answer. Then, as the car left the panorama of the steel-grey sea behind, he said, "Well, let us see. You've had the new teacher, Jairam, a little over a year now. I'll speak to Shukla again."

She'd got rid of Motilalji, partly because of his drink-induced irateness, and this new man, balding, enthusiastic, had taken his place. Jairam came on Laxmi Ratan Shukla's recommendation. He was a family man; he had four children. The third was a daughter, an eight-year-old called Kamala, whom he brought home with him one day. She was dark and quiet. "Brij Mohan," said Jairam, referring to a well-known aficionado and concert organiser, "says she sings like Lata. In ten years . . ." The girl was quiet, but sang without much prompting. "Gao beti," said Jairam—they say that men with a paunch have a cheerful disposition, and this was certainly true of Jairam. "Sing a bhajan for behanji." She launched, in her thin voice, into a Surdas bhajan.

O Govind, O Gopal,
Keep a refuge for me,
I've pledged you my life.

The little girl stared into the distance as she sang. The parrot-like quality was almost touching. But the Lata-like timbre of the child's voice grated on Mrs. Sengupta's ears; it inflamed her, this schooling in replicating this voice, and it also made her despair for Kamala. She imagined that this was what Lata herself might have looked like when *she* was a child, and had been taken by Dinanath Mangeshkar (or so the myth went) to audition for a film-maker; and he had been mesmerised. Lata, too, would have been like this child in her orange frock, expectant and unknown, the progeny of a struggling musical family. But Kamala was not Lata; neither in identity, nor in talent. She was just another girl being asked to live up to her father's dreams.

Jairam was himself a competent teacher, but Mrs. Sengupta wasn't impressed by him. He seemed to lack purpose—except, perhaps, where his daughter was concerned. On that particular day, he'd talked continually about his sons and his daughter, sipped tea and gratefully accepted the snacks offered to him, and gossiped about other singers and music teachers; the morning, Mrs. Sengupta had thought privately, had become a family affair. Mrs. Sengupta didn't like too much conviviality during her music lesson.

It began to rain now, on the office buildings between Worli and Prabhadevi. Under the dark clouds, the sky was changing colour; as on the wing of a bird, one colour fades or deepens into another. He is used to giving orders, thought Mrs. Sengupta of the man beside her, but how incredibly cautious and accommodating he seems before Laxmi Ratan Shukla! The large drops clattered onto the windshield of the Ambassador and melted against the glass. With a tick-tick sound the wipers came to life, and through their swathes the road between Worli and Prabhadevi became visible.

When the first promotion had come after Mr. Deb's death, to Company Secretaryship, almost the first people to know in Bombay were the Neogis. The Senguptas still had few friends in the city. This friendship was a result of an encounter in the fifties, in a foreign land, in England, where Prashanta Neogi had travelled to study art; Apurva Sengupta to peruse Company Law. The story was that they'd met, in fact, on the ship. Two lonely Indians on deck, they'd begun to talk; and Prashanta Neogi still spoke about it with a wifely shrug of the shoulders that went oddly with his large frame. Later, they'd shared a cold room in Croydon for a couple of days, and, the first morning, to his horror, Prashanta had discovered that Apurva had used his toothbrush by mistake. Prashanta spoke of this with bafflement and indulgence, as if it had sealed their friendship for the future.

The Neogis lived on the outskirts; in a house on a lane off Gorbunder Road. A low two-storeyed building; a small dusty driveway; the railway lines visible beyond the houses on the opposite side of the road—it was a very different kind of life from the one the Senguptas had now begun to lead. The Neogis were tenants who occupied the ground-floor flat; their lives were casually artistic and unconventional; neither Prashanta nor his wife Nayana ever wore anything but hand-crafted clothes; they smoked heavily and drank in the evening as a matter of course; there were long, involved sessions of bridge and rummy in the evening. There were almost always guests in the house—filmmakers who were passing through; painters—and one might catch them in the morning, wandering in their pyjamas. "But that's the way we like it," Nayana would say, a woman with a sweet, round Bengali face, made unusual and striking by her height and largeness. "We like people in our house." "People!" Mallika Sengupta would say to her husband. "It's a strange house—not a moment of silence!"

The Neogis were the first to know. Mallika Sengupta called them and said: "I have some news."

"Yes, tell me all about it!" said Nayana, feigning eagerness.

"Apurva has had a promotion. Poor Mr. Deb died suddenly, you know. Mr. Dyer called Apurva day before yesterday to his office and told him to take Mr. Deb's position."

"O that's wonderful!" sang Nayana; she sounded pleased. Both she and her husband had a soft spot for Apurva, the "boy" who'd once erred in using Prashanta's toothbrush. "Thank God that man Dyer has some sense! The things I hear about him . . ."

Of course, Nayana and her husband had an interest in the matter. Their dear friend Apurva's former boss—Kishen Arora—whose company he'd left to join this one: this former boss was a dear friend of theirs. Kishen Arora: a man from Delhi, with a squint, a tall Czech wife, and a cultivated manner. A man who said little. Apurva had realised that his prospects, working under him, were bleak. But when it came to changing jobs, the Neogis had dissuaded him: "That's what Kishen's *like*, silly! He *seems* distant. But he's a man of his word."

That's why every advance Apurva Sengupta made in his new job brought the Neogis both happiness and a momentary embarrassment.

That day, as Motilalji and Shyamji came out from Mrs. Sengupta's house, Shyamji had wondered for a moment what the meaning of the expedition had been. Why had Motilalji taken him there?

He was difficult to fathom, this man.

The answer was obvious, though. Motilalji wanted to impress his brother-in-law. He wanted to show off.

Pyarelal was sitting on the divan in Motilalji's house. He seemed to have been sitting there for a while; he had been eating something. When Shyamji saw him, he blanched slightly; the man always made his pulse beat a little faster. As the two entered, Pyarelal got up, and went quickly to the kitchen to deposit his plate and glass. Always busy, darting from here to there, as if he didn't have a moment's respite; as if he wasn't the parasite he really was. Shyamji couldn't stand his nervous energy, his constant compulsion to turn the humdrum into theatre. But Shyamji called out to him wearily:

"Pyareji!"

He came rushing toward him. He was short—a little more than five feet. In his loose pyjamas and white kurta, all movement.

"Bhaiyya!" he said. Shyamji had lain down on the divan and was no longer looking at him. "Please press my feet. They're aching."

Without a word, Pyarelal sat next to him on the divan and began massaging his calves with both hands. On the wall, a picture of the patriarch: Kishen Prasad. And next to it, a large print of the child Krishna on his knees. Shyamji sighed faintly; almost a sob of relief.

This strange exercise was persisted with for fifteen minutes. Pyarelal went about it as if he were used to it, and this was part of the strangeness. The older man kneading the younger one's calves as if he were a supplicant or a younger relation. And this happening without embarrassment or self-consciousness on Shyamji's part or apparent shame on Pyarelal's. "Theek hai bhaiyya?" said Pyarelal at last. "All right?" "Bas," said Shyamji. "It's better now."

"Must go now," said Pyarelal, getting up quickly. "Have to reach Sion by three o'clock." He spoke as rapidly as he did everything else. That's why he'd stopped by—to replenish himself. He'd have been hungry otherwise on the bus journey. He ate quickly too; some leftover potatoes from the fridge and a couple of rotis from a metal container. On his way out, he confronted Ramesh, the four-year-old who was the youngest of the five children Motilalji had produced, between bouts of drunkenness and hours of imparting, half-heartedly, music training, seemingly without too much strain in the last fifteen years. "Pappi do," Pyarelal said, bending low, offering his face: long, with a slightly hooked nose, a thin moustache above the lip. The boy knew the face but didn't kiss it.

Pyarelal had arrived in Bombay twelve years ago on a railway platform. And then he made straight for Ram Lal's house, and, finding him there, touched his toes passionately, as if it were a reunion, rather than a first meeting. "I am a devotee of yours," proclaimed Pyarelal. "I heard you sing when you came to Mussoorie many years ago, and your voice has echoed in my ears ever since." For some reason, the great man took to him, despite Pyarelal's alarming tendency towards hyperbole and his elusiveness; probably because he needed someone at the time. For Ram Lal, in spite of his great gifts, had not made an impact on Bombay; the appreciation of his gifts was left to a small circle of admirers. Outside of that circle, he was almost—not quite, but almost—a nobody, marked out in a crowd only by the seriousness of his demeanour, his noble forehead, his very reserve. Perhaps, at that time, he needed someone like Pyarelal in the house, and as part of his life.

Pyarelal played the harmonium; he played the tabla; he sang—he was a bits and pieces man: he seemed to do everything fairly well. But most of all he was a dancer: he used to teach kathak in Mussoorie.

One day, Ram Lal, as if he'd been mulling over a bright idea for a while, murmured, "Let us have him as our jamai. He is a good man." Shyamji and his younger brother Banwari were aghast; but Shyamji especially. Must his sister, the Tara he had loved since she was born, marry this vagabond? She was not beautiful; she was dark—did that mean she must be given to this itinerant? Even at the age of twenty-seven, his father still alive, Shyamji had realised that if Pyarelal entered the family he would end up becoming *his* responsibility, a millstone round *his* neck. But he couldn't say as much to his father.

As they were eating, Motilalji said: "What did you think of her?"

Shyamji, putting a piece of roti in his mouth, said: "Of whom?"

"That Bengali lady, bhai," said Motilalji, impatient. "Have you already forgotten her? Mallika."

Shyamji flinched again at the familiar use of the first name. He didn't like it. But it was, he knew, Motilalji's way of dominating his pupil even in her absence; because she could replace him whenever she wished, and because he coveted her patronage as much as she needed him as a teacher, he must salvage his pride by dominating her—by using her first name, which she was too polite to object to—not only during the tuition, but also whenever she was mentioned in conversation; it was as if she had a power to hit back at him which had nothing to do with her, or her actual presence.

Equanimously, Shyamji said: "She seemed a good person."

"Yes, but these people want too much! After two lessons she says to me, 'Motilalji, I have picked up this bhajan now, please give me another one.' I say to her—arrey, first learn to sing it properly!"

He had finished eating. He had very little appetite. In two long sips, he finished his glass of water. Although his wife's cooking was renowned among friends and visitors, he'd become indifferent to it himself.

When Shyamji had first met Motilalji, he—Shyamji—was just eighteen years old. He was a bridegroom; he was getting married to Sumati, Motilalji's sister. Sumati was just a few months younger than Shyamji. Sumati had a lovely face, and the same eyes as her elder brother, except that she had a squint; the squint was considered auspicious.

Directing the marriage, besides caste and community, was, of course, eugenics. Both the retired Ram Lal, with his piercing silence, and the doddering Kishan Prasad, Motilalji's father, for whom death's door was invitingly ajar, had realised that the meeting of the two families promised a gene pool that was full of potential for the musical lineage. In the exchanging of garlands between the bubbly, tomboyish girl and the accomplished young singer, in a way more feminine than his bride, lay the hope of creating a gene for the future.

Pandit Ram Lal's marriage had been similarly arranged. By then he'd transformed from an irresponsible and slightly anxious sensation-seeker into a serious musician—or so it seemed. The dark, stocky woman whom he obediently married had a strong singing voice; a strong voice, period, which could be heard, when she was talking, from a distance. Her uncle on her mother's side was the man—the famous music director—who had composed the tune for the film song "Chanda re ja re ja re." "O go quickly, moon, take this message to my beloved," sang the young Lata. A simple imperishable tune; sometimes still played on the radio. The music director was now dead and all but forgotten.

~

Two years after Apurva Sengupta's company moved office to Nariman Point, the Senguptas themselves moved house. The building was a new one; overnight it strode on to the Malabar Hill skyline, overlooking the Kamala Nehru Park and the expanse of the Arabian Sea. Once there, it was difficult to imagine it hadn't been there before.

Mallika and Apurva Sengupta went to see it one morning; the security guard's cabin was in place already at the entrance, and then the car went up a slope before arriving at the plateau on which the building stood, with a neat strip of lawn on the left.

Heavily, they alighted from the car and encountered the marbled porch, and, in an opening in the wall on the left, a small, interior garden—soil, plants, leaves—whose changeless freedom from the vagaries of seasons would cease to surprise them in the coming years.

There was a double move. The Dyers moved to the seventeenth floor of Block A, a two-tier duplex apartment with an open aquarium on the lower level in which goldfish, orange flickers in the water, darted. The Senguptas moved to the tenth floor of Block D, a large three-bedroom flat. The building was called La Terrasse. It was not a Garden Apartments or a Sea Breeze, which it could have easily been. It was clearly meant to not only look, but to be different.

It was their flat—a childlike happiness gripped the Senguptas. And it wasn't theirs; they saw it as a gift, a gift from life; they wandered, admiring, from room to room, Mrs. Sengupta already imagining alterations—her imagination had *become*, briefly, the flat itself, and the imagination is always, compulsively, altering what it imagines, change and play are its subsistence. And so, for the next six or seven years, the flat—still, as they walked around it on the first night, a half-furnished husk, its walls silken with new paint—became, in a sense, her imagination; she could do with it as she pleased, and felt almost compelled to make pleasure a part of her relationship with it, a pleasure indivisible from constant change. So the narrow balcony at the back, which she only glanced at that night, was later brought into the flat and turned into a study, separated from the dining room by a screen of beads. Other changes were repeatedly made. The flat was theirs: never still, recognisable but not quite hardening into trademark features, never static or motionless.

"How many rooms?" asked Nayana Neogi, following Mallika Sengupta down the small, shadowy corridor between two bedrooms, a glass of gin in one hand.

A constant hubbub in the sitting room behind; a modest get-together had been arranged to celebrate the move, the arrival into the new home. Nayana Neogi, tall in a handwoven cotton sari she'd worn in deliberate haste and clumsiness, had her air of bohemian sophistication intact, a refusal to be awed by this recent spectacle of luxury, but to view the property with friendly sincerity and politeness. She was indifferent to property; her world, and her husband's, was a world of handlooms and recyclable items, of ashtrays made out of inadvertently discarded chunks of wood, of junk fashioned into useful everyday objects or bric-a-brac or even art, a world of small-scale creativity and experiment. She looked upon Mallika Sengupta's back with affectionate superiority; not least because Mallika, a small-town girl, could never, whatever her husband achieved, attain her natural, careless sophistication. Nevertheless, she couldn't suppress a twinge of curiosity.

"Three bedrooms," said Mallika Sengupta with unthinking pride.

"Oh you lucky thing, Mallika!" said Nayana, looking into a bedroom on the left. "Three bedrooms in Malabar Hill! It's beautiful."

The last observation was made quietly, almost a reassurance—that she was partaking of her friend's ascent into these surroundings. By "beautiful" she didn't mean what she meant when wandering about an art gallery, or assessing one of her husband's graphic designs; as an adult sometimes pretends to use a word in a simple, clear, limited way for the benefit of a child, she used the word as the upper reaches of the bourgeoisie thoughtlessly used it, as an uncomplicated acknowledgement of well-being. At the same time, the observation was an afterthought she'd almost come to terms with, without too much ruefulness: about the impossibility of ever possessing anything like this lifestyle.

Later, she went into the drawing room and took up a conversation with her neighbour on the sofa in her lilting convent-taught English. She picked up one of the crisp aubergine fritters that were being served to accompany the drinks. This much she'd grant Mallika; that she had a gift for cooking. It was probably a small-town gift. Her dry chicken curries—her prawns in white gourd—even her daal—all marvellous! The aroma from the kitchen hung among the guests like another visitor; no one remarked on it; no one was unaware of it.

. . .

"It's not that Mallika doesn't have ambition, you know," said Nayana Neogi with quiet certainty, undoing the clips from her hair one night.

"What kind of ambition?" her husband asked, rather surly. He had a drink, the tumbler dewed over with moisture, on the table by the bedside. He was wearing one of the "ethnic" plain tops he often wore: neither a kurta nor a shirt. He turned to look at her without intensity or interest. "You mean to do with Apurva?"

"That, of course," said Nayana, as if the thought had occurred to her long ago. No, she had something else to offer. "No, it's her singing." She placed the clips carefully on the small bedside table. She waited for the remark to sink in. "Bechari, she does have a nice voice," she said. She was more grudging about praising this gift of Mallika Sengupta's than she was about unstintingly giving her her due for her daals and chickens. No response was forthcoming as yet from Prashanta. "But it is rather untrained."

"What's the *point* of having this ambition?" muttered Prashanta Neogi petulantly, after taking a moody sip from the glass. "Where will it get her?" And he put down the glass and stared blankly in front of him. He scratched his arm. He was glowering and seemed to be thinking of something else.

It wasn't clear what had made him say what he had—some grumbling desire to please his wife; contempt for Mallika Sengupta's presumptuousness; a general acrid conviction about fate; or was he in some way being secretly self-referential—speaking of, and to, himself? But he didn't dispute what Nayana had just said; he accepted it as if it were a simple, self-evident truth.

She had been a singer once herself—she had learned in Shantiniketan from Shailajaranjan Majumdar. She had glimpsed the Poet when she was fifteen years old; he was close to death, old, white-maned—she had heard him speak sonorous lines in his thin, clear voice. She had been part of a charmed circle.

Then, in her mid-twenties, she began to lose her voice. It began as a crack in the lower register; she'd clear her throat, gargle secretly at night—because Prashanta had the same bohemian indifference to this crisis that he had to everything else, and crises made him impatient—banned, with an ironical smile, normal conversation for a week, spoke to everyone in whispers, and (this she found most difficult) gave up smoking. The crack did not go away.

Then, gradually, she gave in. She told herself she wasn't giving in, but just putting things in abeyance; but she began to enjoy the benefits of the abeyance, its spacious freedoms, the ambivalent relaxation from the tensions of ambition. At some point, her surrender took on some of Prashanta's casual indifference to "important" things. And she began to smoke again.

Now here was Apurva's wife, disturbing her indifference just a little, a woman from a small town, thrown into the centre of things in Bombay, Mallika with her singing voice, her naivety, and, it seemed to Nayana, the ambition—an implicit backing of herself—which she was herself almost not conscious of.

This twin move, Dyer's and Mr. Sengupta's, and the new proximity it brought between the Chairman and the Head of Finance (to which post Mr. Sengupta had recently been appointed) was seen by many to be a blessing, Dyer's personal blessing on Apurva Sengupta; but the proximity was actually a mixed blessing. It brought the Senguptas into closer contact with what was really a dysfunctional family, a fact they chose to make an effort to ignore since Dyer was at once boss and benefactor.

In private, they sometimes discussed the Dyers with a sort of scandalised wonder. "She was a dancer in Calcutta," he said. "I heard he met her there." "Where?" Mallika Sengupta asked innocently. "In the restaurant on Park Street where she was dancing."

It seemed difficult to connect the woman in the restaurant on Park Street, whom Nirmalya saw, in his mind's eye, in a state of partial undress in a dimly lit dance hall surrounded by shadowy, eager men sitting at their tables, with Julia Dyer. And Nirmalya's imagination furnished him with a younger Philip Dyer, slightly thinner, sitting enigmatically alone at one of the tables. There was the slightest hint of scandal, of speculation, in Apurva Sengupta's voice, that she might be Eurasian. This was left hanging in the air, though, and hardly touched upon; it was just a fleeting, promising thought. Now here was this couple, transmuted, the burra sahib and memsahib, the last vestige of Britannia long after the Raj was over. Julia was small and beautiful; she had somewhat, but not entirely, lost her figure (her dancer's backside—if dancer she had been—had become quite large); she dropped in and out of spells of near-alcoholism—sometimes, in the morning, when she and Mallika Sengupta were having their dutiful convivial chats on the phone, her speech was slurred. But she was never not sober when they met. And they tried not to sit in judgement upon her; Mrs. Sengupta always admiring her for being as beautiful as her name, which she also found particularly beautiful.

From the balcony in front, you could see the sea, Chowpatty beach, the Marine Drive stretching and curving to the right: all that mattered in Bombay was before you; you didn't need to know any more of the city—you took that fickle, flickering, glittering view to be the city itself. The cars were small, busy, and toy-like. The view from the Dyers' flat was the same, but more breathtaking and varied; the cars looked tinier, more numerous, and the white yachts floating on the sea without ever touching it moved with an impulse of their own.

At night, the lights came on in the Marine Drive, a great witch-like celebration of neon and fluorescence, and Mrs. Sengupta cheerfully told her son Nirmalya, as he looked out over the stone bannister, that the row of lights glowing individually around the drive was called the "Queen's Necklace."

. . .

It was to this flat that Shyamji came one day. Mallika Sengupta had been looking for a new teacher. A series of teachers had come to the Cumballa Hill apartment, starting with Chandrashekhar, who used to arrive on a scooter three times a week, a nice man, not hugely accomplished, who worked in an office and gave tuitions in singing. He'd been teaching her as he taught everyone else, with cheerful, encouraging insincerity, till one day he actually listened to her and fell silent in consternation. "Your voice is truly lovely," he said at last; the voice was still ringing in his ear—but this lapse from teacherly propriety never occurred again.

Motilalji, in spite of his gifts, she "got rid of" after he twice came drunk to her lesson. Then there was the famous classical ustad Ghulam Mohammed, who was recommended to her for his immense knowledge; a thin man who wore steel spectacles, he reminded her for some reason of a master tailor—it wasn't difficult to imagine him with a tape-measure around his neck. He taught her nothing, or no songs, at least, but kept giving her vocal exercises; intricate exercises that didn't add up to anything, but which he named, with satisfaction, "designs." "Look at this design," he said; this contributed further to his calm, focussed, tailor-like air. Then, at last, he gave her a song, a geet; "This is a new tuin," he said, and though he taught her the same song for two months, she both liked and was exasperated by his quaint version of the word "tune" and his blithe, dilatory use of it—"Yeh mushkil tuin hai," "It's a difficult tuin," etc. Learning from him was to be in the middle of an unending chapter.

There were others. Jairam, who was past his heyday, and was convinced his daughter would be another Lata; Inderjit, a small flamboyant man, whom, mistakenly, she'd called by name once, instead of "Inderjitji," thus scaring him off possibly with ideas about her romantic interest in him—all these teachers had come and gone from her house. The last teacher who'd come to this new apartment was Dheeraj, a dark man with a pleasant singing voice, a crooner's voice. He began to teach her new geets. He got her to sing a rather "filmi," sentimental song on the radio, not really suited to her style and voice (love songs seldom were), but she sang it with seriousness, too much seriousness, almost: "My many-coloured dreams have all shattered/ Like a mirror." He had a problem with his marriage, though; it was breaking apart. One day he stopped coming. They heard he'd had a stroke. She waited to hear from him; he was untraceable; a month went by. Then, when she'd almost forgotten him, she saw him from her car on the road, looking absent, a stick in one hand.

"Haven't I seen you before?" asked Mallika Sengupta. "I'm sure I've seen you before." Shyamji had been waiting for her, looking beyond the sunken balcony at the sea.

"Didi," he said very courteously, "I once came with my wife's brother, Motilalji. You were in a different flat, then."

"Of course," she said—the day returned to her—and she added, "I remember—he said something like, 'She thinks no end of herself,' and you looked as if you wished you were somewhere else." And she was oddly stirred by the memory of his discomfiture.

That discomfiture fitted with his personality: he was one of the most soft-spoken and pointedly courteous teachers she'd had. Later, she'd hear that people called him "smooth," even "slippery." But her doubts were subsumed by the compassion she'd felt for him right from the beginning; ever since he'd called her, without really knowing her, "didi" and made her an elder sister.

It was seven years since she'd seen him last—and not quite forgotten him. But by this time he was no longer the man who had hovered in the background behind Motilalji. He was becoming, according to unofficial information, one of Bombay's most highly paid teachers; the well-to-do he charged eighty-five rupees per sitting; a huge sum. But they wanted him—among them corporate wives; devout traders and tax defaulters whose anxieties were oddly consoled by music; not to speak of young, ordinary middle-class students who lived in the suburbs and learnt from him in groups of five or six—they wanted him for his melodious voice and his virtuosity. Like the god after whom he'd been named, whose flute was a wand that drew the female cowherds to him, Shyamji's uninsisting, mellifluous singing had drawn one student after another to him in South Bombay.

The boy was now fifteen years old. He'd just finished his school finals; he'd passed with a decent, but not brilliant, first class.

The older he got, and the higher his father rose in the company, the greater the friction that came to exist between him and the life to which he'd been raised. With an adolescent puritanism, he'd almost made it a point to boycott his parents' parties, or to appear in them with a premeditated nonchalance, in a dishevelled state.

It was at this time that the boy ran into Shyamji, as he was flitting from the main door to his bedroom. Shyamji guessed he must be Mrs. Sengupta's son, but couldn't be sure. The boy looked rather intense, bespectacled, a tender goatee—more like down—around his chin. Later, he asked Mrs. Sengupta:

"Didi, is that your son?"

Shyamji was genuinely interested. Because he believed the flat and the way of life inside it to be an inheritance, and he wanted to know who would inherit it. What he'd seen, in the person of this boy, he thought privately, was a bit odd.

"Yes, that is my son," said Mrs. Sengupta, brightening visibly, as if merely to become conscious of the fact again was to experience some form of satisfaction.

"You have no other children, didi?" he asked, softly, as if he were respectful of the ways of the well-to-do, but also very slightly concerned. He couldn't comprehend the impulse to bring only one child into the world, but there were many things about people like Mrs. Sengupta he couldn't quite comprehend.

"No," she said, and called, "Nirmalya, come here!" But the boy was in his room and there was no response. "John," she said, "ask baba to come here."

"Nirmalya": "an offering to the gods"—they'd named him thus because he'd narrowly missed being a stillborn child; he'd been in a stupor in his mother's womb—another two hours and he wouldn't have lived. Even before his inception into the world, it seemed he was delegated a destiny.

He'd come armed with a disability as well; but an invisible one. When he was three and a half years old, a stethoscope had paused, padded around the sternum, then returned to the top-left corner of the chest. The doctor's face had darkened. "There is a murmur," he said, puzzled; it wasn't the kind of sound he'd expected to hear. He'd glanced nervously at the mother, as if expecting to be castigated for speaking out of turn. He was a mere GP after all. Confronted with a happy family, an upwardly mobile family, his first diagnosis was that the fault was in himself, in his instrument. But the murmur wouldn't go away.

At first there was disbelief, then mourning—the preamble to the journey to a heart specialist in a tottering building. Nameplate stacked untidily upon nameplate indicated that at least half the building was occupied by doctors. Once you got out of the giant hencoop of the lift, after the brief journey up a shaft in which only the cords and pulleys were constantly alive and never at rest, you walked down an unpromisingly dark corridor and came to a glass-doored chamber with a small sitting area that was fluorescent-lit and air-conditioned. It was like a world that the building didn't seem to know existed within it.

His father would be dressed in a suit for work. The heart specialist too would be in a suit. As they sat across the table from one another, they'd have the manner of colleagues in tune with each other, the father still with his post-breakfast, corporate, I-know-what-I'm-doing air about him. That air was actually a great comfort to the mother in her printed silk sari, which she'd put on hastily before the appointment; it was however her—with her implacably nervous air, who looked like a child that had been startled by a thunderclap—that the doctor repeatedly addressed, as if it were she who were the patient, and he a family elder who had to persuade her to go to a doctor. Any little thing might make her cry; and the doctor didn't want that to happen in the tranquillity of the chamber.

When Nirmalya was slightly older, and had had further experience of doctors, he asked his father: "Baba, why do these doctors always have their chambers in awful buildings?" He'd always wondered if it was humility or otherworldliness, because the doctors he knew seemed absent-minded, and invariably had bad handwriting. "It's cheap for them," said his father. "They pay very little rent." And at last the logic of these successful doctors seeing him in tottering buildings became clear to him.

As the mother and father waited, he in his dark suit, she in her printed sari, as if they were about to embark on a trip, Nirmalya lay recumbent for twenty minutes on the narrow high bed, while the moist-lipped nozzle connected to the various nodes of the electrocardiogram kissed his skin and ribs wetly. A kindly lady in a white sari moved the nozzle from one point to another on his chest; the little space behind the curtain was ice-cold from the air conditioning. By the time he'd wiped the stuff from himself with a tissue and put on his shirt, he'd grown used to the cold.

These buildings were dark, and the various doctors' chambers were little bigger than large cupboards. But the cupboards were all bright and air-conditioned. After they were finished, the three of them got into the lift and descended into daylight again.

After that, his parents felt temporarily free and lightened. And, since Nirmalya had anyway missed the morning's school, they stopped at a small new café on Marine Lines. Mr. Sengupta, dressed for a business appointment, sitting with wife and child at a table in a café; but it was as if simply emerging from the doctors' building had bequeathed upon him another day. They had chicken sandwiches.

Often, Mrs. Sengupta would think back to that day in January in Calcutta, when Nirmalya was one and a half years old, and she, in Calcutta for two months, had been invited to judge a competition at a music school, where the children would be singing Tagore songs. Her co-judges were two distinguished singers, Sumita Mullick and Banani Ray, and, in a way, it was quite an honour to sit at the same panel as them.

But they—Apurva and Mrs. Sengupta—didn't know what to do with the child; they decided, after a long discussion, to leave him in the car with the ayah. The competition continued longer than expected; it went on and on; one girl after another approached the microphone and sang Rabindranath's lyrics with the utmost solemnity; and Mrs. Sengupta sat ill-at-ease and restless with her co-judges. When they returned to the car, they found that, despite the windows being rolled up, there were mosquitoes inside. The child was howling and angry; he had been bitten. As if he were some sort of deity before which she must be contrite, Mrs. Sengupta bent forward and picked him up from the ayah's lap. "E Ram! E Ram!" she said. A few days later, the child had a fever—it turned out to be the dengue, of which there was an epidemic in Calcutta at the time.

Years later, she would return to that day in Calcutta; the competition, which had now receded into the background; her own neglect, as she saw it; and the dengue, which she could hardly believe had happened to her own child. She'd read that both dengue and rheumatic fever could damage the heart; and she wondered if she were responsible for her son's condition. She could not bear to think it, but she couldn't help thinking it. "No," said the specialist. "This is congenital; the defect was there from birth." Yet she couldn't help thinking of the day of the competition.

"Jumna, will everything be all right?" By "everything" she meant Nirmalya; Nirmalya was twelve years old. She sat on the sofa of the new flat, behind her a new mirror. She looked into the distance; there were tears inside her eyes.

Jumna—who lived in a slum in Mahalaxmi—said: "Why do you think so much, memsaab? Don't you see how well our baba is?" Mallika Sengupta nodded tearfully. She envied Jumna, almost. She envied her her four healthy children. Vipul, Ramesh. Shankar, Asha. Four children who went to a municipal school. Would she, Mallika Sengupta, have changed places with Jumna? Perhaps not. But she would have liked to have had Jumna's easy taking-for-granted, as Jumna bent low before the carpet, jhadu in hand, of her children. And she knew she couldn't have it.

"What do you think will happen?"

And so Jumna had to lay down the jhadu and sit beside the centre table. Mrs. Sengupta was a small statue of pain; Jumna must console her. For a long time they'd just sit together in silence. "Nothing will happen," Jumna said, as if she'd casually dismissed the powers-that-be. "Arrey, what can happen?" Then, slowly, after an interval of brooding and staring into the distance, she'd get back to work.

Jumna lived in the large sprawling slum in Mahalaxmi, not far from the Race Course. In spite of its size, it was invisible from the main road; it had to be arrived at by a couple of narrow by-lanes and gullies. The people at the Race Course and the members of the

Willingdon Club probably didn't know it was there. Once, Nirmalya and the driver had dropped her off on a road next to the Willingdon Club which had a large expanse of untended green on one side. She'd got out of the car, and Nirmalya didn't know in exactly which direction she'd gone. The car had gone back up the road; and when Nirmalya turned back to look, Jumna was already gone, there was only the road and the expanse of overgrown green. But Nirmalya knew now that this—not the exact location, but somewhere here—was where Jumna returned in the afternoons.

Today, it was to Jumna that Mrs. Sengupta turned. It wasn't the first time she'd done so. It was as if the very fact that Jumna possessed almost nothing, that there was nothing, really, she could offer to her employer, that made Mrs. Sengupta turn to her as an inexplicable source of comfort.

"What will happen, then, Jumna?" asked Mrs. Sengupta. Jumna, sitting on the carpet, pulling the aanchal of her sari to cover her head, said, "What will happen? Memsaab, you worry for nothing." Jumna was moved; she was not insincere; the poor have a special ability, after all, to understand the torments of their employers, to empathise with them. It was as if she absorbed some of Mallika Sengupta's pain.

Her real name was Heera. Before she came to work for this family six years ago, a bearded jamadar with red eyes and a paunch used to come in the mornings to clean the bathrooms in the Cumballa Hill flat. While going down the hill one evening, Nirmalya had suddenly seen him from the car, staggering drunkenly on the road. Nirmalya had always wondered what the man did for the rest of the day. "He's a strange man. His kind eat crows," said the driver. "Crows?" Nirmalya was awe-struck. Nirmalya thought of the jamadar sitting in a room, a dead crow in his hand; he was preparing to cook it. One of those crows that sit on parapets, balconies, behind the windows of toilets, and fill the day with their cawing. Nirmalya couldn't decide whether to add a family to the scene—children in the room, sitting next to the jamadar as he began to cook. "Yes, yes, 'they' eat crows," said the driver, and, from the way he said the word, Nirmalya could see the shadowy "they" the jamadar belonged to was, in the driver's eyes, beyond the pale. Then the jamadar was back the next morning, silently wiping the floors.

If the jamadar came from the realm of night and darkness, Jumna came from the world of light. Of course she was a jamadarni, and maybe came from the same caste as the jamadar, but, from the beginning, Mrs. Sengupta had been won over by her demeanour "She's cultured, more cultured than the ladies I meet at parties." This spoke for Jumna's manners and intelligence in that dawn of her employment, and it also spoke for Mrs. Sengupta's own dislike of, and her unease at, the increasing number of company parties she went to. As for Jumna, she'd come, like the jamadar, to wipe the floors, to clean the toilet bowl, but gradually she shed her jamadarni sweeper-woman status. She became all things—confidante; surrogate mother to the boy; slave and friend; part-time servant—and the hands that held the bucket and toilet brush also came to make chapattis. "She makes very good chapattis," said Mallika Sengupta, "she puts them straight on to the gas flame and they swell like balloons."

The boy took it upon himself to educate Jumna. He was also profoundly curious about why she was poor. Already, at eight, though he despised school himself, he was an advocate of the religion of education; he was convinced that going to school could have changed Jumna. They had long and serious dialogues. "Baba, I only went to school till the second class. Then I'd tell my mother I was going to school, but I wouldn't go. I would go somewhere with a friend and come back and say I'd been to school." "And that is why you are in this state now," the boy said, his thesis proved.

During other conversations, Jumna, abandoning her jhadu, would provide more metaphysical explanations.

"It must have been some paap I'd done in my last birth," as if she'd hit upon a reason that was actually plausible, "which is why I'm leading this life in this birth."

"Something you did in your last birth," said the boy, looking at the familiar face of the woman before him. The logic appealed to him. Although his eyes were open, the world went dark for a second, and he wondered who Jumna might have been, and what terrible transgression she might have committed: this person who rang the doorbell at nine thirty in the morning.

"But since you're having such an awful life in this birth," said the boy, leaning forward on the heavy drawing-room chair, "you should have a wonderful life in the next one." He smiled, because it was a joke; but he also hoped it might be true.

"I hope so," she said solemnly, picking up the jhadu. She too was joking; but she didn't completely reject the idea.

"You'll probably live in a palace," said the boy, elaborating. They shared the joke together in the drawing room. In this way, they'd become close. The sorrow of this woman, without his knowing it, had—like something you eat or drink early in life, whose effects become clear only in adulthood—entered and penetrated him.

He wanted to cure her and educate her. When he was still a child, his parents brought him a doctor-set; temporarily, he became her doctor. She was ignorant; she must be treated and warned. "You drink tap water," he accused her. "It has germs." Indeed, she drank tap water in the kitchen, cupping her hand and bending, then wiping her mouth with the back of her hand in absent-minded satisfaction.

So, the treatment commenced. He had to inoculate her. He used the plastic syringe from the doctor-set. Then, to be more thorough, he pricked her with needles from his mother's large dressing table. "Why must you do this, baba?" she asked, genuinely bewildered. "Because you have germs inside you," he replied. She could say nothing to the boy.

Two days later, tearful but smiling, she said to his mother, "Baba is playing doctor. He pricks me with needles." And she showed the marks on her arm. "He's been giving me injections," she said, still smiling.

"I was trying to cure her," the boy said stubbornly.

The treatment stopped.

He was lordly with her, and at home in general, but he was afraid of the outside world. It wasn't fear as much as a shyness of contact—a mild terror of people he already knew. He disliked convivial occasions; he particularly disliked festivals. During Holi, he was the last to go and play; once, when he'd been standing among the furniture in the Cumballa Hill flat, unsure of whether to join the friends who were clamouring outside the main door and indulging in profligate bouts of doorbell-ringing, he was horrified to see, suddenly, purple water trickling underneath the door into the flat; one of the boys outside was busy; it was like a horror film.

He didn't like Diwali either, though he hadn't entirely admitted this to himself. Come Diwali, Apurva Sengupta journeyed dutifully to Teen Batti to bring back a small package of sparklers and firecrackers. Then nighttime, and the dark umbrella of the sky flashing with meteors; but Nirmalya wanted the sky to be quiet again. There was a small back garden in La Terrasse from which his father tentatively launched rockets into the sky. But, while chocolate bombs exploded in the neighbourhood, it was clear that Apurva Sengupta didn't care much for the festival either. When Nirmalya had asked him why he never bought chocolate bombs (because, although he was uneasy with the festival, he was also eager to be part of it), Mr. Sengupta said:

"This is the way businessmen use up their black money," as a pudgy boy in shorts on Little Gibbs Road advanced and swiftly lit a fuse and then ran away again. "They have all that money lying around, they have to find ways of spending it."

A one-night conflagration of undeclared assets! This was one of the revelations of Nirmalya's childhood. Almost all his friends' fathers had "black money." Yet he always sniffed the air when a bomb went off, because he loved the sweet smell of burning explosives.

The boy came out into the sitting room; his mother had called him repeatedly. At fifteen and a half, he had a shadowy goatee under his chin. For more than a year, he'd shaved with pride, even when there was only the slightest evidence of facial hair; standing in front of the bathroom mirror, it was half daydream, in which he felt separate and aloof from his classmates. But now there was a sudden change, and he allowed the goatee to grow. He also allowed his hair to grow. He'd let it grow once before, when he was in school, and had been punished for it; there had been warnings in class, and then an order to stand outside the classroom, and finally a trek to the vice-principal's office. He was disciplined, lectured, his parents notified; he'd had to have a haircut—his mother had forced him to have it cropped. Now he let it grow again; his exams were over; he felt answerable to nobody.

He looked a bit unkempt when he came out to meet the music teacher. He wore a faded kurta with his jeans. But the sandals he wore were expensive, bought from the Taj.

"This is Nirmalya, my son," said Mrs. Sengupta, smiling. Shyamji looked at him critically. He tried to reconcile the boy with the flat, the furniture, the background of the Arabian Sea.

55

. . .

"Baba, listen to this song!" said Shyamji to Nirmalya in a friendly, direct way just as the boy was thinking of going out; it was his second tuition. Shyamji sat alone before the harmonium, pressing the keys, immune to hurry. Behind him, a crow sat on the wide concrete balustrade of the sunken balcony. Reluctantly, Nirmalya lowered himself on the sofa; Shyamji, in his distracted but effective way, had recruited him into his audience.

And right from the beginning, he called Nirmalya "baba," consigning him, albeit affectionately, to the "babalog," the eternal children of the rich. "Listen to this song, didi! You will like it," he said to her with equal candour.

It was the first song he taught her. It was plain but attractive; she'd never heard of the poet—not one of the great names. He began to sing: "Hai aankh wo jo Ram ka darshan kiya kare."

> Those eyes are truly eyes that have seen the Lord.

The song was an admonitory one; he sang it in a low voice.

> Futile are those mouths that remain busy in chatter.
> Those lips are truly lips that utter the name of Hari.

Shyamji had set the words to a simple tune, a tune that, even for a beginner, would be easy to pick up. But there were embellishments in his singing that she carefully noted:

> Jewelled bangles do not lend grace to those hands.
> Those hands are truly hands that are joined in prayer to
> the Lord.

The song was not meant ironically; the words were not a message directed by Shyamji towards the three gold bangles—three of many—that Mrs. Sengupta presently wore round her wrist. The song belonged to the realm of ideal possibility, some other world in which such notions were not only desirable but possible. But the song was just a song; and that world was not *this* world. Nirmalya, sipping a glass of water and listening, didn't even understand all the words.

> Mortal, that man wins immortal fame
> Who sacrifices his life to the love of the Lord.

"Ma, what does balidaan mean?" asked Nirmalya a couple of days later. He was skulking behind her as she, after her bath, was dabbing her face and putting the finishing touches to herself before the dressing-table mirror.

She looked up absently.

"Sacrifice," she said.

Nirmalya heard her sing the song again; and, for some reason, he was interested in finding out what the words meant. One or two of the words had caught his ear; he pieced the song together.

He wasn't quite sure what to think of it. The tune was sugary; and its message so unequivocal that it couldn't be taken quite seriously. And yet, although it was quite a crude song, its meaning startled him. It was as if—because it was only now that he'd put together what the words of the song meant—it was now that he felt himself capable of understanding what it was saying; he almost confused translation with communication; the song had suddenly given to him what it had withheld so far. It penetrated him not through its verbal distinction, but its rapid series of pictures.

Are the hands that pray more beautiful than hands that wear ornaments? Although he himself had never prayed, the question didn't seem merely rhetorical. He saw arms before him, a woman's arms; not disconnected from the body, but the body nevertheless invisible; one set of arms sparkling with three or four bangles; the other set of arms bare. For some reason, the sight—the mental picture—of the bare arms calmed him.

From the sunken balcony he could see Bombay repeatedly; or as much of Bombay as he wanted to see. And the water, which disturbed him without his knowing it, and which, although it was everywhere, he could only look at from the corner of his eye. The sea was a negation of the city's human energies.

Once or twice, in the years he spent at La Terrasse, he dreamt of the sea: this tame accessory, this add-on, to luxury apartments and hotel rooms. It had risen all the way from Elephanta island, like a huge tidal wave swelling from Trombay, in one dream; and the flat he lived in was no longer the flat he knew. From the balcony, he saw the sea approaching with awe and a feeling of doom. But the balcony had become the front rows of a movie theatre, and the flat itself was like the inside of a cinema; a cinema that was elegant and in business, but strangely empty. From the window of the theatre (whose spacious lounge reminded him of the interiors of the Eros or of the Regal), he looked at the gigantic tumult; and then, as if he wasn't alone, he communicated his sense of dread to someone inside with a smile.

Next morning, he woke with a sense of the other world he'd visited still upon him, of having gone and returned from an elsewhere that was familiar, banal, and yet, unexpectedly, magnificently on the brink of destruction: he knew no one survived that flood. When he came out into the drawing room, his eyes smarted with the light. There it was like a drab mercantile fact; the clusters of low and tall buildings from Nana Chowk to the Fort to further away; behind them, like the humps of idle animals, the islands of Elephanta and Trombay. The sea was dull and shining. It was as if the world had exhausted itself, and taken refuge in a surreptitious normalcy. But he was heavy with knowledge.

When Sumit Sen visited Bombay from Calcutta, Apurva Sengupta arranged a recital for him and Mallika Sengupta in a hall in North Bombay. The so-called "expatriate" Bengalis sent out a welcoming party, of course; they wanted to get involved, as they did when any luminary made their way to Bombay from Calcutta. They went to receive him at the station—a gentle, ordinary-looking, bespectacled man who hadn't lost his air of small means and limitations; and his low-key modesty was more a sense of surprised, genuine gratitude at what luck had given him. He emerged from the Gitanjali Express crumpled, but impeccably dressed in the manner of a singer of Tagore songs, in white dhuti and kurta. He folded his hands in a namaskar when the expectant "expatriate" Bengalis approached; if not with garlands, then at least with pleased, vindicated expressions.

Mr. Sengupta had just been made Head of Finance. He was steadying himself after the congratulations; he was weary of the felicitatory food he'd eaten at parties—he felt full all the time. He wanted to get back to work, to the responsibilities that Philip Dyer had quickly divided between Mr. Sengupta and himself. But at the same time, he wanted this performance to go well, both for Sumit Sen and for his own wife; it distracted him.

"Call the newspapers," he said to his personal assistant, the large Das, who was always composed and silently efficacious. "You know that Sumit Sen is well known in Calcutta."

Mr. Das nodded. "He is very well known," he agreed. And, leaving aside some of the day's other work to do with letters and appointments and taxes, he began to make phone call after phone call.

The invitation cards went out. They were sent to the middle-class Bengalis—among them junior employees in Mr. Sengupta's company, who'd been watching his rise from a distance—who lived in Dadar, Khar, Prabhadevi, Mulund. Some of them would have come because Sumit Sen's rendition of Tagore songs in the style of Hemanta was all the rage now in Calcutta; and "expatriate" Bengalis liked to feel they were in touch with their homeland. For this reason they would flock to the Kala Kendra auditorium, and even tolerate Mrs. Sengupta's singing: because, privately, they concluded that the only reason she was singing on that day was because she was Apurva Sengupta's wife. They resented having to make this journey through the traffic lights partly for Mallika Sengupta.

Mallika Sengupta didn't care; she was somewhat contemptuous of the Bengalis who lived in Mulund and Khar. She knew what their "clubs" and cultural programmes, their small-town ideas of recreation, were like. She was not one of them.

Sumit Sen had asked her to sing: so she would. Although she felt a distaste for his unfailingly populist choice of certain Tagore songs, and his sentimental version of Hemanta's already sentimental style, and although he was quite unimpressive-looking, he was, astonishingly, a good man: that rarity. He had, somehow, spontaneously, after listening to her sing, realised what she was, in spite of being the wife of a Head of Finance: an artist. In this itself he was unusual.

. . .

Mrs. Sengupta wore a green jamdani sari; she used to wear it sparingly, and saved it for such occasions. Nirmalya clenched a Panasonic tape recorder by the handle, and entered the hall, feeling rather indispensable and conspicuous, for he'd been entrusted with the mission of getting the performance on tape; not because he wanted to, but because he was so unthinkingly familiar with the "rewind" and "record" and "play" buttons. He focussed fussily on the buttons.

Sumit Sen was in yet another white panjabi and dhuti, with his trademark air of simplicity. One could say that the show was a success: the suburban hall was almost three-quarters full.

For two days afterwards, the tape was played again and again. Out in the sitting room, near the balcony facing the Marine Drive and the indifferent glint of the sea, or inside the bedroom, the Panasonic lay propped against the sofa. Nirmalya's parents listened intently. The muffled world of the auditorium returned, the applause in semi-lit aisles, the rather pedestrian, optimistic energy of Sumit Sen's singing, Mrs. Sengupta's voice, as she sang Atul Prasad, hovering in the ether, all this absorbed and made cloudy by the small microphone.

"Abhay Deshpande was there." Mr. Das, taciturn personal assistant, conveyed this bit of information to Apurva Sengupta with characteristic restraint. "Abhay Deshpande?" said Mr. Sengupta, looking up. Deshpande was a leading music critic; he wrote for the *Times of India* and the *Evening News*. A small, short-sighted man, shaped like a bitter gourd. No one, except those who knew him, recognised him at music concerts.

"But unfortunately," and Mr. Das appeared crestfallen, "I don't think he stayed on for the second half. I think he missed Mallikadi's singing."

"Are you sure?" asked Mr. Sengupta. Mr. Das looked nervous. He nodded.

"I saw him out, Mr. Sengupta," he said. "He was in a hurry."

For some reason, on the next two days, Mr. Sengupta bought a copy of the *Evening News* from a small boy at a traffic junction on Marine Drive. He pored over it carefully as the car stopped at intersections; then set it aside. There was nothing; why had he expected otherwise? The flash of excitement at the Kala Kendra auditorium died; Sumit Sen went back to Calcutta.

He was dictating a letter to his secretary, afternoon sun making the office window radiant, when Mr. Das, purposeful and unstoppable as a weapon in a military arsenal, entered and said with suppressed agitation (because this would surely increase his importance in Mr. Sengupta's eyes): "Abhay Deshpande called." Mr. Sengupta looked up: "Yes?" With unexplained triumph, Das said: "He wants Mrs. Sengupta's bio-data." Mr. Sengupta furrowed his brows; he opened a drawer—fortunately a recent biographical note was at hand.

Then, one day, Apurva Sengupta came back home with a paper in his hand. "Das gave me this," he said. "He's very excited—Abhay Deshpande has written a review." He was beaming; he waved the *Evening News*. She smiled apprehensively; she went past the report on the Chief Minister's transgressions on the first page, the light-eyed girl in the bathing suit on the third page, and kept turning the pages until she came to a headline hovering on the right-hand side, "Bengali Songs Charm Bombay." She didn't know what to make of the small print, the first three paragraphs about Sumit Sen, beginning, "Sumit Sen is all the rage in Calcutta, and one can see why. He sang the songs of the Kaviguru, known to us here in Bombay only from the tunes stolen without any apologies by our music directors, with aplomb in his marvellous and mellifluous voice." The last two paragraphs concerned Mrs. Sengupta: "She has a lovely, melodious voice, soaked in bhakti, and sang the songs of a lesser-known but no less talented composer, Atul Prosad, with command and ease. Many of the songs were set to bittersweet and emotive ragas like Desh and Kafi. Mallika ably brought out the pathos inherent in these ragas."

She closed the paper; her eyes sparkled; she wanted to believe the things he'd said. But Abhay Deshpande's figure receded and receded; she could not grasp it or imagine it. "I thought he left before I started to sing," she said. She tried again to think of him, but the man eluded her. "Mr. Das might have been wrong," she said. She paused, as at a minor conundrum. "Of course, he might have been right . . . What does he look like?" she asked her husband. "I don't know. I haven't seen him," said Apurva Sengupta as he took off his jacket. They decided what to feel—to be happy with the review; to think no more of it.

Prashanta and Nayana Neogi still lived in the rented ground-floor flat with the dusty driveway in Khar. These, the Senguptas' oldest friends in Bombay. But separated from them not only by distance—between the old world of Khar and the sea-facing tall buildings of Malabar Hill—but the different social worlds they now moved in. In fact, the Neogis didn't "move" at all; they stayed put, and people visited them—the same filmmakers and artists, both failed and successful.

And although Khar was far away, the Senguptas sometimes visited on Saturdays; sat in the bedroom, the air-conditioner on, the bamboo chiks keeping out light, as the Neogis' dogs either strutted about, or rested immovably on the floor, tranquil, breathing heaps of bone and hair. Mallika Sengupta appeared to ignore them, but gathered the hem of her sari silently; although she didn't think this in so many words, these animals in the bedroom represented to her the hidden wildness of the Neogis' lives. The dogs, on the other hand, truly ignored everyone, unless a fit of awareness possessed them.

The Neogis had a son, Biswajit, six years older than Nirmalya; the other son, known now only by his pet name, "Tutu," had died when he was seven years old of leukaemia. The Senguptas had never seen this boy; there was a picture of him in the bedroom, a vivid black-and-white close-up of his laughing face. The boy's absence, and the presence of the photograph, haunted the casual cigarette-smoking skein of the Neogis' lives, and always confronted the visitor. When Nirmalya first heard about Tutu from his mother—"They say he was a bright boy, very talented"—he was seven years old himself, and he took a careful second look at the photograph for reasons of his own. He felt a moment of dread; could he die like that, suddenly? The boy in the picture was smiling into the distance; Nirmalya looked to his mother, busy talking to Nayana Neogi, a tea-tray before them, for reassurance. But they were in some other world, on the hallucinatory plane of repetitive, everyday existence. What was death—a sort of permanent blankness? He often wondered what would happen if he fell asleep and didn't wake up again. He'd once had a dream in which he died, and woken up with a sense of foreboding, a deep sense of being metamorphosed. In the dream, he was playing with a friend, Puneet—this small, chuckling boy had since failed his exams and lost a year, and stayed back in the same class; they'd stopped being as close as they used to—Puneet and he were soldiers, possibly American Marines, and they were trying to capture what was either a ship or a submarine. In the gun battle on the green submarine, Nirmalya—and this happened not long before he awoke; the light was already in the curtains—was shot. Puneet couldn't help him; and, at that moment, when Nirmalya was dying, he thought, "This is a dream"; he woke up. But that feeling of draining away, where dying had mingled with the dream's fading into daylight—he found that difficult to shrug off as he put on his socks for school, while John the bearer loomed over him.

The company Mr. Sengupta worked in grew. So they decided to move office again. This time it was a stupendous, time-taking affair; moving from Nariman Point to a tall new upstart building on Cuffe Parade—one of a throng that had appeared where there had been nothing before. At the same time, the Senguptas moved to a huge five-bedroom apartment on the top storey of another one of the new buildings; and, in what seemed a logical but nevertheless breathtaking culmination of his career so far, he took over the company from Philip Dyer. A large laminated black-and-white picture on wood, of Dyer sitting at his chairman's desk, his sideburns flamboyant and prominent, signed in a stylish black scrawl, "To Apurva and family, Philip," as if a gift of some part of himself, even a replica, was to always preside benignly over their lives, was removed a few weeks later from the position it had occupied in the Senguptas' bedroom for three years (where it used to be noted silently by Dyer during parties) and put inside a drawer. No comment was made, or necessary. The company was still partly foreign-owned; but it was, in effect, the end of the last vestiges of the British age.

There was some tension at this time with Dyer—Dyer, who loved Bombay, who loved "India," that mythical composite of colour and smell and anonymous human beings and daylight, who loved being attended to by everyone from peons to businessmen, who, it was said, loved his brief flings with starlets and secretaries, who believed he had in some ways nurtured Apurva Sengupta. The last farewell parties were slightly awkward affairs, full of enforced shoulder-huggings and the sudden, unpredictable moist eye—because people found that emotion could surprise them when they least expected it. (The main bit of gossip at this time was the golden hair that had recently appeared, like a burst of energy, above Dyer's forehead. "It's not a toupee," whispered a director's wife to Mallika Sengupta at a party. "Apparently he had a transplant." There was Dyer, not far from her, gesticulating and displaying the painfully acquired new hair.) Now he was displeased and melancholy at the idea of having to pack his bags after all these decades and leave for London, for "home," with the semi-alcoholic Julia. His children, recently out of boarding school, were no longer in England; the son was somewhere near Dubai, working on an oil rig; the daughter was in her ancient residential boarding school. Philip Dyer, it seemed, had nothing to go back to.

The Senguptas made the move, and he—Apurva—became the new Managing Director. It was around this time that Nirmalya entered into a phase—it was an odd change of mood, a prickliness, that had begun after his school exams—of being ostentatiously ill at ease with the world his father inhabited. Without saying as much, he sat in judgement upon it. He hated the new flat in Cuffe Parade. The first evening, when his parents were busy supervising the packers, he arrived late, and sat in the large drawing room among the semi-finished furniture, asking, "Why did we have to come here?"

He had grown his hair long. It came to his shoulders. He hardly appeared to smile, and never shaved the straggly goatee.

6 7

When his parents threw their first party in the new flat, and just before the first guests began to arrive, congratulating the Senguptas, he went out for a walk. "Where's Nirmalya?" his father asked, exasperated. No one knew.

When he returned, no one asked him where he'd been. His father spotted him and escorted him to the non-executive chairman of the board who'd flown in the previous day from Delhi. Apurva Sengupta had an unnecessarily triumphant air, as if he'd caught a bird of marvellous plumage, and not the untidy boy he had next to him.

"Here he is at last—managed to find him!" he smiled, as if at a hugely funny joke.

The chairman, a tall, fair septuagenarian with bushy eyebrows called Thakore, wasn't impressed. He was a figurehead in the company, but a coveted emblem; and he knew it. His smile was a mixture of politeness and disdain.

"We don't get to see you these days!"

Thakore was slightly threatened by the boy; he sensed a resistance. He wasn't sure if he was getting the respect due to him. His remark was an exaggeration; he'd met the Senguptas' son only once before.

Nirmalya smiled, and, as ever at such moments, said nothing. The silence was infuriating to the chairman.

"So what are you doing these days, young man? In college?" Thakore looked at Nirmalya's hair.

"Junior college," murmured Nirmalya. He was in that zone in which he could pretend he was an undergraduate and no longer a schoolboy, in which he could study in college classrooms and "hang out" in college corridors, without actually beginning his BA until two years later. As far as he was concerned, the important thing was he was not a schoolboy.

"Let me get you a refill, JB," said Mr. Sengupta, and put an arm around Thakore. The bushy-eyebrowed chairman was glad to be led away. Apurva Sengupta took him to the little bar on the far side of the drawing room. Before heading off to the bar, the chairman said (for he liked having the last word):

"We must see more of you, my boy! We haven't got to know each other."

Nirmalya went onto the balcony; the small crowd of two women and a man didn't notice him, or pretended not to notice him, and made no effort to be nice to him, as people did because he was Mr. Sengupta's son. He looked out. It was the sea, of course, the same sea he'd seen for five years from La Terrasse; but he was looking at it from the other side, and it seemed different. In fact, he could see the faint phantom outline of La Terrasse among the different-sized buildings on that side. Darkness had translated the sea into near-invisibility. Ten days after the move, it was as if he were indifferently looking at a relic from his past.

Before moving out of La Terrasse into Thacker Towers (that was the name of this sternly clone-like cluster of buildings) they'd gone scouting around the south side of the city for an appropriate flat for the new managing director: the two of them—Mr. and Mrs. Sengupta, accompanied by a guide delegated by the company, and sometimes Nirmalya.

Dyer was not going to vacate his duplex flat in La Terrasse for Apurva Sengupta; he was going to sell it on behalf of the company—and probably pocket a cut; a parting present to himself before leaving. "Yes, that's why he's selling it," said Mrs. Sengupta. This was a disappointment; they'd been looking forward to moving into the apartment on the seventeenth floor with the goldfish darting in the grey water; where, once the main door opened and you were inside, the staircase swiftly escaped upwards. "No matter, we'll find a better place," said Apurva Sengupta, his face grim but reconciled to the sleight-of-hand by which the duplex flat had vanished. He began to search obdurately for a lavish apartment as a sort of rebuff to the departed Englishman.

But Nirmalya felt bitter and unhappy at the idea of moving house, and wandered sullenly about the flat in La Terrasse as if he were looking for a hiding-place in which to secrete himself, in the hope that he wouldn't be missed.

Looking back (and he was already in a retrospective mood), it seemed—although there was no reason to support this—that he was leaving behind a simpler time in his life, of pure white walls and spacious rooms, where even wealth was less ambivalent. It was as if—and his heart sensed this, not his mind—he was now to be caught up, if not as player then as bystander, in a story of ambition; he wasn't sure whose—perhaps his own, but if not his entirely, then his parents', or other people's, or could it be even the city's itself? The spell of La Terrasse was broken.

Had it only been his imagination? No, even the pigeons who alighted on the sloping concrete bannister of the balcony had succumbed to it; they were conscious of the evident hospitality of the drawing room. Sometimes one of the Senguptas would find one standing there, next to the sofa or on the edge of the carpet; or even seeming to investigate the immense catacomb-like wall-unit on the left, with its various compartments that held, among other things, the record player and speakers that blasted out, at certain times during those years, Nirmalya's burgeoning pop and then rock collection. Innocently it stood there, as if listening for the music that was no longer coming; almost solicitious, but wary if you stopped to look at it, escaping, even before you clapped your hands to shoo it away, with a loud flap of wings, a sound that, long after, would be audible and present to Nirmalya's ear.

. . .

Earlier, when Nirmalya was smaller, and the relationship between the Senguptas and the Dyers was still in its golden period, Mr. Sengupta would cajole his son—sometimes command him—into visiting the Dyers, especially when their son Matthew came "home" from England.

"Matthew's back," Dyer would say cheerily on the phone after a long conversation about more official things. "It would be absolutely lovely for him—and Tina of course—to see Nirmalya again."

Matthew was a nice boy, full of crass jokes and good-natured energy: but a disappointment to his parents. And his parents, especially Philip Dyer, didn't hide their disappointment from him. Dyer treated his son like a semi-literate. "Matthew's spelling's quite atrocious," he'd confided in Apurva Sengupta once, at the end of a discourse of gloomy opinions about Indira Gandhi's nationalising fervour and trade union unrest.

And once, Nirmalya was with the older boy in the study, ensconced by books no one read, a stack of thick faintly shining magazines that Nirmalya wouldn't ordinarily see anywhere else, *Fortune*, *Life*, and *Penthouse*, too, placed neatly on the glass table, signifying other universes that were always just round the corner for the Dyers, the room separated from the sitting room by its absence of natural light and a tinted glass door; Matthew was in the study, wolfing down ice cream from a plate, when his mother had said to him, "I don't think the Murrays would be amused if they saw you eating that way!" The Murrays; a couple in some suburb made mythic by power and distance—Paul Murray was a director in the "parent" company in England, its headquarters in Surrey. Nirmalya, seeing Matthew peer up in hurt surprise from his plate, wondered why his own parents had never issued similar instructions to him. What made the Murrays so important to Matthew's life?

. . .

But Matthew took parental chiding on the chin; he saw them as a source equally of meaningless strictures and endless pocket money; and he'd made a shrewd appraisal of their own shortcomings, and the sort of life, a life created for public consumption, they were leading in India. He himself had a vague longing for the ocean and the deep, to explore the humanless but crowded world underwater; it was only a germ of an idea, but it had already planted itself in his head.

He was only three years older than Nirmalya, but behaved as if he were much older. Part of his independence from people who were much cleverer than he, or who represented success and otherwise dominated him, like his parents, came from his sexual knowledge. He had many girlfriends, and the moral ambiguity of this fact gave him a sort of secret strength. "No girl over sixteen in Britain," he'd told Nirmalya one afternoon, like one who, after discussing several exciting possibilities, returns reluctantly to the sheer ordinariness of things, "is a virgin." This was in response to a stupid question; Nirmalya had asked him, "Do you sleep with your girlfriends?"—for Matthew said he had two, one for weekdays and one for weekends. The reply, an incredible revelation, at first astonished Nirmalya into dumbness; but it also disturbed and excited him physically. Something extraordinary and unmentionable happened to girls in England when they reached sixteen; and the myopic Matthew, in every other way unremarkable, had been inured to it into a state of forgetfulness.

He was the first English boy Nirmalya properly knew. And, because he was English, he was somewhat exotic, as English books were—exotic not in an antique fairy-tale way, but with toffee and jam, mud and physical effluences. Matthew made Nirmalya blink with nervousness. When he was smaller, he'd been loud and unstoppable, like some volatile foreign toy that has a life of its own. Then Nirmalya grew used to the jack-in-the-box energy and wildness, and realised it was essentially harmless. On the whole, it had to be said that Matthew was the friendlier and more simple of the two.

At an early age, Nirmalya had entered Matthew's room on the upper storey and discovered the treasures Philip Dyer had given his son despite being an exacting and sometimes unforgiving father. Among these was a small gramophone, of dimensions that made it look more like a projection of a fantasy than a real object—yet it was not a toy, but played, with precise functionality, Matthew's limited but munificent record collection. Among these was a song, "Mud, Mud, Glorious Mud," which Matthew put on the record-changer repeatedly, and which seemed to emerge from some hitherto unknown bog of English identity, and which Matthew sang along to in an insistent way, with a personal abandonment that made Nirmalya feel uneasy. But there were other wonders that filled him with longing during his brief sojourns in Matthew Dyer's small room; films of the Tramp and Tarzan in bright square packages to be seen at some point on a projector; and thumb-sized toys you could lift in your palm, from which Nirmalya realised that England had the same red postboxes that Bombay had, and the same kind of red double-decker buses.

Matthew had friends in Bombay, rather shady and stupid-looking, but confident from being "experienced"; the sons of some of Philip Dyer's business contacts who escorted Matthew to, and made him pay for, sunless bars and restaurants and discotheques—the Bombay that lay far beyond Nirmalya's purview. He'd developed a taste for Hindi films in their company, for their embarrassing exuberance and their helpless bursting into song, their tearful but happy families and prodigious villains; for two and a half hours they gave Matthew something he found nowhere else.

Now he nurtured an ambition his parents knew nothing about. "I'm going to produce and act in a Hindi film one day." Matthew said this with a smile to Nirmalya, but he was quite serious.

Tina, his sister, went to school in Bombay and was much younger than Nirmalya; eight years old, a child. But the feminine desires and demands that would shape her life had already woken in her, and, almost accidentally, their object was Nirmalya. "I want to marry Nirmalya," she'd said to her mother. To which Julia Dyer replied coldly: "Nirmalya only likes black girls." Candid and inquisitive about the mysterious remark, Tina had passed on the statement to Nirmalya: "Do you only like black girls, Nirmalya—my mother says you do?" and Nirmalya was made speechless by the long passage of history newly written, and condensed into an observation that confused him, and barely managed to mumble something. Tina's desires were genuine and intense, if still out of place at eight. To show her affection, she once lifted her dress in front of Nirmalya and pulled down her panties. Her sudden straightforward insights into Nirmalya sometimes exceeded others', including his own. "I know why you come here," she'd said knowingly. "You want to see my mother's mammas."

When Nirmalya reported the panty episode to his mother, as if he were relating the charming antics with which all eight-year-olds win over the world, she smiled, but was secretly furious. "Is this what working in a company means?" she said to her husband that night. "Is your career so important that our son has to go to that house?"

From the Dyers the Senguptas "inherited" a cook who made continental dishes, a tiny saintly man, a Malyali called Arthur. Arthur was not his real name. His real name was Thambi. He made chocolate cakes, pancakes, steak and kidney pie, stuffed peppers, fruit trifle, macaroni, Christmas pudding. He'd passed through a procession of European households where he'd minted and reproduced this food with an almost unknowing fidelity. Brought into the world in a village in Kerala, he seemed, oddly, to be born for this task. And, yet again, with this latest departure, he was momentarily marooned, momentarily unsure of who'd value his outlandish gift, but was appropriated immediately by the Senguptas before he had time to make up his mind—and the Senguptas would become the first Indian family to benefit from the skills he claimed to have acquired from those slightly exasperated English memsahibs.

The next day, after the party, when John, and Jumna, his assistant, were still putting away, with stately, valedictory meticulousness, the piles of washed dishes, Nirmalya sneaked out for a walk around Thacker Towers. This part of Cuffe Parade had been ocean not very long ago; it was land that had been fairly recently reclaimed. Upon it had appeared Thacker Towers and its sister skyscrapers: a whole family of tall siblings that didn't seem to know one another. And Snowman's Ice Cream Parlour, where different-coloured flavours were frozen inside troughs, a shopping arcade, and the President Hotel with pennants fluttering.

Walking, he was aware of its newness, as if it were the edge of a young planet. It was a strip of land that had encroached on water. And, because of the encroachment, the water had become flat and grey, like macadam; there was hardly a wave in it. Mornings and evenings, it was, for a while, lacquered by light from a sun that rose and set without comment on this part of the universe. One or two gulls hovered in a puzzled way over the water, as if it were a road stretching to infinity, or at least to the other side of Bombay, where you could see La Terrasse among the buildings.

If you walked back down the reclaimed land, you came to the fringes of the old Colaba, with its palm trees and its walls on which sea breezes had left shadows, like bruises that had appeared not overnight, but over years. That was another world, where the sea had once ended; where they'd moved to was only a ten-minute walk away. He was intrigued by the the dead calm of the sea around Thacker Towers. This was not the sea he knew, whose waves had the habit of rising twenty or thirty feet during the monsoons and drenching the cars and buses on Marine Drive. Sometimes, as he stood at its edge, like a traveller newly arrived on a planet, it seemed to be an enormous shadow.

The door was half ajar when Shyamji first arrived at the apartment; so he didn't have to ring the bell to enter. "Didi!" he cried in his sweet high-pitched voice, and looked blankly at the long corridor on his right. "Mallika didi!" He checked his reflection, when he saw it, in the large mirror above the telephone; he ran his fingers through his hair. Then he saw Nirmalya, in a khadi kurta and jeans, his goatee a shadow beneath the chin.

"Baba," he said, "look at this apartment—it is wonderful!"

Mrs. Sengupta, who was just coming down the corridor, said, with a playful approximation of a look of concern:

"He doesn't like it. He tells me he doesn't want to live here."

Shyamji appeared mildly scandalised. He looked closely at Nirmalya.

"But why—why not?"

"I think he liked the old flat—the one in La Terrasse: he liked that better; usko wohi pasand thha."

Nirmalya looked uncomfortable and shy, as if everything his mother had said was a joke, and strangely despondent. But Shyamji nodded seriously, like one who was considering the virtues of a dead relative.

"That flat was nice, certainly. But this one . . ." He was impressed with the little he'd seen of it; it was like a mahal—he'd encountered nothing on this scale before.

. . .

There were flies in the flat. This discovery—of a constant buzzing, a microscopic movement, involved in its own journeys, but coming in your way, challenging and distracting you without even knowing it—this unlooked-for companionship was exasperating. The flies buzzed against windowpanes and flew around your face. You spent a lot of time waving them away. Among other things, they qualified the grand rebuff to Dyer the flat had represented.

Mrs. Sengupta, Nirmalya, even, occasionally, Apurva Sengupta—all attacked them briskly with fly swatters. But it was a losing battle. The flies bred and multiplied in Thacker Towers. And sometimes they sat on surfaces that couldn't be attacked, like a figurine of the Buddha.

They put wire gauzes against the windows, delicate and dun-coloured. They did it on the advice of their friend Prashanta Neogi, who'd done the same to keep out mosquitoes from infesting his ground-floor flat in Khar; for that area was home to tanks of stagnant water. "It's the only way to deal with it," Prashanta had said grimly, drink in hand. Gauze after gauze was put in wooden frames behind the windows in the Managing Director's new flat.

"Where do the flies come from?" A question asked abruptly in the midst of other preoccupations, to do with music, the company, when the buzzing returned to their ears. Because even after the gauze frames, the flat was not flyless.

"It's that machhimar nagar," said Nirmalya, gesturing one morning, prophet-like, toward the sea. The promontory—the fisherman's colony—that featureless strip of sand. Nirmalya had passed it several times on his louche and aimless walks. Bombay, as everyone had learnt in school, had once been seven fishing islands that had been presented by the Portuguese to the British as a part of Catherine of Braganza's dowry; "There was no-*thing* here then," the geography teacher had said, standing before the blackboard, enthralled and relieved for an instant by the sheer recentness of what sometimes seemed eternal: the exercise books, children's voices, chalk dust. "Only these fishermen." Walking down Cuffe Parade on his solitary explorations, Nirmalya saw the hull of an upturned boat on the sand. He saw the nets drying against the sun. He smelled the air.

It was from here that the flies had moved into Thacker Towers.

Now, paintings were hung in the drawing room. Two Jamini Roys, bought eleven years ago for almost nothing, and the B. Prabha—a terracotta village girl with elongated arms—had adorned the walls of the previous flat and were hung again here. The B. Prabha was newly emerging as a status symbol; a curious example of a painter whose stock wasn't high among her peers, but whose work was looked upon with increasing tenderness by the affluent. The Senguptas, too, led to her pictures of smoky huts and indecisive village maidens by a gallery owner, viewed them with simple wonder; the painter herself was present, a gentle soul in a white sari with a green border, unsure of whether to maternally cherish or to broker her brood—the family of images—that surrounded her. When Mrs. Sengupta praised a picture, she murmured, "Thank you," and when they asked her the price, she mentioned it—"Six thousand" or "This one is five thousand"—uninsistingly, with dignity, as if she was telling them its name. The Senguptas were as charmed by the artist as they were by the paintings.

Other pictures were purchased after they moved to this flat—and the cost put down to the "soft furnishings" account. "Soft furnishings" and "entertainment allowance"—these were the two ways in which the company made up for what it couldn't give its directors through the heavily taxed income, cocooning them from the brunt of the non-company world, making it, somehow, less urgent and real. Yet "soft"—as if the fixtures, in a state of semi-fluidity, resisted the solidity of the Midas touch.

. . .

His mother went to the Cottage Industries, wandering aimlessly and liberally on its three levels amidst handicrafts and handlooms, children's playthings made in remote regions of the nation scattered here and there like debris, the dolls limp with concealed life, the horses fished out of some imaginary battlefield and left stranded; she noticed some Moghul miniatures—figures on a white surface.

"Madam, this is ivory," said the saleswoman apologetically.

Ivory! But wasn't ivory illegal—Mrs. Sengupta hardly saw it these days; it was like going down the tunnel of time and glimpsing something decadent and vanished. No, not illegal; but rare. Mrs. Sengupta stared for a couple of moments at the figures: the woman in the brocaded top, the man in an ornate cap, the ageing man holding a rose, the small meeting inside a durbar.

The four miniatures were put down to "soft furnishings."

The miniatures were hung up on one of the walls of the drawing room, not far from a wooden cabinet that housed the music system with its frozen turntable and the muscular wires at the back. Nirmalya guessed that one was Jehangir, the other figure Noor Jehan. The middle-aged person, his whole figure, from top to bottom, in profile, was clearly the Emperor Akbar; or so Nirmalya presumed from the man's appearance. He seemed content, standing in the void of a clearing, pausing for a moment in what looked to Nirmalya like wintry daylight.

Standing alone in the half-empty flat, Nirmalya wondered if the nearest one could come to that kingly world was to be someone like his father—a Managing Director. He saw before him, in his mind's eye, his father in his black suit, going out to the office. Did he feel some of Akbar's poised contentment? Because Akbar, in that painting, standing indecisively, seemed not only to be looking, but listening to something. Did his father, too, secretly, listen to the world?

. . .

A woman called Shalini Mathur came to tinker with and reorganise the flowers in the vases twice every week. She was an expert flower arranger—she had a diploma in flower arrangement—and the company had hired her to do something pretty and slightly different with the flowers every few days in the Chief Executive's flat; to involve these inert, fragrant objects in a delicately changing composition. Shalini came in at about ten thirty in the morning, and began to work; she smiled sweetly at no one in particular, and hardly said anything. She sheared the stalks, trimmed leaves; the vases were always surrounded, while she bent over them, by an autumnal precipitation of disposable plant-life. Pleasant but unremarkable to look at, with thin hair and the efficient but somewhat provisional air of a working woman, always in light chiffon saris that fell upon her like a rag, and rather unexpectedly large-breasted. When she spoke, she spoke to Nirmalya's mother, briefly, and almost out of earshot. Nirmalya couldn't remember having heard her voice.

She leaned forward to place the vases according to some tangible geometry of space, tangible only to her, like a web. The effect was a sort of Japanese calm. When she leaned, the dwarfed aanchal of her sari fell from place; her breasts were full and large.

Jumna, revealing her mauve gums, said, "She has very big 'ball.' Look, look at Arthur—dekho isko, baba. He keeps leaving the kitchen and going into the drawing room." It was true. Arthur would shuffle out into the drawing room, look blankly about him for a few seconds, while Shalini, in the distance, a mixture of professional seriousness and divine obliviousness, hovered behind the flowers, and go back to the kitchen. " 'Baap re, what big ball, what big ball!' he keeps saying," reported Jumna. And, having heard this report, Nirmalya too found himself gravitating towards the drawing room once or twice, casual and anonymous in kurta and pyjamas, with an air of high-minded absentness that recently-turned voyeurs have. Shalini neither acknowledged nor ignored him; her eyes remained downcast but weren't steely or unfriendly. She didn't bristle; she just stiffened slightly, almost imperceptibly as a plant might—partly out of respect for the fact that the ghostly passer-by lurking past was the Managing Director's son; and partly . . . it was something else that was never quite brought to light.

Arthur, with quick small hands (he was a tiny man, well below five feet), made food common in storybooks—cottage pie, pancakes, honey roast ham. But, because the Senguptas didn't eat this kind of food regularly, he found himself with nothing to do. So he became a savant in the kitchen, and browbeat the other servants. "Don't throw them away!" he ordered Jumna, after the flowers Shalini had arranged had shrivelled up, and were gathered funereally from the vases. He fried the petals diligently in masala and oil, and sometimes the servants had no other lunch. "Do you know what he gave us to eat today?" complained Jumna to Mrs. Sengupta one afternoon. "Flowers. Phool. I can't eat them," she said glumly, and stuck out a bit of pink tongue. "They're bitter." "Flowers?" asked Mrs. Sengupta, astonished. "Why?" "He says they're good for you." "But you can't give them flowers, Arthur," said Mrs. Sengupta gently; the old man nodded, his graven, bespectacled face, whose features were quite perfect, expressionless. It was true he was remarkably agile at seventy-four. He believed in the virtues of flower and root.

He knew some English; this made him comic and grand in everyone's eyes, and almost incredible, like a member of the British royalty. One day, when Nirmalya had gone to the Dyers', Matthew had told him, "Arthur's made a chocolate cake for Tina's birthday." "Really?" said Nirmalya. "Yes, I'll show it to you." He took the boy to the kitchen. He opened the fridge and showed Nirmalya a large cake on the second rack, spotlit briefly by the fridge's light, chilled and sealed by its weather. In white, stylish icing, it had inscribed upon it "Happy Birthday Dina." "But . . ." said Nirmalya. His mouth opened in an o. Matthew put a finger to his lips; he closed the fridge judiciously. Arthur called Dyer's daughter "Dina," and that was who she would be, for all purposes, this birthday.

Shyamji had no real interest in objets d'art; pictures of saints or gods or film stars he might take a second look at, but of art for its own sake he didn't have a strong conception. But he was staring at the small durbar scene with interest: not necessarily because it was beautiful, but as if he recognised the people in it.

"Did didi get this?" he asked. "It is new, na?"

Nirmalya nodded.

"Didi really has an eye for things," said Shyamji, looking about him, seeming to take in all the decorations in a glance. Then he became absent-minded, as if he were considering some distant object, something that wasn't in the room. He waited for Mrs. Sengupta to come out into the hall.

Nirmalya had become interested in this man: Shyamji. He still couldn't quite make him out: he'd been observing him from a distance—and listening to him sing, of course. He came almost every other day to the flat; a man who was obviously a master of his craft, and who knew he was one. But not ill-at-ease among the furniture, the mirrors, the accessories to luxury; quite in his element, almost unconscious of his surroundings. Nirmalya was moved by his singing: it was like a spray of rainwater. The phrases were delicate and transient, and almost never, he noticed, sung in the same way twice. Shyamji's ability to spin these beautiful musical phrases out of nothing, thoughtlessly—even, at times, callously, glancing quickly at his wristwatch—was, to Nirmalya, at once wonderful and perplexing.

Nirmalya had formed all kinds of ideas about art, about artists; although he could see that Shyamji was a great artist, he was trying to reconcile him to what his own idea of an artist was. Here was a man in a loose white kurta and pyjamas; a man who put oil in his hair. And, although his music sometimes sounded inspired to Nirmalya, a man who seemed to have no idea of, or time for, inspiration. A man who undertook his teaching, his singing, almost as—a job.

At sixteen, having recently entered Junior College, Nirmalya knew what he wanted to do. He had bought a copy of Will Durant's *The Story of Philosophy*; he carried it with him on buses, occasionally reading or rereading a passage. He also possessed a copy of *Being and Nothingness*; he'd never read beyond three pages in the introduction—they had taken him a week to read, the dense paragraphs were at once numbing and vertiginous—but the words in the title—"being" and "nothingness"—echoed in his head; they seeped into his thoughts. He'd recently become aware of the fact that he existed; and he wanted to get to the bottom of the fathomless puzzle of this new, undeniable truth.

Shyamji fitted neither the model of the Eastern artist, nor that of the Western musician. The Eastern artist was part religious figure, the Western part rebel; and Shyamji seemed to be neither. Shyamji wanted to embrace Bombay. He wanted to partake, it seemed to Nirmalya, of the good things of life; what he wanted was not very unlike what his father or his friends' fathers wanted. Nirmalya couldn't fit this in with the kind of person he thought Shyamji should be.

It was at this time he'd become interested in music; now, when he was poised between wanting to study philosophy, or economics (as his father and his relatives would have preferred him to). "Indian classical music"—the rash of winter concerts in the city was where he'd discovered it; the oboe-like sound of the sarod, a musician in kurta and pyjamas crested upon his instrument; society ladies, saris dipping at the pelvis, the navel peering out with such a gaze of intimacy that he returned it in public; the husbands in silk kurtas, businessmen and executives, wearing ritual fancy dress: the mandatory pretence at being musical. Here, at these concerts, in the midst of this display, he went through the slow, private, educative process, full of humiliation and excitement, of identifying ragas; of mistaking one for another, of being moved by a melody he didn't know. He stirred with recognition at the unmistakable ones, the ones with infallible preambles, Jaijaiwanti and Des; then, ragas like Puriya Dhanashree, with their seemingly antique inaccessibility—his ear began to domesticate them too; they remained mysterious, but became part of his life in the evening. Another discovery came to him with these—that very few people in the audience could tell one raga from another. In fact, the audience constantly threatened to come between him and the music; however sublime the music was, it was as if he couldn't entirely enter its doorway because of his alienated awareness of other people. And yet, everyone, himself included, had, in one way or another, an air of proprietory wisdom about the proceedings. He sat there, appearing to look at no one, but actually noticing more than you'd have thought he had. Once, he'd spotted one of his father's executive friends, whom he'd seen twice at a party at home, a head of a company, in a bright yellow kurta, quite unrecognisable. The man hadn't seen Nirmalya. He went in a torn white cotton kurta and jeans whose bottoms were frayed and hung with threads; he glowered at the audience as he sat by himself.

Sometimes, he'd ask his mother to accompany him. "Ma, come on! I'm going to listen to Kishori Amonkar."

"Oh, all right!" she'd say; secretly pleased. This honour he'd bestowed on her—his attention—was a recent development, a volte-face from the years of attention *he'd* demanded as a child. It was music that had brought about the change; a willingness now to share with her, whom he'd promoted without warning to the status of an equal, the phase of discovery.

He'd ignore her during the performance, hardly speaking to her. Sometimes, she'd fall asleep, tired after a bad night, calmed suddenly by the music. But they were united by the contempt they felt for the audience.

"Look at these fools!" she'd say.

She had the unimpeachable superiority, the spiritual unimpeachability, of one who was deeply gifted but whose gift was a secret. She pretended to be a chief executive's wife, no more. She whispered in his ear, "This music is besura," when the sitar player hit a false note. And when she fell asleep—and this happened only when the music was at its most spontaneous and transporting—Nirmalya, although a little embarrassed, preferred his mother's regression into this childlike, unconscious simplicity to the strenuous exhibition of appreciation by the people in the audience.

Later, after the performance and the applause, there was the long procession outward of smiling, redolent couples, the Deshpandes, Boses, Nanavatis, milling gently behind each other, readying themselves to return to appointed bedtimes and dinners, their pleased stupefaction at the music merging into their general air of contentment. Nirmalya and his mother—hardly aware, as she mingled with the people approaching the exit, of her own short slumber—might run into someone on the way out. "Ah, Mrs. Sengupta!" The tone was familiar, friendly, a little condescending.

The boy brooded in the background as the hall finally emptied, recognising neither the interlocutor nor his mother.

At first, he couldn't understand the singing; the human voice was at once too intimate and foreign to listen to. But he found "instrumental music" pleasant. At the same time, he was slightly repulsed by it. The sweet plucked and pulled notes of the sitar, the liquid rush of sound and excitement the tabla created: all these were already familiar to him—like a line from a poem taught in school that's all but lost its meaning through study and repetition—from bucolic scenes in Hindi films, from government documentaries about road- and dam-building, even from close-up pictures of Mrs. Gandhi cutting ribbons or welcoming foreign dignitaries. These images never quite left him, even when he thought he was wholly absorbed, attentive, listening.

The hall itself—whichever it happened to be—was a strange place; a part of the city, yet with its own weather, seasons, and an eternal daylight in which the audience, once the doors opened, trooped in and took their seats. It was this, perhaps, that made it possible, one day, for Ali Akbar Khan to play Lalit in the evening. The ageing ustad on the stage, struggling with his instrument, his bald pate almost like a sitar's gourd, perfect; producing the notes of Lalit at six o'clock in the evening. A few people stirred uneasily. Nirmalya wasn't unduly troubled; he knew, in an academic way, that Lalit was a morning raga, but he still couldn't quite recognise it, and certainly hadn't internalised it; he still didn't associate Lalit with the first rays of daylight and a certain birdsong. Anyway, he couldn't recall when he'd seen the first rays of daylight, and he didn't care. A few people in the audience leaned over to each other and murmured, "Has the Ustad gone senile?" The morning raga unfolded. The ustad's face was calm like a Buddha's, and stubborn as a child's.

For two days afterwards, he carried this experience of Lalit in the evening inside him like something undigested. Is anything possible in 1980? he asked himself. After a few days, he told Shyamji what Ali Akbar Khan had done. Shyamji shook his head.

"How could he do that?" he said, very grave. "It cannot be done."

But Nirmalya could see from the exaggerated solemnity of Shyamji's expression that his mind was elsewhere.

Nirmalya, unobtrusively but firmly rejecting his father's Mercedes, stood at a bus stop with *The Story of Philosophy* in his hand. He didn't know where he was going. Sometimes he'd go to the college to attend a lecture; to meet a few friends. Sometimes, as if there was an invisible ban on him, he'd just hang about one of the entrances, or roam the environs thoughtfully. If the Mercedes came to pick him up, he ignored it; sometimes it followed him, twenty paces behind him, discreet, trying absurdly to merge with the background, while he walked on, apparently nonchalant, in his khadi kurta and churidar, past peanut vendors and hurrying peons, at one with Mahatma Gandhi Road's disorganised street-life.

He sat in a bus, reading *The Story of Philosophy*; he had trouble subduing his long hair when the bus moved and the breeze came in through the window; he sometimes had to pin it down with one hand. But he read adamantly; and reread the chapter on Croce several times. The work of art precedes actual composition, Croce said; it must be realised in the artist's head, in the brain, before he actually commits it to paper or to canvas. This seemed irrefutable from Nirmalya's own experiences of trying to write poetry; that there was an ideal in his head that he tried his best to incarnate on the page. Meanwhile, people kept coming in and getting off, young Goan women in dresses, college students, Gujarati accountants, men who might be mechanics or drivers, chattering couples. When he arrived at his stop, he'd get off and walk to the tall building with the enormous flat.

"He wants to learn from me? Shastriya sangeet?" Shyamji didn't seem particularly pleased; he was disoriented by the demand. There was puzzlement on his face. No one wanted to learn classical music from him; in fact, he had no disciple in classical music. His son, Sanjay, wanted to learn the guitar; they were going to procure one from Furtado's. Shyamji's wife wanted Sanjay to be a music arranger: "There's money in music arrangement."

"Shastriya sangeet?" said Shyamji, as if he'd not heard the term for years. That difficult continent—why would someone from *this* world want to tread it? The request only confirmed the boy's oddity to him; most other young men and women in Thacker Towers and its neighbouring skyscrapers—he now had a sizeable clientele—wanted to learn ghazals; love songs in simple Urdu (they preferred simple to difficult Urdu) about wine, liaisons, grief. The older women, wives of diamond merchants and exporters, liked to sing bhajans, chanting the names of Radha and Krishna, slipping in and out of tune. And Shyamji had embraced these forms: not only because they'd pay the rent, and for his son's and daughters' weddings (when they came), but because they opened an avenue into the sort of life he wanted—to taste, to partake of. Shastriya sangeet had given him and his father little for the hours, the months, the years they'd put into it. He baulked at being reminded of the fact. These mildly touching songs were a form of currency; classical music—shastriya sangeet—a responsibility.

"I'll teach him," he said reluctantly, addressing Mrs. Sengupta, and looked askance at the boy. "It will be difficult."

. . .

"Shyamji," said the boy—he called him "Shyamji," not "guruji" or "Panditji"; not because he didn't respect him, but because something in him abhorred playing the role (submissive, adoring) of the true disciple—"Shyamji, why don't you concentrate on singing shastriya sangeet? You'd be a great success—there aren't many who can sing classical as well as you do."

If Nirmalya hadn't been Mr. Sengupta's son, Shyamji would have thought the question outrageous. He gazed at Nirmalya with forbearance. He frowned. He was bewildered by the question; he was also slightly amused.

"These ghazals are—cheap," Nirmalya said, implacable in his spectacles and long hair. "And look at the way they sing bhajans these days! Bhajans used to be sung in the temple."

Shyamji assumed an expression of seriousness. "All our music comes from the temple, baba," he said softly. He glanced at his watch, to check when Mrs. Sengupta would come out of her room. "The ease with which I sing these taans," he confided—because he'd just given Nirmalya some vocal exercises—"comes from great labour. I used to practise until I spat blood from my throat." The Arabian Sea glittered outside. Leaning forward on the sofa, he shook his head in consternation at the tenacity he'd had in the past; this other, somewhat uncomfortable and raw self he'd been.

Among Shyamji's students were a Sikh businessman's daughter; a minister's son; the wife of an Air India official; a young student who lived several miles beyond what they thought of as "Bombay," in Ghatkopar; and Biswajeet, a young, tall Bengali from Calcutta, a ghazal artiste on the make. This group—there were other groups and other sittings—sat in a democratic circle round Shyamji twice a week in the Sikh businessman's flat in Thacker Towers. The flat's decor was innovative; the designer had taken his or her inspiration from hotels or restaurants; there was a predominance of red in the sitting room, and a couple of steps led to a raised level, beyond which intimate, sunken spaces had been created for sofas and tables.

But the session with Shyamji didn't take place in the sitting room, which never seemed occupied by anyone, but in a small room. The Sikh's daughter, Priya Gill, was a mixture of the sensuous and the studious; always dressed in a salwar kameez, almost unnaturally fair, frizzy hair drawn tight, myopic, glasses perched delicately on her nose. When she sang, you barely heard her; she whispered in her corner of the room. Shyamji didn't point out to her that she wasn't quite singing; he seemed to hear her perfectly. The minister's son, dressed in a white kurta like the minister, looked like his father—except that the father, Baburao Khemkar, was fat; Raj Khemkar wasn't. He seemed strangely removed from the configurations of destinies and interests—politicians', people's, the state's—that forever attended his father's life. Baburao's picture was in the papers every day; his eyes widened into orbs when he laughed or became angry. Raj Khemkar sang with gusto; this, too, was strange, because those who sang ghazals erred on the side of delicacy and dreaminess. The gusto might be inherited from Baburao Khemkar.

The Air India official's wife, Mrs. Jaitley, had the most powerful voice in the group; but she had trouble hitting the high notes. She liked listening, most of all, to Shyamji when he sang softly; she'd close her eyes, shake her head from side to side. She'd go into a sort of samadhi. The young student who'd come all the way from Ghatkopar would, hunched, stare intensely at Shyamji, as if he'd never seen a man singing before. The Bengali ghazal singer, who wore colourful shirts, was the least weighed down by seriousness; never without a smile on his face.

Nirmalya wasn't part of the group. He'd stumbled upon it once when he was looking for Shyamji in the building, and heard he was taking a class in Mr. Gill's flat. "Baba, sit down for a little while"; but he was awkward in this company. He felt, at once, superior to them, and subtly disadvantaged. Once, when he was standing in the hall on the ground floor, and his long hair had been blown across his eyes, he'd caught Priya Gill, who'd just walked in, and was approaching a lift, exchanging a stealthy smile with her mother.

His own relationship with Shyamji was neither here nor there; he still hadn't started taking regular lessons from him. For one thing, it wasn't a traditional guru–shishya relationship; and this by mutual consent. When Mrs. Sengupta had asked Shyamji, "Should you both go through the ritual?" which would have meant the guru tying the nada, the thread, round the shishya's wrist, and the shishya giving his teacher guru-dakshina, maybe a couple of hundred rupees and a box of sweets, Shyamji said, "There's no need to tie the nada." Shyamji lived in the real world, not in some imagined idea of antiquity.

The boy was slightly disappointed, but relieved.

Nirmalya had a maroon kurta, a dark blue kurta, and a deep green one; handwoven cloth from the spinning wheel. He wore them repeatedly. He wore them with white churidars or blue jeans—the simple clothes a complex uniform, denoting his emergence from the life he'd grown up in. He would have been nothing without them; they were as white or saffron robes are to a holy man—a sign of being removed from the world while being in it, and of allegiance to some order that gave him the vantage point from which to view the ways of ordinary people with distance and tolerance. His appearance exasperated his father, made a certain kind of person wary, and encouraged another sort of person. For instance, although he didn't smoke, he was sometimes offered LSD by a whispering man (at once dropout and visionary) in a corridor when he went inside the college. Oddly, he actually still didn't have a single vice, he wasn't interested in smoking or drinking; but he had the unmistakable air of one who was drifting, of one who'd probably lost his bearings.

Meanwhile, his parents looked better and better—they were in their mid-fifties; they didn't look older than forty. Nirmalya laboured on the meaning of life; he wondered sometimes about the point of existence, the purpose of the universe's inscrutable journey; the universe seemed to him like a variety show on whose no single facet he could focus. He'd discovered a hollowness in the pit of his stomach; it made him feel exceptionally ancient, as if he'd been travelling for centuries. He was consoled by the sight of his parents; as they embraced life, and the company lifestyle, they grew visibly younger. "Life's begun late for your father," said Mrs. Sengupta to Nirmalya. Becoming director, then chief executive, had given Apurva Sengupta a new energy and youth; it wasn't only that his hair had become magically black overnight, or that he was even more handsome than before; he viewed the future, every morning, with a renewed sense of responsibility. Nirmalya felt jaded; the world—the flat; the view from the balcony; Cuffe Parade—caused him pain. He looked unkempt, out of joint, next to his parents.

But, just occasionally, his father fell ill from hard work. He fell ill from sitting too much in the same position. He sat in his suit on the swivel chair, hands on the desk before him. Mr. Sengupta glanced at the files, signed memos, held interviews, had "meetings," and, intermittently, gave dictation. Through all this, he—although his mind was in many places at once—remained mostly immobile. One day, a sharp pain pierced his right arm. Gradually, at work and at home, he found he couldn't move the arm; Nirmalya, who was eleven then, had stared engrossed at the expression on his father's face as he tried to lift it. It was diagnosed as spondylitis; the executive's bane, hours of sitting causing the vertebrae to bear down on a nerve, resulting in excruciating pain. It had happened a long time ago, but Nirmalya could remember it well: his father's stunned look as he was divested of his suit and then his shirt, down to the vest in which Nirmalya often saw him at night. Two weeks of enforced rest at the Breach Candy Hospital, traction weighted down his neck; the executive's bane—hard work, the business of making a company run and earn profits, frozen into the body's prolonged immobility—quite different from an athlete's exhaustion. Dyer came to see his Head of Finance lying on his back; Nirmalya's father smiled at him, teeth gritted because of the traction. "It was the only way to get you to get some rest, A. B.," said the Englishman, his eyes sparkling. "But we need you back soon."

"Sedentary lifestyle": it was at this time that these words permanently became part of Mallika Sengupta's vocabulary. "Sedentary"—no activity at all, it had seemed, but as dangerous, it was revealed, as the most risk-laden act, like mountain-climbing: a brush with mortality, even, while sitting unmindfully upon a chair. She could no longer feel safe or content simply because her husband was seated; death hovered by the seated man as much as, if not more than, it did swimmers at high tide or those who leapt out of aeroplanes for sport. To be seated was to be seeking danger.

Some of Mr. Sengupta's colleagues played golf; a dignified, slow, comradely way of deferring the end of life. Apurva Sengupta almost took it up himself; but could never summon enough enthusiasm, in the end, to see his initiation through, to arrive at dawn before an open space somewhere in the middle of a congested city and discover his companions growing more familiar, less interesting, as it became light. He seldom exercised; the company preoccupied him almost completely. But he was unscarred, as yet, by "the sedentary lifestyle."

Soon after the regime of traction, and the disappearance of the pain, the freeing of his right arm, Mr. Sengupta was up again, off to the office in his black suit in the morning. In the evening, he and Mallika Sengupta went out to parties as they used to; and their acquaintanceship with people who were extremely rich but had a wan, slightly deprived air, who owned roads and factories but whose houses were sparsely furnished, with barely a painting on the wall, whose names were a form of capital but who were themselves unprepossessing and anonymous, the immense diamond earrings on their wives' earlobes always as much a surprise as the weathered walls of their sea-facing apartments—the Senguptas' acquaintanceship with these vintage business families increased.

They went to the Poddars' place, the famous family that built schools and hospitals and named everything after themselves. They found them deceptively ordinary, phantom-like, unremarkable.

"Did you see the glasses in which they gave us sharbat?" murmured Mallika Sengupta. "Beautiful silver glasses—they must be heirlooms." She spoke in a scandalised and disarmed tone, as if people who had so much money had no right to possess beautiful things.

The Breach Candy Hospital intruded upon their lives again. They thought of it as just another benign, well-oiled institution, strangely and courteously obedient to their needs as everything seemed to be to the top-drawer executive; another constituent of a generally friendly environment, from which patients and visitors alike returned like happy churchgoers. It hadn't occurred to them it might be recalcitrant or unpredictable; that it might be witness to a small disruption to afternoons of burgeoning and leisure.

Chandu Prakash Mansukhani, well known everywhere in the nation for CP Tyres. A dashing new type, with a degree from Stanford; modest, confident, quite unlike the clumsy scions and elders of the old business families; someone you could have a brief conversation with at a party and discover that a smile lingered on your lips later—an aftertaste of rightness. It was that combination of things—affluence and taste, money and culture—that seemed destined for one another but were so rarely wedded. He, of all people, had had a chest pain in the afternoon. They—Apurva and Mallika Sengupta—had been to his house several times; two weekends ago, in fact, they'd come into contact with that measured, understated persona again, and marvelled at the rightness of its proportions without saying as much.

One day he had chest pain and the next day he was dead. The doctor had said it was wind.

"Isn't it a shame . . ." said Mrs. Sengupta, thinking of the warmth of that last meeting, a special intimacy which convinced them they knew him better than they did, "they live just opposite Breach Candy Hospital. If only . . ."

No one was immune. Here was a man who belied that leaden word, "industrialist." But he'd eluded them; he had only been forty-two.

"The forties are a bad time," Mallika Sengupta said, looking up from a newspaper, compromised suddenly by fresh knowledge, and—she scared easily—a lurking fear. "Especially for businessmen." She went over her husband's diet—though he was well past fifty—in her head.

Her own singing-practice was affected by the parties. She was being sucked into the vortex and extravaganza of the company Managing Directorship; swallowed, almost willingly, by its current. She couldn't remember what she said at the parties; others' remarks lodged themselves in her brain, but what she said herself she often didn't know. At night, when she returned, she'd be seized by an obstreperous affection, and kiss her son several times where he lay sleeping, waking him up for a moment, although, in the mornings, he never had any memory of her swooping down on him so fiercely in her finery. And then she'd be too exhausted, after changing into her nightie, to take off her make-up, or even all the bangles on her arms; night after night, she'd fall asleep with her make-up on, the blush-on ruddying her fatigued expression, the kohl an outline against her closed eyelids. In the morning, when she sang, she had trouble with her voice; it wavered, weak with underwork, wreaking vengeance for the neglect. She grew impatient and thought, "I can't sing any more. My voice has finally gone," although she knew this wasn't true; that this was a justification, repeated to herself many times in the past, to escape a lifetime's obsession and commitment and seemingly useless labour. And so she neglected it further.

Meanwhile, Nirmalya had plunged into the vocal exercises Shyamji had given him with the zeal of a convert, sitting on the durree-covered floor before the harmonium, pressing the key that gave him the sa with one finger, and chasing after perfection for about an hour. In a way, though he was a beginner, his situation was analogous to his mother's—his voice wouldn't obey him but, unlike her, he had time and energy to spare. Because it could be like a battle; it required physical force to master the exercise. Afterwards, he felt, altogether, drained, satisfied, and defeated.

His transformation, noticed at first by the servants, had given him a mission. He exhorted his mother to get back to singing.

"Ma, you're not practising at all!" he accused her as she slipped on a bangle. "You know what happens to the voice when you don't practise!" She, who had been singing for fifty years to his five months, looked at him with guilty eyes; she was nervous at the way he sprang upon her. "You're spending too much time at these stupid parties."

"I hate going to them. Your father says they're an important part of his job."

She was torn, at these moments, between two influences: her husband, whose wisdom she was guided by, and who, in a way, shaped her life, even her life as an artist; and her son, who'd temporarily assume the role of a guru, always expecting more from her—not more maternal love, but devotion to her art—than she could give, and who seemed to have quite different ideas (he voiced them urgently) from his father about the role singing should play in her existence. There was no quarrel between Nirmalya and Apurva Sengupta about this; they wouldn't even have been aware of the difference of opinion—but while one wished to always listen to his wife sing, and that she should be heard, somehow, by a few others, the other wanted her—it was never clear in what way—to be true to her talent. She, in the middle of this, could take neither Apurva Sengupta's comfortable faith nor her son's impatience seriously; compromise was necessary to lead a life even as unreal as this on an even keel—compromise, which engendered but also tempered disappointment.

Shyamji continued to give her bhajans: these songs that had been written by people whose lives had been wrecked, transformed, by hallucinations. Meera, who'd left her husband the Rana, without sensible justification, it seemed, for the blue god. For her, Krishna was as real as—more real than—the next person. Going through all those rituals of waiting; of shivering at the touch of the wind in expectation of him—it was a form of madness, which she herself at once admitted and refuted by singing, "Log kahe Meera bhai bawri"; "People say Meera's mad." And that remote, unreasoning anguish now entered the drawing room as recreation, and faintly moved the singer ventriloquising Meera's implausible longing.

These songs were made sweet by Shyamji's tunes; and the sound of his harmonium gave them a habitation and background. The tunes were simple, on the whole undemanding, and sometimes he had a formula which he used to make two or three of them.

Mallika Sengupta's voice, for what reason she didn't know, had the rare devotional timbre. She was not religious; she loved life; but when she sang, the true note of religion and renunciation sounded in her voice, as if from the memory of another existence she'd led in some other world. Even now, when she was quite out of practice from the socialising in the evenings, something of Meera's illogical desire came to life in her rather guileless singing.

. . .

He was friends with his parents. When they went to the Taj for their cocktails and dinners, he went with them in high spirits. Of course, he wasn't invited; he said goodbye to them in the lobby in which everything shone. He couldn't help feeling at home in five-star hotels; he'd known them since he was a child. He wandered about, untidy but at ease, a paradoxical master of the terrain; no one challenged him.

After twenty minutes, he walked out and down the wide steps, past the Sikh doormen who'd not long ago deferentially opened the doors of the Mercedes. He first went down the promenade, where couples were leaning against the balustrade toward the water; sometimes there were groups of male friends in limp but apparently unshakeable postures of lassitude, ten- or eleven-year-old soft drink or peanut vendors hoarsely engaged in enterprise; the old and the new Taj looked down at Nirmalya. "Mata pita se toont gaya jo dhaga": Meera's words in the bhajan, "The thread that tied me to Mother and Father has snapped," could never come true for Nirmalya. He would be lost without his parents. All he had were these snatched hours of solitude: his parents, now, might have been in another city.

There was no part of the by-lanes around the Taj that was not alive; the pavement around the Salvation Army guest house, around Barretto and Shepherd's, tailors, where his father had his suits made, around the antique shop. This coughing, whispering life frightened him, but he went out searching for it. The cheap hotels behind the Taj, with old doors and ancient lifts; the beggars, in a huddle of amputated limbs and beedis, beneath the Gateway of India—from there he went back past the Eros cinema all the way to the Gothic building where classical music recitals took place, and easy-to-ignore exhibitions; it was not far from his college; the pavement here was empty but lit.

A woman was sitting on the steps of the building, before a

locked door. She was dressed like a fisherwoman; a basket next to her contained clusters of bananas piled on top of one another.

"Come here," she was saying. Her teeth were betel-stained; she smelled strongly of drink; it was like a gust—a soft, sour mist. Although he'd seen women drinking at parties, he couldn't remember alcohol on a woman's breath before; he was modestly shocked. She was smiling at him with a desolating expectation; she didn't seem to recognise him for what he was, or at all care: his gentleness, his background, which she could never imagine, his upbringing.

"You want to feel my breast?"

"How much?" he asked without emotion, calm with a detached, febrile composure.

"Ten rupees."

This porch was bathed in light sponsored by a reputed business family. Next to them, on the main road, the sides of cars glimmered as they went by swiftly. The spot was bright and unshielded, and he and she were completely visible, but he was sure that no one could see them. She, too, seemed to share the same conviction in her own unmindful way. He sat down next to her. The city closed ranks; ignored them completely. Her breasts, fair but puckered, were already partly out of the blouse; he could see their outline. Once, only, a policeman went past, stopped to scowl unthreateningly for a second, and then walked on as if he were in a hurry to get somewhere.

Back in the Taj, his parents were saying goodbye to an insufferable executive, a man who looked and behaved younger than his years, and who probably saw youthfulness as an irresistible doorway to success. There was the nervous, final eruption of laughter with which these farewells were rounded off, gaiety which could be heard from a long way off. When his mother spotted Nirmalya among the insomniacs loitering in the lobby amidst the opulent, beached furniture, shambolic Arabs and mildly enquiring Europeans and others who seemed to believe it was the middle of the day, it was as if she'd seen a mirage, some beloved phantom who returned to preoccupy her day and night. Something in him, too, was confirmed when he saw his parents; an old and familiar friendship, a trust that had been forged probably in some other birth, some other lifetime, a mutual complicity, that still survived in spite of the distance that had recently separated him from them: he knew he could never completely abandon their world.

"So—how was the party?" he asked, as if it, the party, were a necessary diversion in a relentless journey through the ages. His mother, as she walked with him in new-found contentment to the car, described to him the conversations and exchanges with a peculiar, equanimous gusto, for it had dawned on her suddenly that none of it mattered.

The next morning he woke up, and the previous night's foray receded; the world he knew—his parents' world, which he could pretend to take the greatest liberties with—came back to him in a deceptive neighbourliness. He went to the balcony near his parents' room, where they sometimes had breakfast: now empty and sunlight-bright. He couldn't bear to look at the bedroom; he loathed its decor, its drunken wallpaper. He obdurately looked the other way. Much of the view was the same as the one he'd had from La Terrasse, except it was closer up: the sea beyond the Gateway of India, the dome—the size and colour of an immense pincushion—of the old Taj, before and behind which he'd walked last night, the packed buildings, the islands of Elephanta and Trombay, which, on certain days, did not appear. He blinked at the sun; his eyes were still getting used to the light. That old dream, in which a deluge had risen titanically from behind the islands and covered everything before it, had never left him; and so he regarded the scene with a degree of scepticism, as if it had been hastily put together, as if he were being subjected, once again, to a little deceit that was put on, specially, every morning. The small cars on the Marine Drive disregarded the possibility of apocalypse.

His group comprised an old school friend or two; people brought together by enthusiasms that waxed variably: William Burroughs—more his reputation, and his peers', than the actual work. (In Nirmalya's mind, the name was forever proximate with that of Edgar Rice Burroughs, and therefore had a hint of the unclothed white man and hanging vines and of the mystery of Africa.)

And two Rs: rock music and Rimbaud. And *On the Road*—a land of hobos and destitutes, and wisdom gained through bumming. Nirmalya was the only one among them who was no longer interested in the fantasy; he had already lost interest in rock music; he had tried to read, without reward, *A Season in Hell*, pausing only to wonder at the young man's appetite for words. He was only a little older than Rimbaud had been then, or perhaps the same age; but he felt more tranquil than the Frenchman, changed by his new sense of his country, his air of having journeyed through its millennial blossoming.

His friends were all oddballs in their way; most of them planned to go to America some time in the future and study management and "lay" American women. They had a combination of East Coast mannerisms and snobberies and a San Franciscan carnality; at home, they spoke in their mother-tongues with the parents that hovered in a bewildered way about the house. To their surprise, Nirmalya had begun to burble occasionally about Meera and Tulsi and Surdas. To the others, these sounded too much like relatives from childhood; faintly supernatural, and reproachful, as such relatives are. Only Kabir, among them, was "hip," because he'd been taken up by Ezra Pound. Kabir, the orphan discovered and raised by weavers, they discussed in small doses.

Rajiv Desai's flat in Breach Candy was a meeting place. When Nirmalya and Abhay Sen and Sanjay Nair rang the doorbell at four o'clock, Rajiv—the gangly, light-eyed Rajiv, who strummed the guitar, scored with girls—was asleep. He was in a short kurta and pyjamas; he had, at the moment, a crumpled look common to affluent children.

"Shit," said Sanjay Nair.

Sanjay, wiry and bespectacled, had seen the hard-on underneath Rajiv's pyjamas. Rajiv looked down, surprised by something that flouted his rules of governance. "Shit," he said, getting up. It poked out when he stood up. He rushed into the bathroom as if struck by diarrhoea.

"I often wake up with one of those," he confessed when he came back.

"We *all* wake up with one," said Nair.

"Guys get them when they're hanged, can you believe it?" said Abhay, the short, bright one; his source was, unsurprisingly, Samuel Beckett.

"What shit!"

The topic turned to masturbation. Rajiv Desai transformed it into a game, like golf, that some people could apparently play better than others.

"How far can you shoot?" he challenged, now fully awake, sitting, like a yogi, cross-legged on the carpet. The others seemed puzzled and unnerved by this query; it hadn't occurred to them that achievement could be measured and graded in this way; realisation dawned gradually.

"I've gone three feet—four feet even!" bragged Rajiv. The

others grinned in shock; Nirmalya thought of the state of the toilet in the aftermath of these eruptions.

"OK, what's the worst thing you've ever shagged to?" asked Rajiv. They were now being asked to mine into their darkest, inadmissible recesses, to bring to light what they'd rather deny.

"What's the worst thing *you've* done it to?" said Nair.

Rajiv Desai had been waiting for this question. He glanced quickly around him and said with a sheepish grin:

"The Bible." Although the appearance of God in this conversation was no more real to them than the appearance of Hamlet's father's ghost would have been on a theatre set, it still discomfited them with its hint of malevolence and mystery. They were both impressed and embarrassed by the lengths to which Rajiv would go in his solitary quest for pleasure.

"What's there in the Bible, yaar?" someone asked.

"The Book of Job, yaar," said Rajiv, casual and lascivious. "Job goes to his daughter and sleeps with her. I found it and got turned on."

"What shit! Where's that?" asked Nirmalya.

The tall Desai loped to a drawer and rummaged and took out an old school copy of the book in which, at an early age, Nirmalya had first encountered that stentorian voice, ordering Abraham to sacrifice Isaac. He had never quite forgotten that incorporeal, irrefutable demand.

"Wait a sec, let me find it," said Rajiv, hurriedly turning the fragile pages and poring over the tiny print.

Rajiv, who was now at the Sydenham College of Commerce, knew even less about Indian classical music than Nirmalya had a year ago; he, with his no-nonsense, primate-like, terrestrial concerns, knew nothing about Indian culture. He thought people who went around talking about "Indian" culture oily and pretentious.

In school, again and again, they'd memorised the dates of conquests and kingdoms, Ashoka and Chandragupta, Akbar and Shahjahan; their eyes had rested unseeingly, a hundred times, on faded reproductions of the Red Fort and the Ashoka chakra, emblems that were meant to evolve into fingerprints of their identity, and appeared almost as smudged as fingerprints on the cheap paper of the textbook; they'd read *The Merchant of Venice*, and had never been sure whether to pity Shylock or detest him; both Edgar Allan Poe and G. K. Chesterton had spoken to them, like voices in a seance, one frenzied and uncontrollable, making the classroom giggle and shudder, the other as sweet and reasonable as he was in life. Khushwant Singh too sometimes materialised on their horizon in a puff of smoke, half mischievous clown, half oriental magician. But the Indian poets of antiquity and thereafter, the court poets of emperors and mendicant singers who walked barefoot through the ancient kingdoms—Kalidasa, Kabir, Chandidas, Jayadeva—they'd barely heard of, let alone read or been taught about. And now Nirmalya found it more and more difficult to communicate to his friends the change that was coming upon him as he opened himself to these ragas, and to the telegraphic declarations in Braj Bhasha of the soul's longing written by the nameless or pseudonymous composers of khayals, not to speak of the devotional poets—this was a secret education. His emergence from school had landed him, almost accidentally, in the midst of this indescribable period of learning.

At first he told no one among his Breach Candy friends. Then, quietly—and, later, with increasing stubbornness, a near-stupid insistence—Nirmalya began to preach to Rajiv Desai, a steady undertone of grinding dissent in their usual ecstatic declamations about Nashville and the opening chords of "Horse With No Name" that maddened Desai. He feigned boredom, even imbecility; he made strange faces and looked the other way. At first, he'd taken this talk about ragas and ustads and shrutis as a great betrayal on Nirmalya's part, because Nirmalya, of his friends, had been an erudite supporter of the blues at a time when every object in the universe—not only music, but vegetables, festivities, clothes—was being transmogrified into a condition called "disco." To turn away at this testing time from those magnificent sounds of impecunious Chicago to something that was so formless and god-desiring—it seemed to Rajiv Desai not so much perverse as dishonest.

But sometimes Desai almost gave in; it was as if that secret universe had collided with him, and he had to right himself, shake his head clear, and continue quickly on his way as if nothing had happened. One evening, in a car, Nirmalya sang him two lines from an ancient K. L. Saigal ghazal, his voice sweetly rising above the traffic.

"What d'you think of that?" he asked, ingenuous but merciless.

Desai looked the other way, in the direction of a famous chemist's that was now shut. The tragic mood of the ghazal lingered like an aftertaste in the hot taxi. After a moment, he confessed tersely:

"It's funky."

It seemed to Nirmalya that Rajiv had both opened himself ever so marginally, and then withdrawn immediately, and forever, into the safety of Kemp's Corner and the familiar cartography of Bombay.

Apurva Sengupta decided, again, to court Laxmi Ratan Shukla. Laxmi Ratan Shukla, head of HMV's light music wing ten years ago, and still, immovably, its head. A persona non grata who held the keys to fortune; a person no one had heard of—except the people who queued up to meet him, to convince him, to plead with him, to give them a chance. He would look back at them through his bifocal spectacles, speaking very softly; you had to strain to hear.

Mr. Sengupta, after the board meetings, after socialising with the Tatas, the Poddars, after the poolside cocktails at the five-star hotels, had to readjust himself to Laxmi Ratan Shukla. He was used to the obduracy of this country; used to meeting, in Delhi, after a hurried, solitary, suited breakfast in the hotel coffee shop, some secretary or under-secretary in the ministry near Janpath, about pushing through a new plan for the company that needed government permission. And you needed government permission for everything, in both your personal and professional life—for opening a bank account; for creating a new wing in your firm; for selling a new product. But with Laxmi Ratan Shukla it was slightly different: he was trying to get him to acknowledge, and reward, his wife's talent. There were no clear rules here. And, for this reason, he was prepared to wait indefinitely; and he was prepared to treat Laxmi Ratan Shukla as, at once, an equal and a special person indefinitely.

Laxmi Ratan Shukla didn't know what made him special; he knew, really, that he wasn't special at all; and the strange importance that had been bestowed on him made him perpetually wary. It was almost nine years since he'd muttered, without making eye contact, a half-promise that he might give the go-ahead for Mallika Sengupta to cut a disc of devotionals. They'd reposed their strained faith in the words as if they were a fleetingly heard but mysterious mantra. Nirmalya remembered seeing him in his childhood, drinking tea, eating luchis, and making small, odd noises in his throat, of either satisfaction or discomfort, in their flat near Kemp's Corner. No noticeable progress had been made since that vision; in the nine years that followed, Mallika Sengupta's case had neither moved forward nor backward by an inch.

"She must improve pronunciation," Shukla said. "It is not enough to have *surili* voice. Her pronunciation is still Bengali."

To be a Bengali and to sing in Hindi was, in the eyes of Shukla, an original sin, a stain that would not come off easily. Apurva Sengupta, who usually did little to accommodate time-wasters, listened to him attentively, as if he were explaining an arcane art. He never disagreed with Shukla; he smiled, nodded at Shukla's cryptic wisdom. Mallika Sengupta was repelled by Shukla, and would long ago have had nothing to do with him; but Apurva Sengupta said to her with peremptory, affectionate impatience: "You can't achieve anything if you let your emotions get the better of you." She allowed her mood of frustration to be defused by this bit of paternal advice and was almost convinced by it. The message was clear: it was by having a level head that Mr. Sengupta had got to where he was, and become chief executive. He had survived Dyer; he'd survived many other things, the ups and downs that were part of the legend of his life. But was a level head and patience enough with Shukla?

Mr. Sengupta took Shukla to the Taj for dinner, to Tanjore, the speciality Indian restaurant. Shukla, squat, myopic, almost muscular, and his two daughters, Priya and Sudha, in salwar kameezes, slightly taller than him. Neither was particularly beautiful—in fact, they were quite plain—but they had the charm that young women often have: especially flowers that have grown in a stone's shadow. Shukla was a widower; and, seeing him with his daughters, Nirmalya sensed, for the first time, the void from which he came and which he probably lacked the gift or naturalness to talk about. And yet, the same opaque, bereft-of-ordinary-speech quality that made him so difficult to read to his supplicants, translated, with his daughters, into a strange, impenetrable familiarity, an intimacy that didn't need verbal communication. An ordinary family, without signs of privilege or even a pretence towards being acquainted with these surroundings, the girls accepting the solicitous stewards as temporary incarnations.

They sat at the table on the far end on the right, not far from the platform on which the dancing would begin. There was already a sort of musical background as they sat down, a tinkling of wind-chimes. It might have been taped music, or cutlery being moved. A man dressed in waiter's regalia handed them ornate menu cards, and the two sisters looked at the knife, spoon and fork set before them. Was this meant to be Thanjavur, that place that had burgeoned a thousand years ago, burgeoned and then died, as things do; were they meant to be transported to the splendour of the Cholas?

"I'll have saag paneer," said Laxmi Ratan Shukla at last with a note of diffident affirmation; confessing to a weakness but, equally, exercising his rights. For eating was part of this ritual of establishing his own domain of power in what was Mr. Sengupta's world.

"Do you have butter naan?" he asked the waiter. Tanjore. The dancing had begun. And it continued while they ate after the food was served. Nirmalya tried not to look at her over his shoulder, this woman who wove around the platform, as if unsure she might step over it on to the marble where the waiters were walking past; accompanying her, the tabaliya played looking straight at the eaters at the table, and the singer hunched over his harmonium, singing the stuti to Lord Krishna. No one looked at them; between the doors to the kitchen and the space in which the waiters plied and the guests were seated, they continued to sing and dance and play, as if they were as much a figment of the imagination as the episodes they were enacting from the mythology of the blue god.

"Have some of this," said Priya to Nirmalya. She pushed the copper container of daal towards him. He liked the sisters. They were gently attentive. He nodded. But his father still had not had the gumption to broach the subject of the recording. They concentrated on eating; the food, disappointingly, was unremarkable—only the name of the restaurant, Tanjore, was ambrosial, and promised to transform its taste.

After about forty-five minutes, the dancer and her accompanists left the platform with a mixture of awkwardness and embarrassment; probably to eat where neither guest nor waiter could see them. They completely ceased to exist, and the wind-chimes again became audible; now, paradoxically, they were missed slightly, and Nirmalya caught his mother glancing at the platform, with its harmonium and the outspread sheet on which the singer had been sitting. Dessert arrived; kulfi, for everyone except Nirmalya. Laxmi Ratan Shukla, chipping at his with a spoon, remained unfathomable.

Someone waved at Mr. Sengupta. A man from another company. Apurva Sengupta smiled and waved back. Then he returned to Shukla.

Would anything be achieved with Shukla? The man had his own goals; he was actually a perpetrator of bad taste. He had created Om Prakash Vrindavan—one didn't know if that was his real name—a marketing success, a modern-day saint-poet, a faux Kabir with great lung power. Like the old saint-poets, he composed his own songs, and the last stanza had his signature in it; "Saith Vrindavan," like "Saith Kabir," or "Meera says," and he'd hold the note for "Saith Vrindavan" with his reed-like voice for a full minute. Nouveau riche society ladies trembled; they thought, This is what Kabir must have been like, or Surdas; and they were transported to antiquity without having to vacate the present, or giving up their taste for Hindi film songs.

"The man is an affront to the bhajan," said Mallika Sengupta to her husband one day. She'd met him twice; once in a room above a hall in a house in Dadar, where singers had gathered to "warm up" before a function. He was seated on a rug, wearing saffron as usual, in front of his harmonium, making his wife, a fair, extraordinarily tinselly woman, much younger than him, rehearse some lines in a bhajan with him. She was crooning them in the same thin voice, almost a metallic, machine-like whine, that millions of women had cultivated after Lata. A fan swung forgivingly overhead. She glanced at Mrs. Sengupta without warmth; but Om Prakash Vrindavan interrupted the exercise to do a brief, humble namaskar.

Meanwhile, Laxmi Ratan Shukla had finished most of his kulfi; what remained had melted to a puddle in the base of his bowl.

At any bhajan sammelan, Om Prakash Vrindavan would be the star turn. There he would be, his eyes bulging, his long hair falling smoothly round his face, bent over the harmonium, the whites of his eyes visible during moments of rapture. He was singing the commercial success you could hear every day on the radio; "Meri chadar purani"—"My old shawl." "Saith Vrindavan," he sang, as the ladies glowed with spiritual light. He was clearly another

Kabir; for Kabir, the weaver's son, the shawl or covering, or any piece of cloth, was a symbol of the body—the way it must be woven and made, the ease with which it could be torn—and the work of the loom a symbol of the divine activity of creation, and the sound of the loom—jhini jhini jhini—of the humming of the universe. But Om Prakash Vrindavan's "old shawl"? The thought of it made Mr. Sengupta, sitting in his dark suit in the audience, wrinkle his nose in distaste.

"What's all this about his wrapper?" he said to his wife. "The idea's unpleasant."

They were in a minority, though; the record had sold more than fifty thousand copies.

She knew she could have been famous; but she had opted for the life of a Managing Director's wife. It wasn't only because she'd wanted the easy way out; it was because she couldn't deal with the likes of Shukla; the world was full of Shuklas. She hid behind Apurva Sengupta, almost physically.

And then she'd hear Lata on the radio, and feel a stab of irritation. Lata and Asha, Lata and Asha—the sisters' high-pitched voices, almost indistinguishable from one another, everywhere. This wasn't the India she'd grown up in; India had been transformed into an island, with only one radio station, and she had to listen to the same singers again and again.

Then she'd go to a sari exhibition, and contemplate a Baluchari, or buy a Kanjeevaram. She'd be lost for half an hour in the red and deep blues of the sari.

She knew, after all, she'd made the right decision. Look at Lata in her white sari, unmarried, living like a hermit in Prabhu Kunj. Mallika Sengupta didn't want to be a hermit: she still loved life. At fifty-four, her husband having become Managing Director, she felt she'd just begun to discover existence; she'd accepted the benefits that came with her husband's position without affectation, as if they had always been her due. And Asha, deserted by her husband; Asha Bhonsle, who fell in love with the music director dressed in white, O. P. Nayyar, who then tried to dominate all she did—this seemed to Mallika Sengupta like no life at all; it made her shudder. And to Mallika Sengupta, Lata was no goddess Saraswati, as her admirers claimed, but a lonely woman, too private, not close to anyone. She was glad of her husband, her son, the flat she renovated from time to time: it would be madness to exchange these things that so filled up her day for the fulfilment of some grand personal ambition—she had neither the courage nor the desire to do it.

There was a pall on their lives, though: on the cocktail parties; the flat in Cuffe Parade, the Mercedes; the impulsive purchase of curios. It was the constant, nagging knowledge, like a secret, of their son's health—he wasn't unhealthy, or ill, but the murmur the doctor would hear in his chest every time he put a stethoscope to it, for whatever reason, a cough or the flu, was audible to Mallika Sengupta beneath all she did. It made her regret the name her mother had given him: "Nirmalya"; an offering to the gods. She had no intention of offering him to the gods; of letting them interfere with her life.

When he was a boy, she had a great terror of losing him. Each day she'd send him off to school, hair wet and combed, shirt tucked into laundered half-pants, tie knotted and dangling from the collar, as if she had the merest suspicion that he was on the verge of disappearing forever. She'd read a story recently, in a newspaper, about a kidnapping. These demons could spoil her morning, even when, later, a free spirit at large in the shops from Amarson's in Breach Candy to Sahakari Bhandar in Churchgate, she, hair tied in a bun, wearing a light, printed sari, was buying knick-knacks across the counter.

. . .

The children who ran towards cars in traffic jams were part of her bad dreams in those days. Not just the lepers, whose noses and fingers were wearing away, disappearing inexorably like a bar of soap on a basin; nor the Red Cross volunteers, who came and rattled their tin hypnotically, as if it were a cymbal or tambourine; nor the grimy men in rags that opened on to bits of skin, who were neither maimed nor blind, only forlorn and nameless. It was the children. They knocked on her window with their knuckles and harangued her for change; one child might paw it absent-mindedly with the palm of the hand, as if this were a game and his mind partly elsewhere; another's face might suddenly float into the square, singing, "Give, give, give, haven't eaten"; she waved them away or gave them a coin. What she felt was not compassion; it was inescapable and personal, as if the voices were in her head, inside her life and memory, rather than outside. She was troubled by a recurring fear in her many automobile reveries—what if it were Nirmalya? Constantly, the face of the unknown child knocking petulantly changed, and became Nirmalya's: she could do nothing about it. Among her many secret, absurd obsessions, this was one of the most acute: the snatching away from her, in a moment, of her son; the loss of her life as she knew it. The child, asking her again and again for the coin, was what she couldn't keep out or deny, though she shooed him away with one hand; on the way back from school with Nirmalya, or to the hairdressers', at Kemp's Corner or Chowpatty, the same fear and pity repeated itself, inextricably linked, somehow, to Nirmalya's childhood. Sometimes the light changed from red to orange before she could open her purse; the child was gone; he'd be there tomorrow.

He was now sixteen, this "offering to the gods." He went about with *The Story of Philosophy*; he was reading about Santayana.

The doctors had said there was "no need to touch him" till he was forty.

Apurva Sengupta was a model of reasonableness; he deprecated his wife for being too emotional. He attended board meetings; flew to and from Delhi, wearing his dark suit and aimed towards the sky, and, later, towards home, in an Indian Airlines plane; he brought back home bits of company gossip, and, from the longer journeys, stubs of boarding cards and Parry's lozenges which he presented to Nirmalya like a bribe. "There is nothing to worry about," he said to his wife.

But then he brought with him a yogi; an unbridled, wild-looking bearded man, tame for the moment, with a caste-mark on his forehead, bare-bodied except for a loincloth tucked up above his thighs; accompanied sheepishly by Mr. Sengupta, radiant in his dark suit and tie. He brought the man to the flat in Thacker Towers—Arthur and Jumna speechless after retreating into the kitchen—to tell Nirmalya's future.

Nirmalya felt both sympathy and a hint of contempt for his father's unembarrassed lapse into this experiment, he suddenly realised he was not as calm, as immersed in company life and practicable solutions as he pretended he was. Nirmalya was impatient with the yogi; he was still too young, too newly romantic, to understand, in real life, the irrationalities of filial love. He remembered a line from a poem he'd had to learn in class, a poem he disliked, partly because a man with an Indian, or at least non-European name, had had the temerity to write something about the universal human condition in English called "Night of the Scorpion." A child—an idea, almost, not a flesh-and-blood creature—had been bitten by a scorpion; the grown-ups were trying to save it from death. The poet says: "My father, rationalist, sceptic, tried every curse and blessing . . ." Ramachandra, the swotter, the cleverest boy in class, who sometimes fell asleep on his elbow during lessons from studying at night but was never pulled up by teachers who were nervous that they knew less than he did, had asked shrilly, "Miss, if the father was a sceptic and rationalist, why was he resorting to curses and blessings?" as if he'd tripped the poet up. The others in the class only had a vague idea of what "sceptic" and "rationalist" meant. The question had occurred to Nirmalya too, but he already knew the answer. He thought Ramachandra was showing off.

The yogi consulted Mrs. Sengupta first. He sat magisterially on the edge of the sofa, with Mallika Sengupta in his line of vision. He read the future not by looking at her palm, but staring at the screen of the forehead and then retreating into himself.

"Sangeet," he exclaimed at last; his expression, which refused to register any awe at what he saw around him—paintings; the crystalline vases; even the plump, well-fed cushions on the sofa—held the slightest hint of surprise. "Music!" Mrs. Sengupta looked at her son and husband in both consternation and triumph; though much of the world was ignorant of her gift, this man, undeceived by her sari, her make-up, had discovered what she really was; her destiny, neglected by everyone, including herself, was clear to him.

Then Nirmalya, like something between a reluctant bride and a chastised pupil, was made to sit before him. The man still hadn't moved from the edge of the sofa; red eyes narrowed, the bare back and torso upright. He furrowed his brow, counted on his fingers, some obscure calculus that he kept to himself.

"Unhappiness," he said finally. "You are not happy."

Nirmalya had been waiting for some other news; some prognosis of greatness, at least some glimmer of being singular. But, secretly, he was startled by what the man had said to him without any feeling except, it seemed, one of conviction. Yes, he was unhappy. But how had the man known? Was it an absurdly easy thing to say—would most people recognise unhappiness in themselves if they were told they were unhappy?

"You will not be big director like father," continued the yogi, strangely dismissive now, as if he'd had enough of other people's lives. "Small director."

This, in spite of it being deflating, amused Nirmalya, the measuring of success in this odd vocabulary of directorship. Where had the yogi picked it up? In spite of the dark, brand-like impress of his appearance, which made you think he had stepped out of a storybook, he must have a very particular clientele.

Later, when he'd gone, they—father, mother, and son, each with different degrees of curiosity, awe, and irony—discussed how he might have known Mallika Sengupta was a singer. Were there any musical instruments in the sitting room—a tabla or a harmonium? No, the musical instruments were inside, in a room inaccessible to the yogi. It was an episode their rational minds could neither accept nor leave alone.

But the heart murmur caused Nirmalya's parents less anxiety of late than it once used to. Because a doctor had said Nirmalya needn't be "touched" till he was forty. That seemed a very long time from now, more than a quarter of a lifetime. "Now" was a time of terrace parties, of evening conversation, of daytime drifting between exhibition and hotel lobby and the sitting room at home. Nirmalya at forty—the world would be different then; unrecognisable, but a world in which unthinkable possibilities were a part of the everyday.

Jumna, to whom Mrs. Sengupta used to confide her sorrow, her anxiety, had changed. Her body hadn't aged; but her face had. Seven years ago, her husband, the bewda, had knocked her front teeth out. Each time there was a headline that said, SEVEN DIE IN COUNTRY LIQUOR TRAGEDY, the Senguptas thought of Jumna's husband. When Jumna came in to work, and went into the kitchen to pick up the jhadu, Nirmalya would say to her: "See what happened to these bewdas." "Every evening he goes and drinks bewda," she said, shaking her head, staring at the floor, jhadu in hand. Nirmalya, who'd never seen her husband, pictured him sitting inside a roofed place with tables and an electric light, with men like him who, in this image that flashed upon Nirmalya, had nothing in particular on their minds. When he tried to imagine the liquor that killed these men, gradually or suddenly, it was golden or transparent, like the alcohol he'd noticed being poured out in parties. Then one day he realised it was milky white, like toilet cleaner.

So Jumna's husband came to inhabit Nirmalya's life, a malevolent visitor, unredeemable, present but never there. He never saw him.

One cheerful, company-sponsored morning, the husband came to the flat in La Terrasse. Only a few months ago, Jumna had related how she'd woken up in the middle of the night to find herself soaked: her husband, utterly drunk, had drenched her with kerosene, and was trying with little success to light a match, muttering "Saala! Saala!" in the darkness. Now this man was here in La Terrasse, ensconced in the servants' quarters at the back. Everyone in the house was transformed, as at the advent of a difficult bridegroom; no one, the servants or the Senguptas, knew whether to smile or to be outraged. Jumna had a smile on her lips; you couldn't tell what it denoted—embarrassment, sadness, a strange affection. The man had broken his leg; he'd come to borrow some money.

Nirmalya, twelve years old, was away in school; he narrowly missed seeing him. He desperately wanted to know what Jumna's husband looked like.

"He's quite sober-looking," Mallika Sengupta said. She used the word "sober" to mean "serious." "A very quiet man."

This was the figure of joy in Mrs. Sengupta's and Nirmalya's lives, this woman, more than a decade in their employ, whose own life was like a frayed fabric. Mrs. Sengupta still sought her out when she had a nagging doubt, an anxiety.

Jumna mimicked the other servants wonderfully: she exactly caught their turns of phrase, their vanity, recreated effortlessly

Arthur's frequent curious glances at the mirror. The kitchen and its dramas came alive in her stories. They sat and listened to her and laughed loudly.

Even her tales of hardship seemed intended to seep into their secure, company-engendered lives with a tinge of sadness they would not otherwise have.

This woman who had nothing—they were oddly obliged to her.

The family planning programme had failed Jumna: she had five children. Her husband had not used Nirodh: Nirodh, which was advertised everywhere like a health warning or a royal edict, in cinema halls and on billboards. When he was small, Nirmalya used to upbraid her for adding to India's population, to the number with several zeros he'd memorised in school, each zero the sum-total of fate for almost all the people that number comprised; this, he was certain, like her ignorance of the alphabet and of the facts about the universe he was daily introduced to, was a source of her sorrows.

"Kya karu, baba?" she said, as he sermonised intently. "What can I do?" The matter was, mysteriously, out of her hands.

What was Nirodh? Was it a sort of mixture, or medicine? Was it available in bottles or packets? How exactly did it perform its curtailing purpose?

Jumna went to a government hospital and had a tubectomy; she vanished from work that day. "What could I do," she said. "*He* would never stop." Mrs. Sengupta smiled, relieved. "You've taken the right decision, Jumna," she said, congratulating Jumna for making a shrewd investment.

. . .

"But why did she have so many children?" Nirmalya enquired of the driver. This driver, George, a dashing Tamil Christian, had a drink problem, he had come back to work from lunch, drunk, declaimed to everybody present in the flat, hectored the other servants about their employer, taken off his white shirt with epaulettes—known, in conjunction with his trousers, as the "driver's uniform," a striking ensemble—he'd impatiently divested himself, after his speech, of one half of the uniform and fallen into a deep sleep in the servants' quarters. Later, sober and attempting to shore up his shattered dignity, he'd listened to a description of his behaviour from Apurva Sengupta with a mixture of disbelief and contrition. He also had an eye for women; when driving, he had a habit of speeding up the car brusquely, becoming abruptly focussed, whenever women were crossing, and braking in front of them with a jerk in the nick of time. To Nirmalya's surprise, the women seemed to enjoy the thrust of the car; once they'd recovered from their startlement, they'd smile in complicity at this mockery of their unassailability.

"She too must want it," said George with a lopsided grin.

Usko bhi mangta hai, were his words.

The idea shocked the boy; Jumna, who could never be rich or happy in this life, and who yet seemed to have transcended desire, the idea that Jumna wanted *it*.

"You're teaching Mallika these days." Motilalji had brought up the name after several years. Shyamji flinched: at the use of the first name, the air of—not so much disrespect, as the proprietorial casualness with which it was uttered. It was as if he owned her forever, as he did all his students, the new ones as well as the ones who'd shrugged him off like an old set of clothes. Motilalji, eight years ago, had taken Shyamji to Mallika Sengupta: at that time, *he* used to be her teacher; he had swaggering right of entry into the flat. How quickly that stint had ended, and how long memory was! Mrs. Sengupta shuddered when she thought of Motilalji; but she spoke with sad respect of his gift. "He used to sing beautifully," she said to Shyamji. "When he was sober."

"Yes, twice a week," said Shyamji now, morose and prevaricatory at the observation.

Motilalji had had a stroke a year and a half ago. Part of his face had been paralysed, flesh turned into stone; but it was almost all right now. He was keeping off the drink; sobriety made him taciturn and despondent. Behind him, where he lay supercilious and spent on the divan, knelt the child Krishna; and the smell of his wife's cooking, mixed with traces of sandalwood incense, hung motionless but elusive in the room.

. . .

Shyamji was virtuous in many ways; he had no vice to speak of. People remarked that he didn't drink; he never smoked. His weakness was sweets; he loved eating jalebis with milk.

When he praised this combination to Mrs. Sengupta, she said: "Disgusting! You Marwaris and Punjabis have such awful things for sweets. Jalebis with milk. Halwa made from carrots!"

His other weakness was life itself—life and its material reward. Its great material promise. He didn't want to forgo it.

The idea of withdrawing—into himself, into some temple of art, or some space uncontaminated by the sort of life his richer students led—never occurred to him. Or if it did, it was as a metaphor; something to be admired fervently and solemnly for its truth, while avoided carefully in reality. You couldn't confuse a fiction, however sacred and beautiful it was, with what life could actually offer you. Because life could be bountiful; he observed, every day around him, its generosity and largesse.

The memory of his father made him reverential and nervous. He praised him constantly; at the same time, he was at work all the time to distance himself, in effect, from Panditji's legacy. The immense sacrifice Ram Lal had made for the classical arts! This is what he'd left them in the end, the chawl in King's Circle, from which you could constantly hear the gurdwara loudspeaker.

This was how the story of the family lineage went. Hanuman Prasad and Kartik Prasad—two brothers. No one could say with certainty where Hanuman Prasad got his talent from. His brother, Kartik Prasad, was a farmer. Their mother had a strong and tuneful voice—she used to be heard, before she died, at festivals and at nighttime, singing lullabies in that almost masculine voice.

"That idiot is no help at all," Kartik Prasad would mutter when they were growing up. Where Hanuman Prasad picked up all those compositions from, and how he learnt to sing them, no one knew.

He had been a general nuisance to the family. At night he would lie on his khatiya and look up at the sky. These days he was in the pay of the Bikaner maharaja, and performed in the Jodhpur maharaja's court.

He spent a lot of his time smoking ganja from a chillum. Hanuman Prasad's wife was long-suffering. She bore him two children. The first one they named Trilok; when the second one was born nine years later, they named him Ram Lal. It was during the birth of this child that the woman, who'd anyway been in poor health, died.

An emissary from the court would come to the village and say, "The maharaja wants you," and Hanuman Prasad would disappear for a few days. There was an amusing story about him. After a performance, the maharaja was full of admiration and asked him what he wanted in front of the sabha. Hanuman Prasad asked for some ganja. When Kartik Prasad heard about this, he was outraged. "You know we have an ailing mausi, who brought us up like a mother, and all you can ask for is ganja?" He dealt him a couple of blows. The next time he performed in the court and was asked what reward he wanted, he took five rupees to buy medicine for his aunt. When Kartik Prasad heard of this, he hit him a few more times. "Five rupees?" he shouted. "Is that all you could ask for?" Hanuman Prasad was quite bewildered and angry. He began to realise nothing could satisfy his brother. He nursed a resentment inside.

He bided his time with his usual indifference to exigencies. When he was summoned to the court again, he said after his performance: "I would like a gun." "A gun?" But they didn't question him further; they presented him with a musket encased in wood. When he went home, and his brother asked him what he'd received from the maharaja, Hanuman Prasad said, "A gun." Kartik Prasad was flabbergasted; what did his brother mean? "You've made my life a misery. I'm going to kill you," said Hanuman

Prasad, and displayed the musket. But he had no idea how to use it; in fact, it was doubtful if he'd seen a gun before. "Do you know what it's for?" said Kartik Prasad, and gave him a sharp smack on the head.

That gun lies with the local zamindar to this day.

He died suddenly; they found him dead in his bed, the chillum by his side. Ram Lal was a year old; Trilok, the older son, was ten.

It was Trilok who brought up Ram Lal. Ram Lal was a sickly but indefatigable boy; he had absolutely no understanding of the fact that his father was not alive, and that his mother had died a year ago. He ran about; played with marbles. Meanwhile, his older brother helped his uncle in the field, but never lost the interest in music that the nine years he'd been with his father had brought him. Ram Lal was reluctant to learn anything; nevertheless, Trilok sat and taught him some tunes, like raga Kedar and raga Vibhas. He noticed that although Ram Lal didn't pay the slightest attention during these lessons, he picked up the ragas anyway, and could be heard humming them in the middle of some other activity.

The local zamindar rather liked Trilok's singing. Someone had taken him when he was fifteen to the zamindar's mansion and presented him there, saying, "Sir, listen to him. This is that ganja-addict Hanuman Prasad's older son, and though he works on the field and never learnt from an ustad, you'll find he has something of his father's ability. Besides, he's a very serious boy." And so Trilok, in his sweet, high voice, sang Maand, and, of course, the zamindar was charmed, and gradually, like an inert thing melting, his expression changed as he listened, and he shook his head, nostalgic with some secret yearning. When Trilok finished, he was silent while the boy sat with downcast eyes; then said finally: "Sing something else."

Two years later, Trilok received a harmonium as a gift from the zamindar. It was a black, stout thing with knobs in the front, and bellows at the back which collapsed when you undid the clips on either side, but which had to be pulled constantly, tirelessly, by the dutiful, self-effacing left hand for the keys to burst into sound. And burst they did; it was like having a little band in the house. More and more, Trilok played while the boy Ram Lal sang, in a voice even more high-pitched than his brother's, full-throated and careless, stopping between games or work to suddenly become an instrument that had no other thought or function.

Ram Lal had a fondness for histrionics; he came into his own when he was dancing or playing a part. Gradually, he became known in the villages for playing Majnu, thin, mercurial, a live wire of ardour, in the plangent tale of love and separation between his character and Laila. Still only twelve, he became a player in nautanki, travelling with a ragged theatre group and his brother, who lugged his harmonium around with him, guarding it only a little less scrupulously than he did his younger brother, as they went from village to village, gaping crowd to crowd.

The zamindar had a pain in his chest one day; and he was clutching it with his hand when he died. This left Trilok and Ram Lal more at the mercy of the nautanki group than they'd been before; but it also gave them greater freedom now to travel from village to impassioned nautanki performance in some other village in the evening, and back home again by dawn.

Late in the night after a performance, Trilok was trying to sleep not far from a fire, Ram Lal next to him, both of them covered from head to toe in blankets, and the older brother heard two men from the nautanki warming themselves by the fire speak in low voices:

"Trilok is of no use to us. He's a headache, always behaving like the father of the boy, as if no one else has a right to him. The majnu should be one of ours—he *is* one of ours. *We* are his family."

"That's what I've been saying too."

Then there was only the crackle of wood, and the protracted, drawn-out pleasure of one of the men clearing his throat and expectorating. Trilok did not stir; he lay still as a gunny bag.

"When there is an opportunity we should . . . especially on one of the journeys back . . . fast, and quickly . . ."

"Arrey bhaisaab I will do it."

And one of the men began to sing in a low, cracked voice.

The story goes that Trilok took fright and fled with Ram Lal two days later to Delhi. And they wandered about until they put up at an ashram where Gosain Baba sang. Gosain Baba, long-haired saint, who'd given up worldly success in the royal courts to contemplate the deities he adored, Radha and Krishna.

And he loved the rains. What Malhars he composed! Sughrai Malhar, Adana Malhar . . . the oddest possible combinations.

In the morning, the ten-year-old sat listening to Gosain Baba. He became lost in the music; even his right leg, on which he leaned for an hour as he sat cross-legged, seemed, as awareness returned to him, to be elsewhere, he could not feel it, and it came back to him gradually with a discomfiting tingling sensation. Ram Lal sat still, between the fading of the raga Bhatiyar and his temporary disablement, until he was sure he could get up.

A new seriousness came upon the boy; Trilok had seldom seen him so solemn—not even did the mention of his dead parents or an illness make him as sad. Finally, the boy revealed to his brother the thought that was troubling him; he spoke with the obstinacy of a child who expects to be refused, and, to pre-empt disappointment, becomes glum and implacable:

"Bhaiyya, I want to learn from Babaji."

And Trilok, who was father and mother to the boy, was amused and surprised by this new desire for discipleship, and wondered how long it would possess Ram Lal.

Never one to procrastinate, he went to Gosain Baba and touched his feet, stirring the man from his sluggish spiritual reverie. Ram Lal skulked at the back, a fidgety miscreant.

"Babaji, maharaj," stammered Trilok, "my brother Ram has a good singing voice and a great love of music. All these years he's wasted singing nautanki songs, and now he's ashamed of his ignorance. He wants to learn from you."

"But where is he?" said Gosain Baba.

"Come here ulloo!" said Trilok to the figure standing a few feet away; and the boy, impertinent, at first didn't listen, and then, at his brother's urgent frown, thought it wise to obey.

"I have seen him before," said Gosain Baba, looking at the thin boy tranquilly, with recognition. "What do you know?" he said, addressing Ram Lal directly.

"Very little," intervened Trilok. "In fact, he knows more dance than he does music."

"He will have to forget his dancing for now," said Gosain Baba.

For four years then, the story goes, the boy learnt from Gosain Baba. In that ashram, he practised the ragas endlessly, in a blind, joyous addiction to perfection and the sublime, often sitting down to sing when he shouldn't, after the midday meal, for instance, leaving him with the dyspepsia that would bother him later in life. Already, he was beginning to take very ambitious taans; he created a storm, sudden pent-up torrents of notes, inside the small room.

From the ashram, Trilok and Ram Lal went back to Jaipur. The world was changing; nationalist slogans everywhere exhorting the sahib to leave. The brothers were oblivious. Soon after their return, they got married to two sisters.

Their father-in-law was an extraordinary man. He, Murli Prasad, had been the court dancer at the palace of the Maharaja of

Nepal; his patron had showered him with gifts, jewellery mainly, which he wore and displayed with an indifferent contentment—chains, rings, gold bangles, elaborate earrings even, which dangled proudly from his pierced lobes. A large man with long greying hair, thickset, carrying off the jewellery with an instinctive delicacy. Among his wondrous prizes were the silver ghungroos that the maharaja had once given him, and which he occasionally tied round his ankles, and walked about, replete and musical.

Those ghungroos became Ram Lal's. A bag of silver rupees from Murli Prasad's underground vault was also given to him as the groom-price. All this with a dark, stocky twelve-year-old girl.

In a year, he was bored of the village and of Jaipur and wanted to return to Delhi. A new age was dawning there; huge meetings were being held; the British were leaving. He took a rented room and, without much thought, sold the ghungroos; then satisfied what for some time had been a secret urge—to float a theatre company. A band of ready and unthinkingly devoted disciples gravitated towards him; learnt singing from him, cooked for him, washed his clothes. The rented room doubled as a setting for their rehearsals. The company came to nothing.

In his, and his country's, new-found state of unrest, teetering towards independence, he found a job at All India Radio; as supervisor. He wired his brother-in-law to bring his wife to Delhi; she, who wouldn't look at him at first, soon became, to his wonder, talkative, with an endless number of things to say at any given point of time, as well as forceful and active in more ways than one. In Delhi, a year and a half after that reunion and discovery of one another, a child—a boy—was born to them; and he died almost immediately.

Then, after they had recovered from this first grief, and stopped puzzling over the early evidence of destiny and the hand of God, the young, bereaved mother, still hopeful, suggested: "Should we go to Bombay? Remember my uncle said there is always a place for us there."

Her maternal uncle; who'd already made a name for himself as a music director in the film industry.

Ram Lal, nineteen, did not need much persuading. He was momentarily defeated; but he was hungry to make a fresh start.

The uncle, by wire, asked them to buy tickets to Victoria Terminus.

So began that lineage of music, sketchily. Bits of this story had come to Nirmalya at different points of time. Of how Ram Lal's wife returned to Jaipur when she was with child, and there gave birth to Shyam. Then returned to Bombay with the little mewling infant, who had made her breasts sore, when he was three months old. Two years later, the younger brother Banwari was born, calmer and less importunate than the older child, as if he had accepted from the first the world for what it was. These details—of his teacher and his brother in their most unguarded moments, defenceless, before they became what they were—had, for Nirmalya, the significance of secrets and revelations, as of the birth of kings or holy men in the seemingly unremarkable age we live in. Who knew now, as they went teaching or playing from home to home, of their momentousness? But are not the great among us banal and mortal, even to themselves?

Three years ago, Shyamji began an annual function in his father's memory; to pay respect to Ram Lal's legacy, but also, without being wholly aware of doing so, to tame it, to rework it in terms amenable to him. Because his father's world was not the world Shyamji now lived in; and how could the memorial, in all that it was, avoid reflecting that fact? It must enshrine the past; but it must belong to the present and the future. It was known as the Gandharva Sammelan; Ram Lal's admirers had, towards the middle of his life, in an onrush of slightly belated, sentimental gratitude, given him the title "gandharva." A gandharva is a heavenly singer—there are some singers whose voices are so melodious that they bring to existence, for their listeners, the fictive world of kinnars, gods, and apsaras, from which they seem to be briefly visiting us; and they're identified as gandharvas. Their music brings to this world the message of that other one, to which they'll eventually return. Shivputra Komkali, renamed Kumar Gandharva—"the boy gandharva"—at the age of seven by a shankaracharya for his musical gift, was one such person. Ram Lal was another.

So, around November, Shyamji became peripatetic with a grey-white cyclostyled form for advertisements in his hand: one thousand rupees for a full page in the souvenir, one thousand five hundred for the first page and the back cover, etcetera.

His wish to commemorate his father was acute and sincere; but he was going to hire a hall, and he needed to break even.

Naturally, he approached Mr. Sengupta—in a world without patrons, it's the companies, and the heads of companies, that must provide patronage—for an advertisement. "Sengupta saab," he insisted gently, almost singing, "it is time for the sammelan again this year." "When?" asked Mr. Sengupta. He was busy with other things, burdened by a fall in profits because of intractable trade union activity; the rise of Datta Samant and other inflexible union leaders had coincided unfortunately with his managing directorship; he could remember last year's sammelan, but eleven months had gone by so swiftly, so impatiently, that he couldn't believe it was time for another one. "December," said Shyamji, as ever impeccably patient and polite. "Ninth and tenth."

The form lay on Mr. Sengupta's table for two days, out of place among invitations from the Governor and chambers of commerce; he forgot about it. Then he spotted it, was, for an instant, in a state of blank irresolution, making the instant seem longer than it was, and buzzed for his secretary.

"Tell Nair to do something about it," he said.

But this was not the only time or way in which Shyamji asked for the Senguptas' indulgence, their support. Apurva Sengupta was, at once, patron and honorary elder. There was Shyamji's family, after all; and the extended gaggle, all clamouring with various needs and desires. Sumati, his wife, who would say, "Didi, don't forget my sari!" Shyamji's younger brother Banwari was shy; a near-ink-dark complexion and the buck teeth that marred his otherwise serious, pleasant face crippled him with shyness. Nevertheless, he too became less and less taciturn with the Senguptas—Mallika Sengupta let down her guard as he let down his—and, smiling, covering his mouth and the teeth instinctively, protectively, with one hand, asked for constant "advances" on the tuition fee. He played the tabla solemnly with Mrs. Sengupta; a master of his instrument, Banwari, but forced to subsist on the middle level, to recast himself as one of the many accompanists for "light" music practice-sessions in the drawing room, lowering himself and his instruments on the carpet, his white kurta and pyjamas always photograph-spotless, making his dark skin seem warm and deep, like an ember. On the days he didn't come, Shyamji's brother-in-law, the restive, genie-like Pyarelal, came to play the tabla—Shyamji had seen to it, democratically, that the male members of his family, even the ones he didn't like, had employment. After all, they all had mouths to feed. The sons still too young, too full of unrealistic, swaggering expectation, to work, the daughters mostly unmarried.

The women, wearing chiffon saris, with the ends of the saris covering their heads and part of their faces, like the residue of a veil, seemed too shy to meet the world. They were not in the least so. They were the engine behind their husbands.

Tara, Shyamji's younger sister, sweet-smiling, for many years overweight despite her pious, ostentatious fasts, a small, gold nose-ring piercing one nostril, Tara, whom Ram Lal married off to that jack-of-all trades Pyarelal, was particularly demanding. She was always expecting something from her brother, even when she hadn't said a word. Shyamji could sense it in her endearments, and in her sudden, dreamy grumblings addressed to no one. It was because of her, and because he loved her through the ties of blood and memory, that he'd taken on the responsibility of supporting the mendacious Pyarelal. And Tara, overweight and settling into life, knew it; for her brother, she reserved her most sugary smile.

Then the matriarch, Ram Lal's widow, tiny, barrel-shaped in a white sari, daughter of the bejewelled man who'd once danced before the king of Nepal. Her unspoken edict to Shyamji: always look after your younger brother Banwari, and don't ever forget our Tara.

And Sumati herself, Shyamji's wife, slightly silly and airy-fairy but good-humoured, a little too proud, according to family members, that her husband was doing well.

Finally, Neeta, Banwari's wife, fair, exceptionally pretty underneath the pallu of the sari that she pulled over one side of her face, except that her voice was almost rasping, and she argumentative. A pearl concealed from the world, discontent. She'd have felt she was too good for Banwari with his protruding teeth if he hadn't been Ram Lal's son.

The stage was set after the usual series of trials and errors, the pinning up of pennants by workmen that Shyamji would chance cheerily upon, the final raising of garlands; and now there were floral patterns around the piece of synthetic that said 3rd GANDHARVA SAMMELAN. Rajasthani families—neither entirely of Bombay, nor any more of the scoured landscape of desert and oasis-like villages they'd once come from—wandering busily about in the foyer where men smoked during intermission and boys devoured ice cream, everyone from old crones to children; anyone even distantly related to Shyamji was here. And Shyamji, bowing, joining his palms together in namaskar, gracious in receiving businessmen and their wives, the suited, deceptively modest corporate executives who reigned over companies, and their families. Delegating to his son the task of seating them in the second row or third row or fourth, or sometimes escorting them—for they looked distant and faintly undecided without an escort, these driven, nine-to-nine executives—himself. The occasional inspector-general of police walking in; or politician. A show of intimacy then taking place in the front aisle, the inspector-general hugging the musician and overcoming him momentarily while the wife looked on, smiling. Then anti-climactic murmurs as they were led to their seats.

All this was part of the constant enchantment, the enlargement of life and its prospects for the executives, the businessmen, Shyamji. The sammelan, whatever it achieved, was where these daily premonitions of well-being—that something good was about to happen, that mutual understanding promised mutual benefit—fortuitously came together. All who lived and worked in Bombay believed this as seriously as a dogma or superstition; the music that was to come, or anything else for that matter, was almost secondary to this belief. Ram Lal's portrait, severe, predictably incongruous, was placed at an angle on the right, a garland strung round it. There was a lamp before it, which Shyamji lit on the first day of the sammelan. Another incongruous moment as he bent over the wick—not of introspection, but in which a memory had no time to come to the surface. It was a little like lighting a pyre, the pyre he had lit eleven years ago, an act of reverence and expiation. But now, after the banality of the intervening years and of the day itself, emotion had withered and little remained but the public gesture; Shyamji was distracted—distracted by the air-conditioned auditorium waiting behind him.

The first day was pure classical music and dance, starting with the younger artists' emphatic throat-clearings and improvisatory tentativeness, then, later in the evening, evolving into the familiarity and unapologetic ease of the mature performers; the second day was devoted to "light" music. People tided over the first day somehow; it was the second day they were interested in, because they'd sing themselves then—Shyamji's disciples, from young struggling ghazal singers to businessmen's wives, hot but bright in their saris, naked ears dressed provocatively in gold, whose husbands had put a full-page advertisement in the souvenir. Their relationship with music had begun embryonically, in their prehistory as listeners; they'd hummed along in an undertone with the artists they loved best, or loudly, solitarily, to themselves; and then, at some point, they'd asked themselves the unimaginable, something that wouldn't have occurred to them six months before, or which they didn't have the courage to admit: "Can't *I* be a singer? Can't it be me?" Why should they only listen; why shouldn't they be listened *to*? Once the question was posed so shatteringly, the answer was simple; and led to its own joy, liberation, and trauma. And here, Shyamji, ironically, was to be not so much teacher as mediator; not only to satisfy the middle-class urge for music, but the relentless, childlike longing to *become* the musician (how simply the metamorphosis could be achieved!); to move to centre-stage, at least for fifteen minutes, where the traditional musician previously was.

The lamp was lit, there was a short-lived exhalation of paraffin, the small eye of flame went on burning dutifully, dutifully, no one noticed, but the first day got off to a rather poor start, with Sunder, Shyamji's young son-in-law, dancing kathak for forty-five minutes. Sunder was twenty-two years old; he was married to Shyamji's oldest daughter, and lived in Delhi. Sunder's father had said to Shyamji, "Bhaiyya, you must give your damaad half an hour at least. He's a hardworking boy, and after all he's Ram Lal's granddaughter's husband." Shyamji nodded; the man's logic was irreproachable.

But, though Sunder may have worked hard, he was still raw. For the last two years, his father railed and shouted and cajoled as Sunder tried to master the technical aspects of kathak; he'd not even begun to broach its emotive side, abhinaya, where the dancer, through facial expressions and small gestures of the hand, relives the surprise and tenderness and frustrations of Radha's trysts with Krishna. He was still altogether too gangly; the bells round his ankles sounded too loud when he stamped his feet. It was as if the boy was having a late adolescence.

For forty-five minutes they went on like this, the father, bespectacled, thin, slapping the tabla angrily, Pyarelal playing the harmonium and rapidly saying the bols to which the boy danced. Sunder's wife gaped at him from the audience as he whirled round three times and came to an anxious stop, his eyes still with controlled terror, his body poised like a pin as it hits the ground; the rest of Shyamji's family looked politely uninterested. Really, the boy had no grace at all—he couldn't have entered Radha's body, her movements, if he tried; not his gender, but some anxiety that locked more and more acutely into him made him wooden but volatile, like one of those Rajasthani puppets that, with the yank of the strings, rush everywhere. Perhaps he still hadn't recovered from the long, dusty journey from Delhi in the chair car; he'd arrived, dazed but brimming with hope and impatience, yesterday evening.

Pyarelal was poised on the steps of the foyer—beedi in hand, smoking furiously. He'd just finished his stint playing with Sunder;

his long blue kurta dazzled in the moonlight, though patches of sweat darkened into indigo beneath the underarms. He was furious; he muttered and spewed smoke alternately. Being a parasite on Shyamji, he didn't mind the odd jobs assigned to him; playing the harmonium with Sunder, playing the tabla with this or that person. But then, in between jobs, from nowhere his sense of self-respect returned to him, and, with it, outrage; ingratiatingness replaced by mumbled fulminations.

"Did you see how that boy did his circles? I was afraid he'd fall. Baba, what is the hurry?" He exhaled, looked away and coughed. "It's a difficult art, learn it for five years, ten years. Just because you're the damaad of . . ." His eyes glinted and he lowered his voice, as if he mustn't be heard. "Did you see him when the programme began? He went and touched his father's feet, but he didn't do pranaam to me. Wasn't that an insult?"

He looked at Nirmalya for support—bird-like, his gaze, as of a creature that had been threatened with injury. Nirmalya nodded his most sympathetic and convinced nod.

The final recital of the first day would begin soon; Pandit Rasraj would sing. A small, flamboyant, balding man, he was the only truly eminent artist to perform at the Gandharva Sammelan. With real but not altogether unexhibitionistic humility he laid flowers before Ram Lal's stern portrait. Before beginning, he checked, with a look of tolerant disdain, to see if his disciples' two tanpuras were in tune. Then he closed his eyes and suddenly became immobile. There was utter silence; as if he were Lord Shiva on Mount Kailash. Then, indeed, he plunged into an invocation to Lord Shiva in raga Puriya Dhanashree, very softly at first, his voice a whisper—his performance, at this early point, full of possibility and god-like suspense. Behind his rapturous awareness of the raga was a shrewd assessment of the microphone; for Rasraj, the microphone was the main deity; without anyone becoming conscious of it, it took on preternatural properties. This happened despite, or because of, Rasraj's closed eyes; it was as if the microphone, his real interlocutor, was invisible.

The first seven or eight rows were full, but then more and more empty seats appeared, a random scattering of people: the recital was half-attended. This was because most of Shyamji's "crowd" would come tomorrow, to sing themselves, or to listen to members of their families; they weren't too interested in Rasraj. Besides, the Gandharva Sammelan, despite its grandiose name, wasn't well known. For the last three years it had had no advertisements in the newspapers; the only advertisements were the ones put by students for their firms and enterprises in the programme.

Then the bada khayal began, majestic, resistant to hurry, taking the first steps in its regal elephantine progress: "O blue-throated one, O custodian of the Ganga . . ."

Day two, and the students crowded the wings to sing their two songs each. Some of them were barely trained; but Shyamji had put them in anyway, from a compassion for the weak but eager, and also because they, or their fathers, had put in half-page advertisements. He had a shrewd and tender comprehension of the vanity that made people sing. This was the difference between the age in which he lived and the one Ram Lal had inhabited and taught in; not the age of patronage, this one, in which the landlord and his cognoscenti had, at once, cherished and dominated and learnt from and humiliated the musician. This was the age of democracy; the ordinary person, everyman, was supreme. Deep down, notwithstanding the bowed heads, the affectionate, timorous smiles, the rushed feet-touching, Shyamji understood he and his students were equals; that he was their guru, but also, in this age, their coeval; and the patron had merged into the rights and irreducible power of the common man, not only the right to honour and even own the artist that the patron had, in a sense, reserved for himself, but to do away with the very line that separated artist and ordinary human being. And Shyamji subsisted and thrived on this equality; he mingled among his students as if he were one of them. He oversaw them all, paternal but clear-eyed about his own temporary role—nervous girls in salwar kameezes, pampered daughters of businessmen; young professional singers, already smug, humming intricate modulations to themselves, taking on the mannerisms current these days among the more established singers, the vacuous jerk of the head when the tabla returned to the first beat of the cycle, the curving of the hand while executing a grace-note, tics without which they'd be lost, pretending to be moved by a competitor's mediocre warbling, to be unmoved or momentarily preoccupied when someone else hit a perfect note; elderly ladies in expensive saris, smiling, perspiring, as if in the warmth of paradise, through their make-up. Nirmalya, in goatee and frayed corduroys, trying to mingle in the cat-and-mouse corridors of the wings, escorting his mother backstage, walking past rows of light switches, taking part and yet not taking part.

"This is Sengupta saab's son, Sengupta saab, you know, the MD of . . ." When Shyamji introduced him to some of the people going in and out of the green room, they looked twice at Nirmalya, as if, in spite of his guilty, caught-in-transit appearance, he possessed certain qualities: he was Sengupta saab's son—the famous company was oddly embodied in him, a mark of distinction he wasn't personally responsible for; they didn't need to know his name.

They sat in the third row, Apurva Sengupta, in a dark blue suit, his necktie compressed into a perfect knot, and the untidy, intent son next to him, spectacles gleaming, unremarkable except for his quiet air of exercising judgement.

There, on the stage, was Mrs. Sengupta, cheeks white in the stage lights, turning the pages of the songbook absent-mindedly, as if she'd never find the page; and, next to her, Shyamji, playing the harmonium as he had with all his students, not looking so much tired as far away and vaguely dutiful. A faint hum emanated from the instrument at his fingers.

This was an important moment, both in and out of her social life, this spotlit pause when she was most alone, when she began to sing the first lines to an audience that was never quite listening. The sari she was wearing was a beautiful purple Benarasi, embossed with silver threadwork. In comparison to the other singers and their hurried ambition and swift attunement to the dark of the auditorium, their smiling, convivial namaskars at the end of their two songs, she was like a slightly forgetful royal personage, half-aware of her listeners, in exile, someone from another age. The audience accepted her entry and her brief, incongruous incumbency good-humouredly. But when she sang, Nirmalya couldn't stand it; he felt her voice, amplified and made subtly different, a voice from the past and not her own voice, was sounding too sharp, she was not in practice, she was accompanying her husband to too many parties, from which she'd bring back stories of the Tatas and the Singhanias. He could never listen to his mother calmly during a performance. It was only months, sometimes years, later, when he'd overhear something she'd taped for her own purposes, that he'd be struck by the beauty of her voice, effortlessly fresh and immediate, and wonder why he could never hear it in the present moment.

When she came out into the auditorium, hot, but calm, she whispered, "Mrs. Makhija said to me—You have a wonderful voice!" Nirmalya's father smiled, pleased as much at her spontaneous happiness, at the end of the outing, as at the compliment: "Very good. Very good." She turned to search her son's face for some indication or sign. He didn't smile, only nodded curtly. Later, he was filled with pain for not having been kinder.

. . .

By ten o'clock, it seemed like midnight; the singers had finished—only their teacher remained, Shyamji, singing bhajans to an almost empty hall. His family sat in a cluster—and Apurva and Mallika Sengupta, and Nirmalya, because they so loved listening to Shyamji. Most of the others had gone; they had buses to catch.

In the front row, unmissable because of his largeness, a bearded man, dressed entirely in white, sat shaking his head in appreciation.

"Who's that?" whispered Nirmalya to his father, studying the figure in amusement.

"Hanuman Rao," said his father in a low voice. "Some Congress leader, apparently."

Hanuman Prasad Rao came from a landowning family from a village on the border between Maharashtra and Karnataka; and this was the manner he carried with him—not of a man of the people, but a protector of the people. Dressed always in white, the slightest spot threatened to besmirch not only his clothes, but his reputation. He had huge hands; he could easily have strangled someone with them. An air of foreboding accompanied him; as if, when he'd be struck down, he'd be struck down simply, by a stroke, or a flash of lightning. But, as of now, he looked quietly, assuredly, invincible.

One day he'd discovered Shyamji, and, in his expansive way, become a sort of devotee. "You are the best singer in the country," he said, placing an ample hand upon Shyamji's shoulder, "and some day everyone will know it." Here, too, he had the grandiose, proprietorial air, not unlike that of an explorer who reaches a continent and begins to believe he owns it. His admiration for Shyamji was an extension of his egotism, and possessed the charge, the enchantment, of self-love; Shyamji knew he could withdraw it whenever he wished. He might get bored; or he might take offence for some reason, as people did when they thought they were in love. So Shyamji kept Hanuman Rao happy.

Hanuman Rao was obsessed with films; he loved Dilip Kumar and Raj Kapoor, their youth full of simple rustic joy and unfathomable magic, their openness to the risk of romance and the uncertainty of the changed world; and Hema Malini and Waheeda Rehman, companions in the changed world—he felt beholden to them, these figures of solace and desire. He was moved by the great films, their deep understanding of the importance of sacrifice; his large frame would go still during the great scenes; he would weep.

He also saw that politics was a form of cinema—except that it was real. "They are not the real heroes," he told his wife in private, slapping his chest. "*We* are."

He now had what seemed to him a fantastic idea: he wanted to produce a film and—this seemed like the logical thing to do, given his personality and appearance—to act in it. It didn't matter that he was fifty-one; the movie industry needed a mature protagonist. The film would have the sort of socialist content expected from a Congressman; it would be about a peasant uprising, the overthrowing of a landlord, and he, Hanuman Rao, would play the peasant leader, exiled from his village and then returning to it by subterfuge and bringing about an awakening among the villagers.

"Shyam," he said, for he addressed the singer by his first name, as if he were Shyamji's older brother, "you will be the music director. It's your tunes I hear when I think of the film. It has a wonderful title: 'Naya Rasta Nayi Asha.' " A new road, new hope.

It was Shyamji's good fortune that, although he was an accomplished classical singer, a master, he had a pliable and beautiful voice. This meant it could take advantage of the musical currency of the day, of the songs with which a middle class of faithful, hardworking husbands and vivacious housewives expressed its dreams. It lent itself to ghazals, to their gorgeous banalities about drunken love, about heartbreak and desire, which inordinately moved husbands who seemed generally impervious to passion, and made them sigh; it lent itself also to the pieties of the bhajan, to the worshipful mood, the genuflections to Ram and Krishna that were part of the household created by mother-in-law and daughter-in-law. Shyamji was at the centre of this solemn self-expression. But the beauty of the voice carried with it a seductiveness—in the old days, the masters were right to be wary of mere beauty. It made Shyamji believe he could do, and sing, all things; that he could return to the other needs of his calling later.

"Shyam, you will sing in the film," Hanuman Rao said, the large hand resting on Shyamji's shoulder. "It's my one condition for making you music director. There'll be a special song in the scene in which I rouse the villagers. I want you to sing that song." Hanuman Rao's voice made a rasping sound as the vision formed.

There was no discrepancy at all, as far as he was concerned, that, on screen, he'd burst into song in the ether of Shyamji's voice. He was too grand and determined a man to be bothered by detail.

"Didi!" Shyamji called, as he entered the flat. "Didi—it is ready! I've brought it with me."

He had with him something at once ordinary and charged with unusual significance because of the way he held it—a long-playing record with a bright yellow sleeve. Its back was white, with the names of the songs and details about the film, the music director, the producer, the singers printed neatly, darkly, in English. A third of the yellow side, which was the cover, was enveloped by a looming picture of Hanuman Rao, dressed in white, as he usually was in real life, with what looked like a staff in one hand; behind him, incidental but not negligible, were two smaller figures before a hut—a young woman and a man. Shyamji was dazzled by both the vinyl within and the epic compressed upon the cover; Nirmalya handled the sleeve with diffidence.

"Baba, put it on the record player," Shyamji said, the childlike wonder and impatience barely disguised by the softness of the request—he must have already heard the record twenty times.

A jangly orchestral music filled the room. Shyamji sat with a frown on his face, now and then surrendering to his emotions, staring at the carpet, sighing at the sudden shift of register in the tunes. Mrs. Sengupta and Nirmalya too listened to the record with one ear; but, really, they were more intent upon watching, with a mixture of respect and protectiveness, the spectacle of their teacher listening again to his own music.

"When is the film coming to the theatres, Shyamji? Can we go and see it?" asked Mrs. Sengupta brightly at the end of song number two. She had not the slightest intention of seeing it; the effort it took to be mendacious translated, in her tone, into a sparkling enthusiasm. She hardly ever watched Hindi films; although, like others among her contemporaries and peers, she amused herself sometimes by buying *Filmfare* and reading episodes from the lives of the stars during vacant afternoons—these stories, frivolous and instantly forgettable, were more diverting and less boring than the films themselves.

"It'll be out soon, didi," said Shyamji, humouring Mrs. Sengupta, not daring to distrust either Hanuman Rao or fate. He suspected that, on some strangely moral level, Mrs. Sengupta didn't really care, and didn't want him to care either. "The film is ready."

"Badhai, didi, badhai!" said Sumati, her eyes (she had a squint, but it was the auspicious "Lakshmi" squint, in which one eye tilted slightly in a different direction) bright, her head covered by the end of her chiffon sari. "Congratulations! Your brother is going to be a famous music director!"

What a silly woman, thought Mallika Sengupta (for she herself, having benefited from it, was superstitious about providential benediction—like a dalal on the stock market who watches from below the index fall and rise nervously); the word that described Shyamji's wife—she stored it away to relay it to her husband later—was "fun-loving." Sumati's gaiety seemed to Mrs. Sengupta to be almost an affront. Good fortune, whatever the ebullience you felt within, couldn't for a moment be greeted with levity; it must be welcomed poker-faced, dignified, and serious. To Mallika Sengupta, nervous, too, always about Nirmalya, about any imminent danger to his health, the taking for granted of something that had still not happened was an example of culpable thoughtlessness; her suppression of immediate outward delight at the announcement of good news was, for her, a kind of penance. In Sumati, immediate delight took the form of a sort of innocence. Mrs. Sengupta, her soul inured to holding back, secretly wished Sumati would be sombre and quiet until she had cause for celebration.

. . .

Nirmalya's music lessons were always something Shyamji was doing between things, in a hurry. In the old movies, in the gloom of fake temples or caves made of papier mâché or cardboard, the guru and his disciple spent long hours of struggle, often next to a gigantic graven likeness of Shiva, also made of papier mâché, the god silent and aloof from the trials of human ambition, the guru exacting, sometimes capriciously, both devotion and labour from his young disciple, as a great cobweb grew and grew in one corner, till he finally began to sing in the perfect tone of a famous playback singer. In Thacker Towers, it wasn't like this: nothing in the end can cocoon you from the effort it takes to master something, from the fact that the returns are wrung reluctantly from the energy invested—but neither can you protect yourself from the banal and the everyday that comprise your life and make it safe and familiar for you. The world that Apurva and Mallika Sengupta had made theirs so completely, the proximity of lunch or tea, the servants coming in or going out, qualified the music lesson.

The tape recorder made the process of teaching and learning less messy, more compressed and expeditious, for both the time-pressed guru and his undecided disciple, shackled to the modern life that had formed him, eager to learn, but within the secret, exploratory rhythms of his day. For each day was part purgatory for Nirmalya, where he constantly came close to the sinking spirits of damnation; as well as a time for discovering randomly, with impatient, almost dismissive, exhilaration, the cultures of the world and of history. He had lots to do: read philosophy, and novels in which men suddenly discovered in pubs that existence was *contingent* and *absurd*, that it had occurred almost for no discernible reason, and poems by women who flirtatiously confessed to being besotted with suicide; flick quickly through pornographic books from European social democracies which had pictures taken from dizzying angles accompanied by crowded, shameless texts in German and probably Danish as well as a sort of English, each a short frenetic paragraph, the German full of militantly erect capital letters. In the midst of all this, Shyamji arrived. Nirmalya sat meekly next to him, tape recorder by his side. It doubled as both student and teacher; when Shyamji sang, half carelessly but magically, into the microphone of the Panasonic, as if he were singing into the ear of the immemorial past, it seemed to listen raptly. And then, later, it became a guru; when Nirmalya played back the tape, Shyamji sang through the Panasonic, it became an extension of Shyamji, and yet it could never *be* Shyamji, it was at once less clever than him, and more pliant and amenable than he was. But at least it was always there. In a way, it seemed to occupy its own space, its own domain from which it governed; and it made both guru and disciple independent of—and slightly redundant to—each other.

And so the guru became, to Nirmalya, an ideal figure, a sort of imaginary being, almost unrelated to the fact that his real teacher, Shyamji, was an itinerant with his own compulsions (tuitions, appointments, the hastily improvised recording), who sometimes found it difficult, in the interests of adhering to deadlines, to give Nirmalya the time of day. At what point he began to learn the ragas from the air, from overheard radio programmes, from Shyamji's tapes and the records of other singers, and exactly which ragas he'd learnt from Shyamji and which from the long-playing record of some dead singer—he could no longer tell, or differentiate between the premeditated, routine, or accidental modes of learning. But this was exactly in keeping with what a young man of his privileges had been trained to do: to increasingly exercise his right to construct his own education. The more he learned, the more independent he grew, and the more he developed a taste for independence—that was the arc he was gradually travelling; learning, for people like him, was really an opening up, despite its communal aspects, into solitariness and freedom; and the music lesson couldn't compromise this pattern, it had to somehow merge, chameleon-like, into it. Shyamji understood this instinctively; he knew the boy would make more rigorous demands on himself than he, Shyamji, could have. If he ever felt irritated about the way Nirmalya both adored him and also took his musical education—stubbornly, unapproachably—at least partly in his own hands, it was because he felt slightly threatened by the single-mindedness and fierceness of his competitor, the inner guru in Nirmalya, a product not so much of mystical belief as of a life raised to free will and individual choice. In some ways, though, he didn't altogether mind; it meant he had to take less responsibility. For Shyamji was like a bird that wouldn't be caged; he fluttered, vanished, and reappeared on the horizon.

It was August. All morning, it looked like it was about to rain. The sea was agitated; a single white yacht, sophisticated, flippant, tested the water; the sky was pale grey.

Nirmalya, back from college, grimy, his goatee cloyed with sweat, deliberated with the idea of singing Miya ki Malhar. The weather had put him in a bodily state between anticipation and nostalgia. He sat on the carpet in the huge drawing room, his back against the sofa, the tanpura his parents had bought him before him. Hundreds of years ago, Miya Tansen had lit the lamps in Akbar's court by singing raga Deepak, and had brought drought to the province; then people had begged him to bring rain—he had sung Megh Malhar and clouds had come to the parched land. The miraculous made Nirmalya sceptical, especially as only the innocent and weak and stupid believed in miracles; but the old story, especially in conjunction with the arrival of the monsoons in Bombay, filled him unexpectedly with a fleeting sense of power. He sang the first low notes of Miya ki Malhar—ni dha ni sa—caressing the ni, adrift for a few minutes in the suspense that would lead back to the sa. This raga Tansen had created himself, a simple but immensely effective modulation on Megh Malhar, a patient, prevaricating dwelling on the nether notes before leaping towards the higher: to Nirmalya, it seemed to mirror perfectly the storm's mood, the silent, then deep-throated, build-up, and finally the universal release and relief of the rain. It was not a raga that Shyamji had taught him; he'd picked it up himself, stolen it from repeated hearings of records of Bhimsen Joshi and Amir Khan; it was part of the great inheritance of Tansen and the Moghul Empire and something even older. He checked the window from the corner of his eye: nothing. The weather was jammed and frozen; it wouldn't move. He continued to sing ni dha ni ni sa, overpowered not only by the silliness of his pursuit, but the hugeness of his task—of doing justice to the raga, although he was still in the process of understanding and hesitantly broaching it. A romantic longing possessed him; not to influence and rule the weather, like Tansen, but to be somehow connected to it. After about twenty minutes, he got up, irritable, exhausted. There was still no sign of rain.

He went to the balcony and leaned despondently against the bannister. Pigeons on the parapets of the building circled nervously; many of them sat in ranks, curiously unperturbed by one another, waiting for something to happen.

Then, one day that August, it did rain when he was singing. He'd been practising for ten minutes when large drops that had been journeying for miles spattered loudly against the windowpane, and the glass streamed with grey water. Unfortunately, it wasn't a monsoon raga; it was Bhupali, the verdant, earthly Bhupali, he was very earnestly in the middle of.

"What a nuisance!" said Banwari, fingers tapping without interruption, small, anxious eyes upon the window. "I forgot to bring my umbrella."

Banwari, Shyamji's younger brother, accompanied Nirmalya and Mrs. Sengupta on the tabla. He was, at once, composed-looking and nimble, both utterly static and cunningly responsive: like one of those essences or spirits who move everywhere without changing posture, who alter their shape without announcement or without you noticing it. His smile was fixed, almost meaningless, his eyes not half-closed, just small, his hands, always playing, playing, were awake but machine-like, seemingly disconnected from conscious intent. When the song was finished, Banwari's incarnation altered ever so slightly; it was as if a flesh-and-blood double had taken his place, and immediately decided to savour the air conditioning, the benefits of a physical existence. Conversation ensued; and you noticed his pained civility, bordering sometimes on awkwardness. He still had the awkward air of the young bridegroom who'd lifted the veil off his bride's face to find an impossibly beautiful woman. Banwari hadn't recovered from the burden of having a beautiful wife. Everything he did had an air of pained dignity and self-doubt; he felt compromised by his pitch-dark complexion, his teeth. Then, at his wife Neeta's bidding, he obediently had the two front teeth removed, and replaced by straighter ones: he took the result personally, and was extremely, silently, pleased. Loss or replacement isn't something you can always exhibit or display; but, at first, he glowed for some reason that people couldn't quite understand. He never entirely escaped that memory, though; even now, when he permitted himself a joke during the tea break, he covered his mouth with one hand when he smiled, as if it were haunted by the oversized teeth that had been taken out.

. . .

The other person who accompanied Nirmalya on the tabla and sometimes on the harmonium was Pyarelal, Shyamji's brother-in-law. Shyamji disliked Pyarelal thoroughly; but he doled out favours to him for the sake of his sister.

At one point, three years ago, he'd got Pyarelal an appointment in a music school in Jaipur; but he'd come back suddenly, thinner, sporting a new Nehru jacket, darker—something between a returning prodigal son and a visiting dignitary. So Shyamji would not be so easily rid of his brother-in-law. The Jaipur heat (although he'd been born and had grown up there) had been too much for Pyarelal; he couldn't take it, he said. He'd shown no intentions of leaving Bombay since; the magnetic pull of the city and Shyamji's family made him hover, hover, like an angel who would not be expelled, in his loose kurta and pyjamas and his pointed slippers.

One of the favours Shyamji bestowed on Pyarelal was letting him accompany Mrs. Sengupta and Nirmalya and allowing him to earn sixty rupees per "sitting" for it.

But then Nirmalya began to look forward to his visits. He became attached to the spectacle Pyarelal comprised; punctilious, fussy, qualities, somehow, all the more absurd and acute in him. Pyarelal, in turn, having sensed something with his keen instinct for the unspoken, was effusive in the compliments that Nirmalya so wanted to hear and dreamed were his due:

"Mark my words, baba will be singing these bandishes like a bird in ten years' time!"

And the endless and improbable life-history, which he disclosed readily:

"I used to dance in Raja Man Singh's court . . ."

This sort of thing ordinarily bored Nirmalya; yet Pyarelal, almost an invention, a man not only without status, but without provenance, could never bore him.

"Man Singh's court? When was that?"

A deliberate sip of tea, then:

"I danced before Man Singh when I was four."

And so Pyarelal had a bit of the stardust of the vanished courtly life around him; and he made it seem entirely believable. He was a jetsam of the old world, part of the coterie of artists that had been disbanded with the palaces, or so he fashioned himself for Nirmalya; not like his younger brother-in-law, who'd been shaped by a city of tuitions, and husbands in the background, and fees. And he sensed that Nirmalya, though he belonged to this particular world, was not in harmony with it, and that his own appeal to the boy lay in his anomalousness; he'd quickly discovered in Nirmalya a powerful nostalgia, a thirst for another time and place almost, that made the boy restless and ill-at-ease. Only Pyarelal noticed this nostalgia; and he'd never seen it in any other young person, certainly not in his three sons or any of the students he played with.

He was a self-styled teacher of kathak dance (though Nirmalya had never seen him teach) who'd picked up, as a child, the various arts of singing, tabla-playing, and harmonium accompaniment. An obscure accident in the past—what it was wasn't clear; he'd never specified to Nirmalya—had taken away from him the ability to be a performing dancer; he'd now grandly given himself the name of "kathak teacher and guru," although what he was, in spite of the two or three students he reportedly had, was a loyal practice-session man, banging on the tabla while the dancer memorised her routine, twirled round and thumped the floor with her feet till she got it right.

"Every raga has a roop—a form," he'd say with a very adult wistfulness, as if he'd had a vision of a raga once. "It has a chehra, a face"—and here, with the involuntary dancer's movement, he'd etch the face in the air before him, his own stubbled, hook-nosed face narrow-eyed in concentration—"a body. When you sing Yaman properly, for instance, you can see its form. Yaman comes and stands beside you."

The implication was, of course, that this was not an age in which you saw the raga any more; that for musicians today the raga was an agglomeration of notes, conventions, and rules, to which they brought their subjective passion, their instinct, and different degrees of ability; but to Pyarelal, scratching his chin and imparting his vision to the boy, they were in error—the raga had not only to be played *correctly* or *well*; it had to be courted and pursued.

When Mrs. Sengupta found them talking, Pyarelal smiled with a mixture of mischief and satisfaction, as if two lovers had been interrupted by a friend. If Shyamji happened to find them, he started guiltily and got up.

Unlike many male dancers, there was nothing effeminate about Pyarelal: he was short and sturdy. Wrestling had been one of his passions in his youth; he used to spend hours at the akhara, watching indefatigably as men rolled in the sand, or strained, bull-like, their arms locked around each other; bending introspectively, he'd practise holds and positions. "Being a man" was always important to him, as were its fierce attendant concerns, honour and pride.

His face—thin lips, thin moustache, hooked nose, a small wart beneath one eye, the longish hair combed back from his forehead—was hard and bony. Only the occasionally raised left eyebrow, arched and kept dangling briefly in the course of a conversation, bore testimony to the dancer's art.

"Kathak" derives from "katha" or "story"; Nirmalya hadn't realised this before. Words hoarded meaning like treasure; and Nirmalya was at an age when mere etymology brought to sight and lit up an avenue—whose pull was mysterious and irresistible—he hadn't known had existed. The dancer was not only a virtuoso but a storyteller; this fact was contained in the word "kathak" itself. Sitting on the carpet in the air-conditioned room, the curtains half drawn behind him, Pyarelal showed Nirmalya how Radha would pull the end of the sari before her face to protect herself from prying eyes when she went out into the lanes towards her lover; a motion of the wrist, an avertedness of the eyes, were enough to convey Radha's vulnerability, her racing heart. Nirmalya, in blue jeans and kurta, for the moment seemingly without occupation, education, or future, leaned against a cupboard door as this fifty-four-year-old man tried, at once, to impress him and to do what was surely legitimate: to reveal to him the elements of his craft. Pyarelal shook one foot slightly to remind him that the bells strung round Radha's ankle were too loud; that any moment her mother-in-law might awake and discover her liaison. He never got up from the carpet. Sometimes he whispered the song that told the story, which was really a litany of complaints to the divine, blissfully imperturbable lover who was awaiting her, "How do you expect me to come on this full-moon night, my ankle-bells ring and threaten to wake up my mother-in-law and sister-in-law, etcetera," while his nostrils, as he sang, flared imperceptibly.

When Nirmalya asked Pyarelal to write down for him one of the many songs he had recited or sung for him in the last few months, he discovered that the older man was barely literate. The Devanagari script was largely uncharted terrain, a country Pyarelal felt no pressing need to visit, and which he'd avoided visiting for the greater part of his life with no excessive sense of loss. For Nirmalya's sake, though, he made an attempt, and set down four lines in the exercise book that was Nirmalya's songbook in a faint and almost illegible handwriting. He smiled, as if asking indulgence for a disability (not a serious or harmful one, but a disability nonetheless) for which there was no immediate cure, and which it was in slightly bad taste to discuss.

However much he hid it from the boy, and however much his memories spoke of a spontaneous joy in life, Pyarelal was marked by a sense of inadequacy. All his memories were, strangely, from before his marriage, his restless loiterings between Rajasthan and Dehradun (where he'd lived for four years) and then Bombay, where he'd deliberately inserted himself into Ram Lal's life and then, as Shyamji would have it, got himself married to Ram Lal's daughter. Pyarelal's memories dried up after this; life seemed to have become more real, less surprising, and, somehow, less life-like. He compensated for that sense of inadequacy, his sense of the lack of the respect due to him, in his own way. It was common knowledge that he got drunk in the evenings; and, since everything in a family becomes familiar and then comic, especially to children, this fact became a joke, to Shyamji's children in particular, who, since they were small, had both lovingly and mockingly called him "Puaji," a lisping abbreviation at first, unable as they were then to pronounce "Pyarelalji," and then just an appellation, like "uncle" or "kaka." People seldom mentioned the unfortunate closeness of "Puaji" to "paji," or "wicked," but come evening, and the children in the neighbouring house knew that Puaji became garrulous and beat up Tara, their aunt. In his home, he was unassailable. Who was he? He was Ram Lal's daughter's lord and master, after all. Shyamji didn't, wouldn't, intervene; he was scrupulous about washing his hands of this unpleasantness, as he was about many others. What Pyarelal and his family did in the confines of their four walls was their business.

"What do you talk to him about, baba?" asked Shyamji sadly. He looked calm, but his resentment was essentially stubborn, unappeasable.

Pyarelal had just made an exit, scraping, bowing, saying "Yes, bhaiyya, no, bhaiyya, bilkul, bhaiyya" to Shyamji.

Nirmalya was at a loss for words.

"He's a master of drama," said Shyamji, before Nirmalya could answer his question.

Pyarelal had his own method of exacting, quite ingenuously, revenge on Shyamji; he did it by extolling his father-in-law, the dead Ram Lal.

"The first night of the conference in Calcutta, Bade Ghulam Ali sang Bihag," he recalled with a half-smile, as if the ustad's voice were audible to him. "And then there was Bihag and only Bihag in the air. The second night Panditji"—that was how he referred to Ram Lal—"sang Malkauns. And then there was Malkauns and only Malkauns!"

The son-in-law, who'd arrived out of nowhere and inserted himself into Ram Lal's affections, recounting the dead.

"But what about Shyamji?" asked Nirmalya, his heart brimming with feeling for his often-absent teacher. "He sings wonderfully too, doesn't he?"

"He sings very well, but he's only four annas compared to Panditji," said Pyarelal with a ruminative laugh. Four annas; a mere twenty-five per cent. And since it was the father who was being praised, even Banwari, the younger son, had to nod solemnly when remarks like these were made. Not only Banwari—a swift shadow passed over Shyamji's face when words like "But no one can sing these songs like Panditji" were said, and he'd nod in defeat and add, "He's right, baba, you did not hear my father." It was as if, at such moments, logic deserted him, and the insurmountability of life revealed itself. And the sixteen-year-old would be filled with pity, and at the same time convinced the claim was a lie; that people create lies about the dead to torment the best of the living.

The best of the living: although Nirmalya was convinced his teacher was among the "best," he was disappointed by Shyamji's pursuit of the "light" forms, his pursuit of material well-being. An artist must devote himself to the highest expressions of his art and reject success; he was going to be seventeen, and these ideas had come to him from books he'd read recently, but he felt he'd always known them and that they were true for all time. He put it to Shyamji plainly:

"Shyamji, why don't you sing classical more often? Why don't you sing fewer ghazals and sing more at classical concerts?" Shyamji was always unimpeachably polite. He now turned to study the Managing Director's son's face with curiosity, as if he were reminded again of the boy's naivety.

"Baba," he said (his tone was patient), "let me establish myself so that I don't have to think of money any more. Then I can devote myself completely to art. You can't sing classical on an empty stomach."

Nirmalya had heard a version of this argument in college: that you must first satisfy your physical needs, of food, shelter, clothing, before you can satisfy your psychological ones—like culture. He wasn't persuaded by his guru's words. How did you know when you arrived at that point, when you were safe enough to turn exclusively and fearlessly to the arts? How, and for when, did you set the cut-off date? Nirmalya had never known want; and so he couldn't understand those who said, or implied, they couldn't do without what they already had.

He went to the balcony, considered the view: much-praised, much-prized—more valuable than any of the artefacts inside, it raised, in its daily, innocent rehearsal of daylight and sunset, the price of the apartment to what it was. La Terrasse, white and wide, was in the distance; as was the long strip of beach, like a thin ore of gold, tapering towards the Governor's house.

When you looked straight down from the balcony at dusk, you could see the outlines of people on the edge of the land. Thacker Towers had begun to be repainted before the monsoons, and now work continued in bursts between rainy days. Bamboo scaffolding had been erected around the buildings: and sometimes, when Nirmalya was reading or listening to music in his room, he'd see a man, or men, appear just beyond the balcony, careless as sailors on the top of a mast, seemingly uninterested in his presence.

Word circulated that Mr. Thacker hadn't provided them with toilets—or maybe it hadn't occurred to him that they'd need toilets. It was these men and their families who gathered below at dusk on the edge of land in the shadow of Thacker Towers.

. . .

Almost seventeen, he was leaving his father's world behind—the sitting room behind him, its paintings, ashtrays, curios, vases, the study at the far end with its bound volumes, the dining room with the thick oval glass table, the four bedrooms. Since moving to Thacker Towers, he'd stopped feeling at home. Only the flies, which, in spite of the wire gauze, kept returning, amused him; he eyed the doomed one beadily and killed it heartlessly.

When he was a child, home was escape—from the terrifying terrain of nursery and school, of shiny alphabet charts with their motionless constellation of cats, balls, and vans; of a physical education of running and falling, and singing lessons when you stood like soldiers; and glancing every few minutes at the great hands on the white clockface. But now, his father having assumed the mantle of the Managing Directorship, this flat in Thacker Towers, with all its furniture—the Himalayan peak of his father's career and probably Nirmalya's own material life—was strangely arid to come back to, like a place that could never be properly inhabited, lit by the sun at different points in the day, and by the electric lights heavy with crystals in the evening.

He seemed on the verge of discovering some new definition; he didn't know what it was, but it set him apart, a bit cruelly, but also providentially; and it turned his latent lack of self-belief into a bristly superiority he carried about with him always. Even the servants noticed it.

As he began to shed the meanings he'd grown up with, he busily assigned new ones. He fell almost belligerently in love with an idea, to do with an immemorial sense of his country; and music was indispensable to it. The raga contained the land within it—its seasons, its times of day, its birdcall, its clouds and heat—it gave him an ideal, magical sense of the country; it was a fiction he fell in love with. Having subscribed to the fiction, everything else was a corruption or aberration: the Marine Drive, Thacker Towers, the company his father ran, tea at the Taj Mahal hotel—nothing was "true" enough. Looking, soon after sunset, at the sky above La Terrasse and its neighbouring buildings—careful to deny the Marine Drive and the neon advertisements—he thought of raga Shree and how appropriate it was to this moment, only the latest, in history, in numberless such days' endings—in some place that was both here, and not here, not in Cuffe Parade or Thacker Towers.

A vase catching the light; fresh flowers. Shalini must have come that day to trim the stalks. Teatime; a circle of ladies; one of them, wearing a dress, was English.

Gradually, a thought had begun to niggle in his mind: the ragas had no composer. Where did they come from; and why was no one bothered that the question didn't have an answer? Indian music had no Bach, no Beethoven—why was that? Instinctively, privately, in a confused way, as he looked evening after evening out of the balcony, the notion of authorship came to him—a difficult thought, which he spent some time grappling with. It was the idea of the author, wasn't it, that made one see a work of art as something original and originated, and as a piece of property, which gave it value; it was what made it possible to say, "It belongs to him," or "It's his creation," or "He's created a great work." And this sense of ownership and origination went into how a race saw itself through its artists. He realised, in a semi-articulate way, with a feeling of despair as well as an incongruous feeling of liberation, that this, though, was not the way to understand Indian music; the fact was a secret that dawned on him and which he had to keep to himself. He discussed it with no one; not with Shyamji, although he'd been tempted once or twice to explore the topic with Pyarelal, but had given up before he'd even started. In the meanwhile, as he read his beloved philosophers and poets, he encountered the celebration of genius everywhere—"So-and-so did it first"; "So-and-so did it best"—and he acquiesced in it; but some part of him now, in light of the raga, began to resist it too. Only when rereading Yeats's poem about Byzantium did he appear to find an acknowledgement in what he read of an art without an author, at least in certain lines and phrases: "Those images that yet/ Fresh images beget" and "flames begotten of flame,/ . . . An agony of flame that cannot singe a sleeve." What kind of image could that be, except an image whose author was unknown, and which seemed to have been born of, or authored by, art itself? The lines contained the mystery of what it meant to come into contact with a work of art whose provenance was hidden and, in the end, immaterial. It didn't matter that you couldn't put a signature to that "image." Elsewhere, Yeats had called those images "Presences . . . self-born mockers of man's enterprise"; Nirmalya thought he grasped now what "self-born" meant—it referred to those immemorial residues of culture that couldn't be explained or circumscribed by authorship. It was as if they'd come from nowhere, as life and the planets had; and yet they were separate from Nature. Dimly, he saw that, though the raga was a human creation, it was, paradoxically, "self-born."

The painting of the building was three-quarters complete. The men stood on the scaffolding, sometimes they clung to a pole and stretched to the left or to the right, they moved sideways, they squatted casually on a pole, their rags flapping, almost riding nothingness. They never looked through the glass at the tranquillity within; they were too busy, gossiping, shouting, laughing and showing their teeth (he could see the inside of a workman's mouth, and wondered if he ever spat tobacco from such a great height), all the while at work on that platform. Nirmalya spied on them through the large window. "I couldn't have done it, I couldn't have done it," he told himself, "not if my life depended on it." One of them slipped, fell; Nirmalya heard about it later. He imagined the young man—they were all young—arms beating helplessly against the emptiness. Work went on.

Nirmalya began to see less of his friends. In the twilight world he'd created, or chanced upon, in the intersection of the raga and nature, his friends were intruders; that world accommodated a great part of the universe—sun, dark, rain, the beating of a pigeon's wings, a crow's harsh cry—but it couldn't accommodate Rajiv Desai, Sanjay Nair, and the others.

Without entirely planning to, Nirmalya abnegated "normalcy"; and suffered because of it.

He had moods of withdrawal and renunciation.

"I want to go to the Himalayas," he said, as if he'd given this, and the life he was leading in general, some thought, and decided this was the easiest and most obvious solution. His audience was his mother and Nayana Neogi, the tall bespectacled woman who'd known this family for more than twenty years, and seen Apurva Sengupta transformed from a minor England-returned aspirant into a corporate bigwig with an apartment of seemingly infinite size. She'd reconciled herself to this; her own life with her commercial-artist husband and their pets, and the early thrill of the bohemian manner (she unwaveringly smoked fifteen cigarettes a day, and they lived in the rented ground-floor apartment they'd first occupied twenty-five years ago, and had no property to their name) had become jaded and habit-ridden. Yet habit has the warmth and familiarity of flesh and bone. She was large now, having put on weight in her failed artist's idleness; too large to wear the handwoven saris and rudimentary sleeveless cotton blouses with comfort. Instead, she plunged, these days, into a single loose garment that covered her from shoulder to toe and in which she moved about with a sort of freedom. Her old pets died; new ones entered the ground-floor home. A dachshund, a lovely, large-hearted thing, Nirmalya remembered from his childhood, with its low platform of a body and its charred stub of tail; that had, long, long ago, intended to cross the street outside their house and been run over by a car. But there were other, natural deaths, as cats and fox terriers died in old age and senility; as well as a tragic recent one. Nayana had been lying on the beautifully-crafted divan (so plain you might not notice its beauty) with a kitten nestling at her great back; she'd fallen deep asleep in the afternoon, and turned. Waking up to the sound of sparrows, she, who'd not felt a thing, discovered, distraught, that she'd become the kitten's final darkness and seal. Today, partly with this sorrow, and with the sorrow of her own excessive weight, but buoyant at the change of surroundings, she'd come all the way to the magnificent apartment in Thacker Towers to spend the day with Mallika Sengupta. She was amused to see this boy in the old kurta, whom she'd known since he was a school-going child, standing self-absorbedly before her, the child in him still faintly visible, but also the new, unhappy young man. Ridding it of its cumulus-like appendage of ash, she took a drag on her cigarette; she was oddly moved by his unhappiness.

"Why, Nirmalya? What can you possibly lack? You have everything."

Later, he joined them for lunch and dourly polished off Arthur's fruit trifle.

~

Despite the urge to go to the Himalayas, he also went with his parents to the Taj, and ate chilli cheese toast with them in the Sea Lounge. With a mixture of firmness and practised intimacy, Mr. Sengupta, as he entered, placed an arm on the waiter's shoulder and asked to be led only towards the left to the large sea-facing windows. There they sat at the tables meant for two—for couples or business accomplices; indeed, his parents came here every Saturday, for one unadulterated hour of silent nibbling and tea-stirring punctuated by conversation—and when Nirmalya came with them, he descended oddly on the third, awkward chair that was placed before the table by someone, and waited for the rectangular strips of toast with their swollen topping of cheese flecked with warning red spots.

Never entirely removed from where his parents were, or the areas in which he'd grown up or studied, he could still be spotted—even in the Taj on a Saturday—at different places almost simultaneously, as if these different incarnations of him—in the bookshop, at one end of the lobby, then at another end—all had a mysterious purpose or mission. Once, floating unmindfully, almost contentedly, down the glassy surface of the corridor that connected the old Taj to the new, he saw, and was seen by, a small figure, motionless among elegant passers-by. Pyarelal!

"Pyarelal, what are you doing *here*?" asked the boy, delighted, confused.

Pyarelal grinned as if he had a secret. His pale yellow kurta shone. Then, as Apurva and Mallika Sengupta approached, he dipped low and did a namaskar.

"I have a programme here at six," he explained—he hadn't shaved properly; there was still a bit of grey stubble on the chin. "My student Jayashree Nath performs before tourists. Please come whenever you have the time, baba." Behind him was the church-heavy door of the Tanjore restaurant. It was ajar; through a small gap, Nirmalya peered in to see a waiter in a dark suit, a shadowy, noticeably handsome figure—the restaurant was empty of diners at this time of the day—and a group of what looked like American men and women.

And, indeed, next week, Nirmalya did drop in to Tanjore; he pushed open the door, and was let in by the waiter in the black suit without a word. There were about fifteen tourists in the semi-dark of the restaurant; red-faced women in dresses or trousers, as if congregated in some suburb for a dashing evangelist, or to debate the environmental policies of an industrial house; and large men who were unaccountably shy. When Pyarelal appeared in a businesslike manner, he glanced at the audience, as a great artist resurrected from the dead might regard the living, without surprise, but with restrained curiosity; and then he spotted Nirmalya. He was pleased, and sent him a knowing smile. Bowing, but gazing above the audience's heads, he did an elaborate namaskar, almost as much part of the performance as the dance itself. The tourists stirred vaguely, respectfully, as at the beginning of a speech; they didn't know what the correct response to this was. He sat down before the harmonium with great solemnity; the dignity was expected of him; he'd cast aside the other Pyarelal, the one who was married to Tara, with three children, Puaji to the nephews and nieces, old Puaji, who would never go away, and who lost his temper at night. There was a sound of bells, again, again, and then Jayashree Nath, the bells round her ankles vibrating with every step, appeared on the platform with a young tabla player who ducked his head and glanced goofily at the visitors. She, however, had a far more worldly, assured air, like a tourist guide, cheerful, mechanical, underneath her apsara's appearance; and, in a tourist guide's English, she related the story she was about to perform, the perennially winsome one about Radha going with her friends to the banks of the Yamuna and there being harried by Krishna.

When she began to dance, and Pyarelal, clearing his throat daintily, to croon the words in raga Khamaj into the microphone, the explanation gradually became superfluous. The suburban women's blue eyes sparkled like chips of aquamarine, as if extra interpretation were unnecessary. Repeatedly, surreptitiously, but in a strangely public way, like a lover who wants to make his excitement plain to anyone who cares to notice, Pyarelal glanced at Nirmalya; today's performance was for him. The tourists were never not appreciative; even on bad days, when they danced and sang with less involvement, going through the motions in a way only they were aware of, the tourists' applause was always spontaneous and automatic. This left Pyarelal content but secretly disconnected; he knew he'd been transformed into a fresco, a gilded element in a larger "Indian" experience. Today, Nirmalya's presence gave the performance a hidden competitiveness; they were no longer "Indian" artistes, they felt they needed to show him that they were *good* artistes. So, although the tourists were innocent of this, Pyarelal and even Jayashree Nath and the tabla player were engaged in a give-and-take of concealed pleasure, of revelations and gestures, with the intruder.

. . .

Once, he took Pyarelal upstairs, to the veranda outside the Sea Lounge, where his parents, a couple of splendid potted plants their neighbours, sat on cane chairs having tea. "Pyarelalji, do sit down!" said Mallika Sengupta, as he lowered himself cautiously into the forbidding oasis. "Will you have some tea?" asked Apurva Sengupta, and Pyarelal made one of his exaggerated gestures, humble and overwrought, which could have meant anything. Tea arrived, and Pyarelal watched fastidiously as the waiter poured the weak brew into a china cup; "Bas, bas," he interjected with dignity as the man added milk. He began to relax; thoughtful, but every nerve sensitive, he stirred the tea with a spoon.

Two months ago, Nirmalya and Mallika Sengupta had gone for the first time to Shyamji's house.

"It is very far, didi," Shyamji had warned her, as if she'd suddenly threatened, unreasonably, to journey to a wilderness. "A very small place—we don't have much to show . . ."

"What nonsense!" said Mrs. Sengupta, in total control, as usual, of her decision, distracted by the heat, a neglected spot of powder on the tip of her nose.

Shyamji had recovered instantly and smoothed his hair back as he went out of the apartment; he'd said very sincerely, his pride recollected:

"Please do come, didi. We'd be very happy if you did."

When they arrived finally after an hour and a half in the summer evening, moving from familiar terrain into unfamiliar Matunga, through dust, oil-slicks and traffic past the slums of Dharavi, they found Shyamji in spotless white kurta and pyjamas, and Sumati, smiling, her pallu covering her head, waiting for them.

"Aiye, aiye, didi," said Sumati. "Oh, I'm so glad baba came too. *Vel-come*," she said to him in English. "Kyun, did I say it right?" and laughed loudly.

. . .

Shyamji and Sumati vacated their places on the divan for Mrs. Sengupta and Nirmalya, and sat on an old sofa opposite. Hurriedly, Sumati went inside to make tea; the small sitting room was divided from the kitchen and the bedroom inside by a curtain and a wall. She came out briefly again with a tray with two glasses of water for the visitors and stood before them; they didn't know, for a moment, what to do. Caste was not, of course, the problem; for what can keep you from accepting food and drink in a brahmin's house? No, caste, anyway, was an irrelevance for the Senguptas—but other questions preoccupied them. Shyamji was watching patiently; but the Senguptas didn't drink water that wasn't boiled; they'd agreed amongst themselves to ban all water offered to them outside home, unless, of course, it came from a completely trusted source. Still Sumati, in her innocence, hovered like a spirit of solicitude, a half-smile on her lips; Mrs. Sengupta, hot in her sari, hesitated, then picked up the glass and, as if this were the logical thing to do, placed it on the table in front of her. Nirmalya, faced with the tumbler, retreated almost visibly into his own awkwardness: "No, I'm all right," he said, and Sumati protested in disbelief, "Kya, baba, you don't want water?" and the tumbler returned to the kitchen behind the curtain from where it had come. Behind the divan, on the wall, was Pandit Ram Lal's portrait, utterly still. And, from a distance, you could hear kirtans from the gurdwara's loudspeaker.

And yet how wonderful it was to be in his guru's house, the electric bulbs making the room bright, a room in which visitors were welcomed, but in which the divan where they sat, lightly covered with a sheet, obviously became someone's bed at night. Mrs. Sengupta did most of the talking; Nirmalya was largely silent, as he used to be when he accompanied his mother to the houses of acquaintances as a child; he held Shyamji in too high a regard to ever have a comfortable conversation with him. Besides, what would they talk about? They couldn't discuss music, because it was not discussable; it was a set of rules and commands that had to be passed on and picked up almost unthinkingly. In fact, it wasn't certain Shyamji ever *thought* about the kind of things that Nirmalya considered the province of *thought*; it seemed that his immediate future and that of his children, and, in that context, the business of proper conduct and what was admissible were what exercised Shyamji in his daily life. Nirmalya didn't consider this "thinking"; his own daily life involved an agonising—punctuated by blank phases of stupefaction—over the history that, from the beginning of time, had gone into forming the moment that he now, in 1981, found himself uneasily in. Shyamji would, in all probability, have met these ruminations with incomprehension. The question, then, of having a conversation with Shyamji didn't arise—where would it lead? Nirmalya was happy to be there, to sit and listen, as he often did when his mother talked, while two smoking cups of tea, brown with milk, were placed before them, and he, from time to time, as he sat there, became lost in the difficult, tenuous weave of his own speculations.

The second time Mrs. Sengupta went to Shyamji's house, she found a self-conscious, dark woman, somewhat younger than her, sitting on the divan.

"Didi, this is Ashaji," said Shyamji, with an added carefulness and civility. "She is singing two songs in the film: we are very lucky."

Mrs. Sengupta looked at her again, this woman whose songs were played every day on the radio, and who, with her elder sister, reigned in a dual tyranny over the Hindi film music world. The face was benign, but mask-like; she seemed slightly ill at ease.

"My son is very fond of your singing," said Mrs. Sengupta as she sat down. Asha's face brightened imperceptibly, but the mask-like composure didn't change.

"You should listen to didi some day," said Shyamji, assured, mellifluous. "She has a very beautiful voice."

"Oh I can tell," said Asha, smiling faintly. "Her speaking voice itself is musical to the ear." *Her* speaking voice was a degree louder than a hoarse whisper; the words were spoken with the slow deliberateness of a child.

These words came back to Mallika Sengupta the next day; yes, she was pleased with them, but she dismissed them; it was beneath her to accept such crumbs of appreciation from this woman, who'd appeared to her in the incarnation of an ordinary working person in a plain printed sari. There was no getting round it; she lived in a world wholly separate from Asha's, married happily to a successful man, moving about in sparkling, if occasionally vacuous, circles. But she wondered whether it was accident or destiny or her own hidden desire that had made her what she was. She'd never wanted to be Asha; yet what was it about her own talent that made it meaningless without the happiness she had, and also always made the happiness incomplete?

~

Shyamji's stock had gone up steadily in the last three years: he decided to leave this small rented flat in which he'd lived for decades. Besides, families were growing larger; in neighbouring flats in the row of chawls, Banwari and Pyarelal lived with their wives and children. "Beta, Shyam," said his mother, small but zealous in her widow's white sari, "you must do something, the children are growing up, there is no room any more."

So they left King's Circle; it was almost a wrench, to leave the noise of the gurdwara and the congestion. The task of acquiring the new properties in which the families would now be located, of dividing the money they'd get from their old landlord on vacating their flats in the chawl and using it for this purpose, of applying for loans—all this was left to Shyamji. Pyarelal, barely literate, kept himself in the background (even his withdrawals were dramatic and meant to draw attention), restricting himself to nodding or shaking his head like a deaf-mute when a response was required. On the whole, Shyamji ignored him; his eyes glazed over whenever Pyarelal drifted into the vicinity; but he went about his business stoically, of providing his brother-in-law and his family, besides himself and his brother, with a place to live. Banwari was no help either; he lacked confidence in himself. He continued, silent, decorous, with his old routine, of playing the tabla at various people's houses, practising, quite deliberately, an abnegation of his own from his brother's search, as if there were no change in his life.

"He wants me to be his guarantor," said Mr. Sengupta to his wife at night. He cleared his throat. The lights had been turned off; they were lying on the large bed, talking to each other. The Tibetan rug by the side of the bed, the carpet between the raised wooden floor that surrounded the bed and the way to the cup boards and the bathroom, the swirling wallpaper behind their heads, the faint moth-like glow of the ceiling which they stared at from the pillow, a deeply soothing sight in the day's last wakefulness—all this, as one of them flicked the switch, vanished and was reduced to an aftermath where they were nowhere. Their eyes were open, and they lay wondering; the day's bright magic returned, and its niggling, unresolved questions, loosed from the visible world, hovering like remembered images as their eyes grew used to the dark.

"Guarantor . . . for what?"

"He said to me yesterday—he was very hesitant," here Mr. Sengupta switched to his familiar clumsy version of Hindi, " 'Sengupta saab, I'm applying for a loan to buy the flats. If you are my guarantor, Sengupta saab . . . Anyway, I'll return the bank the money in two or three years.' That's what he said."

They were silent against the equanimous, life-giving, sempiternal background of air conditioning. They weren't entirely happy with Shyamji; he was quick to demand and borrow money from Apurva Sengupta, and to make easy promises to his wife. But he hardly made good those promises; Mallika Sengupta's career as a singer was there—exactly where it had been ten years ago; Laxmi Ratan Shukla was no closer to recording her first disc than when they'd first met him; she still sang, with the purposelessness and dedication of something between a nun and a housewife who's in exile in her own household, the bhajans Shyamji gave her, but mainly at home. "Didi, that voice can make you famous in the world," Shyamji said; but she doubted, during moments of hiatus such as this one, when she was lying on her back, eyes closed, listening, her thoughts everywhere, whether he meant anything he said.

Apurva Sengupta confessed after a few seconds:

"I've decided to sign the form."

"He thinks," Mrs. Sengupta warned her faintly visible husband, "that we have a lot of money. He sees our lifestyle, and thinks we're rich. God forbid that anything should go wrong after he buys the flats . . . You know you have no money." It was the incredible story they kept rehearsing to themselves; that executives like Apurva Sengupta had the perks—the lavish apartment, the Mercedes-Benz, the servants—but, as they saw it and felt acutely, no wealth, no ballast, no substantial material possession, especially in comparison to the people they called, in the simple but expressive language of the age, "businessmen." It wasn't a story that either convinced or appealed to Shyamji.

"Didi, you have to come!" protested Sumati, Shyamji's wife, laughing and shaking, pre-emptively, her head from side to side. "We will not do the grihapravesh without you!"

It was the exaggerated nonsense you expected from Sumati. But Mrs. Sengupta agreed; for she also felt a faint quickening, a sense of being expected, of being special—it was the magic of arrival she loved looking forward to, the sort that attended, for instance, her visit to a poorer relation's house because of some family occasion, when she was at once unremarkable, the same Mallika she'd always been, and transformed and unattainable, the Mrs. Sengupta she was today. The flats had been bought in a housing development far away in Borivli in late November; now, before they were properly occupied, the grihapravesh ceremony—the ritual of making the dwelling auspicious—had to be performed. More nonsense, thought Mallika Sengupta; further expenditure on borrowed money. But, one December morning, they—mother and son (Mrs. Sengupta, giving the lie to her claims of impatience, wearing a carefully chosen Kanjivaram silk, looking like the mistress of some mythic temple), set out in the white Mercedes-Benz; no question of Apurva Sengupta going—he was in meetings all day.

Borivli was only a name to them; they knew it existed somewhere beyond where their conception of the city stopped, but didn't know where it was. Actually knowing anyone who lived in Borivli was out of the question. The driver seemed to be taking them toward the airport, but turned right into a busy junction; he went down a road full of small stops and traders' outlets, then drove down a series of lanes, asking people for directions. It seemed, to their surprise—but, gradually, nothing was surprising—that more and more people lived here. The journey was full of stops and starts, and from time to time Mrs. Sengupta said to Nirmalya, as if she were at the limits of her patience, that Shyamji's family should have known better than to demand they travel to such a remote place. Finally, exhausted by monotony but awed, now and again, by how livelihoods and landscapes were obviously stretching outward, they came to the middle of nowhere, with three new buildings rising before them. They were the sort of building made for the lower-income bracket, plain stone, with only a hint of colour—faint pink—and tiny spaces for balconies. Yet they were noticeably new.

There had been an unseasonal drizzle in the morning, and it had left the ground muddy. Mallika Sengupta had trouble rallying her Kanjivaram round her ankles, and walking to the entrance; her low, two-inch heels marked her wavering, thoughtful progress on the soft ground. "Wait here," she said once, turning round to address the driver, as if she'd accidentally recalled his significance, and wanted to leave him with some instruction or assurance. He, emerging from the car and standing before it in his white uniform and cap, looked lonely and self-sufficient, an emissary who found himself in surroundings unworthy of him. Nirmalya, as he walked to the building, didn't notice that anything was absent, but sensed there was something missing. There were no trees in the circumference that formed the horizon round these buildings.

Children were running up and down the gloomy staircase, yelling loudly and incomprehensibly—thin, not well-to-do, but energetic, stopping momentarily to stare at Mrs. Sengupta with the familiar guileless gaze of people looking at someone who belongs to a different world—admiring, unresentful, a gaze, oddly, almost of recognition; and when Mrs. Sengupta and Nirmalya came to the first floor, they found the door to one of the flats open, and the corridor lit by sunlight. Families of all hues, obviously related to Shyamji, seemed to have come to celebrate the move.

"Didi!" said Banwari's wife, Neeta, when she spotted them, the pallu of her sari, as ever, shadowing a quarter of her face. "Please come in and sit down."

A man in a vest and dhoti was sitting with his back to the balcony, retelling, in a mealy-mouthed way, an episode from the Ramayana; people, among them Shyamji and his mother, had gathered around him, listening. How they loved to be instructed, to be charmed by and surrender to, yet again, the wisdom of a tale they'd heard a hundred times since childhood, to have their moral certitudes reconfirmed!

Then, they—these men, some of whom did nothing else for a living but play the cymbals or the tanpura, ghosts who were too much in love with earthly existence to let go of it, but who also had no proper earthly existence; and their wives—they began to sing the arati, the repetitive, sweet, deeply consoling melodic line that made you want to sing it forever. And it seemed to Nirmalya they'd sing it forever—they went on and on, returning to the same phrase. He and Mrs. Sengupta had moved up; now, Shyamji and his mother stood before them, their backs to them, as the priest made circles in the air with a lamp, the flame flashing on the air and, barely an instant later, on the eye in swift, disappearing arcs, those circles becoming real only when the moment had passed, when seeing had already turned into remembering. Mrs. Sengupta could hear Shyamji's voice clearly, melodious, high-pitched, uninsistent, like a bird's; and then it seemed it was only *his* voice she could hear, and the other voices had become a hum in the background.

It was over; there was anarchy. Children collided with each other and almost knocked down adults in their impatience; Nirmalya and Mrs. Sengupta and others (but the mother and son dealt with a courtesy reserved for no one else; everyone, Shyamji included, was obviously made from the same fabric, while they were made from some other) were taken to another room to eat—chickpeas, cauliflower bhaji, paneer, puris, were served on damp plates placed on the long narrow planks of tables.

"Did you hear Shyamji singing?" asked Mallika Sengupta. "Without tanpura or harmonium or any accompaniment—just the voice: so tuneful!" "Of course," said Nirmalya, scooping up some vegetables with the puri. "But that's what you'd expect from Shyamji, wouldn't you?" "That's the way I used to sing when I was a child. It came naturally," said Mrs. Sengupta. "You don't hear that any more these days."

"Well, there was that man, going on about Hanuman flying in the sky with the Gandhamadan mountain in one hand and about Sita and Lanka," said Pyarelal, standing next to the air conditioner, his kurta-ends fluttering. It was as if he'd been present during that epic moment long before history as we now know it began, and was weary of hearing of such things second-hand. Two days had passed since the grihapravesh ceremony, and he was reminiscing about it; the priest, especially, aroused his ire. He poured tea unhurriedly into a saucer and sipped sweetly from it; he was always uncharacteristically relaxed in the apartment in Thacker Towers, as if it induced in him a state of rumination and stillness. "I was hoping he'd stop, but why should he stop? There were Shyam bhaiyya and mataji, sitting before him with such a look of devotion that they seemed to be falling asleep." As an afterthought, he cleared his throat and added, like one offering a throw-away insight: "The chickpeas were hard." And he moved his jaw involuntarily and glumly, as if his teeth still nagged him. His teeth were vulnerable; chewing intractable material could in an instant rob him of the carefree expression that denoted he was in control of the recalcitrant, milling world he moved in every day.

Pyarelal had got a flat out of this; he wanted the flat, but an odd resentment brewed within, because he felt he had no choice but to take the flat. He was emboldened in the huge Thacker Towers apartment with Nirmalya for company; he could express his innate sense of his own grandeur, before sitting down in front of the tablas again, without self-consciousness; and slip, too, into the odd troubledness that came to him from having a piece of property to his name. In the grihapravesh ceremony, he'd had no standing; he'd ushered in Mrs. Sengupta and Nirmalya to eat, then got bored of hanging around; being humble and attentive around the idiot hordes of relatives didn't suit him—he'd slunk into a corner to smoke a beedi.

No one took much note of Pyarelal. But Nirmalya actually listened to what he said, and took a perversely different view of him. He was in the midst of a discovery when it came to Pyarelal; he was, in a sense, inventing the older man. Later, he'd never be able to recapture the first flush of this excitement, which had aggrandised Pyarelal to him and made him unique, and would see only the mortal, damaged, cringing man. Pyarelal, too, seemed to sense at times that he was caught up in a web of Nirmalya's making, and was unable to, in fact content not to, extricate himself from it; although, once or twice, without even being aware of it, he'd glanced at the boy with a look of incomprehension and almost of sadness, as if some buried part of him wondered how long the spell would last. "Ma," Nirmalya said to Mrs. Sengupta, "he may be hardly able to read and write, but he has what in an educated person would be called a 'critical mind.' " For Pyarelal took nothing as received wisdom, not even the saint-poets. "Tulsi, Kabir—they're wonderful," he'd said. "But Meera? Much of the time there's no merit in what she writes. 'Pag ghungru bandh Meera nachi re'—'Bells strung round her feet, Meera dances'—is that a line worth speaking of?" He looked straight at Nirmalya, as if he'd made an unpleasant remark about Meera's anatomy but was confident nevertheless that what he'd said was fair. Nirmalya was taken aback; for no one he knew thought of whether Meera's lines were good or bad; they celebrated her mythology, the tale her songs narrated, of how she left the Rana, the king she'd been married to, and his palace for the love of Krishna; how, again and again, the Rana tried to poison and kill her; how each time, magically, his attempts were thwarted. All this was as familiar to Nirmalya as a story in a comic book. But now, as Pyarelal stared at him, the famous line "Pag ghungru bandh Meera nachi re" began to sound dead to Nirmalya's ear; Pyarelal had killed it. "Of course, she has *some* good lines," said Pyarelal, his mood changing into one at once imperious and democratic. "Hari, vanquish the world's sorrow,/Rescue the drowning elephant,/Lengthen the garment that covers." Nirmalya understood the allusions compressed in the lines much later—about the elephant, dragged into the water by the crocodile, being rescued by Krishna when it invoked his name; and of how Krishna infinitely extended the yard of cloth that formed Draupadi's sari as Dushasana tried to strip her of it. Meera, in this song, wasn't calling upon the Krishna who was her secret lover, as she did usually, but to Krishna, the vanquisher of the world's sorrows—"jan ke bheer"—and, though Nirmalya was yet to comprehend all this, the music of the words sounded to him distinct from the indisputable flatness of the other line. He stole a glance at Pyarelal. Could it be because this man could barely write that the sounds of words were more audible to him? A theory began to take shape inside his head.

"Not being able to read and write makes life difficult," admitted Pyarelal sadly, one hand on the harmonium.

"All those forms . . ." he said, using the English word and mournfully turning it into *farms*. "All those farms to fill . . ." For the semi-literate musician in Bombay, hemmed in and kept in his place by thickets of bureaucracy, life was a conspiracy of forms.

. . .

But what living in the tiny flat in the chawl in King's Circle for fifteen years had done to him was evident sometimes. Before he sat to play the harmonium with Nirmalya in the boy's small, introspective, neat bedroom, Pyarelal would turn and primly close the bathroom door. If it were ajar behind him, he'd be unable to concentrate on the music; he'd get up in exasperation and shut it. "Why is this open?" The tiles glowed; they gave off a fairy-tale emanation. The basin was encircled by granite and marble; the instruments of washing and defecation were guarded and polished daily by a jamadar like a museum's treasure. Nirmalya wondered why the half-open bathroom door so unsettled poor Pyarelal. It was only after visiting the chawl in King's Circle, and learning more about Pyarelal's and Shyamji's and Banwari's lives, that he understood the stench of a shared toilet, a stench which, given an inch, would insinuate itself into and quietly colonise the house. Pyarelal sniffed the air; he smelled what wasn't there. It was the smell of the toilet in King's Circle that agitated him.

Shyamji fell ill. He'd felt a sudden pressure on his chest, and rubbed it unhappily with one hand; he'd been taken to a nursing home. It was a mild heart attack.

"However did it happen?" asked Apurva Sengupta, phoning his wife in the middle of work. He sounded impatient, as if the knot in his tie felt tight, or his secretary had gestured to him about an appointment; it was three o'clock, a quiet but demanding hour, in which the chief executive, suddenly alone after lunch, has to collect the day around him. "Is he all right?"

Shyamji was only forty-three. He was slightly overweight—Nirmalya had seen him changing his kurta before a programme, the rounded, dark body beneath the vest, the tender, secretive folds of flesh, the brahmin's thread tucked inside: his condition was aggravated by diabetes.

"You must stop him eating sweets," Mallika Sengupta said to Sumati. That irresistible, and, to Mrs. Sengupta, inexplicable urge that people from this particular world had towards jalebis and milk. "If he, a grown man, can't control himself, you, as his wife, must control him."

"Didi, you know that our Shyamji is like the Shyam after whom he was named," said Sumati, with a smile that was lit at once by indulgence and ecstasy. "He'll steal into the kitchen and eat what he pleases—no one can stop him."

There was an idiotic poetry to Sumati's words that infuriated Mallika Sengupta; she recalled, for an instant, the child Krishna stealing into his mother's kitchen to satisfy his truant love of buttermilk. But that Shyam was a god, a diverting figment of someone's imagination, she thought; your husband has just had a heart attack. Sumati was placated and insulated from anxiety by mythology—the mythology of her religion had entered into, and become inseparable from, the mythology of her husband: no real harm could come to him.

The rich of Bombay came to his bedside in the nursing home as he recovered, his head propped against two pillows, a flower vase, a tumbler, and a bottle of water on the table next to him. "Aiye, aiye," he said, as if he were welcoming guests to his abode, his gaze incredibly calm. He was fatigued; but it was reassuring, this arrival of the affluent. Outside, "sisters," figments in white, circulated purposefully in the corridor, sending in, now and again, proprietorial glances through the doorway. At different times, the visitors: Priya Gill and her father, indomitable and inspiring in his Sikh's turban; Raj Khemkar—his father was no longer a minister, but Raj still carried with him the ironical confidence of a minister's son; Mrs. Jaitley, whose husband had been recently promoted to General Manager of Air India—all these, and others like them, brought with them, unthinkingly, the assurance of the everyday and of continuity as they sat kindly by the bed, confirming the solace of the birds and the hopping and buzzing insects outside the window on Shyamji's left.

And the famous; Asha, who said in a hoarse voice (you were always nonplussed, listening to that voice, that it had sung, full-throated, those melodies): "How is he?" and, putting a bangled hand to his forehead: "You have no fever."

. . .

One of the people missing from the bedside was the bearded Hanuman Rao, the Congressman who wore nothing but white. But no one mentioned Hanuman Rao. The film *Naya Rasta Nayi Asha*—a new road, new hope—had been made, but it suddenly seemed unlikely it would ever be released: that the new road would be taken, the hope materialise. Hanuman Rao had fallen out of favour with the powers-that-be in the Congress, puny men in scheming huddles who resented his largeness, metaphorical and physical; an old but niggling case, to do with his role in his constituency during the Emergency, had been brought back into daylight by a member of the Opposition; the Congress had neglected, carelessly, to bail him out—some said the return of the case was instigated by some malevolent force in the Congress itself. Hanuman Rao hadn't been arrested; but his assets were frozen, and the film, alas, was one of those assets. *Naya Rasta Nayi Asha*, soundtrack and all, had been sucked forever into the tunnel of lost prospects; and with it had gone, also, the thousands of rupees that Shyamji had put into it, in the glory and unassailability of having turned, at last, into both "music director" and "playback singer."

"Shyam, I could listen to your bhajans for hours," said Hanuman Rao. "Once the film is released, this voice I love so much will be heard by everyone." Shyamji had been seduced, not just by Hanuman Rao, but by the magic of the colours—perennial, abiding always in a sort of springtime—of celluloid; the loss of its promise, and, with it, his money, had created a vacancy to which he hadn't been able to reconcile himself, and brought a pressure to his heart.

No one mentioned Hanuman Rao's name in that room in the nursing home.

"Saab, we are in need of some money." That's how Shyamji would broach the subject every few months with Apurva Sengupta. Very softly and decorously, not as if he were begging or asking, but sharing a piece of information that had been troubling him. The advance was "adjusted" with the number of "turns" taken teaching Mrs. Sengupta; these English words, with their expeditious, dry clarity, had become part of the parlance. "Adjust ho jayega," said Shyamji, displaying the calm he never deviated from. "It'll get adjusted."

But this calm wasn't only a pose he put on for the benefit of his students or family; it had become a dharma, a philosophy of life. It was partly a strategy of self-defence; he'd begun to suspect (but still didn't wholly believe) that the world he was in love with—Cuffe Parade, Malabar Hill, the mirrored drawing rooms of his older students (plunged by marriage into affluence and anxiety), even the glamour of the film studios—was not quite going to, despite its extravagant, seemingly sincere, gestures of reciprocity, return his love: it had too many other things to do. The thought hadn't formed itself in his head; but the detachment, the calm, had deepened a little.

"Saab, what was the need for this?" he said softly.

This time, money hadn't been asked for; it had been offered; five thousand rupees in a stapled bundle had been placed discreetly by Mr. Sengupta one evening in Sumati's hands.

"We are not rich," Mrs. Sengupta reminded her husband. "In fact, we're poor." Nirmalya heard his mother make this statement with a look of preordained, unshakeable conviction. It might be that she was berating herself and her husband for not having saved enough over the years; or just that she was reminding herself that the job, with its army of attendants and comforts, wasn't forever. The servants themselves seemed blissfully unaware of the fact; symbols of continuity and wealth, they, despite their little quarrels, had the fixity and absence of care that symbols have; Mrs. Sengupta almost envied them their strange abandon.

No, the scandalous remark had a context; it wasn't meant for public consumption, but was a private release, like a curse or a prayer; now, in the early eighties, directors and executives had the satisfaction (as once their English predecessors had) of leading lives that had all the marks of affluence, and a prestige that traders and businessmen lacked: but their salaries were heavily taxed. Most of what constituted the lifestyle belonged to the company; most of the salary belonged to the government of India; and what was theirs (the pay that reached their pockets) was a relatively modest residue. At least that's how Mrs. Sengupta saw it. So she went through the motions and performed the functions of a company housewife and of being the chief executive's wife, and, at the same time, cultivated the detachment of a sanyasinni, an anchorite—even when she was buying a Baluchari or wearing her jewellery—from this way of life. Or so she thought.

Those who seem to be rich feel compelled to behave like the rich. The money they'd given Shyamji, for instance, was given from real concern; they didn't expect it back. But their generosity was complicated by superstition; Nirmalya, in spite of his heart murmur, had developed no symptoms, and they never forgot this fact. Someone was watching over him, and them, and their lives in Thacker Towers in Cuffe Parade; in the shopping arcade in the Oberoi; in the office and on the numerous social occasions that threaded the week—watching others too, possibly, but certainly them. In the midst of everything, they—mainly because of Nirmalya—were sometimes aware of being watched. The lifestyle became partly an enactment; they never quite experienced the luxury, the longed-for benediction, of being able to think it was all there was.

Gradually, Shyamji got better. He felt the need to go back to the world, to embrace it, to win it over, to enjoy it—the old desire and restlessness returned. But it was pre-empted by his family's optimism and impatience; almost as soon as they sensed Shyamji was recovering, they began to make plans for the future. The discontinuity and disjunction Shyamji's illness represented was already a thing of the past.

Some of his students were emigrants. Mainly women, they'd lived for years in England; every winter, sometimes earlier, they'd come back, vaguely doubtful about returning, and at the same time questing, eager with expectation, to Bombay, their husbands following them like mascots. And here, for a month, for two months, they'd fold their cardigans and put them aside in a drawer; they'd stop wearing socks beneath their saris. They should have had a sophisticated and superior air, but they didn't; living in suburban London and its environs made them feel provincial in the whirl of Bombay. Tooting, Clapham, and Surrey were where they lived; one or two lived in Hampstead; in their dowdy saris, they bore no signs of Englishness except an apologetic tentativeness. Now family surrounded them in the crowded flats they were staying in; this didi, that chachi, small, infirm mothers who continued to exist frugally from day to day, nephews and nieces they might have glimpsed as newborns, or not at all.

Music, besides family, is what drew them back—long ago, in the twilight before they left for England, when they were, most of them, newly married and unburdened with children, they used to sing, learn from a teacher. They didn't sing well, but they didn't sing badly; emigration, the hurried departure, the half-hearted, disbelieving resumption of their old life in a new locality and new weather, their mutation into the women they had become, had infinitely deferred their flowering as singers. Decades later, their children and their neighbours' children grown up and "settled," they felt they could resume from where they'd been cut off; their husbands had saved enough money by now to make that yearly journey to the nephews and nieces and the infirm mother. And, unexpectedly, one of the people at the end of that reverse journey was Shyamji.

"You've been unwell, guruji. I hope you're getting the right treatment," said Mrs. Lakhani. She was more affluent than the others—she lived in Frognall Lane. She was unexceptional but reassuring to look at, in spite of the tired eyes and drawn face; years of rearing children, of listening to the silence, of rainy days, of socialising with other Indians, had left her just enough time to satisfy her weakness for music without giving up her friendships. Now, back in this difficult but unforgettable country, she sat, head bowed, as Shyamji, slightly recovered, sat on the bed, having donned a white kurta, and taught her a composition in raga Hansdhwani:

pa ni sa, sa re ga pa ni sa

It was afternoon; not the right time for Hansdhwani. Still, in England, there was no right time at all. Evening and afternoon and morning there were much the same.

"You need a change of air, guruji," said Mrs. Lakhani, once she'd finished singing the notes with him in her soft, unpractised voice, her uncertain tone and his, sweet but undemonstrative after the illness, in unison for a few minutes. "The air over there is very good. Not like here. Even pigeons are fatter there." She smiled at his restrained incredulity. "Come and stay with us. Come and stay with us over there. I will arrange some concerts, I will arrange everything. My friends are dying to listen to you."

This seemed to both Shyamji and his family to be a windfall, a great opportunity. The lady, wan, but always in tasteful, expensive saris, the grey in her hair touching her with an added dignity, began to become more and more visible with Shyamji, with the special, concentrated manner that marks the visitor, a lady with some purpose—perhaps no more than to be in Shyamji's proximity—listening to him, waiting during a recording, discussing something quickly, even, sometimes, self-effacingly going over a song she'd learnt from him. After seeing her in three different places, Nirmalya hummed to his mother: "Who is she?" "I cannot remember her name," she confessed. "She is a student of Shyamji's from England." Nirmalya had overheard her clear her throat and sing once, shyly. "Why does he waste his time with the likes of her?" he asked, the stringent puritan in him provoked. England meant pounds, and pounds were a windfall; they had the power to heal, to renew. "Jao, jao, don't think so much," said Shyamji's mother. But he wasn't thinking; he'd decided to take up the offer—in his courteous, patient way, he had the passport and visa done with Mrs. Lakhani's help. Secretly, he was pleased to be free of his family for the first time, of the gaggle with its needs and requirements and opinions—from his revered mother to that loiterer and dramabaaz Pyarelal. It would be like a rehearsal of sannyas, the last stage when the householder withdraws from worldly duties, except that he wasn't retiring to the forest, he was off to

Frognall Lane: the trip had some of the benefits of renunciation, and also made good business sense. He underwent a transformation; for the passport photo, he abandoned his loose pyjamas and kurta and wore a shirt and trousers. He looked more efficient in this incarnation. He *felt* more efficient, too.

The time of departure was 3 a.m. "There's no point in sleeping," said Shyamji with weary reasonableness to his family. "Haa, Shyam, you sleep on the plane or when you get there. We'll sleep when you've gone," said his mother, even-voiced, hiding some complex apprehension, looking at no one in particular through her thick glasses.

He was leaving on a Saturday; so they rented a VCR from a man on Friday, and two video cassettes, *Dharam Karam* and *Namak Halal*, from one of the stifling video libraries that had sprung up irrepressibly in the interstices of the new buildings, and had brief and bright lives, like fireflies. By eight o'clock the packing was done, various white kurtas and pyjamas and handkerchiefs put in, the puja finished and a red tilak embossed on Shyamji's forehead; they all, Banwari's and Pyarelal's families included, huddled in front of the television set, adults and children spilling on to one another, and began to watch a bad copy of *Dharam Karam*. The volume was high; they seemed unaware of this, and laughed and shouted to each other above the dialogue and violins, talking much of the time, because they'd seen it before; the film wasn't meant primarily to be watched; it was a participant in this gathering as much as they were. Food arrived in the midst of all this, rotis that had swelled in Neeta's deft hands, and vegetables, and, once more, the remnants of the yoghurt that had been set overnight in a bowl made of stainless steel. By the time *Dharam Karam* was over, their eyes ached with the trembling pictures and Banwari felt a bit ill; Shyamji's son Sanjay took out the cassette and lifted the flap and shook his head at the faint line running through the tape; yet they persisted with *Namak Halal*, pushing it into the VCR and watching, agog, as it disappeared into the slot. Sumati laughed with recognition as the titles came on; Shyamji, sitting on an armchair, was now watching the film, and was now elsewhere; his mind travelled far away, then came back to the ear-splitting dialogue (the volume was turned up so they could hear it over their own exchanges), to the room, with everyone in it, abruptly. He was already in a state of departure, but sleep, which he'd dismissed from the occasion, was returning to him like an old habit; he yawned twice, and no one in the loud room noticed. When the film was only halfway through, becoming festive and precipitous a little after midnight, Banwari softly reminded him, "Bhaisaab, we should leave."

Mrs. Lakhani's home was a two-storeyed house with a garden at the back. She manoeuvred the car dexterously into an expectant space in the front; there seemed to be no garage. Then they—she and a curious but slowly acclimatising Shyamji—both got out into the sunlight and shut the doors. A passage on the right, a small half-lit sliver, disappeared somewhere—to the garden, Shyamji found out later. Light came in from that garden into the sitting room. Shyamji had never encountered such silence before, so much composure; so many things everywhere, and not one that looked out of place—the cushions on the sofa, the beer mugs, the plates with pictures of places on them, the orderly crowd of framed photos of ancestors and the Sai Baba and children and grandchildren, a copy of the *Radio Times*, a large upside-down face emblazoned on its cover, upon the table before the sofa. The air had a curious, still smell that was faintly familiar to him and confused him: cumin and asofoetida.

He liked the silence immediately; it didn't oppress him. The next morning he opened his eyes early, and stared at the wall opposite him with a mixture of surprise and panic, but after that, once he heard Mrs. Lakhani call out, ingenuously, "Guruji?" from the kitchen, he quickly, obligingly, exorcised his disorientation and grew used to the weather, the duration of the day. He was happy, in a way carefully contained but spontaneously childlike, to be free of the cacophony he'd left behind. Here, in this weather, he had a momentary but strong premonition of being able to give his music a home, a sanctuary.

She brought him to the harmonium on the upper storey that two years ago she'd ordered and had shipped from India. It too had made a journey, but it had merged into its home and internalised the hardly-broken stillness in the little children's room, empty now. Shyamji ran his fingers over the keys almost blithely; and, finding them alien and hard, furrowed his brow and attacked them with a bit more aggressiveness. Then the instrument and he had made their peace, and he was ready to give his first lesson, and, the next day, to receive Mrs. Lakhani's adoring friends.

He made no attempt to discover London (which he'd, long ago, thought was interchangeable with England) all at once; he was fairly content to walk about Frognall Lane. Dressed in ash-grey trousers, a shirt and new shoes whose tightness he ignored, he walked down the slopes beneath the trees, staring patiently and affectionately at the children—they pretended not to notice him.

"Don't go too far, guruji," warned Mrs. Lakhani.

From the sitting room, he'd look out through the French window into the garden when Mrs. Lakhani had gone to work, leaving him with her daily, good-natured farewell, and he had nothing to do but reign absolutely over a house that was not his own; his complete possession of a place that in no way acknowledged him made him fleetingly nostalgic. "The pigeons *are* fatter here," he thought, watching the traffic of busy birds strutting on the grass. "And so are the sparrows." He'd presumed, previously, that the sparrows at home were universal in size and dimension. He now scrutinised these birds in the garden silently. It was his deceptive, inconclusive way of thinking, before Mrs. Lakhani turned the key in the lock and opened the door, of where he'd come from.

. . .

He emerged, two months later, from the arrivals area at Sahar International airport, blinking in surprise at the sunlight, steering sadly, this man who could neither drive nor cycle, a worn, stuffed burgundy bag with buckles upon a trolley. In the midst of the large crowd, standing in the sun behind flimsy railings and watching the spectacle of passengers coming out one by one and walking down the catwalk before the arrivals exit—in the midst of all this his family was waiting, and broke rank imperceptibly on seeing him; he touched mataji's feet, she blessed him with a detached, immovable satisfaction at something having come full circle, others came forward awkwardly to lightly touch the returning man's toes. The first thing his sister Tara asked, with a sardonic lopsided grin, was:

"What did you bring for me, bhaiyya?"

For some reason, he was disgusted by the question. His eyes, which had had little sleep, stared back at the bright sunlight of the city. Was it being married to Pyarelal that had turned Tara into—a beggar? It wasn't unusual, he thought (walking, like one already beginning to reluctantly embrace the old habitat, towards the line of quarrelling black and yellow Fiats), for wives to take on the characteristics of their husbands. She was no longer little Tara, his sister and Ram Lal's daughter; she was Pyarelal's partner and comrade. But, at a glance, it was true of all of them waiting there for him—they weren't waiting to receive him, they'd been preparing these months to swallow him up; wanting things from him, wanting things, wanting things. It was hot, but he froze inside; he had nothing of himself to give.

His health had improved noticeably after the two summer months in London; he'd lost weight, and felt younger and the better for it. He still hadn't abandoned his new clothes; he came to visit the Senguptas wearing shirt, trousers, and strapped sandals. It was like meeting a man who'd returned from the past, with a new alias and a new future. Beneath the clothes, of course, he was the same man; Nirmalya thought of the quaint English phrase, "in the pink of health," and thought how apposite it was to Shyamji at this moment, incongrous though it was to his complexion.

"It is a good country," said Shyamji moodily. "I would be happy living there. I was thinking, maybe I should move there."

Mallika Sengupta smiled, a little alarmed, although she perfectly understood the sentiment—the sense of possibility, which had come a bit belatedly to him, which suddenly makes things plain; she dismissed the possibility herself, because Shyamji emigrating would leave her without a teacher. But the words disconcerted Nirmalya; all his ideas that were derived from reading books on philosophy and English poetry told him the artist must belong to and practise his art in his milieu. How could Shyamji think of giving up his country so easily? Besides, being a Hindustani classical musician, Shyamji's art was intimately connected to these seasons, *this* light, an intimacy that Nirmalya had not too long ago discovered for himself. After this discovery, which to him had the force almost of a moral revelation, he couldn't understand Shyamji's new-found rootlessness, or the mildly challenging look on his face as he said those words.

But Shyamji didn't leave the country—at least, not permanently. In the following year, he made two more trips to England; his life, and his lifestyle, improved, as if one of those tiny, mute goddesses, whose vermilion-smeared pictures he bowed his head before, had impulsively decided to shower him with bric-a-brac and useful things. So he acquired a second-hand Fiat and employed a young driver to make that long journey from Borivli to various parts of the city.

"Whatever Hari wishes," he'd say, glancing heavenward at the clouds from which the second-hand car had descended.

He arrived at Thacker Towers in it; it saved him the travail of trains and taxis. He was still not a "bada saab"; he couldn't afford an upmarket "vehicle"; but he was proud of the turn in his fate that had brought him his own "vehicle."

Very apologetically, he raised his tuition fees; "What can I do, didi?" he said, with a pained but firm expression, fairly comfortable that what most of them gave him was a fraction of what they spent every day on a decoration, a painting, or a sari.

After his third trip abroad, he had cleared most of his outstanding debts. And he had enough money left over to sell his own flat in

Borivli, and, with that money and some of what he'd recently earned singing for enthusiastic, cushion-propped, sprawling drawing-room audiences in Frognall Lane (how noisy and drink-and-peanut infested that quiet house became during soirees!) and performing in other places in London, he bought a two-bedroom apartment in Versova, facing the sea. This building complex, ventilated and its windows shaken from time to time by sea breezes, was appropriately called Sagar Apartments; it had been built for traders who'd acquired social pretensions and a bit of extra, unaccounted-for money and wanted not to be left out of the property boom; living for years, even generations, next to shops and godowns in humid rooms, they'd developed a longing for the sea. The porch and the corridors leading to the lift were laid with marble, the one stone that, in the city, had the ability to confer prestige indiscriminately upon a habitation. When Shyamji moved here, the building was brand new, and the white surface was still smudged by the footprints of labourers; but his eyes were temporarily, pleasantly, engulfed by that whiteness. With him moved to that smart two-bedroom flat mataji, the mother, and his wife, and his two unmarried daughters and son.

"Papa," said Sanjay, Shyamji's fifteen-year-old son. He spoke softly, but in an abstracted insistent sing-song. "Papa, Motilal mamu's son Kailash was saying that to learn music arrangement properly you have to have a keyboard."

"Hm? Who said?" asked Shyamji, tugged against his will from the wideness of a reverie into the constricted space of this non sequitur. He was full of these absent moments, when he seemed to be thinking neither of his family nor his students.

"Kailash," repeated his son determinedly.

"Bewkoof hai," said Shyamji swiftly, serenely. "He's an idiot."

But Sumati, Shyamji's wife, who was within earshot, smilingly and defiantly took up cudgels on this Kailash's and her son's behalf:

"After all, learning the keyboard now will mean that our Sanjay will be able to become a music arranger by the time he's eighteen, God willing"—she'd had a vision of that moment in the future, it was an image that had a certain power over her—"and"—here her prescience was lit by tenderness—"see how beautifully he already plays the guitar."

All these Western instruments . . . They were glamorous because they'd arrived, intact, after a long journey; once here, they could merge intrepidly into the texture of almost any musical background—it was not as if Shyamji wasn't won over by their virtues and innate youthful qualities himself. A man who could play a Western instrument would always have a livelihood in today's world: so it seemed to the old music families. The tanpura, with its four strings, hadn't lost its magic, but it became more and more difficult to make time for it; still, its sound shocked you every time you heard it—like a god humming to himself, its vibrations difficult to describe or report on, the solipsism of the heavens.

A slim white synthesiser with an apparently interminable row of white and black keys arrived in that room; Sanjay began to toy with it at once—the tinselly cascades of sound introduced a new and slightly embarrassing atmosphere to the small apartment, *filmi*, but upbeat and busy with possibility.

For two days, a series of chords, seemingly arbitrary, but executed in a variety of keys in quick succession, took over life in the little drawing room. People began, eventually, to ignore the boy; from time to time an awareness registered on Shyamji's face in a faint smile, as if his son were a child again, and kept encroaching obstreperously, in his single-mindedness, upon his own concerns—for this is what it had been like when Sanjay could neither walk nor talk, but possessed, in his play, the same glassy-eyed, silent, dogmatic zeal.

The synthesiser dazzled Sanjay, starting from the special

excitement of the name—Yamaha; and, as had been promised, there seemed to be no sound he couldn't extract from it. It was as if an orchestra, minus the heavy, inconvenient corporeality of human beings, lay latent inside it, constantly changing shape, obedient to his fingertips. It was portable; like a wand, he carried it from location to location, room to room.

When Shyamji and Sumati had exchanged garlands when they were eighteen, their respective, impeccable musical lineages had been taken into account to create a gene for the future, a gene which Sanjay, ruffling his hair with one hand, and running the other across the keyboard, represented. But such calculations don't allow for the fact that propensities suppressed in one generation might find freer rein in another, that the gene is self-perpetuating but also self-divided, that it contains within it its own destruction and mutation.

"Music is leaving the house of the ustads, the maestros," an ageing and somewhat pompous singer, a friend of Ram Lal's, had said not long ago to Shyamji, bitterly, as if the younger man were in some way responsible. Shyamji had nodded solemnly, placatingly, in all sincerity; at that moment, he'd thought it safest to be in complete agreement with the octogenarian. But, at this point in his life, he didn't really care—he didn't care exactly where music was located. And he had no pressing worries about whether the splendid but little-known inheritance his father had created would peter out; true, Sanjay hadn't been patient enough to acquaint himself with all the beautiful, difficult compositions, and Shyamji too had become busy of late—but there was time; he was forty-four, Sanjay was sixteen; it would be done, though, of course, it would require diligence and hard work! The gharana was the least of his worries. He cared—he wanted to ensure—that life expanded for him, his children, his children's children, and that when opportunities came or returned—as they seemed to be doing suddenly—he made full and intelligent use of them. And, in spite of himself, he was somewhat won over: without appearing to relent or altering his rhetoric, he was obviously quite pleased with Sanjay's new toy; gingerly, inquisitively, he tried out the keys himself—he was adept at the harmonium—taking stock of its brazen, tinny sound.

Not everyone was happy, though, about Shyamji's move to Sagar Apartments—not, for instance, his younger brother Banwari. Tall, dressed spotlessly in white, naturally affectionate and respectful, but with the innate helplessness and misplaced pride of a younger brother, he circled about, gazing downward, a small area in the sitting room in Borivli, torn between wanting to complain about Shyamji and defending him to his wife and the rest of the world.

"Our father wanted things to be divided equally between us," he grumbled, neglecting to remember that he earned very little in comparison to his elder brother, and that what he did came courtesy of the "tuitions" Shyamji arranged. His eyes were bloodshot, perhaps from lack of sleep—but, actually, they were always a bit red. "I didn't get my full share when we left King's Circle." Suddenly, he looked up, and, in a single god-like gesture, decided to physically shrug off the whole business, and became, at once, sentimental and shrewd: "Anyway, he knows more than I do," managing to sound both utterly sincere and offended, "he is my gurujan."

Pyarelal didn't—couldn't—say anything, although he always had an air about him simultaneously of compliance and complaint; he only raised an eyebrow in judgement, with the dancer's poise and suggestion. But Tara, his wife, grumbled quietly but audibly—everyone carried about with them expressions of fortitude, insider knowledge, and suppressed insights, and did nothing but blink slightly yet tellingly at any mention of Sagar Apartments.

For one thing, the flats in which Banwari and Pyarelal lived with their families—they had two and three children respectively—were too small; rudimentary one-bedroom affairs which had looked welcoming and larger than they really were when they were new but now silently exacerbated their nerves. They lived in them almost festively, investing them with all the bustling, makeshift energy that homes have. But they'd have been ready to go anywhere else. Oddly, they missed the congestion of King's Circle; there was nothing to replace that sense of being surrounded by human activity, with its own untidy ebb and flow, in this environment. There was no nature either; only shops and, from the balcony, the prospect of fresh air. Occasionally, a crow would alight on the balcony, breaking journey between two invisible points in the outskirts of the city, looking into their lives, the assorted jumble of furniture and musical instruments in the small room, before the younger children rushed forward to chase it away. There was no other representative of nature's variety here except this sly intruder.

"No one knows what it takes to travel from this place to the Taj and back twice a week," Pyarelal muttered, and his words embodied, like an epic, the entire terrible, many-stopped journey; by "no one" he meant Shyamji.

But these sentiments weren't conveyed directly to Shyamji; the medium who buzzed them into his ear was his mother, mataji.

"You're doing well, beta, by the grace of God and the good deeds of your father. *Lekin*, beta, don't forget Tara and Banwari."

During Shyamji's absences in England, Pyarelal became both Nirmalya's accompanist and teacher, guiding him about the outlines of ragas, helping him to memorise the compositions Shyamji had taught him. They spent hours together sometimes, from late morning to afternoon, the boy ignoring but protected by his father's existence, the handsome man in the suit, going out of the apartment, then coming back, somewhere on the margins of his consciousness. At such times, the boy was the real monarch, with the day and its luxuries entirely his own, as well as being a fugitive with the small, long-kurtaed older man for company. Just after practising a composition in the raga Yaman, or attempting the complicated, resonating web of Puriya Dhanashri, they would rise and go out onto the balcony to watch the sun set, the orange fragment losing its shape as it touched the horizon, becoming immense, maudlin daubs of colour after it had gone under. Pyarelal would light a beedi with his usual mixture of stealth and furtive theatre, as if all the world had no other concern but to catch him red-handed in the act. Then he would embark on a piece of proselytising, half monologue, in which he'd talk about how the movement of the universe and planets and the pull and push of the tide were all connected to laya, the tempo and rhythm of the compositions they had sung, and were indivisible from it. "*This* is laya," he'd say, gesturing grandiosely toward the water into which the childlike fragment of the sun had disappeared, "this movement of *brahmanda*," obviously transported and moved by his own words, although it was probably excessive to call the view *brahmanda*. By the orange-rimmed ocean, reflecting the light still spread everywhere in the sky, the Marine Drive bristled with droves of impatient cars departing from offices.

He knew, however, never to *presume* to call himself Nirmalya's "guru"; you could see from his face sometimes that he was greedy for acknowledgement, but he knew instinctively where to draw the line; much of his life had been about knowing how far to advance, and when to stop. Importantly, Nirmalya, too, never made the mistake of thinking he was his teacher. Pyarelal was his accompanist, that was all; he was also something else, true, for which Nirmalya's feelings were becoming deeper and more abiding, but that "something else" had no name or official status.

"You should be careful, baba," he said, "about singing 're pa' or 'pa re' in Bhairav. That makes it sound like Shree. This is how Bhairav goes." And he sang, sa re ga ma pa, ga ma dha pa ga ma re sa. This was a morning session—when, once, Pyarelal stayed with them for five days—not long after Nirmalya had finished toast and tea and a glass of sweet lime juice, and Pyarelal had sized up his omelette moodily and made short work of it. The sun that had gone down on one side of the apartment the previous day had risen undisappointingly from the other, and light now illuminated and made plain the various rooms. His voice was a whisper at the best of times; as if singing had become at some point a private pleasure for him, not meant to be overheard by the world, but by certain people only. When he sang for too long, or did taan patterns for Nirmalya's benefit, playing the tabla at the same time (a difficult, foolhardy thing to attempt, singing and playing the tabla at once, an act that Pyarelal plunged into again and again with an unthinking, almost masochistic doggedness), the boy noticed that his voice eventually cracked—the effect both of being out of practice and of relentless beedi-smoking.

When it was evening, and the immense, plush sitting room lit only by a couple of lights, while the great city glittered outside like a chimera, they would descend solemnly upon the sofa and the boy would play him some of his records—not the old collection, part of which had been procured directly from America, rare and precious as the world's treasure, the long haired angelic choirs of Crosby, Stills, and Nash and the others who'd gathered for that sunstruck week at Woodstock, all of which had one day, unaccountably, transformed into so much dross for the boy, but the Hindi film songs which he had discovered belatedly in the twilight of his growing up and adolescence, from the fifties and sixties, when he was not yet born, or was about to be, or had barely come into the world. "Listen to this," said Nirmalya to Pyarelal, and, of course, the older man had already heard the songs from when they'd first been sung, and he nodded and they sat listening gravely as the stylus stopped its hissing and Kishore Kumar began to sing "Chhod do aanchal zamana kya kahega," Nirmalya reiterating his discovery with the satisfaction, almost, of having invented that bygone world, the other, already superannuated, rejuvenated by the rediscovered songs and the younger man's faith in them.

In the acute loneliness of Nirmalya's life, these hours with Pyarelal were animated with actual happiness. For Pyarelal, too, it was an extraordinary transposition; being here, in this apartment. And he worked hard with the boy; he went beyond his brief, although—perhaps even because—he was not his true guru. At lunch, he was never comfortable at the large glass table, with its grid of mats and cutlery carefully laid out, sitting with Mrs. Sengupta and Nirmalya, confronted, in a strange kind of isolation, with the variety of china. Rotis were made for him, because he was not a natural rice-eater, and he tore these delicately, shaking his head slightly, as if he were in a private conversation with the bits of the roti that he dipped in the daal, and as if he could, by keeping his eyes fixed on the plate, wish away the context of the dining room. The thick glass dining table on elaborate legs was the only place where Pyarelal was uneasy; then it was back to discussion, perhaps a temporary parting of ways, then practice again.

The boy was fond of Pyarelal, and, spontaneously and without calculation, took advantage of his love during this residency. "Pyarelal, could you tape the tabla thekas for me?" or "Could you tell me how Asavari goes?"; and the man would comply. Learning with Pyarelal was a form of playfulness, even competitiveness, in which the older man was always surrendering to the younger one. "Well, that taan is too difficult for me; you do it," Pyarelal would say, looking glum and pleased. He wasn't lying; he was exaggerating. His love for the boy made him, during these hours of practice, ingenuously overplay his limitations.

By the end of the fourth day, the boy had actually grown a bit weary of this camaraderie; once or twice, he caught himself wanting to be alone, and tried to keep this fact from himself. But Pyarelal, attuned finely to the unsaid, sensed it, and it hurt him and made him behave badly at dinner with the servants who were intent on serving him daal or chicken, shooing them away peremptorily, or barely acknowledging them in a curt, bureaucratic way, as if they had no business being there—and so further aggravating Nirmalya's belated but untimely sense of being intruded upon.

The next morning, as if to consolidate the illusion that he was going to be with them for many more days, Pyarelal finished his pujas, and, as he'd been doing for the last three days to everyone's slight embarrassment, paraded the flat with three lit incense sticks (from a bundle Mrs. Sengupta had given him), pausing before various icons and deities scattered everywhere in the form of decorations, as well as pictures and portraits of the Senguptas' long-departed parents, closing his eyes, bowing and muttering some sort of a spell, waving the incense sticks, then hurriedly, self-importantly, resuming his tour before suddenly stopping in exactly the same way before the next picture or likeness. This extraordinary demonstration had led, partly, to Nirmalya's frayed nerves; but, on this last morning, he didn't know what to feel—whether to be touched, or thankful that it wouldn't be happening tomorrow.

Before "guru purnima" that year, Tara, Pyarelal's wife, dropped a hint:

"Baba, won't you give your guru something?"

Everywhere that evening, under the light of an immense full moon, disciples and students of a variety of accomplishments would go throughout the city towards their dance or music teachers with yards of raw silk in packets, awaiting to be tailored into kurtas, or with flat red boxes crammed neatly with sweets, the thread with the shop's name faintly printed on it knotted professionally and efficiently round the box; then, with a mixture of apprehension and self-effacement, touch the teacher's feet and leave the packet wordlessly next to him. Nirmalya stared open-mouthed at his extortionist—uncertain of whom she was talking about. She was smiling, so it could all be put down to teasing. The temerity—she obviously meant Pyarelal.

"How dare she!" said Mrs. Sengupta. "You have one teacher—and that is Shyamji. How dare she suggest anything else?"

The boy ruminated on this. And, of course, he wouldn't give Shyamji anything—it would be too formal. He abhorred not so much the act of giving as the exhibition of devotion; he hated excess and the display of something as private, as closely guarded and unquestionable, as his reverence for his teacher. And, happily for him, Shyamji wasn't that *kind* of guru; the almanac and the waning and waxing of the moon didn't in any way interfere with their relationship.

"Well, he *has* helped me a lot," said Nirmalya, divided and in thought. He meant Pyarelal.

"Oh, it's just that Tara wants something—she looks at you and she sees an opportunity," said his mother, exasperated.

Her expression now indicated that she'd lighted upon a simple solution. She rose and went to the cupboard and, parting its slatted doors, put her head into its faintly twinkling darkness for a few silent but busy minutes and eventually took out a sari with a deep pink colour. "It's that synthetic sari I got as a gift that I don't know what to do with." She looked sublimely pleased. He gazed at it with horror, but trusted her, and her knowledge of other people, implicitly; he knew she wouldn't take a false step and embarrass him or herself. "I'll give it to Tara. It's the kind of thing she likes."

There were rumblings in the background Nirmalya was hardly aware of, mild but far-reaching tectonic shifts in the topography of the company, from whose tremors the boy was on the whole insulated.

"That Thakore," muttered Mr. Sengupta, when he'd come back home at six o'clock, as if he'd just had an absolutely stupid argument. This was followed by a reminiscent look of dismayed wonder; he was slightly red-faced, and embarrassed. To all appearances, he'd been made to look foolish in a game of some sort. He was speaking of the non-executive chairman he'd inducted to the board a few years ago, in the euphoria of the first weeks after being appointed chief executive; every gesture, at the time, had seemed not only an exercise of judgement, but of generosity; a new set of peers had come into existence, with whom he was quickly on casual first-name terms, and each one was a friend. "They're not renewing my extension," he said to his wife. She was seated in front of the dressing table; she stared at his reflection behind hers in the mirror, as if he were wandering about in an imaginary room. "What does that mean?" she asked, her lips suddenly thin. Coatless, he shook his head and laughed. "They've created a new post for me—Special Advisor. It means nothing really; I have no executive powers." Then, as was his habit, he decided to round off the news with a positive interpretation—his longevity was dented but not damaged; this was a hiccup; he'd change direction and recover. "I continue to draw the same salary, and I keep this flat for a year." Mrs. Sengupta was silent; then, with a somewhat aggrieved deliberateness, she began to powder the face through which contradictory thoughts were flitting. "I should never have trusted Thakore," he remonstrated with himself, speaking again of the pompous chairman who was not content to be a rubber-stamp. "It seems he conspired with that fool Dick," he was referring to the British shareholder who materialised unfailingly for the Annual General Meeting like some lost, amnesiac member of a scatterbrained royalty, put his arms round the shoulders of the directorial fraternity, sang songs, then vanished again, "and Raman." Raman, soft-spoken, cold, who spoke perfect English, and regularly went with his wife to classical concerts, and looked like he would have been a curator if he hadn't been a corporate executive. "They all have their interests in marginalising me. Raman is the new Managing Director from next Monday," he added without interest or emotion, as if the changes, astonishing in their unexpectedness and finality, had failed, for some reason, to impress or move him. "So you're still the Managing Director?" she asked without irony, like a child who needed to be instructed in these things. He didn't answer her.

That evening, like almost every other evening, they had to go to a party. One part of her mind in a state of febrile blankness, the other part carefully chose a sari from the folded piles and the ones listlessly dangling in their many concentrated colours from hangers, a subdued Chanderi, of a faint glowing green that bordered on white; then, swiftly, efficiently, a drawer unlocked and opened, went through the ritual of jewellery-wearing. It was the humiliation she minded; not of herself, but of her husband; she had outgrown her parents and her brothers and her friends, but not him. In her mind, in spite of his defects, he had always been infallible; to see him deceived like anybody else was shocking. She was almost proud, though, that his most glaring shortcoming was naivety, trusting the wrong people, gauging the others by the standards of his simplicity (for that was how she saw him, as a simple man); or would he have courted Laxmi Ratan Shukla for so long, hoping this taciturn man would produce her disc? Already, she began to make small readjustments to her understanding of the husband she'd known for twenty-nine years. Really, with hindsight, she marvelled that a man as simple as he had been as successful as he was.

They were to have dinner at the Danish Consul's house; the Danish Ambassador, whoever he was, was visiting. The card, with the black, self-conscious, italicised letters embossed on white, had arrived, and the envelope been opened, two weeks ago. Dinners at these Europeans' residences were, at times, a little easier to bear; her hosts instinctively sensed her reserve and dignity, and were unconcerned and ignorant of her small-town background; she had nothing special to say, and they liked her for it. Tonight she had to put on a sort of show; she mustn't think she had only another week as a Managing Director's wife; at the same time, she must be herself. She shivered with contained anger at the thought of running into Raman and his wife; how easily, decorously, unremarkably, everything had changed between yesterday and now for both them and her. Yet nothing had changed; life was as it was.

Often, that evening, as she sat seemingly self-contained and complete with a glass of sweet sherry upon the sofa, she had to control herself. She smiled determinedly and blankly when the Ambassador's wife described to her in fond detail, the homesickness in her voice politely, expertly, transformed into anecdote, her two grown-up children, a son and a daughter, whom she'd left behind in Copenhagen. The Consul's flat was on the third floor of a grand, cool art deco building on an elevation in Breach Candy;

the hosts had kept the windows open for the sea breeze to breathe through their transitory posting and its convivial gatherings, and often Mallika Sengupta found herself being fanned by nature, a vast, gentle solace coming out of nowhere; a large doorway opened invitingly onto the semicircular balcony, a dim promontory that jutted out into the compound's protected darkness.

The food was a diversion; an instance, as ever, of buoyant self-absorption and fantasy in the cricket-infested nighttime of these seven conjoined islands. An invisible cook, quite likely from Kerala, had been given free rein and command. She'd, of course, had no inkling that the Danish had a cuisine; she had a vague conception that they had hams and sausages and cold cuts. But the soup, a milky broth that a bearer took around in bowls, calmed her greatly. They could have served her anything tonight, and she would have connected it with Denmark. Tears formed spontaneously in her eyes; they dried by themselves, no one around her noticing them; even she was hardly aware of them. The change in their lives was a secret, but she wouldn't mind if it weren't; already she'd begun to accept how things would be from tomorrow. The buffet appeared, with its daunting array of cold meat; the eager carnivores made a beeline for it, glasses balanced forgetfully in one hand. Among the long china dishes was one that held a smoky mass, which Mrs. Sengupta paused at, thinking it was some sort of confection. She broke its surface stealthily with a spoon and transferred some to her plate. Eating it later, she was puzzled; it tasted very delicately of fish. It was fish mousse; in all her years, she'd eaten nothing like it.

There was no great change the following day; from afar, Nirmalya could see Jumna squatting at one end of the drawing room, cutting swathes across the floor with the grey wet rag. Nirmalya was unperturbed they'd be leaving Thacker Towers. Then, the day passed and dwindled, the hard glitter of the Arabian Sea and the curving panorama visible from the balcony becoming the inevitable scattered nighttime dazzle.

More and more, he felt philosophy was his future; that he had to have his say on various mysteries—God, Being, consciousness, the self, etcetera. He'd long finished the chapters on Croce and Santayana and Nietzsche in *The Story of Philosophy*; he'd responded with an innocent, assenting delight to the Santayana and the Croce, but Nietzsche and Zarathustra had maddened him with incomprehension. Only Spinoza he'd formed a special fondness for, without understanding him at all, but because it seemed that he'd proved, with a logician's tools, that God and the universe were one thing. What a wonderful hypothesis, and how magical if it should be irrefutable! He turned to a book in his father's study, a Grolier classic (one of a handsome bound set his father had purchased from a distant, once-youthful regard for masterpieces), to read, minutely, the steps in logic by which Spinoza had demonstrated his argument: his mind glazed over. A phrase stood out, "God-intoxicated," which, a note said, had been used once of the seventeenth-century philosopher. Gulp by gulp, in the air-conditioned study, he swallowed civilisation.

As his parents made sketchy and unserious preparations to move to the suburbs after a year, discussing it half-jokingly amongst themselves, he thought increasingly, too, of gods and the divine nature of the universe. At thirteen, he'd dismissed God as a fiction; now, through Tulsidas and Kabir and the pseudonymous authors of the classical compositions, and their constant invocation of Krishna's lips, his eyebrows, his antic childhood, Shiva's tangled locks, his undecipherable moods, silences, and fantastic temper, Nirmalya was made to laugh at how profligate and real the universe of the gods actually was. Unkempt, loitering in Joy Shoes sandals, he was trying to make sense of the anarchic creation of the poets. How messy that world of eternal beings was: Shiva's matted hair infested with the moon and the Ganges, as if they'd nested there like cheap trinkets or bats rustling inside a den or ruin; and all the buttermilk spilt in Yashodha's kitchen as Krishna rummaged clumsily among the utensils. The songs were full of such workaday calamities and disturbances.

As he walked down the driveway and then out of the gates of Thacker Towers, he'd be observed warily by the security guard, and sometimes glanced at, with sudden recognition, by the driver of his father's Mercedes. What was this boy in the kurta all about? Neither the driver nor the guard had quite decided. The guard knew by now that Nirmalya wasn't a student who'd wandered into the compound, but was the son of the man on the twentieth floor who, flickering in his suit, went to work in the white Mercedes.

Nirmalya, now that his sojourn in Thacker Towers was coming to an end, felt more than ever that his home, his calling, were elsewhere. He walked past Snowman's Ice Cream Parlour, where boys in slim-fitting trousers and girls with horizontal bits of midriff afloat playfully above their jeans laughed loudly and devoured the fragile ice-cream cones they held in their hands. Were they laughing at him? Rows of expectant motorcycles stood crowded in the parking space in the centre of the road, booming at the touch of a boy's hand, roaring as he turned his wrist and straddled the taut, muscular epidermis of the seat, always exploding into speed rudely. He didn't care. He was preoccupied with existence itself, with the question almost made nonsensical by repetition, "Why do I exist?"

"The question in itself is not as interesting," he jotted down in a little notebook he'd bought from a small, fragrant, forgettable stationery shop in the shopper's arcade near Thacker Towers, "as the way, or spirit, in which it is posed. 'Why do I exist?' might be the beginning of an intellectual query, a scientific or rational investigation, the answer to be arrived at by reasoning and deliberation, at the end of which there will be no satisfactory answer. Or it might be a cry of pain, '*Why* do I exist?'; here, the answer is no longer important. The answer lies in the question, which is the result of suffering."

He avoided a car and crossed the road. He'd felt pleased after writing those sentences. His sympathies lay with the cry of pain; if someone asked him, What have you suffered? he'd have to say, Very little. Yet, in a mood of visionary despondency, he walked, in his incipient philospher's agony and undecidedness, through this area that was still, every day, changing shape, new lights being added, still newer buildings coming up, with parks thrown willy-nilly in between, for people to explore and circle round in in the evenings, and wildernesses and unkempt places being constantly curtailed, but still surprising you by springing upon you at times. Walking, he found himself before a strange, wide, white building, that seemed to have descended, like many of the other things he'd encountered, laconically from nowhere, providing no explanation or justification; he knew, from some useless snippet of information stored away in his head, that it was called the World Trade Centre. He stood for barely a moment, trying to reconcile himself to the building's apparent lack of function; neither trade nor the world seemed to have anything to do with it. Perhaps it would grow into its name? Was it here that his mother had come visiting briefly two weeks ago, getting out of the car and then advancing in a predetermined way, as if this environment were already familiar to her, through a litter of unused shop space in this ghost town called the World Trade Centre, till she finally arrived at an outlet with two perfectly ordinary human beings, from whom she bought, after giving the matter some, but not too much, thought, tiny stick-on bindis arranged in rows on a piece of paper? And had he been with her, inside? Nevertheless, the building struck him as at once charmless and completely unexpected; he couldn't imagine ever having had anything to do with it. When he returned to the apartment, he heard excited voices coming from the room in which music was usually practised, accompanied by a few incongruous taps on the tabla, and sporadic, short-lived chords on the harmonium. They were taking a break. Shyamji, his face as animated as a child's with speculation, was asking, "Then where will you go, didi? Will it be a different side of the city?" Banwari was sitting Buddha-like on the coir mat, smiling faintly, listening, unmoved by the many revolutions of the earth, his hands still on the tabla. "Come to our side," Shyamji said, biting into a biscuit, entertained, obviously, by this idea of geographical proximity translating into a form of spiritual closeness. "Then you will be near us." And then, suddenly, he spotted the boy by the door, and his expression changed into one of strange, guileless mischief. "Kya, baba, didi says you never liked this area at all?" Shy and exasperating as a new bride, the young vagrant in the narrow churidars and severe-looking khadi kurta smiled and nodded quickly and escaped; avoiding, as ever, ordinary conversation with his guru, never able to see his teacher without reverence, but never, because of his pride, able to behave with the expectedness and ease of a student. "Now where did he go?" Shyamji asked Mrs. Sengupta, puzzled, and, his thoughts already changing, drank from the remaining shallow pool in his cup.

The Bombay Chamber of Commerce was one hundred and three years old, and though nothing now could match the contented but animated milling of suited gentlemen and their wives that the hundredth-anniversary celebrations had comprised—like a reunion of heads of companies and heads-to-be, a reunion in which everyone, magically, conveniently, seemed to have fulfilled their early promise—still, the captains of industry and their bedecked spouses gathered in the basement hall of the Oberoi with their enthusiasm undiminished. A long, breathy speech was made by the President, an amiable duffer, while people laughed both at his jokes and at him, and he beamed at them and continued, relentless; and then the speech ended and everyone was standing, and, in the crowd, there was a subtle insinuation of men in white shirts and black trousers with trays of canapés, receding at the moment of the sighting. Two days ago, Mr. Makhija, secretary of the Chamber, had phoned them; Makhija, whose slow, courteous phone calls and reminders they'd grown used to in the past few years, a doorkeeper to the world of commerce, neither outside it nor, thankfully, quite of it. "Please do come, sir," he had said, a kindly long-distance spy on their lives, and hectorer. There Mrs. Sengupta stood, suddenly having lost her husband; no sign of Makhija either. She held a wine glass half full of mango juice in one hand. The crowd in the large, outstretching room had broken up into circles of men making toasts and telling each other jokes; she was surrounded by people she knew and faces she recognised—it had almost become a habit, this cursory, neutral assignment of names, characteristics, and positions to certain features—and suddenly, far away, she spotted her husband, radiant—he had hardly aged at all—holding a drink aloft nebulously (he drank deceptively, without involvement, and would sip self-importantly and misleadingly from this one glass all morning), his hair as impeccably black as when, on his wife's urgings, he'd begun to dye it twenty-five years ago, only a plume of white in the front held steady all these years like a flame. He was eager as ever, ignoring the bearer of canapés hovering fruitlessly next to him, his expression charged with a strange simplicity and expectancy, and she could not believe that they were not in the middle of things, so impossibly far away the limits of the horizon and emptiness seemed; surely two lifetimes were needed to do justice and give proper shape to, to learn from and perfect, a career of what even now felt like promise and youthfulness? For they were not inheritors of property or fortunes, as the business families were; there was nothing static about what they symbolised; for the Senguptas, the career and the life were what they made of them, constantly surprising, a constant, strenuous, but genuine exploration, and everything that happened before or after these years in the company would be marks announcing what had essentially been their life. They would then disappear, in a way it looked the business families never could. Their life would become memory; their own, and in the minds of people like the ones she ran into at these anniversaries, an immense variety but really a narrow range of faces that seemed, with hindsight, to have been put together, unforgettably, by chance.

. . .

It was a time crowded with celebrations. In November, the great, bizarre event was Chanchal Mansukhani's older son's marriage in a fake village specially created on the lawns on Wodehouse Road, walking distance from the Regal Cinema. People were getting out of cars, urgent men slamming their doors, slow women in organza saris, unsteady on their feet in their jewellery, eager to confer not only wedding gifts but legitimacy upon this man. The Senguptas arrived in a state of minor distractedness and excitement. Chanchal Mansukhani stood, in black suit and dark spotted tie, welcoming the guests, smiling at them whether he recognised them or not, doing namaskar, sometimes taking the palms of their hands uninsistingly in his own, not holding them, but cradling them for a few moments. The donning of the ubiquitous black suit was almost ironical; it was as if it was meant to remind you that he'd made his fortune in textiles, beating to number one place in the market a far better-educated rival of a distinguished political and business lineage; and it was meant to adorn the myth, that this was the son of a man who'd arrived with no belongings at the Victoria Terminus soon after Partition, and who'd worked as both shoeshine boy and coolie. Queueing up to shake hands with him, the creator of Mansukhani Suitings and Shirtings, Apurva Sengupta couldn't decide whether he was a monster or an angel; he had a boneless posture, his edges were rounded and blunted, and the compassionate, maternal smile of a man who'd grown up in a large, disorderly family, an ensconcing microcosm, played on his lips. There were rumours (whether they had credibility or not it was difficult to say) that he'd used hit men and that murder had been useful to him during his remarkably uplifting—for doesn't everyone want the man who reigns to have once been like one of the beggars on the road outside?—rise. How many mill-hands, their means of redressal completely at an end, the tall chimneys empty of smoke, were sitting at home or in idle, despondent groups playing cards because of him? Wedding music filled the background, and returned to them optimistically in the middle of their own words; not the shehnai, but some sort of taped, assuaging expression of the human voice. After the muttered but gracious mantra of the "Congratulations," Apurva and Mallika Sengupta felt they'd dissociated themselves from their host, and they wandered about the lawn entirely as if they'd come here on their own business—although they'd continue to talk about the wedding, with irony and pleasure, for a few days. They stopped at stalls offering kababs; others were distributing, equally generously, but to their surprise, Bombay junk food. Her husband was partly in a trance, with a faint smile on his face, as if there was still a possibility that something might happen. She was possessed by curiosity; she was never brave enough to eat street food except in five-star hotels. She tugged purposefully at his coat sleeve, a small, charming plea (he was elsewhere, and hardly aware); "Come, let's go there," she whispered, pulling him like a small, unappeasable girl towards the pani puris.

Mr. Wilson, from the lower echelons of the company's personnel department, arrived at the flat late one morning. Having been let in, he stood there sheepishly. Then, almost casually, with the enquiring look of a man in a museum, he strolled into the main hall.

News was relayed down the long corridor to the main bedroom, by Arthur, then Jumna, then another, that Wilson was here. Finally, Mrs. Sengupta, fresh from a bath, equanimous for the moment in a tangail, came out from the corridor into the sunlight of the drawing room.

She knew Wilson; as far as she was concerned, he was an odd-job man. When something needed to be done—when she needed to find out if the flight her husband was on was delayed; or to book a private taxi because the driver hadn't turned up—he was the one she got in touch with. He was a big, burly man who spoke English in his brief polite responses with a South Indian accent, rolling his r's and everything else softly; and he got the job done.

"Madam," he said, apologetic, but also as if he were sharing an unpleasant secret, "I must have an inventory done before you move. Which things are belonging to the company, which things are not . . ."

"Wilson," she said quickly, "are you mad? What are you talking about?"

In all these years, his sanity had never been questioned. He was wounded, but he was also ashamed.

"I'm sorry, madam. What can I do?" he said, sullen and obdurate, falling back on the phrase that was a favourite whenever he was in a sticky situation with his superiors. "I have orders from office."

Tentatively, Wilson began to walk around the drawing room, where he'd never been before, either as visitor or guest, with a notepad and pen in his hand. "It's a disgrace," said Mallika Sengupta in a clear voice, as the figure moved further away. "I will complain."

"These will stay," he thought, looking at a rosewood cabinet and the large L-shaped sofa with a qualified but proprietorial eagle eye, as if he'd formed some sort of kinship with them. He barely glanced at the Grecian urn–like table lamps. At a huge stretch of carpet, deep and ruddy, he paused, undecided, and glanced at the paper in his hand. He was in a peculiarly emotional mood, at once self-effacing and blithely, insularly unstoppable. The only time he smiled slightly was at three photographs on a rosewood shelf, a close-up of Mrs. Sengupta's face from ten years ago, her charming uneven teeth showing in her blissful smile, and another of Nirmalya when he was eleven and pudgy, proudly wearing a zip-up T-shirt a relative had sent him from Europe, squinting unthreateningly (those were his last days without spectacles) at the sunlight, with parents on either side, against a wilderness that was actually

Elephanta island; then another one in which Mr. and Mrs. Sengupta and nine-year-old Nirmalya, dressed for the Delhi winter, were posing beside a severe woman with a patient but unprevaricating gaze, who turned out to be Indira Gandhi. A spring came to Wilson's step, a barely noticeable feeling of abandon; till, gradually, once more, he became serious and attentive. Around him, as if he were no more than a fleck of dust, Jumna reached casually with her jhadu for one of the many tables, and then wove herself towards the sofa to plump up a cushion.

When he left, he had the pained, wise air of someone who'd been far happier booking private taxis for Mallika Sengupta, and checking times of flight arrivals and departures. "Thank you, madam," he said, as if he were referring not to the grace of the last half-hour, but redeeming the small role he'd played in her life.

"How is your son?" said a woman whom Mrs. Sengupta knew well from these occasions, a Sindhi businessman's wife. Mallika Sengupta, startled, didn't know where to begin. They had plates of dessert on their laps, the sort of juxtaposition that was becoming increasingly popular in the business and corporate community, honeydew melon ice cream and semi-transparent, plastic-yellow jalebis. "He is reading all the time, very difficult books," she said, laughing. She was always defensive about him. "What will he study?" the woman asked, persistent. "MBA?" Mrs. Sengupta was pleased, cruelly, because she knew her answer would disturb her companion's ingestion. "He says he wants to study philosophy," she smiled. The woman paused, tried to capture, with her spoon, a slippery fragment of ice cream, and said with averted eyes, "Very nice." Then added, as if speaking of a rare condition she was not going to condemn or probe too deeply: "So he is not into money."

To regroup, she asked: "You are leaving this side of the city, Mallika? Where do you plan to go when your husband leaves the company?" "Bombay is such a huge place, and so expensive," said

Mrs. Sengupta, glancing at her reflection to check if her hair was all right; the wall had large glass panels that doubled everything—the fluted frames of the chairs, the doorways opposite opening on to corridors, the hair held ornately in buns or falling darkly upon shoulders, the glow of the chandelier—with various degrees of approval. "My son," she said with secret pride, "says he wants to go somewhere quiet and green."

Finally they left that side of the city forever—too cheap a word, whose meaning you don't quite get to grasp in a lifetime; you only use it self-indulgently, for a luxurious and elegiac sense of closure. Instinctively, they didn't use it; they didn't believe in "forever"—the company had gifted them, almost two decades ago, a permanent sense of the future. Only much later do you learn that there's no going back; learn it, an incontrovertible, minor lesson, not very difficult to grasp, then move on.

This, maybe, was the "quiet, green place" that Nirmalya had been thinking about, but whose existence he'd never really suspected; a lane off one of the downward slopes of Pali Hill, a blue plaque announcing its name hanging by two rings from a pole at the base of the lane, which swung in a monsoon breeze in an intrepid, self-contained way, a gate opening on to a building, a second-storey apartment, three bedrooms, roughly fourteen hundred square feet, just a little more than a third of the flat in Thacker Towers. It was as if, wandering down Thacker Towers, they'd discovered an annexe no one had noticed before, an annexe whose balcony opened on to a silent neighbour, a jackfruit tree—and they'd decided never to return to the main flat.

. . .

The way to the city was long; sometimes it took as much as an hour. Every morning, Apurva Sengupta—he now had a post-retirement job as a consultant in a German firm—went back to it, past the upturned hulls of fishermen's boats on the sand in Mahim, the new Oil and Natural Gas Commission township breeding in the swamp in the background, the Air India maharaja on the left, full of a droll and emphatic sincerity, promising seven flights to London a week; off he went in a sturdy white Ambassador he'd bought from the company, and in which an air conditioner had been fitted. They'd got used to air-conditioned transport, the sealed air, the busy, glinting, ragged world kept at bay by glass; they couldn't, any more, imagine long journeys without it. The air conditioner, however, hadn't been part of the original engine; it had been transplanted in a garage and installed as an extra, and it took something extra out of the machine. Slowly, shamelessly, it was reducing the engine's life. No matter; it gave the Senguptas comfort—every blast of coolness on a hot, uncontainable day was welcome; it turned the interior of the Ambassador into a time capsule, a seamless continuation of their old, familiar life in the Mercedes, which they'd bid farewell to without much of a pang. But, since the air conditioner wasn't built into the engine, it worked off and on, it stopped when the car stopped at traffic lights and went into fan mode, warm air emerged from the slats and brought the Senguptas back to where they were with a wave of irritation. Then, as the light changed to green and the car moved on, there was relief again.

And, in spite of their satisfaction with the new charming little flat, with the quiet lane off Pali Hill and its gulmohur trees with fan-like leaves and churches that emerged silently but busily at the end of a street and reminiscent bungalows that still belonged to Goans, they felt compelled to make the trip, each day, to the centre of Bombay, to Dhobi Talao and Flora Fountain, to partake of their old life: the life they considered shallow and a bit fake. Like interlopers, they arrived, having burnt an hour's worth of fuel on the way, at the club they used to frequent; ordered food, feeling dishevelled after the journey; disappeared into the spacious, forgiving gentlemen's and ladies' bathrooms to splash water on their faces, adjust the bindi on the forehead, smooth their clothes; then, like people who'd been pacified and made whole, returned to their sofa and ate wonton soup and fried rice or a plate of steak sandwiches.

One day, Mrs. Sengupta, an hour after her music lesson, found Shyamji at the top of Pali Hill, determined but anguished, his Fiat uncooperative and impenetrable, he about to push it up the slope, while his driver, collar hanging back from his bare brown neck, stood next to the car, one arm plunged into the window, his hand on the steering wheel. Mrs. Sengupta was seized by a moment of pity; leaning out of her window, she surprised him with, "Shyamji, I will drop you—where are you going?" Nirmalya, her only company in the back, smiled indecisively. Shyamji smiled too, in a pained way, as if neither he nor the second-hand car was to blame, but something more mysterious and inscrutable that had acted up this hot, dazzling morning.

He was grateful, settling into the front seat; he'd have had to take the local train otherwise. "Where are you going now, didi?" he asked, politely, almost an afterthought, delicately adjusting the kurta sleeves which had dark patches beneath the armpits; but with a curiosity that hovered on the brink of wonder, as if he were convinced that her daily routines were bound to be interesting and unpredictable. And, having known Mrs. Sengupta for four years, having been close to the family, he was circumspect and cautiously concerned about the sort of journey she was making now, he didn't want her to ever be too far from what had been her sources of pleasure and well-being. Her reply gladdened him immediately:

"We're going to the club. We'll have lunch there," she revealed in an unflappable sing-song, "and wait for Mr. Sengupta to join us for tea."

So things were more or less as they were, he thought, nodding in assent inwardly, becoming increasingly calm in the interrupted air conditioning after the little incident with the Fiat; this move to the suburbs, the retirement, hadn't really changed anything. After a moment, Mallika Sengupta said:

"In fact, Shyamji, why don't you join us for lunch? If you're not doing anything else?"

Traffic lights changed into a church and into mosques. She was pleased with the idea. Residential buildings with names like Jaijaiwanti and Ahir Bhairav widened into new office blocks; the sea came and went slyly. Shyamji was uncomfortable but full of curiosity.

"Didi," he said, looking at the road ahead of him in Shivaji Park, "will I be allowed in these clothes?" for he was in his usual loose white pyjamas and kurta.

"Of course you will," she said, in a tone that dismissed all imaginary opposition in advance. "There are no dress restrictions."

In the foyer of this old, slate-roofed building, she impatiently signed him into the voluminous register which was open upon a page full of names and signatures and distinguished scrawls, while Shyamji stood beside her, with the mildly questioning furrow on the brow that was almost always present these days, adorned by the remnant of a small orange tika that had been put there by his mother after the morning pujas, neither at a loose end nor relaxed, waiting for something—some embarrassment or unforeseen glitch. The moment didn't come; as you entered the corridor, the members usually looked up from their food or conversation or glass of fresh lime soda to stare at you, but only if they already knew you or thought they should; unashamedly, almost with warmth, certainly without hostility, they rested their eyes on the newcomer, as if they were about to smile; but they had an instinct for not dwelling at all on people or detail that didn't interest them. Hardly anyone noticed Shyamji.

Climbing up the three steps to the veranda, Mallika Sengupta, unaware of Shyamji's discomfiture, clutching her handbag, led the way. They entered the dining hall. Shyamji, decorous, eyes lowered in expectation, and Nirmalya, his chappals making a slight hissing sound as he dragged them on the wooden floorboards, followed. Shyamji would not have understood Nirmalya's embattled defiance, or what he thought he was fighting. He, unimpeachable in his white kurta-pyjamas, had become very serious, and mildly disapproving, as he always was, of any hint of flippancy.

They were surrounded by the din of waiters and executives, lawyers, businessmen. They sat at a table, the menu card, propped up on a holder, upright before them. It said in undistinguished bureaucratic type, "Chicken Xacutti, Brown rice, Daal, Kachumbar salad," and, beneath this, the same list was faithfully repeated, except that "chicken" was substituted with "paneer." And, further below the main course, the terse but inviting addition, "Ginger pudding and custard."

"What will you have, Shyamji?" asked Mallika Sengupta. Waiters were disappearing at the far end of the hall behind a partition that separated kitchen from dining room.

"Vegetarian," he said, simply, as if that would solve all his problems; he glanced around him, bemused. Orders were placed with a tall, swarthy waiter who suddenly loomed before them, nodding and writing with a pencil as Mrs. Sengupta spoke. Then they sat silently for a while, Shyamji toying with and unfolding the napkin, Mrs. Sengupta momentarily contented, as if she were giving him not only lunch, but the club on a platter. Words were unnecessary between teacher and students; finally, as water was being poured from a jug into their glasses, Shyamji enquired, his brow creased, thoughtful:

"Didi, how much does it take to be a member of this club?"

And Mrs. Sengupta felt a pang for him, too brief to be called sadness—again, it was a sort of pity she felt, as when she'd seen him standing absently in the bright sunlight on Pali Hill next to the broken-down Fiat.

"Seven or eight thousand," she said quickly; she noticed the gold-plated buttons on the kurta, the hair combed serenely back. "Mr. Sengupta would know."

He nodded, abstracted and serious.

"Achha hai," he said firmly, dispassionately, as if he didn't mind facing up to the truth, however surprising it might be. "It's a nice place."

Shyamji left them soon after lunch; his series of "tuitions" in this part of the city began from early afternoon. Mother and son approached the sofas on the veranda; they stood against the nets that had been hung along the side to keep out crows, marauding cats, and the cricket ball, waiting to bid farewell to Shyamji.

"Bhojan se anand aa gaya," he said, referring to the food. He smiled affectionately, teasingly, at the boy; then the smile became formal, but nonetheless remained warm, as he turned to look at Mrs. Sengupta. "It was a great joy."

"Shyamji, you did not eat properly," she remonstrated.

"What, didi," he said, upbraiding her gently; his kurta looked as good as new—there wasn't a hint of dishevelment about him.

Nirmalya and his mother sat on one of the sofas, waiting for early afternoon to dilate to teatime. Others were immobile, holding the first evening papers in their hands, with digestion. The nets hadn't succeeded in keeping the club cat-free; they crept to the tables and meowed persuadingly, begging adeptly, without desperation; and the smaller children, who'd already finished school, and were sitting oddly alone in their uniforms, their "house" colours displayed on sashes or badges, or had been briefly reunited with a parent, dropped bits of steak sandwich in their paths, pleased to be showering them frugally with their teatime snacks, which the cats pawed without eagerness. And, on the whole, there were few "dress restrictions"; grown-up men danced slowly past in shorts and strapped sandals; and once, a handsome, well-built teenage boy, taking a short cut between the bathroom and the pool, ran across in swimming trunks, a towel over his shoulders, his hair ink-black and wet, raising a few eyebrows and titters.

At half past four, when an ageing gentleman at a neighbouring table had begun to doze, Apurva Sengupta arrived, his jacket folded over the crook of one arm.

"Ah, there you are!" said Mallika Sengupta, savouring the accident of suddenly spotting him.

And Nirmalya, seeing his father in his post-retirement incarnation, of the world of corporations and yet not quite of it, content to be part of the ghostly transitoriness of the afternoon and teatime as he wouldn't have been before—Nirmalya could sense, almost, as he used to when he was a schoolboy, that they had something in common, which he didn't try to put a name to.

A few of the things that had furnished the apartment in Thacker Towers reappeared now in this small flat. A large oil by the soon-to-be-forgotten Vithal, of two white horses galloping in a green space, a picture with a technicolour air, full of melodramatic energy, hung above the sofa from the wall on the left, and seemed to dominate the room with its drumming of hooves. It had been a coveted acquisition when they'd bought it four years ago. But, otherwise, the drawing room and the flat itself had a crisp, post-retirement elegance; things were scaled down in comparison to the spaces they'd inhabited before, and the arrangement of furniture, carpets, plant-life and decoration was economical and bright.

But there wasn't a place for everything that had left the big company apartment, and some of it found its way to other places. The large green carpet, for instance, had, alas, to be snipped; it was much too big for a drawing room of this size. The snipped bit had swiftly become a rug in Shyamji's flat: welcomed and appropriated there with much delight, with nodding assent at the rightness and inevitability of this transfer, and of course gratitude. Two chairs and a low Sankhera table also quietly travelled there, and an old cupboard had been claimed shyly but impetuously one day by Shyamji's younger brother Banwari ("Didi, what about us?" he'd said at last after a sitting, frowning, mock-offended, like a child trying to charm an elder: "Everything goes to Shyam bhaiyya.").

When Mrs. Sengupta went to visit Shyamji in his flat (it was easier to do so now; the anonymous but impatient developments of Versova weren't too far from Pali Hill), she encountered the snipped-off bit of carpet, not recognising it for a moment, but feeling an odd proprietorial affinity toward it. Severed from its previous expanse, it had merged with and made a home of its present surroundings, a small table stacked with pans looming above it on the left and the detached rectangle of the first-floor veranda opening on to twilight not far from it; once she remembered where it had come from, it gave up its subterfuge and she was buoyant and was translated into a mood of mischief on seeing it. "Arrey, isn't this *my* carpet?" she squinted. The others nodded vigorously at the sensibleness of this query, as if they were just trying to take care of certain things that had been entrusted to them. And there were the two chairs, and the pretty low table with the glass top and the rounded, fluted wooden legs she'd bought years ago from Gurjari. "They are looking nice," she said, so distant a judgement that it was removed from, at once, irony and literal truth.

"Didi," said Sumati, Shyamji's wife, "do sit down," and led her to one of her "own" chairs.

Notwithstanding these gifts, there had been a slight cooling in relations between the Senguptas and Shyamji. The old grievance, that Shyamji hadn't really been serious about enhancing Mrs. Sengupta's prospects as a singer, that he'd never really taken her talent in hand, returned: "After all, what exactly is he doing for *you* that he isn't for all the others?" Nirmalya demanded of Mallika Sengupta, long-haired, immovable, angry. An irritability about the constant ritual of singing-lessons going nowhere from ever since he could remember, from when he was a boy in the flat in Cumballa Hill, trespassing quietly into the bedroom while his mother practised the last song she'd been taught sitting on a bed, her harmonium before her, her distant figure and the look of questing, unworldly dedication on her face captured in the dressing-table mirror, song after song by Meera or Tulsidas or Kabir being added to an already teeming "stock" of songs—the pointlessness of his mother's career as a singer made him brutal. And the relationship between guru and student was complicated by an undertone of suspicion that, after Apurva Sengupta's retirement, Shyamji, always smooth but with an intuition for sensing in which direction the future lay (for how else could he survive?), would have less time for Mallika Sengupta. That was the natural way of things in Bombay after all; it was one of the mild tremors and shocks of post-retirement life here, even for the very well-to-do, this slow orbiting away of the familiar. "His mind is elsewhere. I can feel it," complained Mrs. Sengupta. "He taught me the same song for three sittings, and then he gave me one with a slightly cheap tune. I told him, 'Shyamji, yeh gaana mujhe pasand nahi aaya, I didn't like the song,' and he looked puzzled and irritable and said, 'Achha gaana hai didi, it's a good one.' "

"Do you know that Laxmi Ratan Shukla is dead?" said Mr. Sengupta, faintly disbelieving (as he always was, afresh, on being told that someone had died) but smiling wryly, as if the reason for a particularly long and tiring wait had been finally disclosed to him; he'd just returned from his journey to the city; with his back to his wife, he opened the cupboard and distractedly impaled his jacket upon a hanger.

"What?" cried Mallika Sengupta, looking up and waiting for him to turn and to catch his eye. A strange melange of emotions invaded her; among them was the instinctive realisation that a person's dying was such a simple solution to so many dilemmas and hesitancies, but a solution never seriously considered till it happened and surprised you with its straightforwardness. He'd been

Head of the Light Music wing of HMV when he'd died, though he'd been less on her mind than even two years ago; some people never retire, and become fixed to their employment, like a mask. Very few find out, or even care to, what they were outside it.

"Yes," he nodded. "Two days ago. Died of a stroke."

An employee at HMV he'd run into that afternoon in the lobby of the Taj had paused a moment to break the news, as if Laxmi Ratan Shukla had to, in some form, briefly inhabit these bits of formal chit-chat between them. A couple of minutes of astonishment and slow questioning—"When?" "How?"—and nods and grim phrases, and that was it, they continued urgently in opposite directions. And it almost seemed to Mallika Sengupta that a burden had lifted, that she'd been delivered from waiting for the day this man would be persuaded just that little bit more—that final push—and produce her disc; and surely there must be many others, in whose thoughts Laxmi Ratan Shukla had become a dull and persistent discomfort, who'd been similarly delivered. That day—the day Shukla would pick up the phone and say to her husband, "Sengupta saab, we will do it now; there is a possibility . . ." or rise from his table to say innocuously, with that discomfiting softness, "Sengupta saab, please sit down . . ." and give the go-ahead—that day, it was safe to say, would never come, and she was glad she'd give up, now, whatever attachment she'd had to its arrival.

"Shyamji," she said on the phone, wanting to disabuse him as quickly as possible of any notion he might have had of the man's continuance in the world, "Laxmi Ratan Shukla is no more."

He replied gravely, unfazed, "He never did anyone any good"; the seriousness with which he said this made her laugh later; for her, it became Shukla's epitaph.

For Mr. Sengupta, Shukla's death was, in passing, a day on which to take stock, to understand what music—especially in its incarnation in his wife, his marriage—had meant to him; although there were several other things, to do with the consultancy he was providing the Germans, to preoccupy him in the evening. Had he been too soft, had he given Shukla too much time of day, as Mallika Sengupta seemed to think; would she have fared better if he'd not depended so heavily on this enigmatic man and acted, in his own eyes, with more recklessness? He laughed to himself, as he entered into an imaginary dialogue—composed of strong and inextricable feelings, not words—with his wife and son upon the subject (when he actually had to talk to them about it, he found himself unable to use any but the simplest generalities, which his son infuriated him by dismissing almost immediately); Mallika had wanted recognition, that pure, woebegone desire for a reward for her gift had accompanied her life from the start but never overwhelmed it; but she hadn't wanted to dirty her hands in the music world; she'd wanted to preserve the prestige of being, at once, an artist and the wife of a successful executive. *She* knew, with an uncomplicated honesty, what her worth was; to what extent could she compromise or to which level stoop if others pretended not to? She kept her distance; remaining busy all the time, not a moment's hiatus, busy with the music, busy with the household, busy with Nirmalya's life and Mr. Sengupta's. That had left him with no choice but to pursue Shukla, who'd been more than happy, in his phlegmatic way—if "happy" was a word you could use of him—to be pursued. Apurva Sengupta hadn't *liked* pursuing Shukla; sometimes, he'd found it perplexing and pointless—as a human being, but also as a manager of people and departments. The pursuit had ended; the quarry—though it was Mallika Sengupta who felt more like a quarry herself—had suddenly removed itself, permanently.

Nirmalya—though he still hadn't completed college—wanted to apply to study abroad. "There's no philosophy degree here worth its name," he said, contemptuous and impatient after a day spent loitering intractably around the portals of the college at Kala Ghoda.

He found an ally in his mother, who, otherwise, couldn't bear to let him out of her sight, but who became very serious and nodded at everything he said these days, as if it were of the utmost importance. His mother, who'd disciplined him as a boy when he would plot new and untested devices to "bunk" school, had recently become a sort of acolyte. For thirty years her life had been designed by her husband and by the company; now, like a beacon representing some other order, her son, untidy, brooding, with an opinion about everything, appeared on the horizon.

"He doesn't want to be like *you*," she said, berating Apurva Sengupta, as if he and his kind were a species of obstreperous, careless dinosaur whose day had come.

Mr. Sengupta smiled. He knew that, although his own days might be numbered, his type, the company type, ambitious, brisk, democratic, convinced in the sacred value of entrepreneurship, was bound to flourish—it made him a bit sad, knowing his son had decided not to be part of this proliferation—in a way that dinosaurs never had managed to. His type would populate the world in unforeseen mutations. Money was like a sea-breeze blowing inland; gentle now, but threatening to uproot everything. He, Mr. Sengupta, had never really seen money except in its genteel aspects, had never seen its unbridled form; but he could smell its distant agitation. Nirmalya appeared immune to the smell, or determined to ignore it.

But, surprisingly, Apurva Sengupta felt affectionately about his son's interest in philosophy; just as you might listen to a piece of music which numbs you to the present and makes your nerves tingle to the daydreams of who you were thirty or forty years ago, Mr. Sengupta felt a momentary, youthful enchantment. Then the present returned to him all at once, physically and emotionally; you could not escape being who you were now; he was worried by Nirmalya's intention to study philosophy and the mundane but unavoidable questions it raised. It seemed quite right, and wonderful, to Mr. Sengupta that Nirmalya's first follower was his mother; there was a small but revolutionary change taking place in his family before his very eyes; and who knows—given time, he too might be converted. What was parenthood, after all, but an apprenticeship (a belated apprenticeship in Mr. Sengupta's case) to the possible greatness of one's children?

But to go off to England, as Nirmalya wanted to, soon, insatiable, suddenly, in his conviction that the real hunt for knowledge would begin once he'd transplanted himself there—that passage would require funding; where would the funds come from? Nirmalya was too unworldly, too insulated from the material capriciousness of human existence, to be bothered with these particulars. It was left to Apurva Sengupta, who'd once managed a company, to now manage his son and his unworldliness. Mr. Sengupta would have to quickly review his savings (which, under Mrs. Gandhi's tax regime, had been small, most of it going every month into a strangely futile insurance premium) and apply for educational loans. It was expensive maintaining a saint, a mystic. Wasn't it Sarojini Naidu who'd said—Apurva Sengupta's mind went back to his shabby, peripatetic college days and to the freedom struggle—that it cost a lot of money to keep Gandhi travelling third class? Decades had passed since that remark, exquisite in its irony, had been made and those excitements burnt out into the straight-faced pursuit of well-being in present day existence. Mr. Sengupta smiled as the words—full of a tolerant, even affectionate, mockery he recognised while taking up the task in hand—came back to him.

"King's College, London," he said, returning from work, the look on his face at once querying and pleased, like a boy who suspects, but is not entirely certain, that he's carrying a piece of important news. "Jane says it has a good philosophy department."

"Jane," thin, hesitant, but large-heartedly helpful, was part of an entourage from the Commonwealth office in whose honour a cheerful and efficient business luncheon had been organised that day, in a conference room in the basement of a five-star hotel. The topics covered in the meaningless, happy hum between the suited Indians and the awkward English, some of them making jerky, shy movements of the head, others complacent and impenetrable, had included foreign investment (naturally), mergers, the annual growth rate, trade restrictions, and, between Jane and Apurva Sengupta, for about seven to ten minutes, philosophy departments.

And so Nirmalya became a correspondent, and entered, reluctantly, his first transcontinental communication, in which someone from the department, a Mrs. Sandra Dixon, pleased and ruffled him by writing back to him and sending him, obligingly, an envelope thick with forms. He sat down heavily with them in the morning upon the bed, bending forward, placing them against the hard surface of an exercise book, filling them out laboriously, progressing slowly from rectangle to rectangle, sighing from the start like a sick person (he had a condition close to dyslexia when it came to completing forms; it filled him with a subdued panic and lostness). When it was done, he felt an indescribable sense of liberation, as if he'd never have to do it again; he went on to the veranda to get some air and to survey the unfolding of the everyday. Weekly, now, long white envelopes began to arrive, with postage stamps that had, upon them, a ghostly impression of the head of the Queen of England.

The letter they'd been waiting for but not expecting crept in beneath the door one afternoon with aerogrammes and statements of interest rates: acceptance.

When Nirmalya had ripped open the envelope and excavated the letter, he read, with the same swimming eyes of the unhappy form-filler, the message in the neat, punctilious, by-now-familiar type: "I am pleased to say that . . ." He took it to his mother; she opened her mouth in astonishment and then read it out, in her naive, stumbling, insistent maternal accent, to her husband over the phone.

He went walking around Pali Hill and the lanes of Bandra; in the afternoon, confronting dogs that lay curled up in self-contained, pilgrim-like repose in the middle of a road, or a tyre abandoned on one side without explanation; and in the evening, with the fruit bats hovering overhead. He was in a curious interim phase; unexpectedly leaving his childhood terrors and his adolescent anxieties behind, opening himself, for the first time, to the allure of the world—he was in a state of semi-retirement himself, secretive with his thoughts on books and music and this new locality, nothing to do for much of the time, as he waited to travel to King's College. He had almost no friends—he'd gradually stopped seeing them, one by one—and he undertook his expeditions alone; his parents no longer questioned him about his irregular attendance at college. He was struck by everything here: the warm, loaf-like stones that made up the walls of the Christian schools; the pretty, tissue-paper-like bougainvillea (almost like something mass-produced by a greeting-card manufacturer) by the gates to the Goans' bungalows causing him to stop, undecided, in confusion; at traffic junctions, as lines of cars negotiated transitions from Hill Road to Perry and other roads, sudden crosses rose up like sentinels behind the traffic lights; and churches sprang up between or in the corners of the interconnecting lanes. How different all this was from the Bombay he'd grown up in!

"So you're going to London," said Nayana Neogi, his parents' friend, sitting in a large, loose smock in the small bright sitting room of the new flat. He felt more comfortable now, more at home, with his mother's friends than with his own; he felt they could sense his transformation. "We're so proud of you, Nirmalya." She leaned forward, this woman who was for years familiar to him, large, engrossed, looking for an ashtray.

Now that they were in this part of the city, his parents had begun to see the Neogis more regularly than before: they were a ten-minute drive away. Not only proximity, but the fact that retirement had restored a sort of parity, that to see Apurva Sengupta was to see an old friend, and not so much to visit a "big man," had made things just a little easier; from the early days, when everyone and everything was full of promise, and Nayana's husband a young gifted artist and Apurva a charming, beautiful "chhokra" they were fond of, to the middle period, full of unresolved tensions and contradictions, when it seemed infinite opportunities opened up for the slightly less deserving and mysteriously closed for others, to now, when Nayana Neogi seemed more at peace in her oversized frame and with her superannuated bohemian days, happy with her various pets—so much time had been covered, and was represented, in this simple visit now that the friends lived within a few miles of each other: Khar and Bandra! It was in London, of course, they'd first met in the fifties, when Nayana's husband, Prashanta, and Apurva Sengupta had been students, the former of commercial art, the latter beginning his articleship toward a degree in accountancy: there was that story of how Apurva had, by mistake, on the first night he'd spent at Prashanta's "digs," used—they had taken an instant liking to each other—the latter's toothbrush. This outrageous act of presumption on young Apurva Sengupta's part (for that was how it was seen by the doting

Prashanta) had sealed their friendship for life; but the story of the toothbrush was just a little too old now, almost too pat and rounded, for Prashanta to use it to make a special claim on his friend; but he still recounted it; for him, it still had a kind of music. Over the years, they'd not so much grown apart as been divided by what constituted and defined success: the Senguptas suspected the Neogis secretly resented their "success" only because they clung to one particular meaning of that word. The Neogis felt that Apurva Sengupta had sacrificed his freshness, his mischief, and become predictable in his life-devouring pursuit of conventional fulfilments. But now the Senguptas had moved to this part of the city, the subterranean debate about success had lost its urgency; and Mallika Sengupta had begun to visit, every other day, the rented ground-floor flat, two steps up to a wooden door on the left, where the Neogis continued to live, the black-and-white photograph of their dead, smiling son greeting you as you entered the bedroom, a menagerie of pets—a sleek, supercilious grey cat and, recently, a small family of Pekinese—moving constantly and confidently from kitchen to bedroom to hall, the coir chairs waiting to be occupied by visitors.

Once again, he'd gone out for a walk; he loved the conjunction of foreignness and familiarity in Bandra; he was impelled constantly by a sense of discovery, but also of wonder and recognition, as if he'd once belonged here, to these lanes, these crumbling verandas and families; here were the strange but familiar Goan bungalows again, some of them unsettling him and making him nervous because of the dogs inside that began to bark furiously as he went past; one had a small life-like porcelain dog at the window which stared fixedly at him with a kind of challenge—and he stared back, confident it couldn't leap at him, waiting tensely for it to bark: and, finally, he understood why it was glowering so silently. These figurines and tame beasts, and their semi-visible owners, were the guardians of these lanes. Nevertheless, some of these houses had already been torn down; unintimidating six- or seven-storey buildings with names like Annabella had risen in their places. What the lanes were called was disclosed on the swinging blue plaques found everywhere in the city, usually with the names of Maharashtrian leaders no one knew, and which could well have been invented, so many-syllabled and incredible these unheard-of names were; except that here they bore names of saints—which, too, with the exception of Paul, had a difficult-to-believe fairy-tale ring: Cyril, Leo.

When he came back, he found a woman—he couldn't tell whether she was looking for work, or was just a visitor; whether she was run-down or was really working class—in a pale blue synthetic sari, leaning thoughtfully on the wall at the end of the corridor in front of his parents' bedroom. She was smiling faintly, as if Mrs. Sengupta had said something amusing. "Nirmalya," said his mother when she glimpsed him, "do you know who this is? Do you remember her?"

"How will he remember?" said the woman in Hindi, looking up brightly but pointedly; although his mother had spoken to him in Bengali, she must have guessed at what she meant from the lilt of the question; she had an air of intelligence, of a modest, unhurried alertness.

He looked at her again politely. She seemed embarrassed and happy, and eager to defend him from the charge of forgetfulness.

"Arrey, this is Anju," said his mother, delighted for a moment by the unthinkable simplicity of the situation. "I've told you about her, haven't I? She looked after you when you were two years old."

Ah, so that's who she was! That explained to him her understated but surprising air of recognition, although she couldn't have known him if she'd seen him on the street. Recognition is partly imagination, isn't it, and not knowing what had happened to him in the intervening seventeen years had given her present sighting of him a startling intimacy.

"Do you know," said his mother to Jumna, who was sitting agog, a little puzzled, feeling perhaps a tiny bit excluded, on the carpet—and embarked on the story he'd heard more than a hundred times—"I was feeding baba moong daal and rice, and he was quite a fat greedy child." Both Jumna and Anju laughed together at this frank insight, Jumna showing her gums; Nirmalya looked abashed at being reminded of a time when he was not thin and tortured. "He liked the daal so much he began to dance up and down with pleasure. And he bounced so much that he came straight out of the cot!" "Haa?" said Jumna, sitting up slightly, becoming serious. "He would have fallen to the ground, and I don't know what would have happened, but Anju, who was standing beside me, caught him in an instant." And this woman in the blue sari, looking proud, also became self-effacing and appeared deliberately to melt, as if she had no further claim to this distant miracle.

"Baap re," said Jumna finally. She, who'd looked after Nirmalya for fifteen years, whose skin had been pricked by his needles when he played doctor, whose hair had begun to grey all at once in the last two years, stared at this woman, who'd appeared out of nowhere, and who'd once, instinctively, with an acrobat's grace, prevented serious injury to Nirmalya. Jumna's puzzled smile contained something, a memory and also speculation. She was caught between the past and a present in which she was confronted with this woman, and there was a shadow of disbelief on her face. Anju was still pretty, though a little drawn; almost ghostly in her undecidedness.

"Where do you live now?" Nirmalya asked of his one-time rescuer.

"Baba, not far from here. Juhu Danda," she said, indistinctly gesturing north. "I heard from someone who works in this building that memsaab had moved to this part of the city." She smiled a little, girlish again. "So I decided to come."

Juhu Danda: he knew the place slightly. Their car had passed through it once on the way to the Neogis, when they were going to Khar. There it was, at the end of Carter Road opposite to the one from which he'd just returned; a colony of shanties, with dried bombill hanging between poles, the air awash with the rank, tantalising smell, men in shorts standing in the sea breeze, barefoot children running and playing in the space before the shanties, surveyed dispassionately in a few instants before the car moved on.

When she'd gone, his mother said to him: "Her name's now Saeeda."

"What do you mean?" he asked.

"Well, that's why she left all those years ago, you know. In fact, *we* used to live in Juhu then; your father, on returning from England, got his first job in Bombay, and was given a flat in Juhu. She fell in love with a Muslim and then married him. They *have* to change their religion when they do that, you know." For to marry a Muslim was to not only change your name but to give up your childhood and your future, to pass discreetly into a different world and mode of existence, to, in effect, disappear; only great and impulsive love could, surely, make one justify such an abdication to oneself. And yet was that, strictly speaking, true? After all, here was Anju, older, but still recognisable, the same woman who'd scooped him instinctively in mid-air when he'd leapt out of his cot in his exuberance.

"Is she happy?" he asked; for, briefly, he found Anju's, or Saeeda's, happiness had become his concern.

"Her husband is a strict Muslim but not a bad man, she told me today." Such a belated sharing of confidences! "She herself is not a practising Muslim, but the children were raised strictly. The son is in Dubai, and the younger child is a daughter. Life is sometimes good, sometimes not so good, she said," said Mallika Sengupta, smiling, as if she was relieved that it was at least good in parts.

Anju came again one afternoon, this time with her seventeen-year-old daughter.

"Namaste, memsaab," the girl said to Mrs. Sengupta, and glanced at Nirmalya. Anju, leaning against the wall, looked on as if she was showing off something no one had suspected she had. She herself had obviously been attractive long ago; but the girl was exceptionally lovely to look at; tall, with a large oval face—and the mother seemed pleasurably resigned to being superseded by her daughter. There was a thoughtfulness about her that attracted Nirmalya, a reticence that made her quite different from the lissom girls in narrow trousers and tops, girls from his own social background he passed by every day on the roads, laughing and screaming innocently to each other, as if the world was theirs.

"She's a pretty girl," said Mrs. Sengupta to Anju. Almost slyly, she turned her gaze upon the daughter. "What is your name?"

The girl's eyes were focussed on the carpet. "Salma," she said softly, as if it were a word she did not use often, and then only with care and reluctance.

"Kya karti hai?" Mrs. Sengupta said, speaking to the mother again, with a register of intimacy and a bygone commandingness. "Tell me what she does."

"Memsaab, she's got a few small roles in films," said Anju, creasing her forehead deprecatingly. "Her father doesn't like it, but I said to her—'Do what you have to do, but in today's world be careful.' " She sounded apologetic, but she was a little thrilled as well—overcome, perhaps, by the irresistible, ancient charm of cinema. She was protective of her daughter, but a sort of distance separated them that was not just generational; perhaps she was also a little in awe of her, a little—who knows—envious.

So that was where this girl's modesty, her inner glow, came from: it must be from that extraordinary sense of destiny that both cinema, with its timeless reassurance, and being seventeen give to you. She was set apart—the future had stored something special for her—she'd grown up in Juhu Danda, but she was a flower; lovelier than any other girl Nirmalya had seen for a long time in Bombay.

He saw her on the street once, at the corner of St. Leo Road; she was with a friend; they nodded at each other, he awkwardly, not sure what to make of this Juhu Danda girl. And she came visiting again with her mother—always in cheaply tailored pale green or yellow salwar kameez outfits, looking like an apparition whatever she wore.

He had begun to think of Salma with a kind of yearning; there had been times in the past when he'd almost felt ready for marriage, his tortured, inarticulate heart palpitating for the arrival of the long-awaited instantly-recognised bride: there were occasions he'd grown tense with the as-yet unknown person's imminent arrival.

"Ma," he said to Mallika Sengupta, for she was his one confidant, sitting in the car in a traffic jam between Gorbunder Road and Mahim on one of their trips to the city, "Salma is beautiful, isn't she?" The car had stopped by an old municipal tank it went past almost every day, the railings round it recently painted a garish green.

"Yes, she is," said Mrs. Sengupta, not insincerely, but only half-attentive, as if this conversation couldn't, of course, lead to anything serious.

"Don't you think," he hesitated only for an instant, "that she'd make a very good wife? I mean, generally speaking, *I'd* be happy with a wife like that."

Ah, the future! It was a time when Nirmalya could say anything he wanted about it; he had a magical, careless sense of abandon about the future. And words had begun to come easily to him; he'd just begun to discover he could express any desire, voice any wish.

"Why," said his mother, amused and assured rather than scandalised, as if she knew better than he that this was another of his daydreams, except that now, unlike before, he was at the brink of that age when he could almost turn his daydreams into the life that he, and, by extension, they, would live, "will you carry her away on your white horse?"

Nirmalya looked out of the window to avoid further charges of silliness.

"Such things don't happen in real life," she said, not cruelly, perhaps with a tinge of concern, looking straight ahead as the car began to move. "It isn't possible."

What, then, is possible? He saw himself on a horse, galloping down the curve of Carter Road toward Juhu Danda, and dismissed the idea at least temporarily with a wry smile. Not only books and stories, but real life too has its own verisimilitude against which we keep comparing ourselves. He was bound not by social strictures—in the end, he could not be—but by a sense of plausibility that hung over everything, visible and invisible, and which he came up against daily—not like a wall, but a gentle undefinable limit, circumscribing his new adult life; his feelings for Salma would probably come to nothing, he knew, but not because they were socially inadmissable; the sense of plausibility, pervasive in everyday existence as the conventions of narrative are to a story, curtailed what, after all, might otherwise have been possible, and pleasing.

Then, as suddenly and inexplicably as Anju had first appeared that day in their new flat, they stopped coming—the quiet, beautiful daughter, whom he'd toyed with the idea of falling in love with, and the woman who'd scooped Nirmalya to safety just as he was about to fall. Maybe something had happened; maybe nothing had—maybe somebody had moved out; or hadn't. The Senguptas didn't know; but they stopped coming.

Before that, however, Anju visited them once in the afternoon.

"She had a shooting in Simla, memsaab," she said, lowering herself on the carpet before the bed with a mixture of docility and an old bone-tiredness. "Chunky Pandey is in the film. See."

She'd brought photographs with her today; she took them out of an envelope, one, two, three, four, and passed them silently to Mrs. Sengupta half-recumbent on the bed. The first picture was of Salma and two other girls standing upon a hill, a bit unreal and over-made-up, at a discreet distance from the flamboyant (and largely out-of-work these days) Chunky Pandey in his wide-collar silk shirt. The other three photos were more of the same. It pained Nirmalya that the make-up, and maybe the situation itself, had taken away Salma's glow in the photograph—the glow which was the first thing about her that had struck him, and which was her unique, indisputable and most natural allure—and made her indistinguishable from the other two girls, as well as from the many girls who form the background of the numerous epic scenes in Hindi movies. In each photograph, she looked self-conscious and stiff; and you could feel her stiffness. Nirmalya studied the pictures and returned them to the envelope.

"Bahut achha," he said wryly. "Very good."

He had to have a photograph taken for his passport; and he decided impulsively not to go to a studio in the vicinity, to one of the shops on Linking Road or Hill Road, but—because he needed an instant photo; time was running out—all the way to Churchgate.

He'd begun to use the local train; he'd never learnt how to drive, of course—his childhood had been almost entirely chauffeur-driven, and then a certain laziness about learning to drive after he'd finished school, which was when most of his friends had swiftly acquired the skill, when they were still not eligible for a licence, but were eager and unstoppable: a laziness at that point had coincided with and enlarged into a superiority to do with anything his contemporaries did, anything that was the natural course of events in his father's world or his friends', and he deliberately missed his chance at taking possession of a car. And this refusal had branched out into his indefatigable capacity for walking, which depended on, and emphasised, his increasing, and on the whole self-contained, loneliness, leaving him to explore both the suburbs, the fortuitous ups and downs of Bandra and Pali Hill, and the alleys and familiar roads of the city he'd grown up in, on foot.

He went now, taking a half-empty two o'clock train from Bandra to Churchgate, to the Asiatic department store near the station, because it had the only passport-photo booth in Bombay. Edging past unflappable, prodigious housewives, he paid for a token at a counter and then, avoiding a mirror, climbed expectantly up the stairs. He was suspended momentarily between two levels on which toys, stainless-steel utensils, yards of cloth appeared and disappeared in an exchange of gazes, words, and consultations, the thin salespersons in white taking out and then once again silently returning the folded bales to their places. There, before him, on the first floor, was the booth, flanked by long counters busily selling things. A lone man in uniform advised him sombrely about what he was to do when he was inside: "Be careful not to shut your eyes when the flash goes off"; "Drop the token and stare at the green light before you"; "Adjust the stool to the correct level"; all in a low, inhuman, deadpan voice. "Yes, yes," said Nirmalya, vaguely disturbed; he went in and pulled the curtain, feeling nervous, and also a guilty, solitary excitement, because there's an unmistakable hint of sleaze about cubicles and drawn curtains. Much as he tried, in that narrow island in the milling hubbub of the shop, the flash, both times, went off a moment before he was prepared for it, leaving him feeling somehow chastised when he emerged from the booth. The man, who'd felt snubbed by Nirmalya's "Yes, yes" now had the inevitable tranquillity of the powerful; when the photographs fell with a buzz into the slot, he forbade him with an impersonal, imperious gesture to touch them until a few minutes had passed. Nirmalya dawdled there, distracted, as his image composed itself bit by bit upon the whiteness; when he finally picked up the photos, he saw the sense of being imprisoned inside the cubicle had robbed his face of its strangeness, had made it ordinary and disposable as the paper it appeared on. He felt no attachment to it whatsoever; given a choice, he'd have denied to the passport officer it was his picture.

. . .

"Ma, you know the train's a good way of going to the city," he revealed to Mallika Sengupta. She looked with loving disbelief at her son, as if it were another one of his wild, testing ideas. The train! It wasn't something *they* had ever had any reason to use; when they'd lived in the city and had to visit old friends in Bandra and Khar, the long drive through Breach Candy into Worli and then Cadell Road and Mahim had been the occasion for a magical, purely private, journey, unimpeded, on the whole, by traffic—there were so few businesses, then, on the outskirts—during which the city changed itself several times, seamlessly but unpredictably; and then back again. And now Nirmalya, in his frayed, slightly dirty corduroys (he would *not* put them into the wash) was suggesting trains; almost as a form of enjoyment! How quickly things had changed in the last few years!

They still felt the need, of course, to go to the city three or four times a week; the old life was a fix they suffered almost physically without—despite the prettiness of Bandra, despite their avowed contempt for that existence comprising parties and elaborate hairdos. They took a taxi usually, often with shrill Lata Mangeshkar songs playing from the speakers at the back; or, when Apurva Sengupta was picked up in the morning by a colleague, they followed distractedly in the fitfully cool Ambassador. But it cost money, the journey; hundreds of rupees every week at the Shah and Sanghi petrol station at the corner of Breach Candy and Kemp's Corner. The taxi fare, each time, was almost a hundred rupees.

"And cheap," added Nirmalya. It was not like him to be troubled about such things. Nevertheless, he was aware in a faraway, theological way that there was no company now to foot the bills, and he worried—this was a new and pleasurable anxiety—slightly for his father; and, of course, he quite enjoyed embracing whatever little poverty he could. Travelling by the local train was his way of briefly, innocently, taking on a disguise, of insinuating himself into the life of the multitude.

"Really? Where does it go to?" asked Mrs. Sengupta, enthused mildly by the thought of saving the taxi fare; excited, too, to be in a new partnership in this foray with her son. Besides, the idea of saving money had always exercised the puritan in Mr. and Mrs. Sengupta; the actual practice bored them.

"Churchgate Station," he said.

"Let's try it tomorrow," she replied, negotiating.

They took a taxi—not to the city this time, but to Bandra Station, and, while Mrs. Sengupta hovered in the background, near the entrance, watching vendors, abstracted beggars with bandaged, amputated limbs, and auto rickshaws suddenly roaring back to Bandra, he bought two first-class tickets. This theoretical and implausible luxury gave him much pleasure; ordinary tickets were only two rupees; and, if you paid fifteen rupees more, you travelled first class, which was identical to second, except that the seats were slightly cleaner, and, instead of the raw, ubiquitous perspiration of vegetable vendors, errand boys, and people with part-time employment, you inhaled the odour, mingled with aftershave, of clerks and traders' accountants, their monthly passes (naturally they didn't buy tickets) in their shirt pockets. The compartment was less than half full because it was half past two; he—because she was so nervous about her feet and balance—had to help her up, clasping her hand tightly; once she was in, she looked about her with a mild, puzzled smile, like one who'd entered a somewhat makeshift drawing room at a suburban social gathering, and then allowed herself, elegantly, silently, to be led to her seat. People seemed to recognise her, and looked at her respectfully, as if they knew she was Mr. Sengupta's wife and what that meant; and then returned almost immediately to their own thoughts. She settled into the seat, without comment, trying to experience the strange magic in the compartment, unworried, for the moment, that the seat was hard and that she had a lingering backache. He glanced at her with a deep, uncategorisable love. Just as the train began to move, barefoot children and tiny, intrepid men with fan-like bouquets of pens jumped on board, displaying them briefly to one tolerant but uninterested person after another; the children took around small plastic packets of peanuts, saying, just a little too familiarly, "Timepass?" Mrs. Sengupta looked nonplussed and charmed. "Let's have some peanuts," she said, with an air of someone consenting to behave much more rashly than they normally did. Then, surrendering to the breeze, which generally annoyed her when she was in a car because of what it did to her hair, making her quickly roll the window up, she sat munching peanuts with dignity and an impenetrable delight; until, carefully, entering a different phase in her consciousness of the journey, she put the packet into her leather handbag.

Nirmalya stood by the open doorway, holding, casually, the metal rod he'd lately got accustomed to. "Be careful," she cried. He nodded curtly and looked away, immersed in his own independence. It was a slow train; it gathered speed and immediately lost it; it stopped repeatedly. At every stop, Mrs. Sengupta became dreamy and childlike, her meditation seemed uncomplicated and engrossing, and she was nudged physically out of her reverie only by the jolt the train gave when it started again. Surreptitiously, this experiment saddened her and dampened her spirits; no, she was who she was, she couldn't, at this late stage in her life, become somebody else. She harboured a small panic within her.

"No," she said, getting off, with her son's help again, on to the wide platform at Churchgate Station, the long train motionless beside her, commuters alighting and vanishing unhurriedly towards the gates and exits by the time she'd found her bearings, "this is very nice, but not for me." She smoothed the expensive tangail she was wearing. "You know I've gone round in this city in nothing but a car for the last twenty years," she confessed to her son, as if he'd failed to notice. She smiled in apology, seeming to speak of a way of life she'd had no choice but to accept—that's the way the company had cocooned them all—and how she'd begun to find everything outside it a tiny bit incredible.

She'd taken a change of sari with her for the cocktails that evening, and a jewellery box with a few bangles and small diamond earrings, all in a small plastic bag. She'd refused to give the bag to Nirmalya to carry, nervous that he, in one of his absent, visionary moods, might leave it lying on a seat upon the train.

As ever, like pigeons returning to roost, they got out of the taxi at the gothic archway of the club. Here, at twilight, they were reunited with Apurva Sengupta, in view of members seated on neighbouring sofas, not quite noticing them; and returned to afternoon papers and tea, and fresh lime soda. At the stroke of seven o'clock she went into the cavernous Victorian ladies' dressing room in the club and began to transform herself.

Nirmalya went to see a movie on his own: *Omen II*. It was part of his deliberate cultivation of peculiarity; "What's wrong with seeing a movie by myself?" he said, not so much to others as, defiantly, to himself. Then he stood in a queue and bought one ticket, and climbed up the steps to the hall, liberated by his anonymity, but also feeling the sad undertow of aimlessness that was constantly part of his life. He gradually lost himself in the terror of the film; his heart, his errant heart, beat wildly. And Mallika Sengupta transferred the old sari into the plastic packet, and then put it behind the rear seat of the Ambassador. She was telling her husband about the journey by the local train, laughing at how simple things, things without special distinction or interest, became, for Nirmalya, the son they'd brought up with more than a god-like attention, and put into the best school—how simple things had begun to become for him portentous adventures. "He's excited by what others would find boring, and bored by what they'd find exciting," she said. "It's the way you brought him up. He has no idea of the 'real world,' " the father said, not entirely without pride or admonition. "I worry for him." She'd begun to defend herself, but was interrupted by a child at the traffic lights at Marine Drive crying to her to buy a small garland of mogra flowers.

"No, no," she said, which encouraged the child into assuming a low-pitched whining tone, little more than a whisper: "Take it memsaab, take it memsaab."

She gave in, as she always had ever since she'd discovered the mogra in Bombay. And it was always at this junction that the girl would appear, so that the nocturnal perfume had become associated for her with the traffic lights and the Talk of the Town. She would emboss it on her bun, where, in the dark, it would fit perfectly, like letters of an ancient typeface.

~

The city had begun to glitter; even Pali Hill and Bandra, once cut off, a sanctuary for a different rhythm of life, places in which people lived who were half-hidden, small-scale, even Bandra and Pali Hill sparkled with money. Nirmalya's rejection of the world of corporations he'd grown up in widened into a disgust with the booming city; weddings everywhere; cars in droves thronging at the entrance of some celebration; clusters of families with children shopping late into the evening.

A new shop called "Croissant" had opened on Perry Road; and Nirmalya loved croissants. Walking past its gleaming door, blue and silver in the evening with light, he was tempted to go inside. But then he noticed a group of frenetic children—obviously the children of the labourers who were constructing a building behind the one he lived in: he'd seen the irrevocable, emergent skeleton of the building from the rear balcony of the flat, the labourers rhythmically at work in daytime. White dust rose habitually; he knew these were their children because of that dust, which they bore like signs on their hands and parts of their faces. They were in some excitement; one of them, an obdurate waif-like girl, had created a kind of hammock by lifting and holding the bottom of her dress in front of her, and this tiny hammock was crowded with breadcrust.

Nirmalya had seen the children emerge from the shop; walk noisily down the steps; the others darted away from the girl but were reunited and ran around her in a chattering group, now and then scooping up bits of the crust. Nirmalya was amazed by their pleasure; he stood there, like an idiot, watching them, and taking in the radiance of Croissant from the corner of his eye. He watched as the children danced into the half-completed building off Perry Road, the girl still holding the end of her dress before her. Returning home, he wrote hurriedly in his notebook, shutting out a television that was within earshot, "When the children entered the building site, they became invisible, though I could hear them laughing. The building site, dark with the white dust the labourers had raised, was like the garden in 'Burnt Norton,' where 'the leaves were full of children,/Hidden excitedly, containing laughter.' "

"Let's go and have tea at the Leela Penta," said Mr. Sengupta. Saturday morning, and strange parts of the city beckoned. The Leela was the new hotel, not only a new hotel but a new species of hotel, that had come up in the outskirts. Not like the Sun 'n' Sand, with its respectable, palm-tree-infested charm, overlooking sunsets and quaint horseback rides on the beach, but an excuse, it seemed, for some people to pour money into a freshly built-up wilderness, where you'd least expect it. One morning, Shobha De had surprised them all by describing it as a paradise on the edge of civilisation in a full-page advertisement in the *Sunday Times*. This had made them suspicious; but also, naturally, curious.

"What *is* this place? If Shobha De says it's good, it must be rubbish," said Mrs. Sengupta. And so they set out for tea at eleven thirty. Featureless, intimidating, promising Versova: wide avenues and thickets of tall buildings, even taller than Thacker Towers. This was the city's newest suburb—and was this where, long ago, when Nirmalya was a boy and they used to visit the beach in Marve on certain weekends, was this where a connecting road used to run, with fields and marshes beyond, and with a low-roofed South Indian cafe doing surprisingly bustling business on the roadside, where Nirmalya, with his parents, on the long journey back towards home, had once eaten a dosa, agog with wonder at the black mustard-seed seasoning on the potatoes? So it seemed vaguely, as they went this way; that it had been somewhere here; though there was no evidence of it now.

They arrived, pennant-heralded, at the dun-coloured driveway to the hotel, and got out at the immense porch. A distant gust of chill air greeted them. The hotel, with its line of palm trees, had risen out of nowhere like something in a European fairy tale; it was surrounded largely by waste land. Mr. Sengupta had a lost but cheerfully inquisitive air, like someone who'd been forced to take a long diversion and had stopped accidentally; and the doormen willingly cooperated in this little piece of theatre, and received him accordingly, calming him with smiles and bows as he entered. When they'd walked past the catafalque-like lobby, ignoring the small, glassy-looking men and women behind the reception, and settled into the understated but resplendent chairs in the coffee shop, burrowing finally into the heavy menus before them, running their eyes over varieties of Darjeeling tea and cake named and described in sloping letters, Nirmalya, who was looking out through the large sunlit glass windows into the brown tract of land outside, where, in the distance, a boy was squinting and squatting on the edge of a metal cylinder, said: "Baba, I don't want to eat here."

Apurva Sengupta looked again at his son in surprise, even wonder, as if he were reminded that the boy represented a puzzling, unforeseeable turn in their lives; he couldn't help but laugh, almost with pleasure, as he used to when Nirmalya, as a baby, had first begun to exuberantly and insistently utter nonsense, and it had seemed so momentous to his parents. Then, too, he'd felt that fear mingled with joy, as if he'd never confronted anything comparable before.

"Why, what's the matter?" he asked his son, without anger or condescension—just as he'd reasoned with him at different points in their lives, while cajoling him to go to school, for instance, or when leaning forward to the small unappeasable boy before he got on to a flight.

"I can't eat here," Nirmalya said, shaking his head slowly, the boyish face, little more than a child's in spite of the moustache, full of an inexplicable hurt, the eyes almost tearful. "I can't eat here till Shyamji is able to eat here," he said, eyebrows knitted, still shaking the head ominously.

What was this sudden onrush of love for his teacher—a love he seldom displayed openly? What had happened to this boy, for whom all it took to be happy once was to come home from school? Apurva Sengupta felt a twinge of concern, as he struggled to work his way towards a sense of how his son perceived the world. But they—the parents—didn't argue or admonish; simply tried patiently to understand the truth of this outburst. Returning the ivory-coloured napkin to the table, Mallika Sengupta said: "No, I don't like this hotel either. It has no soul," she concluded determinedly; and the father, still strikingly handsome and kind-looking, fundamentally an optimist and a person of faith, faith in the future, nevertheless wondered at the spectacle of his son, and nodded tentatively in agreement. They pushed the chairs back and rose; Nirmalya had already reached the open doorway of the coffee shop.

Smiling, but with a conviction that they were doing the only logical and admissible thing, the Senguptas followed their son out, leaving the waiters puzzled, Mrs. Sengupta glancing tolerantly, without emotion, at the tray of cakes. They crossed the lobby, forfeiting the usual unconscious abandon and easy familiarity they felt when visiting beautiful, welcoming places in Bombay. The boy, in his faded pink kurta and jeans, was already outside in the heat, distant, self-enclosed, the wind tunnelling through the drive-way blowing into his hair, as he stood oddly adjacent to a gigantic Sikh doorman. "Nirmalya!" said his mother, coming out of the air conditioning and wiping her nose instinctively with a hanky, the merciless semi-developed expanses of Versova trembling in the heat; the Sikh doorman, an anachronistic but unignorable orna-ment, half-turned in her direction with an astonishing jerk of recognition and reassurance and smiled.

Shyamji wasn't well; he'd developed a cough. It interrupted him again and again like a hiccup that wouldn't go away.

"Shyamji, what is this?" asked Mrs. Sengupta suspiciously, looking up from the songbook; her antennae were always tuned to illnesses.

"I don't know, didi," said Shyamji, peeved but distant, as if he were in no way responsible for the tiresome interruption. "I don't have a sore throat."

"You should have it looked at."

Meanwhile, it had begun to rain. June had changed to July without much rainfall, with only, on most days, an expectant, oppressive heat which made the shadows the trees cast in Bandra seem so timeless and seductive; and now, it was suddenly raining in bursts, agitating and disorienting the birds on the balconies, dissolving into a false calm later in which one leaf dripped patiently on to another.

In the midst of this late-arriving, swirling pool of shadow and cloud and wind, Shyamji became, temporarily, a migrant, moving from one suburban location to another, staying with students in Khar or Juhu who wanted to give him space and respite from duties and family while they looked after his needs, while enriching, of course, their own store of songs and even their lives by being near him. Sometimes, Nirmalya and Mrs. Sengupta visited him at these places, getting out of the car after it had been parked on the side of a narrow lane in Khar, the road still moist and muddy with the print of tyre tracks after a brief shower, opening the gate, going in carefully, the scab-rough walls of the old house pale gold with the indecisive, intermittent sun, the small, mali-tended garden outside still wet, the flat leaves shivering with tiny rivulets of water, the bark of the tree seemingly dry and hard; as they approached the door, they could hear Shyamji singing with his students. A young Bengali family—two brothers and a sister—who had musical ambitions and had moved from Calcutta to Bombay for this reason, had rented this apartment.

"Aashun, aashun," cried the older brother when he saw Nirmalya and his mother hesitating at the doorway; because he was well aware they were Shyamji's students, and he knew them slightly.

The harmonium sighed as Shyamji hooked the bellows. "Aiye didi, aiye baba," he said. "Sit down here," he said softly, patting the white sheet that covered the bed. Although he wasn't in the best of health, he was intent on being hospitable; and though he was in a house his students had rented, it was as much his house—perhaps more his—as theirs.

He looked tired, but undemonstratively happy. The fragrance and breath of the rains was always a gift that delighted human beings, and Shyamji was no exception.

In two weeks, in spite of the niggling cough, he was back to accepting invitations and giving in to demands. He said:

"Didi, some people have been asking me to sing in a new Sindhi temple. Will you and baba also sing a song each? I don't want to sing all the songs myself with this cough. Besides, more people should listen to you, didi."

Mrs. Sengupta's role, in her married life, had usually been to sing a song or two on small occasions, after which someone, good-natured and anonymous, would lean towards her and murmur gravely, "I haven't heard a voice like that since Juthika Roy!"; praise that would leave her, each time, happy as a tender seventeen-year-old, but then, as the sense of her body and spirit in time returned to her, essentially unfulfilled. Yet she could never resist adding another nameless venue to the ones her singing-life in Bombay had been dotted with; she agreed now, feeling, in spite of herself, the transient little-girlish excitement and nervousness she always experienced at these moments.

"I must then prepare the song I have to sing," she said, to him but really to herself, very seriously. "Where is the temple?"

"Not far away, somewhere in Versova," he said. "But we will need a car." He'd recently sold the second-hand Fiat. "Will your car be free, didi?" he enquired very quickly, almost a random question. "If we could use it . . ."

Mrs. Sengupta felt a flash of impatience. Did Shyamji really want her to sing, or did he just want to use the car?

"Of course the car will be available," she said, like a fairy godmother speaking of what's most predictable and cursory among her enchantments; and Shyamji looked visibly gratified.

On the afternoon, they set out for the outer reaches of Versova. The macadam road cut deep into a landscape on which nothing much yet had come up, although, here and there, in the dark mud of the monsoons, they noticed the beginnings of construction; on and on they went, in the broad afternoon glare, the tall extinguished lampposts standing in the sun. Finally, the Ambassador, with its cargo of Shyamji, his brother Banwari, Mallika Sengupta, Nirmalya, and the harmonium and tablas secure on their straw rings in the boot, came to the Sindhi temple, which was made of marble; it came to a stop in the dust with a sudden reminiscent whiff of gasoline, the engine over-heated with the air conditioning. A tall, fair man in steel-rimmed spectacles and white kurta and Aligarhi pyjamas ran down the steps to welcome Shyamji, and swooped down on the car door like a melancholy bird: "Aiye, aiye Panditji." He was all humility; and he emphasised it by stooping and lowering his head slightly, drawing attention to his plangent bird-like poise. Everything about him and his clothes seemed fresh and laundered; Shyamji introduced Mrs. Sengupta to him as "my own didi," the wife of the burra sahib of a well-known company ("But you must listen to her sing," he said), and spoke softly of Nirmalya—with a hint of mischief, slyly mocking the obstreperous high-seriousness that the boy carried with him everywhere—as his "true disciple," "asli chela." The tall man nodded in amazement in the approaching dusk, and led them up the steps to where a group of people had been waiting for them, sitting patiently before a raised platform on which there was no human being yet, only an arrangement of microphones. They sat down; tablas and harmonium were brought and placed before them. Almost everyone was dressed in white; they ended up looking, these benign-seeming people, a bit like phantoms (they didn't mean to, of course), inhabiting, as the sun set, a place somewhere between mercantile activity and the afterlife. The new temple itself suggested a similar ambiguity; the white stone it was built from was meant to calm doubts about the everyday world, to suggest abnegation, purity, but to remind you, too, of the benediction of money, that the gods of the affluent demand to be housed expensively. There were no doors in this main area of congregation; and the absence of doorways gave what would otherwise have looked like a hotel lobby the spaciousness of worship. There were no doors, but there were large pillars; in the midst of all this, Mrs. Sengupta's voice, coming from the speaker (she had begun to sing), sounded almost like a child's; a child who had still not seen the world, who was still innocent, who still believed in simple rewards and just dispensations. The sweetness of the voice, and its lack of knowingness, surprised the listeners; the old women, hardened by material expectation, began to sing along softly, as if they'd been won over. Then, when she stopped, they smiled and murmured among themselves, letting her return to being who she was: they didn't want to know her name, as they would if she'd been a professional singer, but glanced sideways at her, at her sari and mascara and bangles, curious, but with no desire to interfere. Now, the boy, long-haired and uneasy, began to sing—an old Surdas bhajan, "Hé Govind, hé Gopal," at which everyone stirred with recognition. He sang quite sweetly, but they found it difficult to relax; he sang with his eyes squeezed tight, as if he were dropping from a great height. After he'd finished, Shyamji seemed to speak a word of encouragement—a "shabaash"—into his ear. The sky outside had reddened. As Shyamji began to sing to the soft background of his harmonium, Mallika Sengupta thought of where she was now, how far away from home, wherever home might be; how *this* was where home had been in the last thirty years, wherever her husband was, or her son, in Malabar Hill, in Cuffe Parade, in Pali Hill, in Versova, wherever she happened to be at that moment, how the old idea and sense of home had faded, and she'd allowed it to fade. Sitting inside the temple, she realised that no place was really alien any more. With part of her attention, she listened to Shyamji; these were the songs she sang away from home, these Hindi bhajans she'd been learning for the last thirty years. If she'd stayed at home, she might probably have sung other songs. Shyamji, now in his second bhajan, coughed twice; the cough irritated him, and he ignored it as he'd ignore a heckler. He cleared his throat, but the cough didn't seem to have anything to do with it; it came back intermittently. The audience didn't mind; Shyamji's music was, to them, anyway, less an aesthetic than a devotional experience; and the flame of their devotion wasn't so easily put out. Nirmalya noticed that the tall man, who looked about forty, who'd brought them in, was shaking his head and weeping copiously as Shyamji sang. It wasn't so much a public display as an outpouring of emotion among people whom he knew too well to feel embarrassed in front of. When Shyamji finally stopped after the fourth song, pointing sketchily to his throat and pleading with a smile to be let off because of his cough, the man swiftly returned to what he'd been like when he'd received Shyamji emerging from the car, normal, cheerful, even official, as if his sorrow had mysteriously faded, or as if he could manage to inhabit two planes of existence, on one of which he could surrender to mourning the pain of life, the other on which he polished his glasses, wore his ironed clothes, and cheerfully carried out all its duties. As the audience dispersed without urgency, he took these visitors, his characteristic graciousness restored, on a small, impromptu tour of the temple, to where the holy book (written, surprisingly, in the Arabic script) was kept, reminding Nirmalya, in a way that had never occurred to him, that the Sindhis were a people without a homeland. Finally, he led them to where boxes of sweets had been kept for them; and, no doubt, out of the sight of others, in a private, invisible moment that nevertheless must have elapsed, paid Shyamji discreetly. But Nirmalya was convinced this man did something terrible every day and that his guilt came back to him in moments like the one that Nirmalya, against his will, had just witnessed. Shyamji looked pleased the session had gone well, and that he'd had use of Mrs. Sengupta's car; though Nirmalya, glancing at the tranquil, slightly out of sorts expression on the face of the sick man, always found it difficult to guess at what his teacher was thinking, what it was he wanted.

Shyamji scratched his cheek (he was a bit untidy; fine needles of stubble spread across the dark skin, making it look almost purple) and told the Senguptas, at the end of another lesson, in a bored, throwaway remark of what had been diagnosed as the cause of the cough: water had collected in his lungs.

Mrs. Sengupta wasn't sure how serious this was; the condition was unfamiliar to her. Water in the lungs; what a nuisance—if it was taken out, would the cough go away? She wasn't unduly worried; Shyamji was in the thick of things, trailing exhaust fumes and traffic lights and junctions as he entered, having moved in an hour from one end of the city to another, gently pushing his hair back as he appeared in the doorway, preoccupied.

"Also, the blood sugar is high," he admitted shamefacedly, delicately lifting his kurta as he lowered himself on to the carpet; he always felt contrite when what he saw to be the superstitions of the educated about health—listen to what the doctor tells you, take your pills, do nothing in excess—when these superstitions proved right, and his own belief, his unspoken but absolute taking for granted of the fact that the supernatural would look out for him (a pale orange thread from a baba, a sort of supplement or insurance policy, was tied round his wrist) seemed, for some reason, not to have worked, at least not this time. Besides (and he didn't elaborate on this to Mrs. Sengupta), he'd been meeting families visiting Sagar Apartments to congratulate him and Sumati for the birth of their second grandson—born to their elder daughter in Delhi in May; how not to finish the rich red swirl of gajar ka halwa on the plate when you were thinking of your own flesh and blood?

"Shyamji!" she admonished him. "You've been eating sweets. Really, you people are so careless!" It wasn't clear whom she meant by "you people"—his family, or a wider category of the similarly blithe and faithful. But she took it up with Sumati when she saw her floating prevaricatingly in their flat in Sagar Apartments.

"Didi, look what's happened to your brother!" said Sumati, in mock consternation, as if discussing a wayward but absorbing child.

"Really, you must take this more seriously," said Mallika Sengupta, small but firm, trying to puncture Sumati's spontaneous attempts to inject levity into the everyday problems of existence. "He *must* take his medicines. And he must stop eating sweets. Jalebis and milk—nothing seems less appetising."

"Don't worry, didi," she replied, "I am going to become like Hitler"; and she became erect, her bangles shook as she drew her aanchal around her and adopted a stern posture, approximating the fierce man, the tiny moustache and the manic disciplinarianism.

"Take him to Dr. Samaddar," said Mrs. Sengupta. "See what he says."

A leading cardiologist on Peddar Road, ensconced in his chamber and standing up and looking out moodily, between receiving patients, at the traffic. She did not like thinking of him; six months ago, he'd examined Nirmalya, distant, avian, circling round him and zeroing in with his stethoscope.

Dr. Samaddar's "chamber" was not far, in fact, from where Motilalji lived—Motilalji, Sumati's elder brother, who'd taught

Mrs. Sengupta and, that morning many years ago, a bit hazy, for him, with alcohol, introduced Shyamji to her.

Sunil Samaddar was a disconcertingly quiet man. Dealing with people who believed he could perform miracles but didn't really listen to him had, to all appearances, tired him and left him largely immune to the unexpected; the great and undisappointingly regular amounts of money he earned each day from speaking the truth had probably made him a little cold.

He made Nirmalya, who loved to go on unhappy, poetic walks, but almost never ran, take the treadmill test; surprised into chasing something that was unattainable, in fact, nameless, the boy embarked on the run silent and unquestioning, stoic in his obscure errand; then, like a young soldier who's unsure of having already outlived his usefulness, he was stripped waist upward, led to one side of a room, and attached to an ECG, and then to the strange gulps and grunts of an echocardiogram; the gulps and grunts, Nirmalya realised (though Dr. Samaddar, hovering in his precise steel-framed spectacles, was ironical and taciturnly remonstrative as a teacher in a school), of his heart.

Seeing her son in this way, gleaming dully next to the machine, brought Mallika Sengupta close to tears; but she couldn't look away. All his promise was reduced to that thinness.

When the family of the Senguptas had recomposed itself before the doctor's table, he said with the clipped, ironical finality he seemed to say everything: "He'll need to have an operation."

They'd heard this before, but each time it thoroughly unsettled Apurva and Mallika Sengupta. Without moving an inch, they drew together silently, like a couple suddenly confronted with oncoming bad weather.

"What kind of operation?" asked Mr. Sengupta, his corporate self-possession not so easily humbled; there was hope until the doctor became more specific.

Dr. Samaddar, looking in a rehearsed way at the notepad

before him, spoke casually, as if he were reading out the name of a common commercial product:

"Open-heart surgery, of course. They're a dime a dozen these days."

Again, silence, and shock; as with all taboos, it was the temerity of mentioning it in what was almost approaching a social conversation that was more outrageous and unforgivable than the taboo itself.

"Does he have to be operated on straight away?" asked Mallika Sengupta, her eyes brimming in wordless reproach, but deliberately making her question an absurd one, and unanswerable in the affirmative. The doctor, though, was on to her game; dryly, he replied, barely tolerant of the nuisance that human emotions represented:

"Well, not straight away; I don't know what you mean by 'straight away'—but there's no getting around it. Better sooner than later. Shubhashya shigram. 'Haste is auspicious.' By forty, he'll *have* to be operated upon."

Forty, again, that magic number—it was as if a demon had begun to materialise, and had melted before it could become fully visible! Nirmalya's parents relaxed imperceptibly, without feeling any happier. But, by the time Nirmalya was forty, all sorts of new technologies would have sprung into existence, open-heart surgery would become obsolete (as they'd been hoping it would for almost twenty years now), like the 78 rpm record and ether (they had witnessed the demise of both), perhaps something as simple as a pill or an intravenous tube would perform the rescue and repair work, travelling like an emissary through the blood, as catheters did these days while performing more minor missions, and the heart, the human heart, would be released from its long history into new possibilities.

"No, they won't touch him," said Apurva Sengupta grimly as they drove down the slope of Peddar Road towards Haji Ali, past the Cadbury's building, which had stood there, incontrovertibly promising sweetness and the white goodness of a glass of milk a day, ever since they'd first arrived in Bombay—Nirmalya, sitting within earshot in the front of the car, absent-minded and calm, as if they were talking about someone else; a cousin or a twin. Neither livelihood nor life was as yet his concern; he still had, glancing from glinting windshield to dashboard to window to the vistas they were quickly passing, the freedom of his moods and startling intimations. Apurva Sengupta, though, spoke not just from paternal emotion, but from the authority of having been a successful man, of having his views listened to, of having run a large company, of knowing a thing or two about the computations that ensured (in conditions that provided little that was helpful or congenial) a company's longevity. He adjusted the knot of his tie irritably, full of a long-standing and ingrained certainty. He may have retired, but being an executive, a man in charge of other men, for so many years had given Apurva Sengupta a sense of conviction and moral weight.

Dr. Samaddar's examination of Shyamji was brief. Looking hesitant and politely suspicious, as if he wasn't sure (like a man who's been given enthusiastic but indecipherable street directions) that he'd arrived at the right place, Shyamji had entered the air-conditioned room with Mr. Sengupta. There he was, only partly at ease with the distinguished man in the black suit and neat striped tie who smelled pleasantly of aftershave. Dr. Samaddar regarded them speculatively.

"This is Pandit Shyam Lal," said Apurva Sengupta, smiling like one continuing an old, recognisable conversation, "a well-known singer. As I said to you on the phone, he's my wife's music teacher."

Dr. Samaddar nodded, as if to say he understood Mr. Sengupta's compulsions. But the nod was oddly premeditated; there was no real sign of memory—either of the dialogue on the telephone, or of Mr. Sengupta himself; memory was something of a misfit in this large room with its motionless framed certificates from fifties' London, and the small plastic figurine of the human heart on the table, its cheeks red and full, its arteries springing from the top stubby and incomplete, like sawn-off antlers. Then, without looking at Shyamji, all the while gazing at the flecked mosaic floor, the doctor listened to the singer's gentle, puzzled description, in Hindi, of his condition.

He gave no indication he'd understood what Shyamji had said. Speaking only one word, "Aiye," he led Shyamji to a high bed on one side of the room. There, as if they were miles away from Apurva Sengupta, the two faced each other in silence, Shyamji, who had perched himself on the bed, then taken off his kurta, and Dr. Samaddar, who stood before him, listening to his heartbeat. Head bowed, in silence; never seeming to actually see the singer, not even when he stared fixedly for a few moments at the dark chest traversed diagonally by the sacred thread or the mournful, patient face, regarding them with the glazed, other-worldly air of someone looking at his reflection in the morning. The stethoscope moving nervously from spot to spot. Apurva Sengupta looked out of the window; he had a great, albeit easily underestimated, capacity for patience, a quality that had been useful to him—more useful even than his skills, his various professional qualifications—from the beginning of his working life. It had given him something that was surprising in one who'd had material success; or perhaps successful people needed to have it more than others: something resembling selflessness. He seemed to be thinking of nothing at all, to be bereft of all sense of boredom, while Dr. Samaddar carefully attached the nodes of the ECG to Shyamji.

Later, unperturbed, the doctor addressed Apurva Sengupta: "Pleurisy hoyechhe."

Mr. Sengupta was surprised by this unconscious—or was it quite deliberate—slip into Bengali. Dr. Samaddar had never claimed any kinship with him; they'd both ignored the fact that they were Bengalis, and had, with one another, opted for the neutrality, the comforting even keel, of English. Now, in the presence of the man sitting on the bed and pushing the silver buttons into the buttonholes of his kurta, it was as if they were suddenly old friends, or something else—who knew? Apurva Sengupta had misgivings about what this meant.

"If we put him in Jaslok"—he gestured to the hospital towering silently on the other side of the road—"we could give him a few more months."

Apurva Sengupta—unexercised; in the generally benign, reasonable mood he experienced when engaged in transactions with others who were as successful in their own fields as he was in his—didn't understand what he meant by "a few more months"; but, because Dr. Samaddar hadn't broken any bad news to him, as he'd threatened to in the case of his own son, he didn't ask for a clarification, and let it pass. In his mind, the doctor's words were transformed to something like—"If we put him in Jaslok, we could make him better in a few months"—or a similar sentence, one that he could understand perfectly and do business with. Shyamji had begun to look unhappy, though, as if Dr. Samaddar were conspiring to force him to break some religious taboo, or to eat meat. He distrusted, fundamentally, allopathic medicine; distrusted it because, in the end, it saved very few, and because he had a hunch that its bases, like the lives of so many of the well-off, were irreligious; and you couldn't be saved unless the means were, in some way, connected to the sacred, and the sacred itself wanted the continuance of your life and good health. He felt detached and impatient, but he sat on the chair, dignified, contained; he wanted to go home.

"What about the cost?" asked Apurva Sengupta.

"I'm a consultant there, I'll take care of it," muttered Dr. Samaddar, as if he were worried his gesture might be mistaken for weakness.

Jaslok Hospital was where Pandit Ram Lal had been admitted twelve years ago, after he'd had two strokes, the second in the taxi in Mulund, groaning "Hé bhagwan" like a saint, full of compassion and endurance even in his suffering, while younger, agitated incarnations of Pyarelal and Shyamji flanked him on either side; the third seizure occurred as he was being bundled into his room in Jaslok—this dark, teeming factory of the living and partially living, with the much-garlanded statue of Ganesh at the entrance, was associated forever for Shyamji with his father's death. Whenever he went past it on Peddar Road, he averted his eyes; often, he wasn't even aware of doing so. Ram Lal had died there, in one of those numberless rooms whose windows were opened very occasionally and hesitantly to let in the sound of the traffic, after a week.

"Sengupta saab," Shyamji said in a couple of days, apologetic, but with the conviction of someone who's finally opened a locked door, and seen something irrefutable, "I cannot go to that hospital."

Nevertheless, he continued teaching; the procession of students and petitioner-relatives entering through the open door a flat permeated with kitchen smells and telephone calls at 10 a.m. The bedsheet-wrapped divan in the sitting room in Sagar Apartments became the place where everyone converged, while the family and the flat orbited around the hour of instruction almost unaware of it. It was not so much a sick-bed as a place of instruction and recovery, the pillow an accessory to a moment of comfort, when Shyamji drew back, relieved, to lean against it. Sometimes, there was no harmonium at all; just singing, and the clapping of hands, as Shyamji, like a magician, brought his naked palms together, always urging the student, made meek but attentive by the very sound of the clapping, to keep abreast of the laya and not to stray from the time-signature. Sitting there in his vest and pyjamas, the laundered white cotton innocently tight against the dark skin, humming briefly to refresh his memory, talking rapidly to justify and explain a new composition, as smells of simmering plantain and cardamom and cinnamon bark dropped into hot oil merged with the kitchen smoke, he was still at the centre of things that constituted his world: news of the city and its changing constellation of politicians, gossip about his students' careers, and the latest on the grapevine about rising property prices. A copy of the *Navbharat Times* lay often on the divan, momentarily neglected. On a small wooden table was a bottle of water, a glass (usually covered by a plastic coaster) freely leaving its faint ring-marks around it, and an economical clutter of pills. He was a marvellous layakar; it was an instinct and genius he'd inherited from the nervous, febrile Ram Lal, a master of the rhythmic permutations of classical music; and so the melee of the flat was always bright with the sound of clapping, and short-lived jubilation and finality. That active, irrepressible brain, running toward every avenue and neighbourhood and opportunity like a dealer with a new product, would compute, in quick succession, the syllables of a composition set to ektaal as well as the interest he'd earn from an investment he'd made a year ago, how much time it would take to pay back the money he'd borrowed recently from a businessman-devotee of the mother Amba, how much this flat would be worth after six months if property prices rose steadily, until, repositioning his pillow, sighing as if after a performance, he curled up on his side and closed his eyes for one hour in the strange, absolute nullity of the afternoon.

Life is a longing for betterment: in that sense, Shyamji was very much alive; he'd sold the second-hand Fiat, but he wanted another car now, one that wouldn't stop and start in bursts and would lift him from his recent, expensive dependence on autos and taxis. But, even at home, suddenly drained of energy and interest, he sometimes lay on his side when teaching a young man who might have journeyed all the way from Marine Lines, the perspiration and heat of the city surrounding him like a nagging but, for the present, bygone impediment, Shyamji propped patiently on an elbow, studying the young arrival with concern, cheek resting against the palm of a hand. He managed to sing from this almost horizontal position, crushing the pillow with his elbow, and kept time by snapping his fingers; of course, Ram Lal's stern portrait, which had moved from King's Circle to Borivli to, now, the wall on the left, the same rose-backgrounded picture that was garlanded and placed at a respectful angle on the stage during the Gandharva Sammelans—the face in this portrait seemed unable to comprehend so much movement, all this recent burgeoning of possibility and material well-being, and the vaguely familiar figure of the sick man, and it seemed to have resigned itself to its location, where it was indispensable, but essentially unnoticed. "Theek hai, let's go over it again," the recumbent Shyamji would sigh at last to the shy, obedient man sitting erect before him. Oddly, disconcertingly, he felt perfectly well when he sang, and this made him briefly doubt both his and everyone else's judgement; something to do with the miracle of song and its pleasure, which, whatever the context, seemed to recognise neither age nor fatigue nor disease, but only its complete union with, and absolute necessity to, the world.

Nirmalya went to him one month before leaving for London, when he was in a state at once valedictory and dutiful and strangely distracted; he kept putting off appointments with Shyamji, but one morning set out without explanation in the Ambassador, a new, inarticulate driver at the wheel, Nirmalya placing, with a mixture of self-consciousness and ironic abandon, the Panasonic two-in-one beside him at the back. His mission was to tape some new compositions and ragas from his guru, to take them with him to the faraway but not entirely unfamiliar country he'd be flying to—something he could practise with for the next eight or nine months, after which he hoped to return home for his vacations. None of this was going to be necessarily spelt out to Shyamji; but clearly this was what was on Nirmalya's mind. It had rained earlier; and the tyres made a minute grinding noise as the car entered the environs of Sagar Apartments, the not quite pukka driveway moist and red and dark, the rubble and bricks of nascent construction projects piled randomly in heaps on its borders. It was rumoured that Rajesh Khanna had booked a property in one of these forthcoming constructions; and though Rajesh Khanna was no longer the kurta-wearing, head-flicking, cherry-lipped beau he once used to be, this piece of unconfirmed information had still raised the esteem of Sagar Apartments in the eyes of Shyamji's family and others. Walking into the flat, Nirmalya found Shyamji with a handsome young ghazal singer in a flowery shirt; he was called Abhijit, a man of some, but not great, talent, who was trying desperately to get a break as a playback singer in films.

"Shyamji," Nirmalya said shyly when there was, at last, a pause in the proceedings, "I want to tape some new compositions." And he angled the Panasonic like an awkward object between himself and the harmonium.

"Do you have Shankara?" asked Shyamji, running his hands through his oiled hair, expansive and grand at this change of register from the common or garden ghazal he'd been teaching to the rarely-visited, flamboyant raga; and when the boy shook his head, he said almost with a kind of glee, "Theek hai, I'll give you a composition in Shankara. But you'll have to practise hard to get it right." And as an afterthought, "I'll also give you Adana. You don't have Adana, do you?" Then, with a look of minor incredulity and puzzlement, as if he'd only just remembered, he asked with a child's ingenuousness: "Baba, when are you leaving?"

"On the twenty-eighth of next month," hummed Nirmalya, shy, holding back, always nervous, in company, of being listened to and noticed.

But Abhijit had, with a disarming matter-of-factness, switched off from the rather highbrow conversation about ragas and international travel, and was crooning a ghazal—not the one he'd just been learning; another one—in an undertone. He was obviously profligate with songs. He was respectfully uninterested in classical music; let the knowledgeable pursue knowledge; what he was after was, simply, melody and success. Someone had told him that his name itself, "Abhijit," had the right sound and weight, the potential to be put into popular circulation; and he now had a quiet faith in his name, and said it undemonstratively but significantly when someone asked him what it was. Glancing once or twice in the direction of the teacher in his vest and the tongue-tied but clearly eager young man, whom he'd met in this flat a couple of times before, he noted with knowing amusement Nirmalya's shabby clothes, already perfectly aware that Nirmalya was a "big officer's" son; Abhijit himself was, of course, always particular about the shirts he wore, and looked quite the hero. Nirmalya, though, was so unremarkably turned out and unprepossessing that it became impossible not to notice him. As he sat down on a chair Abhijit laughed and said:

"Look how simply he dresses!" and shook his head almost fondly—because Nirmalya was wearing a kurta that was torn near the pocket. It was a kurta Nirmalya felt comfortable in, for the last four or five years now he'd been inhabiting some of his clothes as if they were something between skin and makeshift private territory, so close was he to them that he became unaware of their fading materiality, they faded into him, almost—he was now in a kurta that he'd worn, as usual, too often.

Shyamji nodded briskly, and murmured, while positioning the tape recorder away from the bellows of the harmonium and before him, "Woh sant hai"—invoking the old word, which was used of saints and poets and the mad or unworldly. Abhijit smiled; he had light cat-like eyes, and they gleamed in pleasure and in crystalline agreement. Shyamji wasn't mocking Nirmalya; "Is the tape in place?" he asked, almost woeful, looking up from the mysterious, stealthy window of the TDK cassette. He found Nirmalya odd, and his disdain of the whirl and glitter of the city a bit tiresome. He hadn't been able to understand it. He couldn't quite see why the boy had to make it a point to head in a direction quite different from the world he'd been fortunate enough to be born into; it was childishness, that's what it was: once or twice, he'd wanted to say to him, Why, baba, aren't your parents good enough for you? Isn't what they gave you good enough? And to add in a tone of guidance and patience, Be happy, baba, that you're blessed with what you have. But in the last two or three months, he'd become strangely indulgent towards the boy; and, though he hardly thought about it or spent time comprehending it, something about him moved Shyamji against his will. There had been a loosening within, a gradual breaking down of a barrier that had circumscribed, without Shyam Lal even knowing it, everything he'd done; and this change, this forgiving erosion, had expressed itself in his sudden urge to give to the boy whatever compositions he demanded so quietly but insistently, set to these magnificent, ever-returning ragas, ragas you thought you could do without for the time being, but which had a way of coming back to you, the compositions his father had once created and dazzled his listeners with, and which Shyamji imparted to his students with the utmost evasiveness and pusillanimity.

Eyes closed, his face young and tranquil, as it always was during these opening phrases, Shyamji began to sing Shankara into the small whorl of the microphone. Nirmalya and Abhijit sat, one on a chair and the other on a razai rug, and listened; the older student smiling, quite open to being moved and nudged by the unexpected incursion of the notes of a raga. Nirmalya frowned in concentration, as if he couldn't hear properly, or as if he was trying seriously to shut out the sounds coming from the kitchen or the compound of Sagar Apartments. Of course, Shyamji had probably misunderstood him—just as Nirmalya had often misunderstood Shyamji, reverencing the artist with preconceived but urgent notions of what an artist's life and behaviour must be like: he'd constructed and created his own Shyamji, and had been bemused and exacting when, again and again, the two Shyamjis had failed to come together. Similarly, it was possible Shyamji had misunderstood his young, politely obdurate student; had mistaken the tear above the pocket for a genuine sign of renunciation. Maybe, not having quite entered the world of the young in Malabar Hill and Altamount Road and Colaba (his own son's world was noticeably different), he didn't see that it was an affectation, a necessary phase that some of the children of the rich pass through. Or maybe he'd taken all those ambiguities into account recently and still decided that, in his eyes, Nirmalya was an unusual and uncharacteristic sort of young man.

"What can you do with a man who won't be treated?"

Mr. Sengupta shook his head and smiled; in a post-retirement moment on Saturday morning, having a cup of tea with his wife in the small but spruce drawing room (the Sea Lounge was too far away these days to drive to every weekend), he was speaking (stirring the sugar in the mild infusion) as he always had, as the voice of sanity and reasonableness. And this was partly why Mrs. Sengupta found in him such an anchor, an axis around which her universe turned; because sanity and reasonableness were binding, but were so hard to find.

In the Sea Lounge, they'd cover topics from the banal to the most worrying, as, one by one, portions of chilli cheese toast disappeared from the plate, and replenishments of Darjeeling tea were poured. Now, with the same lingering mixture of concern and aimlessness, they discussed how someone who had a problem and had been offered a solution to it could reject that solution so easily out of hand. What kind of a man was this, paralysed, at the end of the twentieth century, by the sort of absurd superstition they'd seen around them, and left behind, as children? Sipping their tea, they became momentarily silent, experiencing an obstinate knot of irritation and pity, while exhortatory birdcall and human voices burst into the drawing room from the balcony on the right.

But Apurva Sengupta hadn't quite washed his hands of Shyamji; he was defeated, for the time being, by his soft-spoken intransigence. To not want to be admitted into a private hospital free of cost because his father had died there . . . he couldn't take it seriously; he would persuade Shyamji. But not now, there was no point in coercion; he'd put it off for a few days.

Pyarelal was concerned; at least, he looked more worried than Shyamji's family did. Part of the reason was that he disagreed with the family he'd married into on everything; and this exhibition of concern was seen as a further instance of making trouble, of being negative and perverse in what was, on the whole, an optimistic, well-networked period for Shyam Lal, of—and this was the most characteristic Pyarelal-like vice—drawing attention to himself.

"These fools!" he complained to Nirmalya with the contempt of the clear-sighted. "They talk about movies and that minister's son and this new hotel." Then, with a preoccupied, martyred look, he pushed at a bad tooth with his tongue.

After which, satisfied with his prodding, he added, his mood changing at once to exasperation and comedy:

"He sings that song at the end of each programme. The boring Kabir bhajan: 'At least see to it, lord,/that when my life leaves my body,/I have the name of Govind on my lips.' Do you know what Durgaji"—referring to a relative, a fairly well-known singer of qawwalis—"calls it?" He grinned; then was wracked immediately by a beedi-smoker's cough; but he shook off the tremor that passed through his body in a businesslike way, as if it had happened to someone else, and resumed: "He calls it 'Shyam's national anthem.' " He looked at Nirmalya, a look of irony and entreaty exchanged among partners with similar persuasions and agendas. "Arrey, tell him to stop singing it, baba"—for he'd really had enough of the tearful paean.

Although, like everyone else, Pyarelal believed it was only a matter of time before his brother-in-law was better, he'd begun to feel a subterranean fear; was it an intuition of the end? It came to him in the middle of the tedious and demanding everyday, while scratching his stubble or nagging at a tooth, or boarding a BEST double-decker in the afternoon, standing at attention with a self-conscious jerk of the head if he didn't get a seat, this unsettling intimation of the void. But it didn't last long; Bombay said to him, as the bus lurched ahead: "Don't be silly. Life goes on; it has always gone on." But then, when he'd finally found a seat, there might be a delay; the bus coming to a halt, the cars next to it frozen, their occupants' elbows sticking resignedly out of the windows; impatient, grandiosely peremptory, always as if he were playing a part, he'd glance at his steel-banded wristwatch, shake his head; then—thank God!—the bus would begin to inch forward, and menacingly approach, then pass by, a roadside congregation of people, strangely, for the most part, focussed and silent; an accident, the windshield of the Fiat was smashed; this time, there was no intimation, no premonition, just the urge to return to, as soon as possible, the homeward-bound traffic, a quick averting of the eyes and the obligatory muttering of a prayer for no one—no one known, encountered, or imagined—another solitary, wondering shake of the head (again, as if an audience were looking), and the perspiration on the forehead drying as the bus picked up speed and a sea-breeze blustered in through the window. So Pyarelal, in his better moments humming a film tune that had been following him persistently all day, returned home.

The suitcase had been packed: the deep, folded layer of winter clothes, a dark suit that Nirmalya had vowed never to wear, small and diminished inside the suitcase, but possessing, nevertheless, a buttoned-up authority even without a body inside it, trousers—including a couple of frayed, disintegrating corduroys that his mother had at first slyly neglected to put in, and which he'd had to bargain for, with the steely persuasiveness of a counsel and, finally, the relentlessness of a madman. Into the smaller suitcase went *The Story of Philosophy*, with its psychedelic borders in yellow and orange and blue, the strip of black along the bottom of the jacket, and the comforting, pain-numbing mantra of names on the back, Kant, Schopenhauer, Nietzsche, Santayana; it was a book he'd outgrown since he'd picked it up from a shelf in a bookshop three years ago, but he still needed it as a pacifier. The cheap, commercial binding that held together these great lives and speculations was falling apart; page one hundred and seventeen, from the chapter on Francis Bacon, which he'd glanced at and skipped, had dislodged itself in protest. Yet, armed with Will Durant, although he felt—had always felt, really—somewhat superior to him, to his success, to his solemn trust in Western civilisation, to his somewhat gauche devotion to his wife, proclaimed on the second page—armed with Will Durant, he still hoped to make the journey into the unknown and into deliverance.

He hadn't finished discovering Bandra. It was here, as he circled the roads with their cottages, the courtyards swept and empty and the gardens overgrown with weeds and flowers, or came up against a stone cross or the warm wall of a church, it was here that his fierce world-denying self began to understand the pleasures of the earthly. Strange that he should embrace the earthly amidst so many signs of transcendence: the cross, the church. But this is what Bandra meant to him.

His father too, and his mother—how different they were in this location! They were the same as ever, of course; but he felt they were more his own now. The grey that had slowly appeared in his mother's hair in the last few years was only visible if you looked hard at it; otherwise, she was changeless. But she liked the quaintness of these environs; "It reminds me of the town in which I grew up," she said, not elaborating.

When it rained here, you were aware not only of the rain, but of the other houses, the lane itself, the trees: the disappearing, panicky birdcall, the creak of a gate, loitering schoolboys breaking into a run. And, after the shower, the gulmohur blossoms would have fallen from branches on certain parts of the road with a particular exactness and economy, precise carpets of bright red only in those sections of the lane where the gulmohur trees stood, then, an hour later, becoming pink, then, after another hour, a soiled pink fading into the tarmac's perennial, unsentimental grey. Inside, of course, the household duties of cooking, cleaning, changing bedsheets, were always unobstreperously unfolding. He was going to leave his parents quite tranquil in these surroundings; they seemed, temporarily, like long-standing citizens of these lanes; they appeared to feel no loss for the Bombay they'd left behind, and would never return to now except for a previously decided and pondered-upon part of the day.

The building his father had bought the flat in had risen, naturally, where a cottage had stood once; so, in a sense, they were a part of the change that was now coming to this lane, as were the others who'd bought flats in the building. Most of the Senguptas' neighbours were Sindhis—toughened by hard work and migration, but also boisterous and benign with new money. Mr. and Mrs. Sengupta were on cordial terms with them; but, the moment they entered their own flat, their neighbours hardly existed, and their world, instead of closing in and becoming a microcosm, expanded idiosyncratically through the windows and balcony, embracing the old houses opposite, the lanes that ran parallel to theirs, and the invisible horizon. Nirmalya didn't really mind the families who lived opposite or on the other floors, he liked them for their openness; he liked them better than the polished, cocky corporate types he'd grown up among. But he wasn't always sure whether to be amused or affronted by their taste and their sense of display.

A week was all that remained for his departure; and a friend, Mihir, who'd been with him in school and was studying for an engineering degree in Calcutta, had, unxpectedly, made enquiries about his address and come to visit. His childhood was splintering now; different elements of it were being blown towards directions and places that were unthinkable then; and it always surprised him when one of those splinters returned to him, and took the trouble to look him up.

"You sort of dropped out of circulation, yaar," Mihir said, as they stood in patient, forbearing camaraderie on the balcony. "But I thought I'd find out what you're doing these days." He chuckled, as if taken aback by an act of transgression from a person he'd always suspected was capable of anything. "I didn't realise you were off to the UK."

"What are your own plans?" asked Nirmalya—partly because they were at the stage of their lives when "plans" were important, when everyone around him was working overtime on a sifting and sorting out of destinies; but also because he'd reached that age when he was curious whether old, rapidly anachronistic friendships could be turned into alliances, when he'd realised that allies had become more important to him than friends. Yet, for all his hints, he had few friends, and even fewer allies. "Joining an engineering firm—going abroad?"

"Probably do management," said Mihir, embarrassed and aggressive at once, because they'd wanted to be poets and artists two years ago, adding, "Philosophy-tilosophy is not for me."

"I thought you were quite interested in it," Nirmalya reminded him, anxious that the undefined cause had lost, again, a possible recruit, but confirmed in his own singularity.

"Oh, that's OK to *patao* the chicks!" laughed Mihir loudly, vastly amused that anyone could think it had another purpose; and Nirmalya laughed too, at the validity of the suggestion, slightly apologetic that he hadn't pursued its ample possibilities.

They were startled from their lugubrious sharing of thoughts by firecrackers. "Gosh!" said Mihir; for a simple bang had woken him up to where he was. People Nirmalya knew vaguely by sight were rushing out of the porch, laughing breathlessly, long, festive kurtas shimmering, setting alight coils of serpent-like firecrackers that then exploded, in a rapid series of white flashes and spent smoke, deafeningly and endlessly. When one coil had burnt itself out, or even before, a tall young man would light another and, giggling as if at an old man's unintimidating scolding, jump away as it began to go off.

"Shit," said Mihir, trying to ignore the noise suavely, like an officer in the middle of artillery, "that's black money, you know."

The fragrance of burning crackers filled their nostrils. A man in a radiant sherwani and turban—the younger son of a family that lived on the second floor, transformed without forewarning into a bridegroom—walked stiffly towards a nervous but obedient horse that had appeared in the lane, and mounted it. Nirmalya was about to speak, but a fresh burst of crackers took his breath away; pigeons, now almost accustomed to the general atmosphere of disturbance, took off again lazily from the neighbouring mango tree.

"This is what the Jews must have been like," said Mihir, his youthful, good-natured face (he wasn't handsome, but something about him drew you to him) expressionless with irony, leaning on the bannister as they watched the family dancing in the lane, "before the Nazis came along."

Nirmalya, already silenced by the crackers, was made speechless by the observation. A great gust of history seemed to blow towards him, threatening to spoil the idyll, but passed him by without harming him. What exactly did Mihir have on his mind; and in his heart? The fanfare, in its own quite organised way, moved left, probably towards some hall where the wedding would take place; the bridegroom, his face now covered by the screen of flowers dangling from the turban, sat still and lifeless on the horse, while the revellers, snapping their fingers and dancing round him, kept drawing more and more family members, the ones staying aloof and dignified in the background, into the dance; and it took these initiates only a second or two to cast off their aloofness and dignity, and to be converted to the pleasure of being a public spectacle. How many times in their life would they be asked to dance, after all? The horse would have looked ancient and fairy-tale-like, had it not been conveying, in spite of itself, its very animal discomfiture and unsureness to the onlooker. It was a relief to finally see it go, and the euphoric humans as well, towards the wedding. "Beautiful place," said Mihir, when it was quiet again (only the two latecomers, plump fifteen-year-old girls in gleaming white silk dresses, ran out to the lane to search for the lost party). "Your parents are lucky to have a flat here." Glancing cannily at Nirmalya, he added: "So much nicer than Cuffe Parade—don't like Cuffe Parade at all." They lingered on the balcony for ten minutes, letting the scene, the lane, the trees, melt into twilight. Nirmalya felt a strange pang: it was more time he wanted, he half-realised, without the desire really breaking to the surface; a little more time to be with Mihir, more time before going to England, more time for the day itself to last. He mourned the fact that the day could not be longer.

Two days after he'd left, Shyamji came to the Senguptas' flat. The curtains were parted to let in the hot, bright light of early October.

"What, has baba gone?" he asked, looking slowly around him, as if the boy just might materialise from behind the furniture.

Although he was so dark, his face was pale and scourged this morning, as if he'd powdered it; his feet, beneath his pyjamas, seemed to be swollen. He hobbled comically into the sitting room scattered with curios and pristine ashtrays.

"Oh, he reached there day before yesterday," Mallika Sengupta said—it was almost an announcement; not just for Shyamji, but for the world, if it cared to listen. "We spoke for a short while on the telephone . . ." She went into a momentary reverie. "The flat is so quiet now." Bleary-eyed, she asked—for her sleep had gone awry ever since she'd waited, in the airport, for Nirmalya to be airborne at three in the morning; she'd woken up yesterday and today at half past three, her mind on fire as she wondered where her son would be twenty years from now, eyes shut, determined not to notice the dawn stealthily coming to the windows—"Shyamji, will you have some tea before we start?"

Shyamji, who looked like he hadn't been sleeping too well himself, his cheeks puffy, frowned as if he'd been challenged and said: "Why not, didi?"

So cups, trembling faintly, and the pot and strainer were brought to the sitting room on a wooden tray, and they sat, at eleven o'clock in the morning, the mother, sombre with reminiscence, and her teacher, drinking tea without any milk in it, each cup made wonderfully palatable with a sachet of Equal.

"You know, he said to me on the phone day before yesterday, 'Tell Shyamji to be careful. He isn't looking too well.' "

Shyamji sipped his tea, smiled ruefully: "He is my biggest critic. He keeps a stern eye on me."

It was true; had been true in the last four years, with those recurrent queries made in the glassy whirl of life in Cuffe Parade. Nirmalya's frequent, awkward questions to Shyamji—"Why don't you sing more classical?"—his high-minded disenchantment, from the transcendent vantage-point of Thacker Towers, with the music scene—"Why are bhajans and ghazals sung in this cheap way these days?"—had earned him a nickname, "the critic." It was a bit of leg-pulling; Nirmalya enjoyed it. "Baba is a big critic," Shyamji would say, pretending to be very thoughtful. And yet Nirmalya, in this incarnation, had managed to make him slightly uneasy. A couple of years ago, late one morning in Thacker Towers, the boy, with obviously no real anxieties to plague him, had asked, genuinely exercised, "Why don't you sing classical more often?" and Shyamji had tried explaining, with a patience he reserved for the pure-hearted but naive, "Baba, you cannot practise art on an empty stomach. Let me make enough money from these lighter forms; and then I'll be able to devote myself entirely to classical." A perfectly workable blueprint. But, to Shyamji's discomfort, "the critic" had not replied, but looked at him beady-eyed, as if to say, with a seventeen-year-old's moral simplicity and fierce dogmatic conviction: "That moment will never come. The moment to give yourself to your art is now."

Jumna—this woman who'd come to their house seventeen years ago as a cleaner of bathrooms, elegant, measured, twenty-six, whom Mrs. Sengupta, in the first flush of company life, had pronounced a "cultured woman, more cultured than the women I meet at parties"—this Jumna, already tired and resigned before she'd touched the jhadu, sat down on her haunches on the sitting-room carpet. One small eye sparkled with moisture. She'd been coming late every day for a month, the ends of her sari trailing behind her as she swept guiltily in like a phantom at eleven o'clock; Mrs. Sengupta was not happy with her.

"Memsaab," said Jumna, trying to reason with this familiar person shaking her head who was part employer, part perhaps comrade, "it's too long a distance from Mahalaxmi to this part of the city. Bahut vanda hota hai—too much hassle. Why cause all this gichir-michir and gussa? Let me retire now, memsaab."

Her hair was all grey, the metal strands falling on both sides of the parting and gathered at the back—this woman to whom Mallika Sengupta often used to turn, in the sea-facing heaven of La Terrasse, for solace, of whom she used to think, "Well, in some ways she's luckier than I am."

She sat before her on her haunches, patient in her campaign.

"What are you saying, Jumna," said Mrs. Sengupta, hardly listening. "How can you give up a good job in this way? Do you think they're to be plucked from trees? And you're much younger than I am."

She said this complacent in the knowledge that she looked so much younger than Jumna; time hadn't hurt her substantially since the flash had gone off in the studio in 1971 and illuminated that face with two surreptitious pearl-like crooked teeth and the fashionable dangling earrings falling from the earlobes; and Jumna (who'd circled that photograph and dusted it many times) knew it was only appropriate that this should be so, knew, without envy, that Mrs. Sengupta had been blessed by the powers that governed lives (it was enough, for her, to have come into contact with such a being), and she now indulged, as she always did, Mrs. Sengupta's blitheness. As a rule, the poor age more quickly than the affluent; time, and life, move, for them, at another pace, "like a relapse after a long illness." In fact, Jumna's eldest son, after joining Jaslok Hospital as a sweeper two years ago—temporary employment, but imminently to be made permanent ("You must educate your children," the ten-year-old Nirmalya, who quailed at the thought of school, once preached to Jumna; but her son had, in a doomed, helpless way, dropped out of his municipal school in the seventh standard)—this son had contracted jaundice and died a year ago. The awful husband—"Your sufferings in this birth will probably make your next birth a happy one," Nirmalya had instructed her when he was seven—that lame bewda who'd knocked out her teeth and drenched her with kerosene, intent to set fire to her one night: he too had died, hunted down by cirrhosis, two years ago. Now Jumna had had enough of making that tedious journey from Mahalaxmi; her left eyelid closed upon moisture; she wanted to go to the free optician for a pair of long-awaited spectacles.

"I'll find employment in the city," she reassured her unconvinced employer, and then, like a charm against refusal, reiterated a by-now ancient, barely-respected excuse. "The train to Bandra takes long, and sometimes I miss the train."

He kept going to the window of the little room, almost habituated now to its odd smell of carpet and fittings and the faint hovering ghost of a cigarette smoker; it was a concourse of people he wanted to see, but each time found other windows reflecting the modest light, and a courtyard on which it rained often. From the beginning, he was struck by the excess of silence; and he began to realise that his famous love of solitude was not real, that he loved company and noise much more than his own thoughts. He ate badly; half-eaten green apples, bitten into without pleasure, were thrown into the waste-paper basket; he went into the kitchen like a mouse at three o'clock in the afternoon, when there was no one else there, and put a Ginsters' Cornish pasty into the oven. It smelled awful; but it was an absurdly, almost cheeringly, simple solution, and the rank but appetising smell made him impatient with hunger; the first bite always burnt his lips. Later, dead with solitariness, he switched on the kettle to make himself a cup of tea, its rumble growing like an approaching storm and chastising him and making him nervous, until the entire room filled with its roar. He needn't have worried; it became silent, like everything else, including the plumbing behind the walls—where, as a matter of fact, the real pulsations of the place seemed to be hidden. The steam emerging from the spout pleased him; as any signal of life, even from things not really alive, had begun to please him.

Disturbingly free, for a student, of a plan of action or an impending deadline, he poured the water into a mug and watched the colour swim away unhurriedly from a tea bag.

He was unhappy—and undecided for the first ten days about practising. "At least I'm alone in this room," he thought, granting himself the luxury of asking for the one hundredth time, "What on earth possessed me to come to this country?" He'd always envied Goopy and Bagha, the two buffoons, for their magic nagra shoes, which could transport them in an instant from one kingdom to another; London made him ache with such impossible longings. And just when he'd grown used to listening to the silence and its thin, unvarying pitch, he heard, one grey afternoon, his neighbour in the next room, coughing. Nirmalya was trapped; he froze at his table; his heart plummeted suddenly. The cocoon-like fabric of rumination and subterfuge he'd spun around himself in the first week was unravelled by this bodiless presence, whom he couldn't see, but who became, in his or her ordinariness, a focus of Nirmalya's suspicions and speculations. For an interminable fifteen minutes after hearing the solitary, but astonishingly candid, cough, Nirmalya kept very quiet, newly aware of every sound. The changing light from morning to afternoon, as he sat petrified in his room, took on a despondent significance.

Then he ran into his neighbour in the corridor at midday, and saw he'd been imagining a monster. A large, chunky, brown-haired man stuffed unevenly into a sweater like a pillow in a pillowcase, he'd clearly just woken up, and was on his way to do something necessary in the toilet. "Hello," he nodded to Nirmalya, his hair ravaged and made untidy with sleep, his freckled face full of a simple, childlike trust as he made his way through the corridor.

. . .

Tentatively, Nirmalya began to sing; hitting the sa, but no more than murmuring the note, feeling foolish too, afraid, almost, of being thought mad. Like many other singers, he too, in an unthinking ritual, took off his wristwatch and placed it beside himself before he began, as if he were about to dive into water, or embark on a journey for which there must be some form of material evidence and record; the white dial, he noticed, sighing deeply from the pressure of some unspecified responsibility, said five past ten. He began with the Asavari composition Shyamji had sung for him once, which then, quickly bringing out the two-in-one, he'd taped, then run over in secret with the maternally nurturing Pyarelal, a sweet, melancholy piece. Outside his window, the sun was waning; a very different sun from the one he was used to. What sense, he asked himself, does it make to sing Asavari here? Yet he steeled himself, his voice much louder, magnified, in the deceptive late-morning hall-of-residence silence.

His tutor, a middle-aged man in a tweed jacket, grey-black hair combed back to announce a thinker's forehead (his name was Dickinson, an elegant interlocutor who seemed, on principle, not to have produced anything of note), wanted to cure Nirmalya of his philosophical hunger. He responded to his intensity with a cup of tea and a tin of biscuits, never forgetting to round this off with the question that effectively stemmed the questions his student might have asked: "Sugar?" He approached Nirmalya's unspoken sense of civilisational crisis as a doctor might a hypochondriac's ailment, wryly, warily, not wishing in any way to offend. "Existence is not the chief problem of philosophy," he said, tolerant, good-humoured, as if he were breaking news that had long gone stale, "language is. But of that, more later."

Exploring the epicentre of London, with its cinemas, Anne Summers lingerie shops, ghostly doner kebab outlets and overcrowded sandwich-purveying delicatessens, its windows displaying the slashed prices of electrical goods or silent constellations of wristwatches, its private sex shops with indigo-blue doors, he entered a narrow sunlit avenue called Charlotte Street. Here, utterly despondent, walking past grim buildings, he found himself face to face with a barber's shop in a corner. "A haircut is long overdue," he thought; but hesitated, desolate, conscience-stricken, on the pavement. His hair, straight on the whole, a glimmering black, in which mysterious waves appeared as it descended the tide-mark of the collar, was precious to him. Yet, resolved to tackle the unpleasant but necessary ceremony head-on, he entered the shop, hung his deep-sea-fisherman's anorak from a hook, and sat down upon a sofa beside two other obedient victims who were pretending to read. He was beckoned, finally, with a forefinger; and as the Italian smashed the white cloth against the air like a child's magician, he, before removing his spectacles, checked his reflection sadly in the mirror. "Just a trim, please," he said, diffident, for a moment, that he must make this deeply felt plea in a language he had no proprietorial right to—and because he, and his whole being, were now in the barber's hands. The barber paid no attention; unsmiling, as detached as a blind man, he flashed his scissors and ran the comb through Nirmalya's hair as if stroking a musical instrument. Then, like one who knew exactly what he was doing, he chopped off a great deal of the hair, as its young owner sat helplessly still. The hair which Nirmalya had started growing after school, this emanation, no less peculiar than a halo, which he allowed to be touched by complicit hands only once in two and a half months, lay irrevocably on a dark floor in Charlotte Street.

Two weeks later, as if in penitence, and in a moment's hurtling recklessness, he shaved his moustache and his goatee; the face he saw above the basin was completely "normal," surprisingly pleasant-looking, almost certainly respectable. He felt a great relief, and an irrepressible desire to laugh—delighted to return to the human race, to all the ambitions and desires it decreed were valid, and which he, too, surreptitiously shared. His razed but gleaming cheeks protested at the slap and sting of Tabac.

"There's an invitation, ji—from outside Bombay," said Sumati, adjusting the curve of her aanchal as she replaced the handset in its cradle. Shyamji was on the divan, his head propped on the palm of one hand, talking animatedly to a relative, an old man in white who sat on the carpet in a way that made it seem he could see all the way to the horizon. "From Dongri. Some bada officer posted there lagta hai—I think 'Collector'-hi was what he said—his daughter is getting married. He said he'll pay twenty thousand rupees and, arrey wa, first-class fare for you and Banwari and Pyareji. For you to sing, saheb, the night after the wedding for a small group of friends."

Shyamji frowned more and more at Sumati's unflagging cheer. Dongri was a nowhere place; but twenty thousand rupees!

"He says he heard you sing in Khemkar saab's house and is mad about your singing," she continued softly, caught in the vision of a time when she used to sit hunched in the background, face partially concealed by the aanchal, listening, her husband singing to a hall packed with government servants and businessmen, when Khemkar was no longer Chief Minister, but still a person of influence. She was very proud of her husband. Her indulgent, teasing adoration used to irritate the other relatives.

"What did you tell him?" he asked, half-listening to what she'd said. He used the familiar "tu": married for more than twenty years, they were like a sister and a brother who'd almost approached an understanding about living with each other; half the time, they didn't notice one another, except in fleeting glances of recognition, or with mild distaste and weariness. "Arrey, Suman, why didn't you give *me* the phone?" He only excavated her pet name to address her when he was close to exasperation.

"Lo!" she said with a gruff laugh, drawing back in wonder as the old visitor gaped open-mouthed. "*You* are the one who does not want to take phone calls, and now *you* are the one to change your mind without telling anyone else. Tell me, is that right?" she asked, smiling, shifting her benign, blessed squint towards the old man. She was careful, while rebutting her husband, to use "aap," investing it at once with respect and a mischievous reproachfulness.

"I said you'd let him know tomorrow," she added, as she vanished into the bedroom.

He was silent for a short while, neither saying anything after her or to the old relative, taking determined refuge, instead, in one of his ever-returning reveries.

The idea of travelling to Dongri quickened him; three fingers forming a chord, D sharp, on the harmonium, he crooned a ghazal—what did people listen to these days but ghazals? He decided to tell Banwari the next day: a tiny bit of good news that he deliberately delayed passing on.

In the morning, though, he had an irregular heartbeat, and, coming out of the bathroom, fresh from the effort of evacuation, he felt dizzy. The cardiologist who was now seeing him (arranged for by a student, one of the many who comprised the inexhaustible drove of new learners), Dr. Readymoney, paid him a visit (three hundred rupees he'd charge him at the end, Shyamji knew; there was no way out) and, with a fastidious, metronomic gaze, took his pulse. "Telephone hai?" he asked, in that richly musical Parsi Hindi, which had Sumati swooning over him in haste and anxious nodding compliance. He made a terse, polite call to have the music teacher admitted into a private nursing home in Versova.

Shyamji wasn't overly worried. There was every chance he'd be better in a month's time for Dongri and the Collector's daughter and the wedding audience; he could smell that house; no need to refuse the Collector—if that's what he was—this very moment. "Tell him I'm on a trip when he calls," he instructed his wife, sombre and moral, thinking it was the least consequential and most effective lie possible in the circumstances. Two middle-class disciples had been marshalled along with Dr. Readymoncy; they hovered by the doorway and ran up and down the stairs, quite oblivious of the lift; he—his family—was in his students' hands; he was safe. Sumati, too, was unworried by the truant heartbeats; the sight of Shyamji's students was a source of great pride and comfort, of almost a lulling rightness. She was smiling, as ever, at the way the different pieces were coming together. "Remember to take the pills!" she cried out as an afterthought.

As he was being moved out of the ambulance in the cornice-and-lawn-bordered compound of the nursing home, his mind, not taking in the birdcall at all, was working at a terrific speed; he was comparing the costs of the treatment with his earnings and what he could expect from his students, and he was on the brink of arriving at a figure, like a musician, goose-fleshed, coming to the end of the allocations in a cycle of laya. Then he felt tired and closed his eyes, murmuring, "Hé bhagwan"—almost a pleasurable blankness, as he entrusted his volition to the men around him, and was suddenly carried forward.

The flat in Sagar Apartments was in morningtime disarray. The forgiving pre-luncheon fragrance of worship, sandalwood incense, had spread from Mataji's secretive, jealously-attended shrine in the bedroom to the sitting room. The maidservant was bent, a wet and dripping sheaf of spinach bunched in one fist. When Nisha, the youngest daughter, powdering her dark, acned cheeks, heard, she cried in terror—"Papa!"—as she used to when she'd see bandicoots scurrying into the chawl in King's Circle, and fainted. Sumati, her daughter's head on her lap, sprinkled water on her face, intent, proper, ceremonial; she revived, dazed by her mother's face, by the closeness of the ceiling, by the daylight, the cawing. "Hai Ram, hai Ram," Sumati said. "Kuchh samaj me nahi aa raha hai!" She was lost. Of all the children in the family, Nisha was the least musical; she was learning, with an elemental buoyancy, to be a hairstylist. She was supposed to leave in half an hour for her training, curling her fingers, in a cramped and artificially nocturnal interior, around people's hair.

Mataji, in her white widow's sari, sat on the divan, silent, worship peremptorily abandoned, as if every part of her had been cut out of stone.

It was Banwari who called Mallika Sengupta; eyes bloodshot, nervous, he'd been making phonecall after phonecall, like a businessman desperate to trace a product on the market, his pale fingernail curving round the dial of the phone. She'd just been instructing a maidservant, one of Jumna's many temporary, and inadequate, replacements in the last two months, to fold a sari she'd taken off before going to sleep. The young woman stood behind her, with childlike simplicity pinning down one end of this striking sari with her chin. Mallika Sengupta and her husband had gone to a party last night on the other side of the city, and returned late, exhausted, to the nighttime idyll of Bandra.

"See what has happened to your brother, didi!" said Banwari, his voice, as ever, hoarse, but passionate with bewilderment and injustice.

She had not heard from Shyamji for two weeks—an unusual neglect, to do with Nirmalya's absence, of the steadfast, placatory role the music lesson played in her day. Instead, she'd been going to the Neogis', not altogether happy to be there, watching Nayana Neogi, large in her smock, reigning in her inert way over the bed, she herself in the wicker chair, never, even now, completely sans the aura of the successful executive's wife, surrounded by lackadaisically incumbent dogs, and one self-assured feline who appeared and faded at will. Sometimes, when Nayana (both of them having run out of chit-chat) lay worryingly silent—was she napping?—Mallika, in the remote presence of her old friend, took out a brand-new aerogramme from her handbag, and began to fill its paper-aeroplane-like folds with her large, impatient English handwriting: "Our shona Nirmalya . . ." This was what retired life should be like; but Mallika Sengupta could never accept her life as a superannuated one, and soon wanted to get back home; but wondered, too, at how everything at the Neogis' had been reassembled after the disaster of the rains, when water had flooded this ground-floor flat, as it did every monsoon, making Prashanta Neogi walk about ankle-deep in the sitting room, rescuing the avant-garde ashtrays, gathering up an armful of old spotted copies of *Imprint* (for which he once worked), Nayana, a dog cradled in her own arms, warning him: "Arrey baba, be careful of the electric wires!" "We'll have to vacate this flat," she confessed to Mallika, comfortably retrospective now, and semi-horizontal on the bed. "The water's become too much of a nuisance; it's not safe here any more": but where would they go? Property prices were incredible; and what savings did a retired commercial artist have? "The only safe place to go is upstairs," she concluded, metaphorical but subversive at the end of her worldly tenancy; she was loosening her ties in a way that Mrs. Sengupta could not. But the rhythm of these social exchanges had become, for Mallika Sengupta, a substitute for the music. She'd once again begun thinking of Shyamji, lately, with a mixture of puzzlement and suspicion: he'd made use of her as he'd used his other students, but, in return, had failed to back her in the way he should have. The disciple wants nothing of the guru but knowledge; but Shyamji was not a teacher in the mythological sense. He lived in a world of transactions. He expected his students to promote him; his students expected him to promote them; it was a relationship of interdependence at once less calculating, less final, and more human—with all the oscillations of judgement and misunderstandings that humans are prone to—than one might be led to believe.

Her husband was sealed in a meeting; trembling in the universe-illuminating mid-morning light, she changed into a sari and rushed out, hoping to catch up with the procession that Banwari had said, before disconnecting, was about to embark with the body toward a crematorium. "Which crematorium, Banwariji? How to get there?": relieved, and the brunt of the news tempered, by the banalities of the quest. Once in the back of the Ambassador, she passed on, in her familiar summations so confusing to drivers (as if facts and destinations were beneath her), but noticeably emotional, the directions Banwari had given her with a peculiar, protective calmness. Half an hour passed as the hallowed, leaf-encircled, church-dotted streets of Bandra changed, and changed again, into the dusty edges of a metropolis of small retail outlets, large hoardings, cars tense and quiet at traffic lights. Then, past a dark, stifled PCO distributing the manna of long-distance calls to those who were hungry for the sound of the human voice, and the large, inviolate sanctum of a temple to Lakshmi, she saw a sizeable but straggly group, some of whom she knew, by sight or name or personally, joined together by their common, day-to-day pursuit of music, undertaken with varying degrees of intensity, or simply for its soothing, medicinal qualities, by, too, a currency of ghazals and bhajans that had been circulating among them, and, by choice, but as good as inadvertently, to the fate of a man who now occupied their thoughts and had left them temporarily baffled and disoriented. "He's gone in," said Dr. Kusum Deshpande sadly, a paediatrician who'd been a student of Ram Lal in another time, a "guru behan"—a sister by virtue of having had the same guru—of the man who might as well have entered that doorway (such was the almost comic wistfulness of her words) to keep an appointment. She and Mallika Sengupta were the only women in the company, both educated, out of place, not women in the traditional sense (who were discouraged, as children might be, from being anywhere near the pyre, as if they might catch an infection); these two could not cry, but only have a conversation, and discuss—a look of utter disbelief on Mrs. Sengupta's face, a faint, wise smile on Dr. Deshpande's—the irrationality of what had occurred. She was six years older than Shyam; remembered him as a taciturn, precocious boy in and out of the room in which she used to sit and learn bandishes from the thin, idiosyncratic, but jubilant Ram Lal. "He was so talented," she said in English, shaking her head, struck by the memory of the boy, and the immediacy of his incursions into the room. "He would have been famous." The men around them were largely silent, mistaking physical discomfort for emotional dislocation, pushing back the collars of their shirts, not knowing what to do, waiting, again, to be needed or required.

~

Along with an invitation to join a discussion on the second coming of Christ by members of the New Church, a scribbled note on the back of a scrap of circular from Mr. Dickinson, asking whether the time of the next tutorial could possibly be changed, a terse pamphlet, full of exclamation marks and a smudged picture of Winnie Mandela, exhorting the reader to become one of the many who no longer ate South African oranges, there was, in Nirmalya's pigeonhole, an aerogramme, a silent traveller from India, its blue peering out from amidst the white and yellow. Surprisingly, it bore his father's small, ornate handwriting. Despite directions provided to the recipient, the aerogramme always threatened to come apart in Nirmalya's hands as he tore it open. Exhuming its contents like something that had been hidden in a magic box, he found a message written in a formal, somewhat stiff style, the style of a man who'd grown more used to officialese than to personal disclosure; but it masked deep emotion, the emotion of a father who'd successfully protected his son from the world, and wanted to continue to protect him. "Such things happen," he wrote. "Your Shyamji didn't know where his best interests lay." He spoke of Shyamji as if he'd committed a minor transgression, something that could be forgiven and forgotten.

Shyamji was in a hurry, thought Nirmalya; as he read—ignored by students in the common room who hardly knew him, who were bending, congregating, spontaneously breaking away—he felt, for once, poised and centred in his aloneness, and his eyes filled with tears too fine and crystalline for anyone to have noticed, while, as ever, he sat in judgement upon his teacher. Taking a Tube from the Strand, numb, like everyone else on the train, but vivid with a secret grief that made him, in his own eyes, separate from the other commuters, and suddenly immune to the awkwardness of exile, he got off finally at Tottenham Court Road, and wandered, as he often did without rhyme or reason, among the crowds and theatres, but this time to clear his thoughts. He'd wanted too much too soon, he thought, as he upbraided his dead teacher for his impatient—even irresponsible—departure. What would Nirmalya, guruless, do now? And what was that "too much"? Certain of what it was, he didn't—couldn't—specify it to himself.

Three months later, he was in the lane off Pali Hill, relieved to be back home for the excess and heat of summer in this sloping, tapering neighbourhood. When Banwari and Pyarelal came to see him, he said, "The weather over there is so gloomy, I don't feel like singing most of the time. I try to sing Purvi, and I think: what's the point? Pyarelalji, the light isn't right. Ekdum theek nahi hai. Some days in London, evening doesn't come, because it's like evening from the morning onward." Pyarelal nodded vigorously, delighted, not because he understood exactly what Nirmalya meant, but because he expanded with pride while listening to him hold forth; Banwari seemed non-committal and suffused with responsibility, as if he were weighing, with exaggerated gravity, Nirmalya's words.

Nirmalya was happy to see Banwari and Pyarelal, quickened as of old with a simple wonder at their reappearance. They were like friends; he'd never felt that tension with them that he had with

Shyamji, where his feelings had been complicated, set on edge, by reverence and expectation. But he noticed that, despite their cheerfulness, they were oddly at a loss at their own juxtaposition, courteous elders of the bridegroom's party where the bridegroom had gone missing, leaving them embarrassed and clearing their throats; Shyamji's death had disoriented them—the intensely shy younger brother, and the garrulous, fidgety older man who'd married into the family and felt shackled to it ever since.

"Baba looks nice with the haircut, doesn't he?" said Pyarelal, looking at Banwari, as if the thought had just dawned on him, as if Nirmalya were not present but a thing of the past, and they were reminiscing about him.

There was a faint smile on Banwari's lips, suggesting matters concerning "baba" were beyond the realm of mere truth and observation, as he agreed.

"He used to talk about you a lot before he died," said his mother, as the young man strode about in his pyjamas in the sitting room with a cup of tea in his hand at ten thirty in the morning. He was still under the spell of jet lag, its early-morning startlements, its creeping heaviness. He'd woken up at dawn, looked for a while at the milky light outside the window, which had grown so beloved to him in his absence, and didn't know when he'd fallen asleep again. "He told me, 'Baba will make a mark in the world.' " Nirmalya, uncomfortable, uncertain of where to store this prophecy, listened to his mother repeat the dead man's words as if they had a special mystery, a magic; as if they weren't about him. Mallika Sengupta, leaning forward in a low chair in her housecoat (how she loved to sit with her son at breakfast!) was tearful; she'd become maudlin after moving to Pali Hill with her husband's retirement.

The doorbell rang. The young servant opened the door, and a conversation of stops and starts, of monosyllables and broken sentences, could be heard taking place in an undertone; Mrs. Sengupta, naturally curious, naturally suspicious, followed. "Achha?" she could be heard exclaiming in disbelief; and then re-entered the sunlit perfection of the sitting room, as if she couldn't keep the news from her son, displaying a mango in one hand, a faint stain like a shadow on one side of the skin. "This is from the tree in our compound," she said to Nirmalya, who was still immune to the taste of the fruit. "The watchman"—the invisible interlocutor outside the door—"has given us a few"; more pleased than if it were a lottery draw.

"He needn't have died," said Nirmalya, shaking his head, chasing the thoughts that had been preoccupying him since she'd got up. "It was nothing but stupidity." He finished the tea. He saw Shyamji's life, in the last few years, as a series of errors in judgement: choosing glamour over art, light music over classical, death over life. It wasn't diabetes or even heart disease that had killed him; it wasn't drink, or the hidden self-destructive impulse that finished other artists—Shyamji was a calm, reasonable man, who had no vices. It was wanting too much from life. "Why was he in such a hurry?" he said irritably to Mrs. Sengupta, as she stood there, solemnly listening, still delicately cupping the fruit. "Why couldn't he wait?"

"Didi, baba," said Pyarelal in an urgent, sheepish whisper, pretending to underplay the importance of his announcement, "my student Jayashree Nath—you've seen her, baba, in the Taj—will be dancing at the Little Theatre on the fifteenth. Please come. I want some samajhdaar, knowledgeable people in the audience. Baba is very samajhdaar—yes, absolutely!"

And so Nirmalya, who'd been conferred the status of "critic" by Shyamji, and Mrs. Sengupta, whose long, distracted line of music teachers since she moved to Bombay appeared to have abruptly and finally disbanded with Shyamji's death—they, mother and son, in their old, persistent companionableness, were persuaded to set out that evening for the National Theatre of the Performing Arts, which hovered like a bleached fragment in their memory, because they used to see the white squat building across the waves every day from the balcony of Thacker Towers. An hour's journey on the way, an hour in the Little Theatre, an hour returning; a quarter of the day, at the very least, spent on the cause of Jayashree Nath. But, getting ready, they were busy with anticipation; Mrs. Sengupta, as ever, consuming the last twenty minutes applying the finishing touches to her face. It meant going to the other end of the city, where the land shrank into the sea: where Nirmalya had grown up, and dreamed, and looked out on the curving drive to school, and seldom been happy. Tara, Pyarelal's wife, was waiting in the aisle of a hall in which people were still settling into seats; she said, "Aiye, didi, aao, baba, your gur"—but she checked herself quickly before she said "guru"—"your Pyarelalji was so excited that you're coming." As Tara seated Nirmalya and Mrs. Sengupta in the second row, she bent and, kohl-blackened eyes narrowing with her familiar teasing smile, said in Nirmalya's ear: "See, your Pyarelalji's new student Madhu is sitting next to you—woh jo film star." Once seated, Nirmalya glanced deftly to his right. He'd heard about Madhu; she'd acted in one film; it had been a great success. And she—a diminutive young woman, fair and light-eyed, pretty but not unusual, as ordinary as a college girl—was learning kathak dance from Pyarelal. Her chaperone, her mother, sat next to her—now, where had he read about her? It was a long time since he'd turned the pages of the magazines of film gossip his mother used to subscribe to when he was a child, skimming them objectively for a stray piece of titillating data. And now they took the stage, Pyarelal, stiff and small with reflected glory, then a wiry, bespectacled man who, aloof with what looked like a secret source of amusement, went and sat before the harmonium, and, anklets resonating, Jayashree Nath. Everyone clapped; Madhu joined her small, angelic hands to give them a warm ovation. Pyarelal, from behind the tablas, saw Nirmalya—the sort of glance of recognition, satisfaction, and subterfuge that's exchanged between accomplices separated by crowds in busy places.

"That's Motilalji!" whispered his mother.

She was looking straight at the wiry man, who'd begun to sing, straightaway climbing the high notes. Her teacher, who used to miss his lessons because he'd be fast asleep, lulled and sedated by drink in the mornings, who used to take some time during each lesson to both praise and insult her in his casual, perfunctory way: Sumati's elder brother, Shyamji's brother-in-law, who, late one morning, had taken the reticent "Shyam" to her flat in Cumballa Hill with its long veranda of potted plants just because he wanted to show off—*I have rich students like these.* How embarrassed and compromised Shyamji, poor man, had been; and always uncomfortable, quick to move on to some other subject, on being reminded of that first visit.

"So he's singing again," she ruminated, not sure whether to feel surprised or intrigued.

Nirmalya listened carefully as he sang the thumri about Radha venturing towards the banks of the Jamuna; he'd heard Motilalji had once been a great singer, but, in the flat in Cumballa Hill, he'd been more interested in hide and seek, the "servants' quarters," and imaginary exigencies and companions. But, sober and recovered, this voice, whose actual timbre Nirmalya could hardly recall, lacked pliability and freshness, though he realised, once or twice with a thrill of recognition, that there were flashes of the old gift.

There were no microphones; the auditorium boasted special acoustics that were usually disappointing. And so, when Pyarelal spoke the bols of the tabla rapidly, or recited two lines from an Awadhi poem to his own grand tabla slapping, Nirmalya thought he'd have to strain to hear, but was surprised today that Pyarelal was clearly audible. The two items that followed the weaving of the thumri were staples of kathak dance, almost clichés; but novel and compelling to Nirmalya, who, silently watching the narratives dilate and ebb before him, still had a child's innocence and enthusiasm about the world of Indian art: whatever was beautiful was incomparable, and endlessly more exciting than anything to be found in a European museum. It was the moment of Radha's sringar: and as the wiry man sang, practised, unhesitating, noticeably without inspiration, Radha adorned herself before her tryst, consulting a mirror she held in her hand, examining herself from one angle, then another. The entire audience—kind-hearted Parsi ladies, buttoned-up marketing executives and their wives, men from advertisement agencies, fresh from composing copy, older couples from "cultured" families, with the sheen of some rare substance about them, brazen regulars who'd strayed in for the air conditioning, all the usual migrants who made up an audience for a performance, preferring, for an hour, this interior to the shelter of home—everyone in the hall attended, for five minutes, to the beauty of Radha's toilette, giving her the utter privacy to make herself up bit by bit.

Then, after satisfied applause, there was the episode of Draupadi's rape—Yudhishthir's last throw of the dice, accompanied by a dire, confirming thump on the tabla by Pyarelal; Shakuni's bronchial laughter, his head thrown back; and then, for the millionth time since this story was born, Dushasana enlisted to strip Draupadi of the yard of cloth that covered her. And there was Krishna, beatific, almost smug, effortlessly extending the yard of cloth that the hapless Dushasana, puzzled, then vanquished, by the length of the sari, kept trying to pull off. And Nirmalya, lost in his seat in the spectacle, couldn't help admiring the way Jayashree Nath, despite her unrelenting Hindi-film-style jerks of the head, became, disconcertingly, about a quarter of the cast of the Mahabharata. It was striking how what was really a magic trick, something worthy of a circus, had been transformed by Jayashree Nath and Pyarelal and Motilalji and kathak dance into an instance of the terrifying but undeniable dependence of human beings on divine intervention. Everyone was moved; it was as if, teetering on the brink of disaster, they'd glimpsed the smirking Krishna and fallen back into the safety of Bombay, the air-conditioned auditorium, the soft but resolute seats, and the knowledge that, outside, the cars were parked silently in rows by the Arabian Sea.

Nirmalya and Mrs. Sengupta went backstage, through a door from which people were already emerging, sated, having passed on their congratulatory messages. The artists now had ridiculous bouquets in their arms. Tara, large in a maroon sari, was standing next to Pyarelal; and Pyarelal, flushed with the congratulations and the performance, spotted them and said:

"Aao, aao, baba, tell me—what did you think?"

He spoke to the young man, still marked by the pathos and specialness of one who'd come back from "foreign," as if *he* were the celebrity, or mysteriously, but inevitably, was about to become one.

"Wonderful," said Mrs. Sengupta.

"Thanks for coming," said Jayashree Nath to Nirmalya in English, in her brisk all-purpose tourist-guide manner, where the veneer of confidence was a sort of defence mechanism, her face, from close quarters, grotesquely exaggerated and motionless with paint. "He speaks so much about you!" And Pyarelal, girded by Tara and two of his sons, dark boys wearing high-power spectacles, found time to blush at these words, realising his feelings were being described.

"Mallika?" a dry and perfectly audible voice said; and Mrs. Sengupta turned, smiling, and saw the thin stern man in white kurta and pyjamas. Motilalji—sober but still impudent as ever, with the temerity to address her by her first name! Not the slightest hesitation about him, or respect for the passage of time; he may as well have been drunk. She felt a wave of exasperation; but also girlish wonder, at seeing him after all these years. "How are you Motilalji?" she asked; and she was actually concerned; nervous he might drop dead from his previous excesses before her. "Aren't you going to do pranam, Mallika?" The impudence—asking her, she who was older than him, to touch his feet! It was as if he'd derive some sort of pleasure in extracting an obeisance from the bada sahib's wife, not least because *she* had the audacity to be conscious of her abilities as a singer.

As at the parties she went to, she pretended she hadn't heard; and, outraged though she was, she was also amused that he hadn't changed. He, too, pretended, the next instant, he hadn't spoken; it was as if everything had happened, in a flash, on a different, unverifiable plane of existence. There was nothing to do but continue the exchange of pleasantries and information, and let the small moment of theatre pass. "Bas chal raha hai. Pulling along," he confessed without enthusiasm, upright and dead as a plank of wood, a prisoner amidst the mundane.

Now, after Shyamji's death, Banwari and Pyarelal, the latter in his joking, persistent way, the former with the sweet-faced presumption of entitlement that family members have, began to make increasing demands on the Senguptas—for loans, for advance payments which they couldn't hope to "adjust" or return—as if (and this was implicit, but a constant undercurrent) the death were a justification.

"Why?" asked Mrs. Sengupta, as Pyarelal stood before her with a suitably contrite face after having asked her for three thousand rupees.

She thought, "He doesn't realise we don't have black money. He sees a lifestyle, has seen it for years, but doesn't see what it takes to maintain it."

"Tara is not well," he said, pulling an interesting face—ever the performer. "She's in the nursing home, didi. Bilkul thheek nahin hain. Doctor says it might be an ulcer."

Those all-night vigils, fasts, and prayers! Years later, the sore hidden inside bringing pain.

"Which nursing home?" asked Mrs. Sengupta sceptically.

"Why, Laad Nursing Home," said Pyarelal, clearing his throat, as if it were a world-famous institution. "Run by Dr. Laad."

"Pray more," she said, shaking her head, but picking up the key to the cupboard. "Perform more fasts!"

Pyarelal too shook his head from side to side, at the stubborn idiocy of the world as well as at the startling, uncomfortable insights "didi" offered sometimes. He listened for the key turning in the lock.

Nirmalya sat on the carpet in the living room and tuned the tanpura; his palm ensconced each giant, resistant key, and, with a deep breath, he tightened it with the distant attentiveness of an engineer. It had been standing, like a forgotten heirloom or a stopped clock, upright and untouched in its place in his bedroom for more than nine months now. Pyarelal, fussy, witch-like, chattering constantly, had turned the keys and loosened the strings before Nirmalya had left for England, so that they wouldn't snap in his absence. Now Nirmalya tightened the strings that had been resting, suspended in a reptilian twilight, turning his face away as he did so; he'd seen Pyarelal doing the same, narrow his eyes nervously and avert his face as the string grew tighter and tighter with a droll but ominous twang, because it could snap sometimes, and sting viciously.

The tuning went off without event or injury; only the lint that had accumulated on the strings flew out in small, lazy particles as he began to play. The sound filled his ear, the four strings combining to create not only a single vibration, but a world. It was a world without time, and Nirmalya was alone in it; he forgot, for the moment, the confusion and distress he'd felt when he'd heard Shyamji had died. And then, as he kept playing, his predicament returned to him, the real world intruded into the world of sound the strings had created: he was without a teacher—he didn't know where to go from here. "What should I sing?" he wondered; because his tanpura-playing was a preamble, a doorway into the world of the raga, but he was content to sit, dazed and speechless, at that doorway, to wait in that world of sound, to be undecided about what to practise. A minute passed; a surprisingly soothing breeze reminded him that it had rained last night, clattering on the back of the air conditioner, making him think for a second, as he lay in bed, of the tin roofs of houses he used to stay in when visiting relatives in small towns as a child. "Malhar—it has to be a Malhar, of course," he thought. He allowed the tanpura, aloof sentinel, to embrace and envelop him.

"She doesn't smile any more," said Mrs. Sengupta, her face stricken, like a child's. "She has not smiled since that day."

Ram Lal's widow—that sturdy and unstoppable woman in the white sari. Mallika Sengupta was momentarily overcome; the pain of a mother at her son's death—she'd lived it many times in her imagination; and now to see it so plainly before her!

"How did you hear about it?" he asked, drawn again and again to the same story, the story of that day; and she recited it, tremulous and obedient.

"And upon reaching there I found Kusum Deshpande—you know her, the doctor," said Mrs. Sengupta. "She was very kind," she observed, as if it was she who had somehow been the victim of a misunderstanding. Then, speaking to him in the old, quietening, timeless voice with which she used to tell him stories as the evening ended and he was already, mentally, in exile, at his desk in the classroom, "None of the women of the family were there"—she meant the crematorium—"the women don't go there, Nirmalya."

In his mind, Rajasthan, from where the family had originally come, was mixed up with spectacular tales of sacrifice from abandoned textbooks, of newly widowed women leaping or being pushed on to a funeral fire. Would Sumati, two hundred years ago, have become a woman of pure soul, and burned while Banwari and

Pyarelal watched in terror and humility and adoration? The fantasy, in which he couldn't quite picture the protagonists, only the pure white sari and the flames, ran away with him.

No, here, in Bombay, things had to take their tried and tested course; the small, forthcoming celebrations of which life was constituted. Sumati went to a jeweller's to look at dainty gold bangles for newborn children, frozen, glimmering but shrunken, resting on the red velvet; for her eldest daughter, who lived in Delhi, was eight months pregnant.

After Shyamji's death, Pyarelal received a new lease of life. After the first dawning of doubt and anxiety—for he'd been shamelessly dependent on Shyamji—he'd emerged into a teeming world where he was no longer under Shyamji's protective umbrella.

It was around this time that he'd acquired Madhu, the one-film-old star, who'd stepped down from her brief tenancy in the firmament, and had come to him to refine her skills in kathak. She was like a being from a fairy-tale kingdom, but what Pyarelal saw before him was a talented dancer and an average, middle-class suburban woman, alight with ambition. And she could dance; she was already accomplished in kathak when she discovered Pyarelal, had conquered, with her mother standing guard shadowily behind her, the competition circuit. Something about the man's gestures, the subtlety of his style in abhinaya, which could lift him from his hyper-tense, beedi-smoking, traffic-negotiating, itinerant state into becoming Radha herself, and the compositions in his store, all these drew Madhu to him; so he became her "guru"—unofficially, of course, as he for the most part seemed destined to be: never quite acknowledged, but constantly turned to. There was another Pyarelal somewhere in the city, a well-known dance teacher from

Banaras who got mentioned occasionally in the *Times of India*; Pyarelal would dismiss him peremptorily with a flick of the hand when people rang him up to congratulate him.

"Woh doosra hai," he'd say. "He's not me."

And he'd be incensed when people thought that Madhu's teacher was this other obtrusive and recurring Pyarelal.

"I will present Madhu in a performance," he promised Nirmalya, as they stood together on the balcony of the flat in Bandra, his beedi lit and shrinking, nature rustling about them. "You will miss it, baba, because you're going back to London"—by which he meant not the city, but a distant place, more distant than Russia (which he'd visited in the fifties as part of a government-sponsored entourage, bringing back with him pictures of himself in a warm black sherwani, standing, slight as a snowflake, next to Sitara Devi). "I wish you could have been here—it'll be wonderful!"

"What about Ashaji?" Nirmalya asked Pyarelal, ingenuous as ever, always flummoxed by human behaviour. They were discussing the troubled financial circumstances, the fresh uncertainty, this family had fallen into after Shyamji's death. But what of Ashaji—the great playback singer who still crooned into people's dreams, the one who'd sung for the eternally shelved film *Naya Rasta Nayi Asha*? With such admirers, legends themselves, after all, surely there wasn't cause for worry?

"She cried a lot," said Pyarelal, grave, histrionic in his ponderousness, as if her tears were a form of capital which few people ordinarily saw her part with. "She called bhabhi on the phone and cried."

But Pyarelal, Nirmalya discovered, was clear-eyed and undeceived about Madhu. For, on this visit back home, he'd been seeing billboards displaying giant-sized versions of her, as the car went into Haji Ali toward the sea and the mosquito-frail worshippers weaving their way in the rain through the wave-lashed path to the mosque. There she was at the corner of Haji Ali, newborn and windswept like Venus, the gods and mortals agog around her, about to spring her second film on the world, exposing a bit of midriff—and when he'd asked Pyarelal how seriously she took her dance in comparison to the movies (for surely to be an "artist," if you had the talent, was superior to being a "star"), Pyarelal, taking a drag on the leaf-stub of his beedi, had said:

"Baba, Madhu knows exactly what she wants. She wants to be recognised by people when she walks down the street. She has the talent, but I don't know how long she'll keep dancing."

And he took another hungry drag; while Nirmalya puzzled over this logic and on the apparently calculated, short-lived movement of Madhu's small ghungru-wearing feet.

It was during these vacations that the song in the new movie, with the infectious words "Tin tin na tin, yeh ratein rangeen" to which she'd danced a pert athletic number, became a big hit and was on everyone's lips, or at the very least invaded everybody's ears, even in Bandra—its tinny, electric chorus flowing in waves from a radio in the evening, across the chirruping of bats—confirming her fame and charm.

Pyarelal was returning to his small flat in Borivli after the Wednesday presentation at Tanjore in the Taj, where Jayashree Nath danced before the American tourists under his hawk eye and to his ever-dependable singing and tabla playing. By the time he was near home, walking punctiliously in his nagra shoes past the peeling, frayed poster of *Gini and Jony* on a much-urinated-upon wall, the many-hued paper exfoliating around Mehmood's mournful face, heading towards the dark, inhabited avenue, all of whose lamp posts were lightless except two, it was after ten; the sweat and press of the local train and the lurching of the bus were gradually leaving him. He'd smoothed his long yellow kurta after getting off on the platform. As he was crossing the road to the compound that led to his building, avoiding, with jaw set, the potholes the rain had thrown before him, it seemed a bat flew out of the darkness and swooped down upon him; he was knocked to the ground.

He couldn't understand at first what had happened; he was at a loss; he only heard the snarl in his ear, withdrawing, fading. He sat there for a while, mulling the incident over and over; and then two or three people, he realised, had picked him up—he wasn't really too heavy—and taken him to the flat, portable and voluble in his wet clothes. With every movement, worryingly, there was pain; his pyjamas, he saw to his disapproval when he was in the flat, were soaked with blood.

There was excited chatter, the sort of chorus you heard during weddings and departures, when everyone wanted to drown everyone else out, neighbours looked in, serious-faced phonecalls were made; he listened to some of it, still and bent with the ennui of inevitability. No, not a bat; it was obvious an auto rickshaw had borne down on him in the badly lit lane, knocked him down, driven away.

"The suburbs have too many autos," said a neighbour, a clerical officer, a kind man, thin as a reed, but an unbending one. "All kinds of miscreants are driving them."

Pyarelal, in his mind's eye, saw the bat's face, human in its internecine suddenness, appearing, and vanishing forever.

"What kind of hospital is it?" asked Nirmalya, speaking of the place that Pyarelal had been transferred to. "I've never heard of it." He was beginning to feel, again, the stealthy, irresistible pull of afternoon and twilight; everything around him, including the geckos and fruit bats, was whispering to him to stay, but he was going to leave in twelve days. Only this morning, while ambling toward Hill Road to buy medicine for his mother, he'd watched, struck, as a skeletal vendor in white had picked up a cob of corn from a basket, and ripped the closed umbrella covering it, then singed it on a fire till it was covered in a shadow of soot, with all the while a boy waiting for the spent crescent of lime to be scraped upon it. This basket of corn was among the largesse of the monsoons; but he'd had neither the time nor the urge to stop for a cob.

"It's a government hospital," said Mr. Sengupta, as, without urgency, he buttoned a bush shirt with a floral print (the sort of fabric Nirmalya would never permit within inches of his skin) that his wife had bought him. (Her taste, even now, after her husband's retirement, was unapologetically youthful.) "There's no reason why you should have heard of it."

A government hospital! Free care—but poor facilities. For Nirmalya, a government hospital was preceded by its reputation, by a premonition of its municipal, functional interior of transits and departures. Nirmalya wrinkled his nose, as if he could smell the phenyled corridors in the distance.

Once they had reached this awful but equably accommodating place—the government hospital was a handsome colonial building, and still had a residue of that air of stern justice that the Raj must have once appeared to have—they went to the first floor to the general ward. A large room on the left surprised them, with about ten beds, each quite near the other. Pyarelal—his bed wasn't too far from the corridor—seemed to be taking a nap on this narrow, high, iron contraption; his eyes were shut. When the nurse told him he had visitors—"Dekho kaun aya"—he opened them immediately. He'd been shaved in the morning; there was no shadow on the cheeks. They murmured their questions, Mallika Sengupta more probing and reproachful than the other two, as if the accident were somehow a result of a lapse in Pyarelal's judgement, Nirmalya standing close to where the man's legs were swathed in a green sheet, feeling that unexplainable childlike inner ease he experienced whenever he was close to him. Pyarelal answered in a sprightly way, admitting to his guilt with good humour; it was a bad fracture. Nirmalya kept glancing at the next bed, where a man, pretending to be deaf, was eating diligently from a metal tray carved into tinny crevasses that contained peas, subzi, roti, and daal that was drying into cold scabs at the edges. There was a smell of onions. To be so focussed on the hospital food, bent forward in that buttonless white shirt and loose pyjamas everybody here had to inhabit, seemed terribly lonely to Nirmalya, one man joined to the other by the camaraderie of exile; it was like having to deny, for that moment, what had nurtured and made you.

"And food?" asked Mrs. Sengupta, frowning, challenging him.

Pyarelal smiled, the smile of a man who knew he was free. He gestured to a humble tiffin-carrier on the floor tucked next to his bed.

"Food comes from home, didi," he said, deprecating but content.

A week later, Pyarelal was relocated in the tinctured safety of Dr. Karkhanis's nursing home, a cramped room with three beds that could be partitioned at will by frayed green curtains, a Voltas air conditioner shuddering in one wall, no windows anywhere so that visitors and convalescents were shielded from the contamination of daylight, connections behind the bedhead for monitors if they were needed, a little bedside table for a glass of water, Marie biscuits, and a banana: a chilly, nocturnal, crowded haven. The name of this orthopaedic surgeon sounded too perfectly apposite to Nirmalya not to be made up—"Karkhanis" from "karkhana" or "factory": it was as if, improbably, the man and his very lineage specialised in spare parts for the body.

"He's fine," said the shambolic doctor when he had a moment to speak, with the succinctness of a harried but polite young man. "The wound is taking time to heal though. It's a common problem with chronic smokers." And then, having imparted an implicit sense of understanding in the perspiring overcrowded corridor next to the lift, he, with a deft, not impolite, movement had shaken off the possibility of the next question, and was gone.

Nirmalya saw the bandaged leg later, as he stood next to the bed along with his mother and Tara, as she drew the screen to blot out the incumbent on a neighbouring chair, a man with well-combed hair with shirt buttons open up to just above the stomach, keeping vigil next to a puzzlingly well-looking woman.

"Give them space," Pyarelal ordered Tara; she, suddenly yielding and obedient, stepped backward to make way for the visitors.

The lower leg beneath the pyjama was supported by a metal splint that had been screwed, it appeared to Nirmalya, on to the bone of the shin and ankle; an intimate streak of blood, like betel juice, had dribbled on to the dressing.

"Well, you won't be able to play the tabla with me next week," said Nirmalya, pressing his arm with the urgency of their early conversations, an urgency that returned in deceptive waves whenever they were together. Hidden in that clasp were all sorts of things; the first onrush of love, faded misunderstandings, mutual suspicion, and the memory of the transformation, the sense of possibility, that music brings. They'd once held that knowledge like a secret. "I was thinking of sitting for some practice. Maybe I can ask your son to play." Pyarelal's son had learnt the tabla; it was going to be his profession too, the gharana deepening, continuing, then losing itself in the mundane.

Pyarelal at once looked apologetic, a bit confused—probably because he was no one's guru. He'd taught people a few things, yes, but he had no official status. He'd taught Nirmalya many things, but Nirmalya's guru was Shyamji; he didn't dispute that. In private, he said to Tara: "Arrey, what did Shyam teach him? *I* taught him much more!" And then the two of them, the small, darting man who could be full of pestilential fury, the large smouldering wife, became silent and heavy for a minute, probably for very different reasons.

Later, at the close of the year, as the gentle month of December approached, bright and polished, the sweatiness of October gone, the sun descending marginally early on Marine Drive, Banwari, Shyamji's younger brother, and Shyamji's son Sanjay went about half-heartedly trying to set up the Gandharva Sammelan. They would soon be here from California, Zakir Hussain and Ali Akbar Khan and Ravi Shankar, the proscenium was being erected in the St. Xavier's quadrangle, you'd have to plan the evenings accordingly with the thin, bangled girls in their shawls and blue jeans. It was a matter of prestige, in the midst of all this, to try to keep the Gandharva Sammelan going. But the irony of having to place Shyamji's portrait next to Ram Lal's! For Sumati, that framed picture, taken in London, in Wembley, by a student, the face in it patient, not absolutely convinced by the moment, waiting for the click of the shutter—that picture, in these last months, had become for the newly lost and unmindful Sumati a mute companion.

Banwari, brushing his hair back, his absent gaze riveted to the mirror before he opened the door, and Sanjay, his head bowed, set out to scout for advertisements and donations; they went to the homes of former students, did their inaugural namaskars, descended upon drawing-room sofas, shook their heads and gazed heavenwards while accepting condolences. But most of the students didn't want to sing. The sammelan, even with its crowded, inbred glamour, in which every singer was like a blessed and exceptional son or daughter in a single remarkable family, had lost its impetus. "Not this year," said Mallika Sengupta, while Mr. Sengupta sat some distance away on the same sofa, not unsympathetic, in fact, perfectly democratic in his sympathies, understanding at once the dead man's brother's and son's requirements as well as his wife's reservations. The whole burden of opening the hardback songbook again—its spine had begun to break like an old, tattered hive—was too much for her. These bhajans hadn't gone forever, no; Meera's agonies over her phantom god, Tulsi chanting and chanting the name of Ram; she was confident they'd return to her. But she didn't want to have anything to do with them just yet. "And, Banwariji," she added, glancing at her husband in a way that suggested he couldn't speak for himself, "please don't ask Sengupta saab for an advertisement. You know he's not with the company any more."

Pandit Rasraj, the one eminent singer who performed regularly at the sammelan, and was distantly related to the family (their forefathers had, fifty years ago, stirred out of the scoured desert landscape of Rajasthan and set out for this brittle, teeming metropolis), said: "I cannot sing before Shyam's picture. No, I can't do that. He was very dear to me. No, I cannot sing before his picture." He shook his head from side to side, as he sometimes did when he sang. He sounded bitter—almost as if he envied Shyamji. Rasraj was now almost an icon. The classical musician has a short creative shelf life; that is, there's a relatively brief period in which his creative powers and his visibility coincide. Pandit Rasraj was now in his second phase, of canonisation, and it promised to be long. He was losing his spontaneity and mastery in music; but, otherwise, he had every reason to be content. But he was strangely impatient. "No, no, I can't sing before Shyam's picture," he said.

"Karkhanis has failed," wrote Mrs. Sengupta in a letter in her large-hearted scrawl. "What kind of doctor is he? Pyarelal keeps having to go back to the nursing home."

It was March now. Despite reading Frege and Wittgenstein, Nirmalya was still not cured of metaphysics; the world, for him, hadn't been demystified. Which was why he continued to rail against it secretly and blame it as if it were an errant and immoral object. Cross and lonely, he went out. The leaves had barely begun to come back to the parks in London, to Regent's and Hyde Park, to the neat green but shorn barricades near Buckingham Palace. But it was still cold. He did not see the leaves returning; he looked straight through the frail physical outline of things into their essence as if he had X-ray vision; and he went about everywhere, in rain and shine, in the hooded, grey, featureless anorak.

Ah, the embrace of poverty! It was much less attractive here than it was at home; you felt the fight was going unnoticed, somehow. Yet he kept at it, glowering in the Kentucky Fried Chicken, the metallic beat of the music in his ear as he retired, anonymous, to a corner and emptied a sachet of sugar into the styrofoam cup.

News of Pyarelal's bad health kept penetrating the ennui of exile. "What kind of nursing homes are these?" wrote his mother, and her outrage was audible to his inner ear. "They are running a business, that is all." That nursing homes were businesses like any other was clearly a revelation to her. The wound in the leg had lingered; Pyarelal had been admitted to hospital again; there had been a complication, and he'd contracted jaundice.

Nirmalya sighed as he refolded the aerogramme. He sat and looked straight in front of him. Where did this sudden melancholy come from? Was it Pyarelal, or the light outside, or the way in which Shyamji had gone abruptly? Or was it something without history, a dull, buzzing ache which had first announced itself to him during his transformation from a child into a young man, and which had no present and immediate cause?